# The Collected Supernatural and Weird Fiction of Mrs. Molesworth

# The Collected
# Supernatural and Weird
# Fiction of
# Mrs. Molesworth

Including Two Novelettes 'Unexplained' and
'The Shadow in the Moonlight'
and Thirteen Short Stories
of the Strange and Unusual

Mrs. Molesworth

LEONAUR

*The Collected*
*Supernatural and Weird*
*Fiction of*
*Mrs. Molesworth*
*Including Two Novelettes 'Unexplained' and*
*'The Shadow in the Moonlight'*
*and Thirteen Short Stories*
*of the Strange and Unusual*
by Mrs. Molesworth

FIRST EDITION

Leonaur is an imprint
of Oakpast Ltd

Copyright in this form © 2011 Oakpast Ltd

ISBN: 978-0-85706-621-3 (hardcover)
ISBN: 978-0-85706-622-0 (softcover)

**http://www.leonaur.com**

# Contents

# Lady Farquhar's Old Lady

## A True Ghost Story

(A story from *Four Ghost Stories*).

"*One that was a woman, sir; but, rest her soul, she's dead.*"
I myself have never seen a ghost (I am by no means sure that I
wish ever to do so), but I have a friend whose experience in this
respect has been less limited than mine. Till lately, however, I had
never heard the details of Lady Farquhar's adventure, though the
fact of there being a ghost story which she could, if she chose,
relate with the authority of an eyewitness, had been more than
once alluded to before me. Living at extreme ends of the country, it is but seldom my friend and I are able to meet; but a few
months ago I had the good fortune to spend some days in her
house, and one evening our conversation happening to fall on
the subject of the possibility of so-called "supernatural" visita-
tions or communications, suddenly what I had heard returned
to my memory.

"By the bye," I exclaimed, "we need not go far for an authority on the question. You have seen a ghost yourself, Margaret. I
remember once hearing it alluded to before you, and you did
not contradict it. I have so often meant to ask you for the whole
story. Do tell it to us now."

Lady Farquhar hesitated for a moment, and her usually bright
expression grew somewhat graver. When she spoke, it seemed to
be with a slight effort.

"You mean what they all call the story of 'my old lady,' I suppose," she said at last. "Oh yes, if you care to hear it, I will tell it

7

you. But there is not much to tell, remember."

"There seldom is in *true* stories of the kind," I replied. "Genuine ghost stories are generally abrupt and inconsequent in the extreme, but on this very account all the more impressive. Don't you think so?"

"I don't know that I am a fair judge," she answered. "Indeed," she went on rather gravely, "my own opinion is that what you call *true* ghost stories are very seldom told at all."

"How do you mean? I don't quite understand you," I said, a little perplexed by her words and tone.

"I mean," she replied, "that people who really believe they have come in contact with—with anything of that kind, seldom care to speak about it."

"Do you really think so? do you mean that you feel so yourself?" I exclaimed with considerable surprise. "I had no idea you did, or I would not have mentioned the subject. Of course you know I would not ask you to tell it if it is the least painful or disagreeable to you to talk about it."

"But it isn't. Oh no, it is not nearly so bad as that," she replied, with a smile. "I cannot really say that it is either painful or disagreeable to me to recall it, for I cannot exactly apply either of those words to the thing itself. All that I feel is a sort of shrinking from the subject, strong enough to prevent my ever alluding to it lightly or carelessly. Of all things, I should dislike to have a joke made of it. But with you I have no fear of that. And you trust me, don't you? I don't mean as to truthfulness only; but you don't think me deficient in common sense and self-control—not morbid, or very apt to be run away with by my imagination?"

"Not the sort of person one would pick out as likely to see ghosts?" I replied. "Certainly not. You are far too sensible and healthy and vigorous. I can't, very readily, fancy you the victim of delusion of any kind. But as to ghosts—are they or are they not delusions? There lies the question! Tell us your experience of them, anyway."

So she told the story I had asked for—told it in the simplest language, and with no exaggeration of tone or manner, as we sat there in her pretty drawing-room, our chairs drawn close to the fire, for it was Christmas time, and the weather was "seasonable." Two or three of Margaret's children were in the room, though not within hearing of us; all looked bright and cheerful, nothing mysterious. Yet notwithstanding the total deficiency of ghostly accessories, the story impressed me vividly.

"It was early in the spring of '55 that it happened," began Lady Farquhar; "I never forget the year, for a reason I will tell you afterwards. It is fully fifteen years ago now—a long time—but I am still quite able to recall the *feeling* this strange adventure of mine left on me, though a few details and particulars have grown confused and misty. I think it often happens so when one tries, as it were *too* hard, to be accurate and unexaggerated in telling over anything. One's very honesty is against one. I have not told it over many times, but each time it seems more difficult to tell it quite exactly; the impression left at the time was so powerful that I have always dreaded incorrectness or exaggeration creeping in.

"It reminds me, too, of the curious way in which a familiar word or name grows distorted, and then cloudy and strange, if one looks at it too long or thinks about it too much. But I must get on with my story. Well, to begin again. In the winter of '54-'55 we were living—my mother, my sisters, and I, that is, and from time to time my brother—in, or rather near, a quiet little village on the south coast of Ireland. We had gone there, before the worst of the winter began at home, for the sake of my health. I had not been as well as usual for some time (this was greatly owing, I believe, to my having lately endured unusual anxiety of mind), and my dear mother dreaded the cold weather for me, and determined to avoid it.

"I say that I had had unusual anxiety to bear, still it was not of a kind to render me morbid or fanciful. And what is even more to the point, my mind was perfectly free from prepossession or association in connection with the place we were living in, or the people who had lived there before us. I simply knew nothing whatever of these people, and I had no sort of fancy about the house—that it was haunted, or anything of that kind; and indeed I never heard that it *was* thought to be haunted. It did not look like it; it was just a moderate-sized, somewhat old-fashioned country, or rather seaside, house, furnished, with the exception of one room, in an ordinary enough modern style. The exception was a small room on the bedroom floor, which, though not locked off (that is to say, the key was left in the lock outside), was not given up for our use, as it was crowded with musty old furniture, packed closely together, and all of a fashion many, many years older than that of the contents of the rest of the house.

"I remember some of the pieces of furniture still, though I think I was only once or twice in the room all the time we were there. There were two or three old-fashioned cabinets or bureaux; there was a regular four-post bedstead, with the gloomy curtains still hanging round it; and ever so many spider-legged chairs and rickety tables; and I rather think in one corner there was a spinet. But there was nothing particularly curious or attractive, and we never thought of meddling with the things or 'poking about,' as girls sometimes do; for we always thought it was by mistake that this room had not been locked off altogether, so that no one should meddle with anything in it.

"We had rented the house for six months from a Captain Marchmont, a half-pay officer, naval or military, I don't know which, for we never saw him, and all the negotiations were managed by an agent. Captain Marchmont and his family, as a rule, lived at Ballyreina all the year round—they found it cheap and healthy, I suppose—but this year they had preferred to pass the winter in some livelier neighbourhood, and they were very glad to let the house. It never occurred to us to doubt our landlord's being the owner of it: it was not till some time after we left that we learned that he himself was only a tenant, though a tenant of long standing.

"There were no people about to make friends with, or to hear local gossip from. There were no gentry within visiting distance, and if there had been, we should hardly have cared to make friends for so short a time as we were to be there. The people of the village were mostly fishermen and their families; there were so many of them, we never got to know any specially. The doctor and the priest and the Protestant clergyman were all newcomers, and all three very uninteresting. The clergyman used to dine with us sometimes, as my brother had had some sort of introduction to him when we came to Ballyreina; but we never heard anything about the place from him. He was a great talker, too; I am sure he would have told us anything he knew. In short, there was nothing romantic or suggestive either about our house or the village. But we didn't care. You see we had gone there simply for rest and quiet and pure air, and we got what we wanted.

"Well, one evening about the middle of March I was up in my room dressing for dinner, and just as I had about finished dressing, my sister Helen came in. I remember her saying as she came in, 'Aren't you ready yet, Maggie? Are you making yourself extra smart for Mr. Conroy?' Mr. Conroy was the clergyman; he was dining with us that night. And then Helen looked at me and found fault with me, half in fun of course, for not having put on a prettier dress. I remember I said it was good enough for Mr. Conroy, who was no favourite of mine; but Helen wasn't satisfied till I agreed to wear a bright scarlet neck-ribbon of hers, and she ran off to her room to fetch it.

"I followed her almost immediately. Her room and mine, I must, by the bye, explain, were at extreme ends of a passage several yards in length. There was a wall on one side of this passage, and a balustrade overlooking the staircase on the other. My room was at the end nearest the top of the staircase. There were no doors along the passage leading to Helen's room, but just beside her door, at the end, was that of the unused room I told you of, filled with the old furniture. The passage was lighted from above by a skylight—I mean, it was by no means dark or shadowy—and on the evening I am speaking of, it was still clear daylight.

"We dined early at Ballyreina; I don't think it could have been more than a quarter to five when Helen came into my room. Well, as I was saying, I followed her almost immediately, so quickly that as I came out of my room I was in time to catch sight of her as she ran along the passage, and to see her go into her own room. Just as I lost sight of her—I was coming along more deliberately, you understand—suddenly, how or when exactly I cannot tell, I perceived *another* figure walking along the passage in front of me.

"It was a woman, a little thin woman, but though she had her back to me, something in her gait told me she was not young. She seemed a little bent, and walked feebly. I can remember her dress even now with the most perfect distinctness. She had a gown of gray clinging stuff, rather scanty in the skirt, and one of those funny little old-fashioned black shawls with a sewed-on border, that you seldom see nowadays. Do you know the kind I mean? It was a narrow, shawl-pattern border, and there was a short tufty black fringe below the border. And she had a gray poke bonnet, a bonnet made of silk 'gathered' on to a large stiff frame; 'drawn' bonnets they used to be called. I took in all these details of her dress in a moment, and even in that moment I noticed too that the materials of her clothes looked *good*, though so plain and old-fashioned.

"But somehow my first impulse when I saw her was to call out, 'Fraser, is that you?' Fraser was my mother's maid: she was a young woman, and not the least like the person in front of me, but I think a vague idea rushed across my mind that it might be Fraser dressed up to trick the other servants. But the figure took no notice of my exclamation; it, or she, walked on quietly, not even turning her head round in the least; she walked slowly down the passage, seemingly quite unconscious of my presence, and, to my extreme amazement, disappeared into the unused room.

"The key, as I think I told you, was always turned in the lock—that is to say, the door was locked, but the key was left in it; but the old woman did not seem to me to unlock the door, or even to turn the handle. There seemed no obstacle in her way: she just quietly, as it were, walked *through* the door. Even by this time I hardly think I felt *frightened*. What I had seen had passed too quickly for me as yet to realise its strangeness. Still I felt perplexed and vaguely uneasy, and I hurried on to my sister's room. She was standing by the toilet-table, searching for the ribbon.

"I think I must have looked startled, for before I could speak she called out, 'Maggie, whatever is the matter with you? You look as if you were going to faint.' I asked her if she had heard anything, though it was an inconsistent question, for to *my* ears there had been no sound at all. Helen answered, 'Yes:' a moment before I came into the room she had heard the lock of the lumber-room (so we called it) door click, and had wondered what I could be going in there for. Then I told her what I had seen. She looked a little startled, but declared it must have been one of the servants.

"'If it is a trick of the servants,' I answered, 'it should be exposed;' and when Helen offered to search through the lumber-room with me at once, I was very ready to agree to it. I was so satisfied of the reality of what I had seen, that I declared to Helen that the old woman, whoever she was, *must* be in the room; it stood to reason that, having gone in, she must still be there, as she could not possibly have come out again without our knowledge.

"So, plucking up our courage, we went to the lumber-room door. I felt so certain that but a moment before, someone had opened it, that I took hold of the knob quite confidently and turned it, just as one always does to open a door. The handle turned, but the door did not yield. I stooped down to see why; the reason was plain enough: the door was still locked, locked as usual, and the key in the lock! Then Helen and I stared at each other: *her* mind was evidently recurring to the sound she had heard; what *I* began to think I can hardly put in words.

"But when we got over this new start a little, we set to work to search the room as we had intended. And we searched it thoroughly, I assure you. We dragged the old tables and chairs out of their corners, and peeped behind the cabinets and chests of drawers where no one *could* have been hidden. Then we climbed upon the old bedstead, and shook the curtains till we were covered with dust; and then we crawled under the valances, and came out looking like sweeps; but there was nothing to be found. There was certainly *no one* in the room, and by all appearances no one could have been there for weeks. We had hardly time to make ourselves fit to be seen when the dinner-bell rang, and we had to hurry downstairs. As we ran down we agreed to say nothing of what had happened before the servants, but after dinner in the drawing-room we told our story.

"My mother and brother listened to it attentively, said it was very strange, and owned themselves as puzzled as we. Mr. Conroy of course laughed uproariously, and made us dislike him more than ever. After he had gone we talked it over again among ourselves, and my mother, who hated mysteries, did her utmost to explain what I had seen in a matter-of-fact, natural way. Was I sure it was not only Helen herself I had seen, after fancying she had reached her own room? Was I quite certain it was not Fraser after all, carrying a shawl perhaps, which made her look different? Might it not have been this, that, or the other? It was no use. Nothing could convince me that I had *not* seen what I had seen; and though, to satisfy my mother, we cross-questioned Fraser, it was with no result in the way of explanation. Fraser evidently knew nothing that could throw light on it, and she was quite certain that at the time I had seen the figure, both the other servants were downstairs in the kitchen.

"Fraser was perfectly trustworthy; we warned her not to frighten the others by speaking about the affair at all, but we could not leave off speaking about it among ourselves. We spoke about it so much for the next few days, that at last my mother lost patience, and forbade us to mention it again. At least she *pretended* to lose patience; in reality I believe she put a stop to the discussion because she thought it might have a bad effect on our nerves, on mine especially; for I found out afterwards that in her anxiety she even went the length of writing about it to our old doctor at home, and that it was by his advice she acted in forbidding us to talk about it anymore.

"Poor dear mother! I don't know that it was very sound advice. One's mind often runs all the more on things one is forbidden to mention. It certainly was so with me, for I thought over my strange adventure almost incessantly for some days after we left off talking about it."

Here Margaret paused.

"And is that all?" I asked, feeling a little disappointed, I think, at the unsatisfactory ending to the "true ghost story."

"All!" repeated Lady Farquhar, rousing herself as if from a reverie, "all! oh, dear no. I have sometimes wished it had been, for I don't think what I have told you would have left any long-lasting impression on me. All! oh, dear no. I am only at the beginning of my story."

So we resettled ourselves again to listen, and Lady Farquhar continued:—

"For some days, as I said, I could not help thinking a good deal of the mysterious old woman I had seen. Still, I assure you, I was not exactly frightened. I was more puzzled—puzzled and annoyed at not being able in any way to explain the mystery. But by ten days or so from the time of my first adventure the impression was beginning to fade. Indeed, the day before the evening I am now going to tell you of, I don't think my old lady had been in my head at all. It was filled with other things. So, don't you see, the explaining away what I saw as entirely a delusion, a fancy of my own brain, has a weak point here; for *had* it been all my fancy, it would surely have happened *sooner*—at the time my mind really was full of the subject.

"Though even if it had been so, it would not have explained the curious coincidence of my 'fancy' with facts, actual facts of which at the time I was in complete ignorance. It must have been just about ten days after my first adventure that I happened one evening, between eight and nine o'clock, to be alone upstairs in my own room. We had dined at half-past five as usual, and had been sitting together in the drawing-room since dinner, but I had made some little excuse for coming upstairs; the truth being that I wanted to be alone to read over a letter which the evening post (there actually was an evening post at Ballyreina) had brought me, and which I had only had time to glance at.

"It was a very welcome and dearly-prized letter, and the reading of it made me very happy. I don't think I had felt so happy all the months we had been in Ireland as I was feeling that evening. Do you remember my saying I never forget the year all this happened? It was the year '55 and the month of March, the spring following that first dreadful 'Crimean winter,' and news had just come to England of the *Czar's* death, and everyone was wondering and hoping and fearing what would be the results of it. I had no very near friends in the Crimea, but of course, like everyone else, I was intensely interested in all that was going on, and in this letter of mine there was told the news of the *Czar's* death, and there was a good deal of comment upon it.

"I had read my letter—more than once, I daresay—and was beginning to think I must go down to the others in the drawing-room. But the fire in my bedroom was very tempting; it was burning so brightly, that though I had got up from my chair by the fireside to leave the room, and had blown out the candle I had read my letter by, I yielded to the inclination to sit down again for a minute or two to dream pleasant dreams and think pleasant thoughts. At last I rose and turned towards the door—it was standing wide open, by the bye. But I had hardly made a step from the fireplace when I was stopped short by what I saw. Again the same strange indefinable feeling of not knowing how or when it had come there, again the same painful sensation of perplexity (not yet amounting to fear) as to whom or what it was I saw before me.

"The room, you must understand, was perfectly flooded with the firelight; except in the corners, perhaps, every object was as distinct as possible. And the object I was staring at was not in a corner, but standing there right before me—between me and the open door, alas!—in the middle of the room. It was the old woman again, but this time with her face towards me, with a look upon it, it seemed to me, as if she were conscious of my presence. It is very difficult to tell over thoughts and feelings that can hardly have taken any time to pass, or that passed almost simultaneously. My *very* first impulse this time was, as it had been the first time I saw her, to explain in some natural way the presence before me. I think this says something for my common sense, does it not?

"My mind did not readily desert matters of fact, you see. I did not think of Fraser this time, but the thought went through my mind, 'She must be some friend of the servants who comes in to see them of an evening. Perhaps they have sent her up to look at my fire.' So at first I looked up at her with simple inquiry. But as I looked my feelings changed. I realised that this was the same being who had appeared so mysteriously once before; I recognised every detail of her dress; I even noticed it more acutely than the first time—for instance, I recollect observing that here and there the short tufty fringe of her shawl was stuck together, instead of hanging smoothly and evenly all round. I looked up at her face.

"I cannot now describe the features beyond saying that the whole face was refined and pleasing, and that in the expression there was certainly nothing to alarm or repel. It was rather wistful and beseeching, the look in the eyes anxious, the lips slightly parted, as if she were on the point of speaking. I have since thought that if *I* had spoken, if I *could* have spoken—for I did make one effort to do so, but no audible words would come at my bidding—the spell that bound the poor soul, this mysterious wanderer from some shadowy borderland between life and death, might have been broken, and the message that I now believe burdened her delivered. Sometimes I wish I could have done it; but then, again—oh no! a *voice* from those unreal lips would have been too awful—flesh and blood could not have stood it.

"For another instant I kept my eyes fixed upon her without moving; then there came over me at last with an awful thrill, a sort of suffocating gasp of horror, the consciousness, the actual realisation of the fact that this before me, this *presence*, was no living human being, no dweller in our familiar world, not a woman, but a ghost! Oh, it was an awful moment! I pray that I may never again endure another like it. There is something so indescribably frightful in the feeling that we are on the verge of being tried *beyond* what we can bear, that ordinary conditions are slipping away from under us, that in another moment reason or life itself must snap with the strain; and all these feelings I then underwent.

"At last I moved, moved backwards from the figure. I dared not attempt to *pass* her. Yet I could not at first turn away from her. I stepped backwards, facing her still as I did so, till I was close to the fireplace. Then I turned sharply from her, sat down again on the low chair still standing by the hearth, resolutely forcing myself to gaze into the fire, which was blazing cheerfully, though conscious all the time of a terrible fascination urging me to look round again to the middle of the room. Gradually, however, now that I no longer *saw* her, I began a little to recover myself. I tried to bring my sense and reason to bear on the matter. 'This being,' I said to myself, 'whoever and whatever she is, *cannot harm* me. I am under God's protection as much at this moment as at any moment of my life. All creatures, even disembodied spirits, if there be such, and this among them, if it be one, are under His control. *Why* should I be afraid? I am being tried; my courage and trust are being tried to the utmost: let me prove them, let me keep my own self-respect, by mastering this cowardly, un-reasonable terror.'

"And after a time I began to feel stronger and surer of myself. Then I rose from my seat and turned towards the door again; and oh, the relief of seeing that the way was clear; my terrible visitor had disappeared! I hastened across the room, I passed the few steps of passage that lay between my door and the staircase, and hurried down the first flight in a sort of suppressed agony of eagerness to find myself again safe in the living human compan-ionship of my mother and sisters in the cheerful drawing-room below. But my trial was not yet over, indeed it seemed to me afterwards that it had only now reached its height; perhaps the strain on my nervous system was now beginning to tell, and my powers of endurance were all but exhausted.

"I cannot say if it was so or not. I can only say that my agony of terror, of horror, of absolute *fear*, was far past describing in words, when, just as I reached the little landing at the foot of the first short staircase, and was on the point of running down the longer flight still before me, I saw *again*, coming slowly *up* the steps, as if to meet me, the ghostly figure of the old woman. It was too much. I was reckless by this time; I could not stop. I rushed down the staircase, brushing past the figure as I went: I use the word intentionally—I did *brush* past her, I *felt* her. This part of my experience was, I believe, quite at variance with the sensations of orthodox ghost-seers; but I am really telling you all I was conscious of.

"Then I hardly remember anything more; my agony broke out at last in a loud shrill cry, and I suppose I fainted. I only know that when I recovered my senses I was in the drawing-room, on the sofa, surrounded by my terrified mother and sisters. But it was not for some time that I could find voice or courage to tell them what had happened to me; for several days I was on the brink of a serious illness, and for long afterwards I could not endure to be left alone, even in the broadest daylight."

Lady Farquhar stopped. I fancied, however, from her manner that there was more to tell, so I said nothing; and in a minute or two she went on speaking.

"We did not stay long at Ballyreina after this. I was not sorry to leave it; but still, before the time came for us to do so, I had begun to recover from the most painful part of the impression left upon me by my strange adventure. And when I was at home again, far from the place where it had happened, I gradually lost the feeling of horror altogether, and remembered it only as a very curious and inexplicable experience. Now and then even, I did not shrink from talking about it, generally, I think, with a vague hope that somehow, some time or other, light might be thrown upon it. Not that I ever expected, or could have believed it possible, that the supernatural character of the adventure could be explained away; but I always had a misty fancy that sooner or later I should find out *something* about my old lady, as we came to call her; who she had been and what her history was."

"And did you?" I asked eagerly.

"Yes, I did," Margaret answered. "To some extent, at least, I learnt the explanation of what I had seen. This was how it was: nearly a year after we had left Ireland I was staying with one of my aunts, and one evening some young people who were also visiting her began to talk about ghosts, and my aunt, who had heard something of the story from my mother, begged me to tell it. I did so, just as I have now told it to you. When I had finished, an elderly lady who was present, and who had listened very attentively, surprised me a little by asking the name of the house where it happened. 'Was it Ballyreina?' she said. I answered 'Yes,' wondering how she knew it, for I had not mentioned it.

"'Then I can tell you whom you saw,' she exclaimed; 'it must have been one of the old Miss Fitzgeralds—the eldest one. The description suits her exactly.'

"I was quite puzzled. We had never heard of any Fitzgeralds at Ballyreina. I said so to the lady, and asked her to explain what she meant. She told me all she knew. It appeared there had been a family of that name for many generations at Ballyreina. Once upon a time—a long-ago once upon a time—the Fitzgeralds had been great and rich; but gradually one misfortune after another had brought them down in the world, and at the time my informant heard about them the only representatives of the old family were three maiden ladies already elderly. Mrs. Gordon, the lady who told me all this, had met them once, and had been much impressed by what she heard of them.

"They had got poorer and poorer, till at last they had to give up the struggle, and sell, or let on a long lease, their dear old home, Ballyreina. They were too proud to remain in their own country after this, and spent the rest of their lives on the Continent, wandering about from place to place. The most curious part of it was that nearly all their wandering was actually *on foot.* They were too poor to afford to travel much in the usual way, and yet, once torn from their old associations, the travelling mania seized them; they seemed absolutely unable to rest. So on foot, and speaking not a word of any language but their own, these three desolate sisters journeyed over a great part of the Continent.

"They visited most of the principal towns, and were well known in several. I daresay they are still remembered at some of the places they used to stay at, though never for more than a short time together. Mrs. Gordon had met them somewhere, I forget where, but it was many years ago. Since then she had never heard of them; she did not know if they were alive or dead; she was only certain that the description of my old lady was exactly like that of the eldest of the sisters, and that the name of their old home was Ballyreina. And I remember her saying, 'If ever a heart was buried in a house, it was that of poor old Miss Fitzgerald.'

"That was all Mrs. Gordon could tell me," continued Lady Farquhar; "but it led to my learning a little more. I told my brother what I had heard. He used often at that time to be in Ireland on business; and to satisfy me, the next time he went he visited the village of Ballyreina again, and in one way and another he found out a few particulars. The house, you remember, had been let to us by a Captain Marchmont. He, my brother discovered, was not the owner of the place, as we had naturally imagined, but only rented it on a very long lease from some ladies of the name of Fitzgerald. It had been in Captain Marchmont's possession for a great many years at the time he let it to us, and the Fitzgeralds, never returning there even to visit it, had come to be almost forgotten.

"The room with the old-fashioned furniture had been reserved by the owners of the place to leave some of their poor old treasures in—relics too cumbersome to be carried about with them in their strange wanderings, but too precious, evidently, to be parted with. We, of course, never could know what may not have been hidden away in some of the queer old bureaux I told you of. Family papers of importance, perhaps; possibly some ancient love-letters, forgotten in the confusion of their leave-taking; a lock of hair, or a withered flower, perhaps, that she, my poor old lady, would fain have clasped in her hand when dying, or have had buried with her. Ah, yes; there must be many a pitiful old story that is never told."

Lady Farquhar stopped and gazed dreamily and half sadly into the fire.

"Then Miss Fitzgerald *was* dead when you were at Ballyreina?" I asked.

Margaret looked up with some surprise.

"Did I not say so?" she exclaimed. "That was the point of most interest in what my brother discovered. He could not hear the exact date of her death, but he learnt with certainty that she was dead—had died, at Geneva I think, sometime in the month of March in the previous year; *the same month, March '55, in which I had twice seen the apparition at Ballyreina."*

This was my friend's ghost story.

# Witnessed By Two

(A story from *Four Ghost Stories*).

"But tomorrow—tomorrow you will keep for me. I may expect you at the usual time?" said young Mrs. Medway to her old friend Major Graham, as she shook hands with him.

"Tomorrow? Certainly. I *have* kept it for you, Anne. I always said I should," he answered. There was a slight touch of reproach in his tone.

She lifted her eyes for half a second to his face as if she would have said more. But after all it was only the words, "Goodbye, then, till tomorrow," that were uttered, quietly and almost coldly, as Major Graham left the room.

"I can't quite make Anne out sometimes," he said to himself. "She is surely *very* cold. And yet I know she has real affection for me—*sisterly* affection, I suppose. Ah, well! so much the better. But still, just when a fellow's off for heaven knows how long, and—and—altogether it does seem a little overstrained. She can't but know what might have come to pass had we not been separated for so long—or had I been richer; and I don't think she could have been exactly in love with Medway, though by all accounts he was a very decent fellow. She is so inconsistent too—she seemed really disappointed when I said I couldn't stay today. But I'm a fool to think so much about her. I am as poor as ever and she is rich. A fatal barrier! It's a good thing that she *is* cold, and that I have plenty of other matters to think about."

And thus congratulating himself he dismissed, or believed that he dismissed for the time being, all thought of Anne Medway from his mind. It was true that he had plenty of other things to occupy it with, for the day after tomorrow was to see his departure from England for an indefinite period.

Mrs. Medway meantime sat sadly and silently in the library where Major Graham had left her. Her sweet gray eyes were fixed on the fire burning brightly and cheerfully in the waning afternoon light, but she saw nothing about her. Her thoughts were busily travelling along a road which had grown very familiar to them of late: she was recalling all her past intercourse with Kenneth Graham since the time when, as boy and girl, they had scarcely remembered that they were not "real" brother and sister—all through the pleasant years of frequent meeting and unconstrained companionship to the melancholy day when Kenneth was ordered to India, and they bade each other a long farewell! That was ten years ago now, and they had not met again till last spring, when Major Graham returned to find his old playfellow a widow, young, rich, and lovely, but lonely in a sense—save that she had two children—for she was without near relations, and was not the type of woman to make quick or numerous friendships.

The renewal of the old relations had been very pleasant—only too pleasant, Anne had of late begun to think. For the news of Kenneth's having decided to go abroad again had made her realise all he had become to her, and the discovery brought with it sharp misgiving, and even humiliation.

"He does not care for me—not as I do for him," she was saying to herself as she sat by the fire. "There would have been no necessity for his leaving England again had he done so. It cannot be because I am rich and he poor, surely? He is not the sort of man to let such a mere accident as that stand in the way if he really cared for me. No, it is that he does not care for me except as a sort of sister. But still—he said he had kept his *last* evening for me—at least he cares for no one else *more*, and that is something. Who knows—perhaps tomorrow—when it comes to really saying goodbye——?" and a faint flush of renewed hope rose to her cheeks and a brighter gleam to her eyes.

The door opened, and a gray-haired man-servant came in gently.

"I beg your pardon, ma'am," he said apologetically; "I was not sure if Major Graham had gone. Will he be here to dinner, if you please?"

"Not tonight, Ambrose. I shall be quite alone. But Major Graham will dine here tomorrow; he does not leave till Thursday morning."

"Very well, ma'am," said Ambrose, as he discreetly retired.

He had been many years in the Medway household. He had respected his late master, but for his young mistress he had actual affection, and being of a somewhat sentimental turn, he had constructed for her benefit a very pretty little romance of which Major Graham was the hero. It had been a real blow to poor Ambrose to learn that the gentleman in question was on the eve of his departure without any sign of a satisfactory third volume, and he was rather surprised to see that Mrs. Medway seemed this evening in better spirits than for some time past.

"It's maybe understood between themselves," he reflected, as he made his way back to his own quarters. "I'm sure I hope so, for he's a real gentleman and she's as sweet a lady as ever stepped, which I should know if anyone should, having seen her patience with poor master as was really called for through his long illness. She deserves a happy ending, and I'm sure I hope she may have it, poor lady."

"Tomorrow at the usual time," meaning five o'clock or thereabouts, brought Kenneth for his last visit. Anne had been expecting him with an anxiety she was almost ashamed to own to herself, yet her manner was so calm and collected that no one could have guessed the tumult of hope and fear, of wild grief at his leaving, of intense longing for any word—were it but a word—to prove that all was not on *her* side only.

"I could bear his being away—for years even, if he thought it must be—if I could but look forward—if I had the *right* to look forward to his return," she said to herself.

But the evening passed on tranquilly, and to all appearance

pleasantly, without a word or look more than might have been between real brother and sister. Kenneth talked kindly—tenderly even—of the past; repeated more than once the pleasure it had been to him to find again his old friend so little changed, so completely his old friend still. The boys came in to say goodnight, and "goodbye, alas! my lads," added their tall friend with a sigh. "Don't forget me quite, Hal and Charlie, and don't let your mother forget me either, eh?" To which the little fellows replied solemnly, though hardly understanding why he patted their curly heads with a lingering hand this evening, or why mamma looked grave at his words.

And Anne bore it all without flinching, and smiled and talked a little more than usual perhaps, though all the time her heart was bursting, and Kenneth wondered more than ever if, after all, she *had* "much heart or feeling to speak of."

"You will be bringing back a wife with you perhaps," she said once. "Shall you tell her about your sister Anne, Kenneth?"

Major Graham looked at her earnestly for half an instant before he replied, but Anne's eyes were not turned towards him, and she did not see the look. And his words almost belied it.

"Certainly I shall tell her of you," he said, "that is to say, if she ever comes to exist. At present few things are less probable. Still I am old enough now never to say, '*Fontaine, je ne boirai jamais de ton eau.*' But," he went on, "I may return to find *you* married again, Anne. You are still so young and you are rather lonely."

"No," said Anne with a sudden fierceness which he had never seen in her before, "I shall *never* marry again—*never*," and she looked him full in the face with a strange sparkle in her eyes which almost frightened him.

"I beg your pardon," he said meekly. And though the momentary excitement faded as quickly as it had come, and Anne, murmuring some half-intelligible excuse, was again her quiet self, this momentary glimpse of a fierier nature beneath gave him food for reflection.

"Can Medway have not been what he seemed on the surface, after all?" he thought to himself. "What can make her so vindictive against matrimony?"

But it was growing late, and Kenneth had still some last preparations to make. He rose slowly and reluctantly from his chair.

"I must be going, I fear," he said.

Anne too had risen. They stood together on the hearthrug. A slight, very slight shiver passed through her. Kenneth perceived it.

"You have caught cold, I fear," he said kindly; for the room was warm and the fire was burning brightly.

"No, I don't think so," she said indifferently.

"You will write to me now and then?" he said next.

"Oh, certainly—not very often perhaps," she replied lightly, "but now and then. Stay," and she turned away towards her writing-table, "tell me exactly how to address you. Your name— is your surname enough?—there is no other Graham in your regiment?"

"No," he said absently, "I suppose not. Yes, just my name and the regiment and Allagherry, which will be our headquarters. You might, if you were *very* amiable—you might write to Galles—a letter overland would wait for me there," for it was the days of "long sea" for all troops to India.

Anne returned to her former position on the hearthrug—the moment at the table had restored her courage. "We shall see," she said, smiling again.

Then Kenneth said once more, "I *must* go;" but he lingered still a moment.

"You must have caught cold, Anne, or else you are very tired. You are so white," and from his height above her, though Anne herself was tall, he laid his hand on her shoulder gently and as a brother might have done, and looked down at her pale face half inquiringly. A flush of colour rose for an instant to her cheeks. The temptation was strong upon her to throw off that calmly caressing hand, but she resisted it, and looked up bravely with a light almost of defiance in her eyes.

"I am perfectly well, I assure you. But perhaps I am a little tired. I suppose it is getting late."

And Kenneth stifled a sigh of scarcely realised disappointment, and quickly drew back his hand.

"Yes, it is late. I am very thoughtless. Goodbye then, Anne. God bless you."

And before she had time to answer he was gone.

Ambrose met him in the hall, with well-meaning officiousness bringing forward his coat and hat. His presence helped to dissipate an impulse which seized Major Graham to rush upstairs again for one other word of farewell. Had he done so what would he have found? Anne sobbing—sobbing with the terrible intensity of a self-contained nature once the strain is withdrawn—sobbing in the bitterness of her grief and the cruelty of her mortification, with but one consolation.

"At least he does not despise me. I hid it well," she whispered to herself.

And Kenneth Graham, as he drove away in his cab, repeated to himself, "She is *so* cold, this evening particularly. And yet, can it be that it was to hide any other feeling? If I thought so—good God!" and he half started up as if to call to the driver, but sat down again. "No, no, I must not be a fool. I could not stand a repulse from *her*—I could never see her again. Better not risk it. And then I am so poor!"

And in the bustle and hurry of his departure he tried to forget the wild fancy which for a moment had disturbed him. He sailed the next day.

But the few weeks which followed passed heavily for Anne. It was a dead time of year—there was no special necessity for her exerting herself to throw off the overwhelming depression, and strong and brave as she was, she allowed herself, to some extent, to yield to it.

"If only he had not come back—if I had never seen him again!" she repeated to herself incessantly. "I had in a sense forgotten him—the thought of him never troubled me all the years of my marriage. I suppose I had never before understood how I *could* care. How I wish I had never learnt it! How I *wish* he had never come back!"

It was above all in the afternoons—the dull, early dark, autumn afternoons—which for some weeks had been enlivened by the expectation, sure two or three times a week to be fulfilled, of Major Graham's "dropping in"—that the aching pain, the weary longing, grew so bad as to be well-nigh intolerable.

"How shall I bear it?" said poor Anne to herself sometimes; "it is so wrong, so unwomanly! So selfish, too, when I think of my children. How much I have to be thankful for—why should I ruin my life by crying for the one thing that is not for me? It is worse, far worse than if he had died; had I known that he had loved me, I could have borne his death, it seems to me."

She was sitting alone one afternoon about five weeks after Kenneth had left, thinking sadly over and over the same thoughts, when a tap at the door made her look up.

"Come in," she said, though the tap hardly sounded like that of her maid, and no one else was likely to come to the door of her own room where she happened to be. "Come in," and somewhat to her surprise the door half opened and old Ambrose's voice replied—

"If you please, ma'am———" then stopped and hesitated.

"Come in," she repeated with a touch of impatience. "What is it, Ambrose? Where is Seton?"

"If you please, ma'am, I couldn't find her—that is to say," Ambrose went on nervously, "I didn't look for her. I thought, ma'am, I would rather tell you myself. You mustn't be startled, ma'am," and Anne at this looking up at the old man saw that he was pale and startled-looking himself, "but it's—it's Major Graham."

"Major Graham?" repeated Anne, and to herself her voice sounded almost like a scream. "What about him? Have you heard anything?"

"It's *him*, ma'am—him himself!" said Ambrose. "He's in the library. I'm a little afraid, ma'am, there may be something wrong—he looked so strange and he did not answer when I spoke to him. But he's in the library, ma'am."

Anne did not wait to hear more. She rushed past Ambrose,

across the landing, and down the two flights of steps which led to the library—a half-way house room, between the ground-floor and the drawing-room—almost before his voice had stopped. At the door she hesitated a moment, and in that moment all sorts of wild suppositions flashed across her brain. What was it? What was she going to hear? Had Kenneth turned back half-way out to India for *her* sake? Had some trouble befallen him, in which he had come to seek her sympathy? What *could* it be? and her heart beating so as almost to suffocate her, she opened the door.

Yes—there he stood—on the hearthrug as she had last seen him in that room. But he did not seem to hear her come in, for he made no movement towards her; he did not even turn his head in her direction.

More and more startled and perturbed, Anne hastily went up to him.

"Kenneth," she cried, "what is it? What is the matter?"

She had held out her hand as she hurried towards him, but he did not seem to see it. He stood there still, without moving—his face slightly turned away, till she was close beside him.

"Kenneth," she repeated, this time with a thrill of something very like anguish in her tone, "what is the matter? Are you angry with me? *Kenneth*—speak."

Then at last he slowly turned his head and looked at her with a strange, half-wistful anxiety in his eyes—he gazed at her as if his very soul were in that gaze, and lifting his right hand, gently laid it on her shoulder as he had done the evening he had bidden her farewell. She did not shrink from his touch, but strange to say, she did not feel it, and some indefinable instinct made her turn her eyes away from his and glance at her shoulder. But even as she did so she saw that his hand was no longer there, and with a thrill of fear she exclaimed again, "*Speak*, Kenneth, *speak* to me!"

The words fell on empty air. There was no Kenneth beside her. She was standing on the hearthrug alone.

Then, for the first time, there came over her that awful chill of terror so often described, yet so indescribable to all but the few who have felt it for themselves. With a terrible though half-stifled cry, Anne turned towards the door. It opened before she reached it, and she half fell into old Ambrose's arms. Fortunately for her—for her reason, perhaps—his vague misgiving had made him follow her, though of what he was afraid he could scarcely have told.

"Oh, ma'am—oh, my poor lady!" he exclaimed, as he half led, half carried her back to her own room, "what is it? Has he gone? But how could he have gone? I was close by—I never saw him pass."

"He is not there—*he has not been there,*" said poor Anne, trembling and clinging to her old servant. "Oh, Ambrose, what you and I have seen was no living Kenneth Graham—no living man at all. Ambrose—he came thus to say goodbye to me. He is dead," and the tears burst forth as she spoke, and Anne sobbed convulsively.

Ambrose looked at her in distress and consternation past words. Then at last he found courage to speak.

"My poor lady," he repeated. "It must be so. I misdoubted me and I did not know why. He did not ring, but I was passing by the door and something—a sort of feeling that there was some-one waiting outside—made me open it. To my astonishment it was he," and Ambrose himself could not repress a sort of tremor. "He did not speak, but seemed to pass me and be up the stairs and in the library in an instant. And then, not knowing what to do, I went to your room, ma'am. Forgive me if I did wrong."

"No, no," said Anne, "you could not have done otherwise. Ring the bell, Ambrose; tell Seton I have had bad news, and that you think it has upset me. But wait at the door till she comes. I—I am afraid to be left alone."

And Mrs. Medway looked so deadly pale and faint, that when Seton came hurrying in answer to the sharply-rung bell, it needed no explanation for her to see that Mrs. Medway was really ill. Seton was a practical, matter-of-fact person, and the bustle of attending to her mistress, trying to make her warm again—for Anne was shivering with cold—and persuading her to take some restoratives, effectually drove any inquiry as to the cause of the sudden seizure out of the maid's head. And by the time Mrs. Medway was better, Seton had invented a satisfactory explanation of it all, for herself.

"You need a change, ma'am. It's too dull for anybody staying in town at this season; and it's beginning to tell on your nerves, ma'am," was the maid's idea.

And some little time after the strange occurrence Mrs. Medway was persuaded to leave town for the country.

But not till she had seen in the newspapers the fatal paragraph she knew would sooner or later be there—the announcement of the death, on board Her Majesty's troopship *Ariadne* a few days before reaching the Cape, of "Major R. R. Graham," of the 113th regiment.

She "had known it," she said to herself; yet when she saw it there, staring her in the face, she realised that she had been living in a hope which she had not allowed to herself that the apparition might in the end prove capable of other explanation. She would gladly have taken refuge in the thought that it was a dream, an optical delusion fed of her fancy incessantly brooding on her friend and on his last visit—that her brain was in some way disarranged or disturbed—anything, anything would have been welcome to her. But against all such was opposed the fact that it was not herself alone who had seen Kenneth Graham that fatal afternoon.

And now, when the worst was certain, she recognised this still more clearly as the strongest testimony to the apparition not having been the product of her own imagination. And old Ambrose, her sole confidant, in his simple way agreed with her.

"If I had not seen him too, ma'am, or if I alone had seen him," he said, furtively wiping his eyes. "But the two of us. No, it could have but the one meaning," and he looked sadly at the open newspaper. "There's a slight discrimpancy, ma'am," he said as he pointed to the paragraph. "Our Major Graham's name was 'K. R.' not 'R. R.'"

"It is only a misprint. I noticed that," said Anne wearily. "No, Ambrose, there can be no mistake. But I do not want any one— not *any one*—ever to hear the story. You will promise me that, Ambrose?" and the old man repeated the promise he had already given.

There was another "discrimpancy" which had struck Anne more forcibly, but which she refrained from mentioning to Ambrose.

"It can mean nothing; it is no use putting it into his head," she said to herself. "Still, it is strange."

The facts were these. The newspaper gave the date of Major Graham's death as the 25th November—the afternoon on which he had appeared to Mrs. Medway and her servant was that of the 26th. This left no possibility of calculating that the vision had occurred at or even shortly after the moment of the death.

"It must be a mistake in the announcement," Anne decided. And then she gave herself up to the acceptance of the fact. Kenneth was dead. Life held no individual future for her any more—nothing to look forward to, no hopes, however tremblingly admitted, that "someday" he might return, and return to discover—to own, perhaps, to himself and to her that he did love her, and that only mistaken pride, or her own coldness, or one of the hundred "mistakes" or "perhapses" by which men, so much more than women, allow to drift away from them the happiness they might grasp, had misled and withheld him! No; all was over. Henceforth she must live in her children alone—in the interests of others she must find her happiness.

"And in one blessed thought," said the poor girl—for she was little more—even at the first to herself; "that after all he *did* love me, that I may, without shame, say so in my heart, for I was his last thought. It was—it must have been—to tell me so that he came that day. My Kenneth—yes, he was mine after all."

Some little time passed. In the quiet country place whither, sorely against Seton's desires, Mrs. Medway had betaken herself for "change," she heard no mention of Major Graham's death.

One or two friends casually alluded to it in their letters as "very sad," but that was all. And Anne was glad of it.

"I must brace myself to hear it spoken of and discussed by the friends who knew him well—who knew how well *I* knew him"—she reflected. "But I am glad to escape it for a while."

It was February already, more than three months since Kenneth Graham had left England, when one morning—among letters forwarded from her London address—came a thin foreign paper one with the traces of travel upon it—of which the superscription made Anne start and then turn pale and cold.

"I did not think of this," she said to herself. "He must have left it to be forwarded to me. It is terrible—getting a letter after the hand that wrote it has been long dead and cold."

With trembling fingers she opened it.

"My dear—may I say my dearest Anne," were the first words that her eyes fell on. Her own filled with tears. Wiping them away before going on to read more, she caught sight of the date. "On board H.M.'s troopship *Ariadne*, 27th November."

Anne started. Stranger and stranger. *Two* days later than the reported date of his death—and the writing so strong and clear. No sign of weakness or illness even! She read on with frantic eagerness; it was not a very long letter, but when Anne had read the two or three somewhat hurriedly written pages, her face had changed as if from careworn, pallid middle age, back to fresh, sunny youth. She fell on her knees in fervent, unspoken thanksgiving. She kissed the letter—the dear, beautiful letter, as if it were a living thing!

"It is too much—too much," she said. "What have I done to deserve such blessedness?"

This was what the letter told. The officer whose death had been announced was not "our Major Graham," not Graham of the 113th at all, but an officer belonging to another regiment who had come on board at Madeira to return to India, believing his health to be quite restored. "The doctors had in some way mistaken his case," wrote Kenneth, "for he broke down again quite suddenly and died two days ago. He was a very good fellow, and we have all been very cut up about it. He took a fancy to me, and I have been up some nights with him, and I am rather done up myself. I write this to post at the Cape, for a fear has struck me that—his initials being so like mine—some report may reach you that it is *I*, not he. Would you care very much, dear Anne? I dare to think you would—but I cannot in a letter tell you why. I must wait till I see you. I have had a somewhat strange experience, and it is possible, just possible, that I may be able to tell you all about it, *vivâ voce*, sooner than I had any idea of when I last saw you. In the meantime, goodbye and God bless you, my dear child."

Then followed a postscript—of some days' later date, written in great perturbation of spirit at finding that the letter had, by mistake, not been posted at the Cape. "After all my anxiety that you should see it as soon as or before the newspapers, it is really too bad. I cannot understand how it happened. I suppose it was that I was so busy getting poor Graham's papers and things together to send on shore, that I overlooked it. It cannot now be posted till we get to Galles."

That was all. But was it not enough, and more than enough? The next few weeks passed for Anne Medway like a happy dream. She was content now to wait—years even—she had recovered faith in herself, faith in the future.

The next Indian mail brought her no letter, somewhat to her surprise. She wondered what had made Kenneth allude to his perhaps seeing her again before long—she wondered almost more, what was the "strange experience" to which he referred. Could it have had any connection with her *most* strange experience that November afternoon? And thus "wondering" she was sitting alone—in her own house again by this time—one evening towards the end of April, when a ring at the bell made her look up from the book she was reading, half dreamily asking herself what visitor could be coming so late. She heard steps and voices—a door shutting—then Ambrose opened that of the drawing-room where she was sitting and came up to her, his wrinkled old face all flushed and beaming.

"It was me that frightened you so that day, ma'am," he began. "It's right it should be me again. But it's himself—his very own self this time. You may believe me, indeed."

Anne started to her feet. She felt herself growing pale—she trembled so that she could scarcely stand.

"Where is he?" she said. "You have not put him into the library—anywhere but there?"

"He would have it so, ma'am. He said he would explain to you. Oh, go to him, ma'am—you'll see it'll be all right."

Anne made her way to the library. But at the door a strange tremor seized her. She could scarcely control herself to open it. Yes—there again on the hearthrug stood the tall figure she had so often pictured thus to herself. She trembled and all but fell, but his voice—his own hearty, living voice—speaking to her in accents tenderer and deeper than ever heretofore—reassured her, and dispersed at once the fear that had hovered about her.

"Anne, my dear Anne. It is I myself. Don't look so frightened;" and in a moment he had led her forward, and stood with his hand on her shoulder, looking with his kind, earnest eyes into hers.

"Yes," he said dreamily, "it was just thus. Oh, how often I have thought of this moment! Anne, if I am mistaken forgive my presumption, but I can't think I am. Anne, my darling, you *do* love me?"

There was no need of words. Anne hid her face on his shoulder for one happy moment. Then amidst the tears that *would* come she told him all—all she had suffered and hoped and feared—her love and her agony of humiliation when she thought it was not returned—her terrible grief when she thought him dead; and yet the consolation of believing herself to have been his last thought in life.

"So you shall be—my first and my last," he answered. "My Anne—my very own."

And then she told him more of the strange story we know. He listened with intense eagerness, but without testifying much surprise, far less incredulity.

"I anticipated something of the kind," he said, after a moment or two of silence. "It is very strange. Listen, Anne: at the time, the exact time, so far as I can roughly calculate, at which you thought you saw me, I was *dreaming* of you. It was between four and five o'clock in the afternoon, was it not?"

Anne bowed her head in assent.

"That would have made it about six o'clock where we then were," he went on consideringly. "Yes; it was about seven when I awoke. I had lain down that afternoon with a frightful headache. Poor Graham had died shortly before midnight the night before, and I had not been able to sleep, though I was very tired. I daresay I was not altogether in what the doctors call a normal condition, from the physical fatigue and the effect generally of having watched him die. I was feeling less *earthly*, if you can understand, than one usually does. It is—to me at least—*impossible* to watch a deathbed without wondering about it all—about what comes after—intensely. And Graham was so good, so patient and resigned and trustful, though it was awfully hard for him to die. He had every reason to wish to live.

"Well, Anne, when I fell asleep that afternoon I at once began dreaming about you. I had been thinking about you a great deal, constantly almost, ever since we set sail. For, just before starting, I had got a hint that this appointment—I have not told you about it yet, but that will keep; I have accepted it, as you see by my being here—I got a hint that it would probably be offered me, and that if I didn't mind paying my passage back almost as soon as I got out, I had better make up my mind to accept it. I felt that it hung upon *you*, and yet I did not see how to find out what you would say without—without risking what I *had*—your sisterly friendship. It came into my head just as I was falling asleep that I would write to you from the Cape, and tell you of Graham's death to avoid any mistaken report, and that I might in my letter somehow feel my way a little. This was all in my mind, and as I fell asleep it got confused so that I did not know afterwards clearly where to separate it from my dream."

"And what was the dream?" asked Anne breathlessly.

"*Almost precisely what you saw,*" he replied. "I fancied myself here—rushing upstairs to the library in my haste to see you—to tell you I was not dead, and to ask you if you would have cared much had it been so. I saw all the scene—the hall, the staircase already lighted. This room—and you coming in at the door with a half-frightened, half-eager look in your face. Then it grew confused. I next remember standing here beside you on the hearthrug with my hand on your shoulder—*thus*, Anne—and gazing into your eyes, and struggling, *struggling* to ask you what I wanted so terribly to know. But the words would not come, and the agony seemed to awake me. Yet with the awaking came the answer. *Something* had answered me; I said to myself, 'Yes, Anne does love me.'"

And Anne remembered the strange feeling of joy which had come to her even in the first bitterness of her grief. She turned to the hand that still lay on her shoulder and kissed it. "Oh, Kenneth," she said, "how thankful we should be! But how strange, to think that we owe all to a dream! *Was* it a dream, Kenneth?"

He shook his head.

"You must ask that of wiser people than I," he said. "I suppose it was."

"But how could it have been a dream?" said Anne again. "You forget, Kenneth—Ambrose saw you too."

"Though I did not see him, nor even think of him. Yes, that makes it even more incomprehensible. It must have been the old fellow's devotion to you, Anne, that made him sympathise with you, somehow."

"I am glad he saw you," said Anne. "I should prefer to think it more than a dream. And there is always more evidence in favour of any story of the kind if it has been witnessed by two. But there is one other thing I want to ask you. It has struck me since that you answered me rather abstractedly that last evening when I spoke about your address, and asked if there was any other of the name in your regiment. Once or twice I have drawn a faint ray of hope from remembering your not very decided answer."

"Yes, it was stupid of me; I half remembered it afterwards. I should have explained it, but it scarcely seemed worthwhile. I did know another Major Graham might be joining us at Funchal, for that very day I had been entrusted with letters for him. But I *was* abstracted that evening, Anne. I was trying to persuade myself I didn't care for what I now know I care for more than for life itself—your love—Anne."

# Unexplained

(A story from *Four Ghost Stories*).

## PART 1

*For facts are stubborn things.*—SMOLLETT.

"Silberbach! What in the name of everything that is eccentric should you go there for? The most uninteresting, out-of-the-way, altogether unattractive little hole in all Germany? What can have put Silberbach in your head?"

"I really don't know," I answered, rather tired, to tell the truth, of the discussion. "There doesn't seem any particular reason why anybody ever should go to Silberbach, except that Goethe and the Duke of Weimar are supposed to have gone there to dance with the peasant maidens. I certainly don't see that that is any reason why *I* should go there. Still, on the other hand, I don't see that it is any reason why I should *not*? I only want to find some thoroughly country place where the children and I can do as we like for a fortnight or so. It is really too hot to stay in a town, even a little town like this."

"Yes, that is true," said my friend. "It is a pity you took up your quarters in the town. You might have taken a little villa outside, and then you would not have needed to go away at all."

"I wanted a rest from housekeeping, and our queer old inn is very comfortable," I said. "Besides, being here, would it not be a pity to go away without seeing anything of the far-famed Thuringian Forest?"

"Yes, certainly it would. I quite agree with you about everything except about Silberbach. *That* is what I cannot get over.

You have not enough self-assertion, my dear. I am certain Silberbach is some freak of Herr von Walden's—most unpractical man. Why, I really am not at all sure that you will get anything to eat there."

"I am not afraid of *that* part of it," I replied philosophically. "With plenty of milk, fresh eggs, and bread and butter, we can always get on. And those I suppose we are sure to find."

"Milk and eggs—yes, I suppose so. Butter is doubtful once you leave the tourist track, and the bread will be the sour bread of the country."

"I don't mind that—nor do the children. But if the worst comes to the worst we need not stay at Silberbach—we can always get away."

"That is certainly true; if one can get there, one can, I suppose, always get away," answered Fräulein Ottilia with a smile, "though I confess it is a curious inducement to name for going *to* a place—that one can get away from it! However, we need not say any more about it. I see your heart is set on Silberbach, and I am quite sure I shall have the satisfaction of hearing you own I was right in trying to dissuade you from it, when you come back again," she added, rather maliciously.

"Perhaps so. But it is not *only* Silberbach we are going to. We shall see lots of other places. Herr von Walden has planned it all. The first three days we shall travel mostly on foot. I think it will be great fun. Nora and Reggie are enchanted. Of course I would not travel on foot alone with them; it would hardly be safe, I suppose?"

"Safe? oh yes, safe enough. The peasants are very quiet, civil people—honest and kindly, though generally desperately poor! But you would be *safe* enough anywhere in Thuringia. It is not like Alsace, where now and then one does meet with rather queer customers in the forests. So goodbye, then, my dear, for the next two or three weeks—and may you enjoy yourself."

"Especially at Silberbach?"

"*Even* at Silberbach—that is to say, even if I have to own you were right and I wrong. Yes, my dear, I am unselfish enough to hope you will return having found Silberbach an earthly paradise."

And waving her hand in *adieu*, kind Fräulein Ottilia stood at her garden-gate watching me make my way down the dusty road.

"She is a little prejudiced, I daresay," I thought to myself. "Prejudiced against Herr von Walden's choice, for I notice everyone here has their pet places and their special aversions. I daresay we shall like Silberbach, and if not, we need not stay there after the Waldens leave us. Anyway, I shall be thankful to get out of this heat into the real country."

I was spending the summer in a part of Germany hitherto new ground to me. We had—the "we" meaning myself and my two younger children, Nora of twelve and Reggie of nine—settled down for the greater part of the time in a small town on the borders of the Thuringian Forest. Small, but not in its own estimation unimportant, for it was a "*Residenz*," with a fortress of sufficiently ancient date to be well worth visiting, even had the view from its ramparts been far less beautiful than it was. And had the little town possessed no attractions of its own, natural or artificial, the extreme cordiality and kindness of its most hospitable inhabitants would have left the pleasantest impression on my mind. I was sorry to leave my friends even for two or three weeks, but it was *too* hot! Nora was pale and Reggie's noble appetite gave signs of flagging. Besides—as I had said to Ottilia—it would be too absurd to have come so far and not see the lions of the neighbourhood.

So we were to start the next morning for an excursion in the so-called "Forest," in the company of Herr von Walden, his wife and son, and two young men, friends of the latter. We were to travel by rail over the first part of the ground, uninteresting enough, till we reached a point where we could make our way on foot through the woods for a considerable distance. Then, after spending the night in a village whose beautiful situation had tempted some enterprising speculator to build a good hotel, we proposed the next day to plunge still deeper into the real recesses of the forest, walking and driving by turns, in accordance with our inclination and the resources of the country in respect of *Einspänners*—the light carriage with the horse invariably yoked at one side of the pole instead of between shafts, in which one gets about more speedily and safely than might be imagined.

And at the end of three or four days of this, weather permitting, agreeably nomad life, our friends the Waldens, obliged to return to their home in the town from which we started, were to leave my children and me for a fortnight's country air in this same village of Silberbach which Ottilia so vehemently objected to. I did not then, I do not now, know—and I am pretty sure he himself could not say—why our guide, Herr von Walden, had chosen Silberbach from among the dozens of other villages which could quite as well—as events proved, indeed, infinitely better—have served our very simple purpose. It was a chance, as such things often are, but a chance which, as you will see, left its mark in a manner which can never be altogether effaced from my memory.

The programme was successfully carried out. The weather was magnificent. Nobody fell ill or footsore, or turned out unexpectedly bad-tempered. And it was hot enough, even in the forest shades, which we kept to as much as possible, to have excused some amount of irritability. But we were all sound and strong, and had entered into a tacit compact of making the best of things and enjoying ourselves as much as we could. Nora and Reggie perhaps, by the end of the second day, began to have doubts as to the delights of indefinitely continued walking excursions; and though they would not have owned to it, they were not, I think, sorry to hear that the greater part of the fourth day's travels was to be on wheels.

But they were very well off. Lutz von Walden and his two friends—a young baron, rather the typical "German student" in appearance, though in reality as hearty and unsentimental as any John Bull of his age and rank—and George Norman, an English boy of seventeen or eighteen, "getting up" German for an army examination—were all three only too ready to carry my little boy on their backs on any sign of over-fatigue. And, indeed, more than one hint reached me that they would willingly have done the same by Nora, had the dignity of her twelve years allowed of such a thing. She scarcely looked her age at that time, but she was very conscious of having entered "on her teens," and the struggle between this new importance and her hitherto almost boyish tastes was amusing to watch.

She was strong and healthy in the extreme, intelligent though not precocious, observant but rather matter-of-fact, with no undue development of the imagination, nothing that by any kind of misapprehension or exaggeration could have been called "morbid" about her. It was a legend in the family that the word "nerves" existed not for Nora: she did not know the meaning of *fear*, physical or moral. I could sometimes wish she had never learnt otherwise. But we must take the bad with the good, the shadow inseparable from the light. The first perception of things not dreamt of in her simple childish philosophy came to Nora as I would not have chosen it; but so, I must believe, it had to be.

"Where are we to sleep tonight, Herr von Walden, please?" asked Reggie from the heights of Lutz's broad shoulders, late that third afternoon, when we were all, not the children only, beginning to think that a rest even in the barest of inn parlours, and a dinner even of the most modest description, would be very welcome.

"Don't tease so, Reggie," said Nora. "I'm sure Herr von Walden has told you the name twenty times already."

"Yes, but I forget it," urged the child; and good-natured Herr von Walden, nowise loath to do so again, took up the tale of our projected doings and destinations.

"Tonight, my dear child, we sleep at the pretty little town— yes, town I may almost call it—of Seeberg. It stands in what I may call an oasis of the forest, which stops abruptly, and begins again some miles beyond Seeberg. We should be there in another hour or so," he went on, consulting his watch. "I have, of course, written for rooms there, as I have done to all the places where we mean to halt. And so far I have not proved a bad courier, I flatter myself?"

He paused, and looked round him complacently.

"No, indeed," replied everybody. "The very contrary. We have got on capitally."

At which the beaming face of our commander-in-chief beamed still more graciously.

"And tomorrow," continued Reggie in his funny German, pounding away vigorously at Lutz's shoulders meanwhile, "what do we do tomorrow? We must have an *Einspänner*—is it not so? not that we are tired, but you said we had far to go."

"Yes, an *Einspänner* for the ladies—your amiable mother, Miss Nora, and my wife, and you, Reggie, will find a corner beside the driver. Myself and these young fellows," indicating the three friends by a wave of the hand, "will start from Seeberg betimes, giving you *rendez vous* at Ulrichsthal, where there are some famous ruins. And you must not forget," he added, turning to his wife and me, "to stop at Grünstein as you pass, and spend a quarter of an hour in the china manufactory there."

"Just what I wanted," said Frau von Walden. "I have a tea-service from there, and I am in hopes of matching it. I had a good many breakages last winter with a dreadfully careless servant, and there is a good deal to replace."

"I don't think I know the Grünstein china," I said. "Is it very pretty?"

"It is very like the blue-and-white that one sees so much of with us," said Frau von Walden. "That, the ordinary blue-and-white, is made at Blauenstein. But there is more variety of colours at Grünstein. They are rather more enterprising there, I fancy, and perhaps there is a finer quality of china clay, or whatever they call it, in that neighbourhood. I often wonder the Thuringian china is not more used in England, where you are so fond of novelties."

"And where nothing is so appreciated as what comes from a distance," said George Norman. "By Jove! isn't that a pretty picture!" he broke off suddenly, and we all stood still to admire.

It was the month of August; already the subdued evening

lights were replacing the brilliant sunshine and blue sky of the glowing summer day. We were in the forest, through which at this part ran the main road which we were following to Seeberg. At one side of the road the ground descended abruptly to a considerable depth, and there in the defile far beneath us ran a stream, on one bank of which the trees had been for some distance cleared away, leaving a strip of pasture of the most vivid green imaginable.

And just below where we stood, a goatherd, in what—thanks possibly to the enchantment of the distance—appeared a picturesque costume, was slowly making his way along, piping as he went, and his flock, of some fifteen or twenty goats of every colour and size, following him according to their own eccentric fashion, some scrambling on the bits of rock a little way up the ascending ground, others quietly browsing here and there on their way—the tinkling of their collar-bells reaching us with a far-away, silvery sound through the still softer and fainter notes of the pipe. There was something strangely fascinating about it all—something pathetic in the goatherd's music, simple, barbaric even as it was, and in the distant, uncertain tinkling, which impressed us all, and for a moment or two no one spoke.

"What is it that it reminds me of?" said Lutz suddenly. "I seem to have seen and heard it all before."

"Yes, I know exactly how you mean," I replied. "It is like a dream;" and as I said so, I walked on again a little in advance of the others with Lutz and his rider. For I *thought* I saw a philosophical or metaphysical dissertation preparing in Herr von Walden's bent brows and general look of absorption, and somehow, just then, it would have spoilt it all. Lutz seemed instinctively to understand, for he too for a moment or so was silent, when suddenly a joyful cry arose.

"Seeberg!" exclaimed several voices; for the first sight of our temporary destination broke upon the view all at once, as is often the case in these more or less wooded districts. One travels for hours together as if in an enchanted land of changeless monotony; trees, trees everywhere and nothing but trees—

one could fancy late in the afternoon that one was back at the early morning's starting-point—when suddenly the forest stops, sharply and completely, where the hand of man has decreed that it should, not by gradual degrees as when things have been left to the gentler management of nature and time.

So our satisfaction was the greater from not having known the goal of that day's journey to be so near. We began to allow to each other for the first time that we were "a *little* tired," and with far less hesitation that we were "*very* hungry." Still we were not a very dilapidated-looking party when the inhabitants of Seeberg turned out at doors and windows to inspect us. Reggie, of course, whom no consideration could induce to make his entry on Lutz's shoulders, looking the freshest of all, and eliciting many complimentary remarks from the matrons and maidens of the place as we passed.

Our quarters at Seeberg met with the approval of everybody. The supper was excellent, our rooms as clean and comfortable as could be wished.

"So far," I could not help saying to my friends, "I have seen no signs of the 'roughing it' for which you prepared me. I call this luxurious."

"Yes, this is very comfortable," said Herr von Walden. "At Silberbach, which we shall reach tomorrow evening, all will be much more homely."

"But that is what I like," I maintained stoutly. "I assure you I am not at all *difficile*, as the French say."

"Still," began Frau von Walden, "are you sure that you know what 'roughing it' means? One has such romantic, unpractical ideas till one really tries it. For me, I confess, there is something very depressing in being without all the hundred and one little comforts, not to say luxuries, that have become second nature to us, and yet I do not think I am a self-indulgent woman."

"Certainly not," I said, and with sincerity.

"If it were necessary," she went on, "I hope I should be quite ready to live in a cottage and make the best of it cheerfully. But when it is not necessary? Don't you think, my dear friend, it would perhaps be wiser for you to arrange to spend your two or three weeks *here*, and not go on to Silberbach? You might return here tomorrow from Ulrichsthal while we make our way home, by Silberbach, if my husband really wishes to see it."

I looked at her in some surprise. What possessed everybody to caution me so against Silberbach? Everybody, that is to say, except Herr von Walden himself. A spice of contradiction began to influence me. Perhaps the worthy Herr had himself been influenced in the same way more than he realised.

"I don't see why I should do so," I said. "We expect really to enjoy ourselves at Silberbach. You have no reason for advising me to give it up?"

"No, oh no—none in particular," she replied. "I have only a feeling that it is rather out of the way and lonely for you. Supposing, for instance, one of the children got ill there?"

"Oh, my dear, you are *too* fanciful," said her husband. "Why should the children get ill there more than anywhere else? If one thought of all these possibilities one would never stir from home."

"And you know my maid is ready to follow me as soon as I quite settle where we shall stay," I said. "I shall not be alone more than four-and-twenty hours. Of course it would have been nonsense to bring Lina with us; she would have been quite out of her element during our walking expeditions."

"And I have a very civil note from the inn at Silberbach, the *Katze*," said Herr von Walden, pulling a mass of heterogeneous-looking papers out of his pocket. "Where can it be? Not that it matters; he will have supper and beds ready for us tomorrow night. And then," he went on to me, "if you like it you can make some arrangement for the time you wish to stay, if not you can return here, or go on to any place that takes your fancy. We, my wife and I and these boys, *must* be home by Saturday afternoon, so we can only stay the one night at Silberbach," for this was Thursday.

And so it was settled.

The next day dawned as bright and cloudless as its predecessors. The gentlemen had started—I should be afraid to say how early—meaning to be overtaken by us at Ulrichsthal. Reggie had gone to bed with the firm intention of accompanying them, but as it was not easy to wake him and get him up in time to eat his breakfast, and be ready when the *Einspänner* came round to the door, my predictions that he would be too sleepy for so early a start proved true.

It was pleasant in the early morning—pleasanter than it would be later in the day. I noticed an unusual amount of blue haze on the distant mountain-tops, for the road along which we were driving was open on all sides for some distance, and the view was extensive.

"That betokens great heat, I suppose," I said, pointing out the appearance I observed to my companion.

"I suppose so. That bluish mist probably increases in hot and sultry weather," she said. "But it is always to be seen more or less in this country, and is, I believe, peculiar to some of the German hill and forest districts. I don't know what it comes from—whether it has to do with the immense number of pines in the forests, perhaps. Some one, I think, once told me that it indicates the presence of a great deal of electricity in the air, but I am far too ignorant to know if that is true or not."

"And I am far too ignorant to know what the effect would be if it were so," I said. "It is a very healthy country, is it not?"

"For strangers it certainly is. Doctors send their patients here from all parts of Germany. But the inhabitants themselves do not seem strong or healthy. One sees a good many deformed people, and they all look pale and thin—much less robust than the people of the Black Forest. But that may come from their poverty—the peasants of the Black Forest are proverbially well off."

A distant, very distant, peal of thunder was heard at this moment.

"I hope the weather is not going to break up *just* yet," I said. "Are there often bad thunderstorms here?"

"Yes; I think we do have a good many in this part of the world," she replied. "But I do not think there are any signs of one at present."

And then, still a little sleepy and tired from our unusual exertions of the last three days, we all three, Frau von Walden, Nora, and myself, sat very still for some time, though the sound of Reggie's voice persistently endeavouring to make the driver understand his inquiries, showed that he was as lively as ever.

He turned round after a while in triumph.

"Mamma, Frau von Walden," he exclaimed, "we are close to that place where they make the cups and saucers. Herr von Walden said we weren't to forget to go there—and you all *would* have forgotten, you see, if it hadn't been for me," he added complacently.

"Grünstein," said Frau von Walden. "Well, tell the driver to stop there, he can rest his horses for half an hour or so; and thank you for reminding us, Reggie, for I should have been sorry to lose the opportunity of matching my service."

The china manufactory was not of any very remarkable interest, at least not for those who had visited such places before. But the people were exceedingly civil, and evidently very pleased to have visitors; and while my friend was looking out the things she was specially in search of—a business which promised to take some little time—a good-natured sub-manager, or functionary of some kind, proposed to take the children to see the sheds where the first mixing and kneading took place, the moulding rooms, the painting rooms, the ovens—in short, the whole process.

They accepted his offer with delight, and I wandered about the various pattern or show rooms, examining and admiring all that was to be seen, poking into corners where any specially pretty bit of china caught my eye. But there was no great variety in design or colour, though both were good of their kind, the Grünsteiners, like their rivals of Blauenstein, seeming content to follow in the steps of their fathers without seeking for new inspirations. Suddenly, however, all but hidden in a corner, far away back on a shelf, a flash of richer tints made me start forward eagerly.

There was no one near to apply to at the moment, so I carefully drew out my treasure trove. It was a cup and saucer, evidently of the finest quality of china, though pretty similar in shape to the regular Grünstein ware, but in colouring infinitely richer—really beautiful, with an almost Oriental cleverness in the blending of the many shades, and yet decidedly more striking and uncommon than any of the modern Oriental with which of late years the facilities of trade with the East make us so familiar. I stood with the cup in my hand, turning it around and admiring it, when Frau von Walden and the woman who had been attending to her orders came forward to where I was.

"See here," I exclaimed; "here is a lovely cup! Now a service like that *would* be tempting! Have you more of it?" I inquired of the woman.

She shook her head.

"That is all that remains," she said. "We have never kept it in stock; it is far too expensive. Of course it can be made to order, though it would take some months, and cost a good deal."

"I wish I could order a service of it," I said; but when I heard how much it would probably cost it was my turn to shake my head. "No, I must consider about it," I decided; "but I really have never seen anything prettier. Can I buy this cup?"

The woman hesitated.

"It is the only one left," she said; "but I think—oh yes, I feel sure—we have the pattern among the painting designs. This cup belonged to, or rather was an extra one of, a tea-service made expressly for the Duchess of T——, on her marriage, now some years ago. And it is curious, we sold the other one—there were two too many—to a compatriot of yours (the gracious lady is English?) two or three years ago. He admired them so much, and felt sure his mother would send an order if he took it home to show her. A tall, handsome young man he was. I remember it so well; just about this time of the year, and hot, sultry weather like this. He was travelling on foot—for pleasure, no doubt—for he had quite the air of a *milord*. And he bought the cup, and took it with him. But he has never written! I made sure he would have done so."

"He did not leave his name or address?" I said; for the world is a small place: it was just possible I might have known him, and the little coincidence would have been curious.

"Oh no," said the woman. "But I have often wondered why he changed his mind. He seemed so sure about sending the order. It was not the price that made him hesitate; but he wished his lady mother to make out the list herself."

"Well, I confess the price *does* make *me* hesitate," I said, smiling. "However, if you will let me buy this cup, I have great hopes of proving a better customer than my faithless compatriot."

"I am sure he *meant* to send the order," said the woman. She spoke quite civilly, but I was not sure that she liked my calling him "faithless."

"It is evident," I said to Frau von Walden, "that the good-looking young Englishman made a great impression on her. I rather think she gave *him* the fellow cup for nothing."

But after all I had no reason to be jealous, for just then the woman returned, after consulting the manager, to tell me I might have the cup and saucer, and for a less sum than their real worth, seeing that I was taking it, in a sense, as a pattern.

Then she wrapped it up for me, carefully and in several papers, of which the outside one was bright blue; and, very proud of my acquisition, I followed Frau von Walden to the other side of the building containing the workrooms, where we found the two children full of interest about all they had seen.

I should here, perhaps, apologise for entering into so much and apparently trifling detail. But as will, I think, be seen when I have told all I have to tell, it would be difficult to give the main facts fairly, and so as to avoid all danger of any mistaken impression, without relating the whole of the surroundings. If I tried to condense, to pick out the salient points, to enter into no particulars but such as directly and unmistakably lead up to the central interest, I might unintentionally omit what those wiser than I would consider as bearing on it. So, like a patient adjured by his doctor, or a client urged by his lawyer, to tell the whole at the risk of long-windedness, I prefer to run that risk, while claiming my readers' forgiveness for so doing, rather than that of relating my story incompletely.

And what I would here beg to have specially observed is *that not one word about the young Englishman had been heard by Nora.* She was, in fact, in a distant part of the building at the time the saleswoman was telling us about him. And, furthermore, I am equally certain, and so is Frau von Walden, that neither she nor I, then or afterwards, mentioned the subject to, or in the presence of, the children. I did not show her the cup and saucer, as it would have been a pity to undo its careful wrappings. All she knew about it will be told in due course.

We had delayed longer than we intended at the china manufactory, and in consequence we were somewhat late at the meeting-place—Ulrichsthal. The gentlemen had arrived there quite an hour before; so they had ordered luncheon, or dinner rather, at the inn, and thoroughly explored the ruins. But dinner discussed, and neither Frau von Walden nor I objecting to pipes, our cavaliers were amiably willing to show us all there was to be seen.

The ruins were those of an ancient monastery, one of the most ancient in Germany, I believe. They covered a very large piece of ground, and had they been in somewhat better preservation, they would have greatly impressed us; as it was they were undoubtedly, even to the unlearned in archæological lore, very interesting. The position of the monastery had been well and carefully chosen, for on one side it commanded a view of surpassing beauty over the valley through which we had travelled from Seeberg, while on the other arose still higher ground, richly wooded, for the irrepressible forest here, as it were, broke out again.

"It is a most lovely spot!" I said with some enthusiasm, as we sat in the shade of the ruined cloisters, the sunshine flecking the sward in eccentric patches as it made its way through what had evidently been richly-sculptured windows. "How one wishes it were possible to see it as it must have been—how many?—three or four hundred years ago, I suppose!"

Lutz grunted.

"What did you say, Lutz?" asked his mother.

"Nothing particular," he sighed. "I was only thinking of what I read in the guide-book, that the monastery was destroyed—partly by lightning, I believe, all the same—by order of the authorities, in consequence of the really awful wickedness of the monks who inhabited it. So I am not sure that it would have been a very nice place to visit at the time you speak of, gracious lady, begging your pardon."

"What a pity!" I said, with a little shudder. "I do not like to think of it. And I was going to say how beautiful it must be here in the moonlight! But now that you have disenchanted me, Lutz, I should not like it at all," and I arose as I spoke.

"Why not, mamma?" said Reggie curiously. I had not noticed that he and his sister were listening to us. "They're not here *now*—not those naughty monks."

"No, of course not," agreed practical Nora. "Mamma only means that it is a pity such a beautiful big house as this must have been *had* to be pulled down—such a waste when there are so many poor people in the world with miserable, little, stuffy houses, or none at all even! That was what you meant; wasn't it, mamma?"

"It is always a pity—the worst of pities—when people are wicked, wherever they are," I replied.

"But *all* monks are not bad," remarked Nora consolingly. "Think of the Great St. Bernard ones, with their dogs."

And on Reggie's inquiring mind demanding further particulars on the subject, she walked on with him somewhat in front of the rest of us, a happy little pair in the sunshine.

"Lutz," said his father, "you cannot be too careful what you say before children; they are often shocked or frightened by so little. Though yours are such healthy-minded little people," he added, turning to me, "it is not likely anything undesirable would make any impression on them."

I particularly remember this little incident.

It turned out a long walk to Silberbach, the longest we had yet attempted. Hitherto Herr von Walden had been on known ground, and thoroughly acquainted with the roads, the distances, and all necessary particulars; but it was the first time he had explored beyond Seeberg, and before we had accomplished more than half the journey, he began to feel a little alarm at the information given us by the travellers we came across at long intervals "coming from," not "going to St. Ives!" For the farther we went the greater seemed to be the distance we had to go!

"An hour or thereabouts," grew into "two," or even "three" hours; and at last, on a peculiarly stupid countryman assuring us we would scarcely reach our destination before nightfall, our conductor's patience broke down altogether.

"Idiots!" he exclaimed. "But I cannot stand this any longer. I will hasten on and see for myself; and if, as I expect, we are really not very far from Silberbach, it will be all the better for me to find out the *Katze*, and see that everything is ready for your arrival."

Frau von Walden seemed a little inclined to protest, but I begged her not to do so, seeing that three able-bodied protectors still remained to us, and that it probably was really tiresome for a remarkably good and trained pedestrian like her husband to have to adapt his vigorous steps to ours. And comfort came from an unexpected quarter. The old peasant woman, strong and muscular as any English labourer, whom we had hired at Seeberg to carry our bags and shawls through the forest, overheard the discussion, and for the first time broke silence to assure "the gracious ladies" that Silberbach was at no great distance; in half an hour or so we should come upon the first of its houses.

"Though as for the *Katze*," she added, "that was farther off—at the other end of the village;" and she went on muttering something about "if she had known we were going to the '*Katze*,'" which we did not understand, but which afterwards, "being translated," proved to mean that she would have stood out for more pay.

Sure enough, at the end of not more than three-quarters of

an hour we came upon one or two outlying houses. Then the trees gradually here grew sparser, and soon ceased, except in occasional patches. It was growing dusk; but as we emerged from the wood we found that we were on a height, the forest road having been a steady, though almost imperceptible, ascent. Far below gleamed already some twinkling cottage lights, and the silvery reflection of a small piece of water.

"To be sure," said young von Trachenfels, "there is a lake at Silberbach. Here we are at last! But where is the *Katze*?"

He might well ask. Never was there so tantalising a place as Silberbach. Instead of one compact, sensible village, it was more like three or four—nay, five or six—wretched hamlets, each at several minutes' distance from all the others. And the *Katze*, of course, was at the farther end of the farthest off from where we stood of these miserable little ragged ends of village! Climbing is tiring work, but it seemed to me it would have been preferable to what lay before us,—a continual descent, by the ruggedest of hill-paths, of nearly two miles, stumbling along in the half light, tired, footsore past description, yet—to our everlasting credit be it recorded—laughing, or trying to laugh, determined at all costs to make the best of it.

"I have no feet left," said poor Frau von Walden. "I am only conscious of two red-hot balls attached somehow to my ankles. I daresay *they* will drop off soon."

How thankful we were at last to attain to what bore some faint resemblance to a village street! How we gazed on every side to discover anything like an inn! How we stared at each other in bewilderment when at last, from we could not see where, came the well-known voice of Herr von Walden, shouting to us to stop.

"It is here—*here*, I say. You are going too far."

"Here," judging by the direction whence came the words, seemed to be a piled-up mass of hay, of proportions, exaggerated perhaps by the uncertain light, truly enormous. Was our friend buried in the middle of it? Not so. By degrees we made out his sunburnt face, beaming as ever, from out of a window behind the hay—cartful or stack, we were not sure which; and by still further degrees we discovered that the hay was being unloaded before a little house which it had almost entirely hidden from view, and inside which it was being carried, apparently by the front door, for there was no other door to be seen; but as we stood in perplexity, Herr von Walden, whose face had disappeared, emerged in some mysterious way.

"You can come through the kitchen, ladies; or by the window, if you please." But though the boys and Nora were got, or got themselves, in through the window, Frau von Walden and I preferred the kitchen; and I remember nothing more till we found ourselves all assembled—the original eight as we had started—in a very low-roofed, sandy-floored, tobacco-impregnated sort of cabin which, it appeared, was the *salle-à-manger* of the renowned hostelry "*zur Katze*" of Silberbach!

Herr von Walden was vigorously mopping his face. It was very red, and naturally so, considering the weather and the want of ventilation peculiar to the *Katze*; but it struck me there was something slightly forced about the beamingness.

"So, so," he began; "all's well that ends well! But I must explain," and he mopped still more vigorously, "that—there has been a slight, in short, a little, mistake about the accommodation I wish to secure. The supper I have seen to, and it will be served directly. But as to the beds," and here he could not help laughing, "our worthy host has beds enough"—we found afterwards that every available mattress and pillow in the village had been levied—"but there is but one *bedroom*, or two, I may say." For the poor Herr had not lost his time since his arrival. Appalled by the want of resources, he had suggested the levy of beds, and had got the host to spread them on the floor of a granary for himself, the three young men, and Reggie; while his wife, Nora, and I were to occupy the one bedroom, which luckily contained two small beds and a sort of settee, such as one sees in old farmhouses all over the world.

So it was decided; and, after all, for one night, what did it matter? For one night? that was for me the question! The supper was really not bad; but the look, and still worse the smell, of the room where it was served, joined no doubt to our excessive fatigue, made it impossible for me to eat anything. My friends were sorry, and I felt ashamed of myself for being so easily knocked up or knocked down. How thoroughly I entered into Frau von Walden's honestly-expressed dislike to "roughing it"! Yet it was not only the uncivilised look of the place, nor the coarse food, nor the want of comfort that made me feel that one night of Silberbach would indeed be enough for me.

A sort of depression, of fear almost, came over me when I pictured the two children and myself alone in that strange, out-of-the-world place, where it really seemed to me we might all three be made an end of without any one being the wiser of it! There was a general look of squalor and stolid depression about the people too: the landlord was a black-browed, surlily silent sort of man, his wife and the one maid-servant looked frightened and anxious, and the only voices to be heard were those of half-tipsy peasants drinking and quarrelling at the bar.

To say the least, it was not enlivening. Yet my pride was aroused. I did not like to own myself already beaten. After supper I sat apart, reflecting rather gloomily as to what I could or should do, while the young men and the children amused themselves with the one piece of luxury with which the poorest inn in Thuringia is sure to be provided. For, anomalous as it may seem, there was a piano, and by no means an altogether decrepit one, in the sandy-floored parlour!

Herr von Walden was smoking his pipe outside, the hay being by this time housed somewhere or other. His wife, who had been speaking to him, came in and sat down beside me.

"My dear," she said, "you must not be vexed with me for renewing the subject, but I cannot help it; I feel a responsibility. You must not, you really *must not*, think of staying here alone with those two children. It is not fit for you."

Oh, how I blessed her for breaking the ice! I could hardly help hugging her as I replied—diplomatically—

"You really think so?"

"Certainly I do; and so, though perhaps he won't say so as frankly—so does my husband. He says I am foolish and fanciful; but I confess to feeling a kind of dislike to the place that I cannot explain. Perhaps there is thunder in the air—that always affects my nerves—but I just feel that I *cannot* agree to your staying on here."

"Very well, I am quite willing to go back to Seeberg tomorrow," I replied meekly. "Of course we can't judge of the place by what we have seen of it tonight, but no doubt, as far as the inn is concerned, Seeberg is much nicer. I daresay we can see all we want by noon tomorrow, and get back to Seeberg in the afternoon."

Kind Frau von Walden kissed me rapturously on both cheeks.

"You don't *know*, my dear, the relief to my mind of hearing you say so! And now I think the best thing we can do is to go to bed. For we *must* start at six."

"So early!" I exclaimed, with a fresh feeling of dismay.

"Yes, indeed; and I must bid you goodbye tonight, for after all I am not to sleep in your room, which is much better, as I should have had to disturb you so early. My husband has found a tidy room next door in a cottage, and we shall do very well there."

What sort of a place she euphemistically described as "a tidy room" I never discovered. But it would have been useless to remonstrate, the kind creature was so afraid of incommoding us that she would have listened to no objections.

Herr von Walden came in just as we were about to wish each other goodnight.

"So!" he said, with a tone of amiable indulgence, "so! And what do you think of Silberbach? My wife feels sure you will not like it after all."

"I think I shall see as much as I care to see of it in an hour or two tomorrow morning," I replied quietly. "And by the afternoon the children and I will go back to our comfortable quarters at Seeberg."

"Ah, indeed! Yes, I daresay it will be as well," he said airily, as if he had nothing at all to do with decoying us to the place. "Then goodnight and pleasant dreams, and——"

"But," I interrupted, "I want to know *how* we are to get back to Seeberg. Can I get an *Einspänner* here?"

"To be sure, to be sure. You have only to speak to the landlord in the morning, and tell him at what hour you want it," he answered so confidently that I felt no sort of misgiving, and I turned with a smile to finish my goodnights.

The young men were standing close beside us. I shook hands with Trachenfels and Lutz, the latter of whom, though he replied as heartily as usual, looked, I thought, annoyed. George Norman followed me to the door of the room. In front of us was the ladder-like staircase leading to the upper regions.

"What a hole of a place!" said the boy. "I don't mind quite a cottage if it's clean and cheerful, but this place is so grim and squalid. I can't tell you how glad I am you're not going to stay on here alone. It really isn't fit for you."

"Well, you may be easy, as we shall only be here a few hours after you leave."

"Yes; so much the better. I wish I could have stayed, but I *must* be back at Kronberg tomorrow. Lutz could have stayed and seen you back to Seeberg, but his father won't let him. Herr von Walden is so queer once he takes an idea in his head—and he *won't* allow this place isn't all right."

"But I daresay there would be nothing to hurt us! Anyway, I will write to reassure you that we have not fallen into a nest of cut-throats or brigands," I said laughingly.

Certainly it never occurred to me or to my friends what *would* be the nature of the "experience" which would stamp Silberbach indelibly on our memory.

We must have been really very tired, for, quite contrary to our habit, the children and I slept late the next morning, undisturbed by the departure of our friends at the early hour arranged by them.

The sun was shining, and Silberbach, like every other place, appeared all the better for it. But the view from the window of our room was not encouraging. It looked out upon the village street—a rough, unkempt sort of track—and on its other side the ground rose abruptly to some height, but treeless and grassless. It seemed more like the remains of a quarry of some kind, for there was nothing to be seen but stones and broken pieces of rock.

"We must go out after our breakfast and look about us a little before we start," I said. "But how glad I shall be to get back to that bright, cheerful Seeberg!"

"Yes, indeed," said Nora. "I think this is the ugliest place I ever was at in my life." And she was not inclined to like it any better when Reggie, whom we sent down to reconnoitre, came back to report that we must have our breakfast in our own room.

"There are a lot of rough-looking men down there, smoking and drinking beer. You *couldn't* eat there," said the child.

But, after all, it was to be our last meal there, and we did not complain. The root coffee was not too unpalatable with plenty of good milk; the bread was sour and the butter dubious, as Ottilia had foretold, so we soaked the bread in the coffee, like French peasants.

"Mamma," said Nora gravely, "it makes me sorry for poor people. I daresay many never have anything nicer to eat than this."

"Not nicer than this!" I exclaimed. "Why, my dear child, thousands, not in Germany only, but in France and England, never taste anything as good."

The little girl opened her eyes. There are salutary lessons to be learnt from even the mildest experience of "roughing it."

Suddenly Nora's eyes fell on a little parcel in blue paper. It was lying on one of the shelves of the stove, which, as in most German rooms, stood out a little from the wall, and in its summer idleness was a convenient receptacle for odds and ends. This stove was a high one, of black-leaded iron; it stood between the door and the wall, on the same side as the door, and was the most conspicuous object in the room.

"Mamma," she exclaimed, "there is the parcel you brought

away from the china place. What is it? I wish you would show it me."

I gave a little exclamation of annoyance.

"Frau von Walden has forgotten it," I said; for my friend, returning straight to Kronberg, had offered to take it home for me in her bag for fear of accidents. "It does not matter," I added, "I will pack it among our soft things. It is a very pretty cup and saucer, but I will show it to you at Kronberg, for it is so nicely wrapped up. Now I am going downstairs to order the *Einspänner*, and we can walk about for an hour or two."

The children came with me. I had some trouble in disinterring the landlord, but at last I found him, of course with a pipe in his mouth, hanging about the premises. He listened to me civilly enough, but when I waited for his reply as to whether the *Einspänner* would be ready about twelve o'clock, he calmly regarded me without speaking. I repeated my inquiry.

"At twelve?" he said calmly. "Yes, no doubt the gracious lady might as well fix twelve as any other hour, for there was no such thing as a horse, much less an *Einspänner*, to be had at Silberbach."

I stared at him in my turn.

"No horse, no carriage to be had! How do people ever get away from here then?" I said.

"They don't get away—that is to say, if they come at all, they go as they came, in the carriage that brought them; otherwise they neither come nor go. The lady came on foot: she can go on foot; otherwise she can stay."

There seemed something sinister in his words. A horrible, ridiculous feeling came over me that we were caught in a net, as it were, and doomed to stay at Silberbach for the rest of our lives. But I looked at the man. He was simply stolid and indifferent. I did not believe then, nor do I now, that he was anything worse than sulky and uncivilised. He did not even care to have us as his visitors: he had no wish to retain us nor to speed us on our way. Had we remained at the "*Katze*" from that day to this, I don't believe he would have ever inquired what we stayed for!

"I *cannot* walk back to Seeberg," I said half indignantly, "we are too tired; nor would it be safe through the forest alone with two children."

The landlord knocked some ashes off his pipe.

"There may be an ox-cart going that way next week," he observed.

"Next week!" I repeated. Then a sudden idea struck me. "Is there a post-office here?" I said.

Of course there was a post-office; where can one go in Germany where there is not a post and telegraph office?

"The telegraph officials must be sadly overworked here," I said to myself. But as far as mine host was concerned, I satisfied myself with obtaining the locality of the post-office, and with something like a ray of hope I turned to look for the children. They had been amusing themselves with the piano in the now empty room, but as I called to them, Reggie ran out with a very red face.

"I wish I were a man, mamma. Fancy! a peasant—one of those men who were drinking beer—came and put his arm around Nora as she was playing. '*Du spielst schön,*' he said, and I *do* believe he meant to kiss her, if I hadn't shaken my fist at him."

"Yes, indeed, mamma," said Nora, equally but more calmly indignant. "I certainly think the sooner we get away the better."

I had to tell them of my discomfiture, but ended with my new idea.

"If there is a post-office," I said, "the mail must stop there, and the mail takes passengers."

But, arrived at the neat little post-house—to reach which without a most tremendous round we had to climb up a really precipitous path, so called, over the stones and rocks in front of the inn—new dismay awaited us. The postmaster was a very old man, but of a very different type from our host. He was sorry to disappoint us, but the mail only stopped here for *letters*—all *passengers* must begin their journey at—I forget where—leagues off on the other side from Silberbach. We wanted to get away? He was not surprised. *What had we come for?* No one ever came here. Were we Americans! Staying at the *"Katze"*! Good heavens! "A rough place." "I should rather think so."

And this last piece of information fairly overcame him. He evidently felt he must come to the rescue of these poor Babes in the wood.

"Come up when the mail passes from Seeberg this evening at seven, and I will see what I can do with the conductor. If he *happens* to have no passengers tomorrow, he *may* stretch a point and take you in. No one will be the wiser."

"Oh, thanks, thanks," I cried. "Of course I will pay anything he likes to ask."

"No need for that. He is a *braver Mann*, and will not cheat you."

"We shall be here at seven, then. I would rather have started to walk than stayed here indefinitely."

"Not *today* anyway. We shall have a storm," he said, looking up to the sky. "*Adieu. Auf Wiedersehen!*"

"I wish we had not to stay another night here," I said. "Still, tomorrow morning will soon come."

We spent the day as best we could. There was literally nothing to see, nowhere to go, except back into the forest whence we had come. Nor dared we go far, for the day grew more and more sultry; the strange, ominous silence that precedes a storm came on, adding to our feelings of restlessness and depression. And by about two o'clock, having ventured out again after "dinner," we were driven in by the first great drops. Huddled together in our cheerless little room we watched the breaking loose of the storm demons. I am not affected by thunder and lightning, nor do I dread them. But what a storm that was! Thunder, lightning, howling wind, and rain like no rain I had ever seen before, all mingled together.

An hour after it began, a cart, standing high and dry in the steep village street, was hidden by water to above the top of the wheels—a little more and it would have floated like a boat. But by about five, things calmed down; the few stupid-looking peasants came out of their houses, and gazed about them as if to see what damage had been done. Perhaps it was not much after all—they seemed to take it quietly enough; and by six all special signs of disturbance had disappeared—the torrents melted away as if by magic. Only a strange, heavy mist began to rise, enveloping everything, so that we could hardly believe the evening was yet so early. I looked at my watch.

"Half-past six. We must, mist or no mist, go up to the post-house. But I don't mind going alone, dears."

"No, no, mamma; I *must* go with you, to take care of you," said Reggie; "but Nora needn't."

"Perhaps it would be as well," said the little girl. "I have one or two buttons to sew on, and I *am* still rather tired."

And, knowing she was never timid about being left alone, thinking we should be absent half an hour at most, I agreed.

But the half hour lengthened into an hour, then into an hour and a half, before the weary mail made its appearance. The road through the forest must be all but impassable, our old friend told us. But oh, how tired Reggie and I were of waiting! though all the time never a thought of uneasiness with regard to *Nora* crossed my mind. And when the mail did come, delayed, as the postmaster had suspected, the good result of his negotiations made us forget all our troubles; for the conductor all but *promised* to take us the next morning, in consideration of a very reasonable extra payment. It was most unlikely he would have any, certainly not many passengers. We must be there, at the post-house, by nine o'clock, baggage and all, for he dared not wait a moment, and he would do his best.

Through the evening dusk, now fast replacing the scattered mist, Reggie and I, light of heart, stumbled down the rocky path.

"How pleased Nora will be! She will be wondering what has come over us," I said as the *Katze* came in view. "But what is that, Reggie, running up and down in front of the house? Is it a sheep, or a big white dog? or—or a child? Can it be Nora, and no cloak or hat? and so damp and chilly as it is? How can she be so foolish?"

And with a vague uneasiness I hurried on.

Yes, it was Nora. There was light enough to see her face. What had happened to my little girl? She was white—no, not white, ghastly. Her eyes looked glassy, and yet as if drawn into her head; her whole bright, fearless bearing was gone. She clutched me convulsively as if she would never again let me go. Her voice was so hoarse that I could scarcely distinguish what she said.

"Send Reggie in—he must not hear," were her first words—of rare unselfishness and presence of mind.

"Reggie," I said, "tell the maid to take candles up to our room, and take off your wet boots at once."

My children are obedient; he was off instantly.

Then Nora went on, still in a strained, painful whisper—

"Mamma, there has been a *man* in our room, and——"

"Did that peasant frighten you again, dear? Oh, I am so sorry I left you;" for my mind at once reverted to the man whom Reggie had shaken his fist at that morning.

"No, no; not that. I would not have minded. But, mamma, Reggie must never know it—he is so little, he could not bear it—mamma, it was *not* a man. It was—oh, mamma, I have seen a *ghost!*"

## PART 2

"A ghost," I repeated, holding the poor trembling little thing more closely. I think my first sensation was a sort of rage at whomever or whatever—ghost or living being—had frightened her so terribly. "Oh, Nora darling, it couldn't be a ghost. Tell me about it, and I will try to find out what it was. Or would you rather try to forget about it just now, and tell me afterwards? You are shivering so dreadfully. I *must* get you warm first of all."

"But let me tell you, mamma—I *must* tell you," she entreated piteously. "If you *could* explain it, I should be so glad, but I am afraid you can't," and again a shudder passed through her.

I saw it was better to let her tell it. I had by this time drawn her inside; a door in front stood open, and a bright fire caught my eyes. It was the kitchen, and the most inviting-looking room in the house. I peeped in—there was no one there, but from an inner room we heard the voice of the landlady hushing her baby to sleep.

"Come to the fire, Nora," I said. Just then Reggie came clattering downstairs, followed by Lieschen, the taciturn "maid of the inn."

"She has taken a candle upstairs, mamma, but I've not taken off my boots, for there's a little calf, she says, in the stable, and she's going to show it me. May I go?"

"Yes, but don't stay long," I said, my opinion of the sombre Lieschen improving considerably; and when they were out of hearing, "Now, Nora dear, tell me what frightened you so."

"Mamma," she said, a little less white and shivering by now, but still with the strange strained look in her eyes that I could not bear to see, "it *couldn't* have been a real man. Listen, mamma. When you and Reggie went, I got out a needle and thread—out of your little bag—and first I mended a hole in my glove, and then I took off one of my boots—the buttoning-up-the-side ones, you know—to sew a button on. I soon finished it, and then, without putting my boot on, I sat there, looking out of the window and wondering if you and Reggie would soon be back. Then I thought perhaps I could see if you were coming, better from the window of the place outside our room, where the hay and bags of flour are." (I think I forgot to say that to get to our room we had to cross at the top of the stair a sort of landing, along one side of which, as Nora said, great bags of flour or grain and trusses of hay were ranged; this place had a window with a somewhat more extended view than that of our room.)

"I went there, still without my boot, and I knelt in front of the window some time, looking up the rough path, and wishing you would come. But I was not the least dull or lonely. I was only a little tired. At last I got tired of watching there, and I thought I would come back to our room and look for something to do. The door was not closed, but I think I had half drawn it to as I came out. I pushed it open and went in, and then—I seemed to feel there was something that had not been there before, and I looked up; and just beside the stove—the door opens *against* the stove, you know, and so it had hidden it for a moment as it were—there, mamma, *stood a man*! I saw him as plainly as I see you. He was staring at the stove, afterwards I saw it must have been at your little blue paper parcel. He was a gentleman, mamma—quite young. I saw his coat, it was cut like George Norman's.

"I think he must have been an Englishman. His coat was dark, and bound with a little very narrow ribbon binding. I have seen coats like that. He had a dark blue neck-tie, his dress all looked neat and careful—like what all gentlemen are; I saw all that, mamma, before I clearly saw his face. He was tall and had fair hair—I saw that at once. But I was not frightened; just at first I did not even wonder how he *could* have got into the room—now I see he *couldn't* without my knowing. My first thought, it seems so silly," and Nora here smiled a little, "my first thought was, 'Oh, he will see I have no boot on,'"—which was very characteristic of the child, for Nora was a very "proper" little girl,—"and just as I thought that, *he* seemed to know I was there, for he slowly turned his head from the stove and looked at me, and then I saw his face. Oh, mamma!"

"Was there anything frightening about it?" I said.

"I don't know," the child went on. "It was not like any face I ever saw, and yet it does not *sound* strange. He had nice, rather wavy fair hair, and I think he must *have been* nice-looking. His eyes were blue, and he had a little fair moustache. But he was so *fearfully* pale, and a look over all that I can't describe. And his eyes when he looked at me *seemed not to see me*, and yet they turned on me. They looked dreadfully sad, and though they were so close to me, as if they were miles and miles away. Then his lips parted slightly, very slightly, as if he were going to speak. Mamma," Nora went on impressively, "they would have spoken if *I* had said the least word—I felt they would. But just then—and remember, mamma, it couldn't have been yet two seconds since I came in, I hadn't yet had *time* to get frightened—just then

68

there came over me the most awful feeling. I *knew* it was not a real man, and I seemed to hear myself saying inside my mind, 'It is a ghost,' and while I seemed to be saying it—I had not moved my eyes—while I looked at him———"

"He disappeared?"

"No, mamma, he did not even disappear. He was just *no longer there*. I was staring at nothing! Then came a sort of wild fear. I turned and rushed downstairs, even without my boot, and all the way the horrible feeling was that even though he was no longer there he might still be coming after me. I should not have cared if there had been twenty tipsy peasants downstairs! But I found Lieschen. Of course I said nothing to her; I only asked her to come up with a light to help me to find my boot, and as soon as I had put it on I came outside, and ran up and down—it was a long time, I think—till you and Reggie came at last. Mamma, *can* you explain it?"

How I longed to be able to do so! But I would not deceive the child. Besides, it would have been useless.

"No, dear. As yet I cannot. But I will try to understand it. There are several ways it may be explained. Have you ever heard of optical delusions, Nora?"

"I am not sure. You must tell me;" and she looked at me so appealingly, and with such readiness to believe whatever I told her, that I felt I would give anything to restore her to her former happy fearlessness.

But just then Reggie came in from the stable.

"We must go upstairs," I said; "and Lieschen," turning to her, "bring up our supper at once. We are leaving very early tomorrow morning, and we will go early to bed."

"Oh, mamma," whispered Nora, "if only we had not to stay all night in that room!"

But there was no help for it, and she was thankful to hear of the success of our expedition to the post-office. During supper we, of course, on Reggie's account, said nothing of Nora's fright, but as soon as it was over, Reggie declaring himself very sleepy, we got him undressed and put to bed on the settee originally intended for Nora. He was asleep in five minutes, and then Nora and I did our utmost to arrive at the explanation we so longed for. We thoroughly examined the room; there was no other entrance, no cupboard of any kind even. I tried to imagine that some of our travelling cloaks or shawls hanging on the back of a chair might, in the uncertain light, have taken imaginary proportions; that the stove itself might have cast a shadow we had not before observed; I suggested everything, but in vain. Nothing shook Nora's conviction that she had seen something *not* to be explained.

"For the light was *not* uncertain just then," she maintained; "the mist had gone and it had not begun to get dark. And then I saw him *so* plainly! If it had been a fancy ghost it wouldn't have looked like that—it would have had a long white thing floating over it, and a face like a skeleton perhaps. But to see somebody just like a regular gentleman—I could never have *fancied* that!"

There was a good deal in what she said. I had to give up my suggestions, and I tried to give Nora some idea of what are called "optical delusions," though my own comprehension of the theory was of the vaguest. She listened, but I don't think my words had much weight. And at last I told her I thought she had better go to bed and try to sleep. I saw she shrank from the idea, but it had to be.

"We can't sit up all night, I suppose," she said, "but I wish we could. I am so dreadfully afraid of waking in the night, and—and—*seeing him there again.*"

"Would you like to sleep in my bed? though it is so tiny, I could make room and put you inside," I said.

Nora looked wistfully at the haven of refuge, but her good sense and considerateness for me came to the front.

"No," she said, "neither of us would sleep, and you would be *so* tired tomorrow. I will get into my own bed, and I *will* try to sleep, mamma."

"And listen, Nora; if you are the least frightened in the night, or if you can't sleep, call out to me without hesitation. I am sure to wake often, and I will speak to you from time to time."

That was the longest night of my life! The first part was not the worst. By what I really thought a fortunate chance it was a club night of some kind at Silberbach—a musical club, of course; and all the musically-gifted peasants of the countryside assembled in the sanded parlour of the *Katze*. The noise was something indescribable, for though there may have been some good voices among them, they were drowned in the din. But though it prevented us from sleeping, it also fairly drove away all ghostly alarms.

By twelve o'clock or thereabouts the party seemed to disperse, and all grew still. Then came some hours I can never forget. There was faint moonlight by fits and starts, and I not only found it impossible to sleep, I found it impossible to keep my eyes shut. Some irresistible fascination seemed to force them open, and obliged me ever and anon to turn in the direction of the stove, from which, however, before going to bed, I had removed the blue paper parcel. And each time I did so I said to myself, "Am I going to see that figure standing there as Nora saw it? Shall I remain sane if I do? Shall I scream out? Will it look at *me*, in turn, with its sad unearthly eyes? Will it speak? If it moves across the room and comes near me, or if I see it going towards Nora, or leaning over my Reggie sleeping there in his innocence, misdoubting of no fateful presence near, what, oh! what *shall* I do?"

For in my heart of hearts, though I would not own it to Nora, I felt convinced that what she had seen was no living human being—whence it had come, or *why*, I could not tell. But in the quiet of the night I had thought of what the woman at the china factory had told us, of the young Englishman who had bought the other cup, who had promised to write and never done so! What had become of him? "If," I said to myself, "if I had the slightest reason to doubt his being at this moment alive and well in his own country, as he pretty certainly is, I should really begin to think he had been robbed and murdered by our surly landlord, and that his spirit had appeared to us—the first compatriots who have passed this way since, most likely—to tell the story."

I really think I must have been a little light-headed some part of that night. My poor Nora, I am certain, never slept, but I can only hope her imagination was less wildly at work than mine. From time to time I spoke to her, and every time she was awake, for she always answered without hesitation.

"I am quite comfortable, dear mamma, and I don't think I am very frightened;" or else, "I have not slept much, but I have said my prayers a great many times, and all the hymns I could remember. Don't mind about me, mamma, and do try to sleep."

I watched the dawn slowly breaking. From where I lay I could see through the window the high mound of rough stones and fragments of rock that I have described. At its foot there was a low wall loosely constructed of these same unhewn blocks, and the shapes that evolved themselves out of this wall, beside which grew two or three stunted trees, were more grotesque and extraordinary than I could describe.

They varied like the colours in a kaleidoscope with the wavering and increasing light. At one time it seemed to me that one of the trees was a gipsy woman enveloped in a cloak, extending her arm towards me threateningly; at another, two weird dogs seemed to be fighting together; but however fantastic and fearsome had been these strange effects of light and fancy mingled together, I should not have minded—I knew what they were; it was a relief to have anything to look at which could keep my eyes from constantly turning in the direction of that black iron stove.

I fell asleep at last, though not for long. When I woke it was bright morning—fresher and brighter, I felt, as I threw open the window, than the day before. With the greatest thankfulness that the night was over at last, as soon as I was dressed I began to put our little belongings together, and then turned to awake the children. Nora was sleeping quietly; it seemed a pity to arouse her, for it was not much past six, but I heard the people stirring about downstairs, and I had a feverish desire to get away; for though the daylight had dispersed much of the "eerie" impression of Nora's fright, there was a feeling of uneasiness, almost of insecurity, left in my mind since recalling the incident of the young man who had visited the china factory.

How did I know but that some harm had really come to him in this very place? There was certainly nothing about the landlord to inspire confidence. At best it was a strange and unpleasant coincidence. The evening before I had half thought of inquiring of the landlord or his wife, or even of Lieschen, if any English had ever before stayed at the *Katze*. If assured by them that we were the first, or at least the first "in their time," it would, I thought, help to assure Nora that the ghost had really been a delusion of some kind. But then, again, supposing the people of the inn hesitated to reply—supposing the landlord to be really in any way guilty, and my inquiries were to rouse his suspicions, would I not be risking dangerous enmity, besides strengthening the painful impression left on my own mind, and this corroboration of her own fear might be instinctively suspected by Nora, even if I told her nothing?

"No," I decided; "better leave it a mystery, in any case, till we are safely away from here." For, allowing that these people are perfectly innocent and harmless, their even telling me simply, like the woman at Grünstein, that such a person *had* been here, that he had fallen ill, possibly died here—I would rather not know it. It is certainly not probable that it was so; they would have been pretty sure to gossip about any occurrence of the kind, taciturn though they are. The wife would have talked of it to me—she is more genial than the others—for I had had a little kindly chat with her the day before, *à propos* of what every mother, of her class at least, is ready to talk about—the baby!

A pretty baby too, though the last, she informed me with a sort of melancholy pride, of four she had "buried"—using the same expression in her rough German as a Lancashire factory hand or an Irish peasant woman—one after the other. Certainly Silberbach was not a cheerful or cheering spot. "No, no," I made up my mind, "I would rather at present know nothing, even if there is anything to know. I can the more honestly endeavour to remove the impression left on Nora."

The little girl was so easily awakened that I was half inclined to doubt if she had not been "shamming" out of filial devotion. She looked ill still, but infinitely better than the night before, and she so eagerly agreed with me in my wish to leave the house as soon as possible, that I felt sure it was the best thing to do. Reggie woke up rosy and beaming—evidently no ghosts had troubled *his* night's repose. There was something consoling and satisfactory in seeing him quite as happy and hearty as in his own English nursery. But though he had no uncanny reasons like us for disliking Silberbach, he was quite as cordial in his readiness to leave it.

We got hold of Lieschen, and asked for our breakfast at once. As I had told the landlady the night before that we were leaving very early, our bill came up with the coffee. It was, I must say, moderate in the extreme—ten or twelve *marks*, if I remember rightly, for two nights' lodging and *almost* two days' board for three people. And such as it was, they had given us of their best. I felt a little twinge of conscience, when I said goodbye to the poor woman, for having harboured any doubts of the establishment. But when the gruff landlord, standing outside the door, smoking of course, nodded a surly "*adieu*" in return to our parting greeting, my feeling of unutterable thankfulness that we were not to spend another night under his roof regained the ascendant.

"Perhaps he is offended at my not having told him how I mean to get away, notwithstanding his stupidity about it," I said to myself, as we passed him. But no, there was no look of vindictiveness, of malice, of even annoyance on his dark face. Nay, more, I could almost have fancied there was the shadow of a smile as Reggie tugged at his Tam o' Shanter by way of a final salute. That landlord was really one of the most incomprehensible human beings it has ever been my fate to come across, in fact or fiction.

We had retained Lieschen to carry our modest baggage to the post-house, and having deposited it at the side of the road just where the coach stopped, she took her leave, apparently more than satisfied with the small sum of money I gave her, and civilly wishing us a pleasant journey. But though less gruff, she was quite as impassive as the landlord. She never asked where we were going, if we were likely ever to return again, and like her master, as I said, had we been staying there still, I do not believe she would ever have made an inquiry or expressed the slightest astonishment.

"There is really something very queer about Silberbach," I could not help saying to Nora, "both about the place and the people. They almost give one the feeling that they are half-witted, and yet they evidently are not. This last day or two I seem to have been living in a sort of dream or nightmare, and I shall not get over it altogether till we are fairly out of the place;" and though she said little, I felt sure the child understood me.

We were of course far, far too early for the post. The old man came out of his house, and seemed amused at our haste to be gone.

"I am afraid Silberbach has not taken your fancy," he said. "Well, no wonder. I think it is the dreariest place I ever saw."

"Then you do not belong to it? Have you not been here long?" I asked.

He shook his head.

"Only a few months, and I hope to get removed soon," he said. So *he* could have told me nothing, evidently! "It is too lonely here. There is not a creature in the place who ever touches a book—they are all as dull and stupid as they can be. But then they are very poor, and they live on here from year's end to year's end, barely able to earn their daily bread. Poverty degrades—there is no doubt of it, whatever the wise men may say. A few generations of it makes men little better than——" He stopped.

"Than?" I asked.

"Than," the old philosopher of the post-house went on, "pardon the expression—than pigs."

There were two or three of the fraternity grubbing about at

the side of the road; they may have suggested the comparison. I could hardly help smiling.

"But I have travelled a good deal in Germany," I said, "and I have never anywhere found the people so stupid and stolid and ungenial as here."

"Perhaps not," he said. "Still there are many places like this, only naturally they are not the places strangers visit. It is never so bad where there are a few country houses near, for nowadays it must be allowed it is seldom but that the gentry take some interest in the people."

"It is a pity no rich man takes a fancy to Silberbach," I said.

"That day will never come. The best thing would be for a railway to be cut through the place, but that, too, is not likely."

Then the old postmaster turned into his garden, inviting us civilly to wait there or in the office if we preferred. But we liked better to stay outside, for just above the post-house there was a rather tempting little wood, much prettier than anything to be seen on the other side of the village. And Nora and I sat there quietly on the stumps of some old trees, while Reggie found a pleasing distraction in alternately chasing and making friends with a party of ducks, which, for reasons best known to themselves, had deserted their native element and come for a stroll in the woods.

From where we sat we looked down on our late habitation; we could almost distinguish the landlord's slouching figure and poor Lieschen with a pail of water slung at each side as she came in from the well.

"What a life!" I could not help saying. "Day after day nothing but work. I suppose it is not to be wondered at if they grow dull and stolid, poor things." Then my thoughts reverted to what up here in the sunshine and the fresh morning air and with the pleasant excitement of going away I had a little forgotten—the strange experience of the evening before. It was difficult for me now to realise that I had been so affected by it. I felt *now* as if I wished I could see the poor ghost for myself, and learn if there was aught we could do to serve or satisfy him! For in the old orthodox ghost-stories there is always some reason for these ee-rie wanderers returning to the world they have left. But when I turned to Nora and saw her dear little face still white and drawn, and with an expression half-subdued, half-startled, that it had never worn before, I felt thankful that the unbidden visitor had attempted no communication.

"It might have sent her out of her mind," I thought. "Why, if he had anything to say, did he appear to her, poor child, and not to me?—though, after all, I am not at all sure that *I* should not have went out of my mind in such a case."

Before long the post-horn made itself heard in the distance; we hurried down, our hearts beating with the fear of possible disappointment. It was all right, however, there were *no* passengers, and nodding *adieu* to our old friend, we joyfully mounted into our places, and were bowled away to Seeberg.

There and at other spots in its pretty neighbourhood we pleasantly enough spent two or three weeks. Nora by degrees recovered her roses and her good spirits. Still, her strange experience left its mark on her. She was never again quite the merry, thoughtless, utterly fearless child she had been. I tried, however, to take the good with the ill, remembering that thorough-going childhood cannot last forever, that the shock possibly helped to soften and modify a nature that might have been too daring for perfect womanliness—still more, wanting perhaps in tenderness and sympathy for the weaknesses and tremors of feebler temperaments.

At Kronberg, on our return, we found that Herr von Walden was off on a tour to the Italian lakes, Lutz and young Trachenfels had returned to their studies at Heidelberg, George Norman had gone home to England. All the members of our little party were dispersed except Frau von Walden.

To her and to Ottilia I told the story, sitting together one afternoon over our coffee, when Nora was not with us. It impressed them both. Ottilia could not resist an "I told you so."

"I knew, I felt," she said, "that something disagreeable would happen to you there. I never will forget," she went on naïvely, "the dreary, dismal impression the place left on me the only time I was there—pouring rain and universal gloom and discomfort. We had to wait there a few hours to get one of the horses shod, once when I was driving with my father from Seeberg to Marsfeldt."

Frau von Walden and I could not help smiling at her. Still there was no smiling at my story, though both agreed that, viewed in the light of unexaggerated common sense, it was most improbable that there was any tragedy mixed up with the disappearance of the young man we had heard of at Grünstein.

"And indeed why we should speak of his 'disappearance' I don't know," said Frau von Walden. "He did not write to send the order he had spoken of—that was all. No doubt he is very happy at his own home. When you are back in England, my dear, you must try to find him out—perhaps by means of the cup. And then when Nora sees him, and finds he is not at all like the 'ghost,' it will make her the more ready to think it was really only some *very strange*, I must admit, kind of optical delusion."

"But Nora has never heard the Grünstein story, and is not to hear it," said Ottilia.

"And England is a wide place, small as it is in one sense," I said. "Still, if I *did* come across the young man, I half think I would tell Nora the whole, and by showing her how *my* imagination had dressed it up, I think I could perhaps lessen the effect on her of what she thought she saw. It would prove to her better than anything, the tricks that fancy may play us.

"And in the meantime, if you take my advice, you will allude to it as little as possible," said practical Ottilia. "Don't *seem* to avoid the subject, but manage to do so in reality."

"Shall you order the tea-service?" asked Frau von Walden.

"I hardly think so. I am out of conceit of it somehow," I said. "And it might remind Nora of the blue paper parcel. I think I shall give the cup and saucer to my sister."

And on my return to England I did so.

★ ★ ★ ★ ★

Two years later. A very different scene from quaint old Kronberg, or still more from the dreary "*Katze*" at Silberbach. We are in England now, though not at our own home. We are staying, my children and I—two older girls than little Nora, and Nora herself, though hardly now to be described as "little"—with my sister. Reggie is there too, but naturally not much heard of, for it is the summer holidays, and the weather is delightful. It is August again—a typical August afternoon—though a trifle too hot perhaps for some people.

"This time two years ago, mamma," said Margaret, my eldest daughter, "you were in Germany with Nora and Reggie. What a long summer that seemed! It is so much nicer to be all together."

"I should like to go to Kronberg and all those queer places," said Lily, the second girl; "especially to the place where Nora saw the ghost."

"I am quite sure you would not wish to *stay* there," I replied. "It is curious that you should speak of it just now. I was thinking of it this morning. It was just two years yesterday that it happened."

We were sitting at afternoon tea on the lawn outside the drawing-room window—my sister, her husband, Margaret, Lily, and I. Nora was with the schoolroom party inside.

"How queer!" said Lily.

"You don't think Nora has thought of it?" I asked.

"Oh no, I am sure she hasn't," said Margaret. "I think it has grown vague to her now. You know she spoke about it to us when she first came home. You had prepared us, you remember, mamma, and told us not to make too much of it. The first year after, she *did* think of it. She told me she was dreadfully frightened all that day for fear he should appear again. But since then I think she has gradually forgotten it."

"She is a very sensible child," said my sister. "And she is especially kind and sympathising with any of the little ones who seem timid. I found her sitting beside Charlie the other night for ever so long because he heard an owl hooting outside, and was frightened."

Just then a servant came out of the house, and said something to my brother-in-law. He got up at once.

"It is Mr. Grenfell," he said to his wife, "and a friend with him. Shall I bring them out here?"

"Yes, it would really be a pity to go into the house again—it is so nice out here," she replied. And her husband went to meet his guests.

He appeared again in a minute or two, stepping out through the low window of the drawing-room, accompanied by the two gentlemen.

Mr. Grenfell was a young man living in the neighbourhood, whom we had known from his boyhood; the stranger he introduced to us as Sir Robert Masters. He was a middle-aged man, with a quiet, gentle bearing and expression.

"You will have some tea?" said my sister, after the first few words of greeting had passed. Mr. Grenfell declined. His friend accepted.

"Go into the drawing-room, Lily, please, and ring for a cup and saucer," said her aunt, noting the deficiency. "There was an extra one, but someone has poured milk into the saucer. It surely can't have been you, Mark, for Tiny?" she went on, turning to her husband. "You *shouldn't* let a dog drink out of anything we drink out of ourselves."

My brother-in-law looked rather comically penitent; he did not attempt to deny the charge.

"Only, my dear, you must allow," he pleaded, "that we do not drink our tea out of the *saucers.*"

On what trifling links hang sometimes important results! Had it not been for Mark's transgressing in the matter of Tiny's milk we should never have learnt the circumstances which give to this simple relation of facts—valueless in itself—such interest, speculative and suggestive only, I am aware, as it may be found to possess.

Lily, in the meantime, had disappeared. But more quickly than it would have taken her to ring the bell, and await the servant's response to the summons, she was back again, carrying something carefully in her hand.

"Aunt," she said, "is it not a good idea? As you have a tea-spoon—I don't suppose Tiny used the spoon, did he?—I thought, instead of ringing for another, I would bring out the ghost-cup for Sir Robert. It is only fair to use it for once, poor thing, and just as we have been speaking about it. Oh, I assure you it is not dusty," as my sister regarded it dubiously. "It was inside the cabinet."

"Still, all the same, a little hot water will do it no harm," said her aunt—"provided, that is to say, that Sir Robert has no objection to drink out of a cup with such a name attached to it?"

"On the contrary," replied he, "I shall think it an honour. But you will, I trust, explain the meaning of the name to me? It puzzles me more than if it were a piece of ancient china—a great-great-grandmother's cup, for instance. For I see it is not old, though it is very pretty, and, I suppose, uncommon?"

There was a slight tone of hesitation about the last word which struck me.

"I have no doubt my sister will be ready to tell you all there is to tell. It was she who gave me the cup," replied the lady of the house.

Then Sir Robert turned to me. Looking at him full in the face I saw that there was a thoughtful, far-seeing look in his eyes, which redeemed his whole appearance from the somewhat commonplace gentlemanliness which was all I had before observed about him.

"I am greatly interested in these subjects," he said. "It would be very kind of you to tell me the whole."

I did so, more rapidly and succinctly of course than I have done here. It is not easy to play the part of narrator, with five or six pairs of eyes fixed upon you, more especially when the owners of several of them have heard the story a good many times before, and are quick to observe the slightest discrepancy, however unintentional. "There is, you see, very little to tell," I said in conclusion, "only there is always a certain amount of impressiveness about any experience of the kind when related at first hand."

"Undoubtedly so," Sir Robert replied. "Thank you very much indeed for telling it me."

He spoke with perfect courtesy, but with a slight absence of manner, his eyes fixed rather dreamily on the cup in his hand. He seemed as if trying to recall or recollect something.

"There should be a sequel to that story," said Mr. Grenfell.

"That's what I say," said Margaret eagerly. "It will be too stupid if we never hear any more. But that is always the way with modern ghost stories—there is no sense or meaning in them. The ghosts appear to people who never knew them, who take no interest in them, as it were, and then they have nothing to say—there is no *dénouement*, it is all purposeless."

Sir Robert looked at her thoughtfully.

"There is a good deal in what you say," he replied. "But I think there is a good deal also to be deduced from the very fact you speak of, for it is a fact. I believe what you call the meaninglessness and purposelessness—the arbitrariness, one may say, of modern experiences of the kind are the surest proofs of their authenticity. Long ago people mixed up fact and fiction, their imaginations ran riot and on some very slight foundation—often, no doubt, genuine, though slight—they built up a very complete and thrilling 'ghost story.' Nowadays we consider and philosophise, we want to get to the root and reason of things, and we are more wary of exaggeration.

"The result is that the only genuine ghosts are most unsatisfactory beings; they appear without purpose, and seem to be what, in fact, I believe they *almost* always are, irresponsible, purposeless will-o'-the-wisps. But from these I would separate the class of ghost stories the best attested and most impressive—those that have to do with the moment of death; any vision that appears just at or about that time has *generally* more meaning in it, I think you will find. Such ghosts appear for a reason, if no other than that of intense affection, which draws them near those from whom they are to be separated."

We listened attentively to this long explanation, though by

no means fully understanding it.

"I have often heard," I said, "that the class of ghost stories you speak of are the only thoroughly authenticated ones, and I think one is naturally more inclined to believe in them than in any others. But I confess I do not in the least understand what you mean by speaking of *other* ghosts as 'will-o'-the-wisps.' You don't mean that though at the moment of death there is a real being—the soul, in fact, as distinct from the body, in which all but materialists believe—that this has no permanent existence, but melts away by degrees till it becomes an irresponsible, purposeless *nothing*—a will-o'-the-wisp in fact? I think I heard of some theory of the kind lately in a French book, but it shocked and repelled me so that I tried to forget it. Just as well, *better*, believe that we are nothing but our bodies, and that all is over when we die. Surely you don't mean what I say?"

"God forbid," said Sir Robert, with a fervency which startled while it reassured me. "It is my profound belief that not only we are something more than our bodies, but that our bodies are the merest outer dress of the real ourselves. It is also my profound belief that at death we—the real we—either enter at once into a state of rest temporarily, or, in some cases—for I do not believe in any cut-and-dry rule independently of *individual* considerations—are privileged at once to enter upon a sphere of nobler and purer labour," and here the speaker's eyes glowed with a light that was not of this world. "Is it then the least probable, is it not altogether discordant with our 'common sense'—a Divine gift which we may employ fearlessly—to suppose that these real 'selves,' freed from the weight of their discarded garments, would leave either their blissful repose, *or*, still less, their new activities, to come back to wander about, purposelessly and aimlessly, in this world, at best only perplexing and alarming such as may perceive them? Is it not contrary to all we find of the wisdom and *reasonableness* of such laws as we *do* know something about?"

"I have often thought so," I said, "and hitherto this has led me to be very sceptical about all ghost stories."

"But they are often true—so far as they go," he replied. "Our natures are much more complex than we ourselves understand or realise. I cannot now go at all thoroughly into the subject, but to give you a rough idea of my will-o'-the-wisp theory—can you not imagine a sort of shadow, or echo of ourselves, lingering about the scenes we have frequented on this earth, which under certain very rare conditions—the state of the atmosphere among others—may be perceptible to those still 'clothed upon' with this present body? To attempt a simile, I might suggest the perfume that lingers when the flowers are thrown away, the smoke that gradually dissolves after the lamp is extinguished! This is very, very loosely and roughly the *sort* of thing I mean by my 'will-o'-the-wisps.'"

"I don't like it at all," said Margaret, though she smiled a little. "I think I should be more frightened if I saw that kind of ghost—I mean if I thought it that kind—than by a good, honest, old-fashioned one, who knew what it was about and meant to come."

"But you have just said," he objected, "that they never do seem to know what they are about. Besides, why should you be frightened?—our fears, ourselves in fact—are the only thing we really need be frightened of—our weaknesses and ignorances and folly. There was great truth in that rather ghastly story of Calderra's, allegory though it is, about the man whose evil genius was himself; have you read it?"

We all shook our heads.

"It is ignorance that frightens us," he went on. "In this instance think of the appearances we are speaking of as almost of the nature of a photograph, or the reflection in a looking-glass. I daresay we should have been terrified by these, had we not grown used to them, did we not know what they are. Somebody said lately what appalling things we should think our own *shadows*, if we had suddenly for the first time become aware of them."

"I don't mind so much," said Margaret, "when you speak of ghosts as a sort of photograph. But——" she hesitated.

"Pray say what you are thinking."

"Just now when you said how incredible it was that *real souls* should return to this earth, you only spoke of good people, did you not?"

In his turn Sir Robert hesitated.

"It is difficult to draw a line even in thought between good and bad people," he said, "and, thank God, it is not for us to do so. 'To my Maker alone I stand or I fall.' There is evil in the best; there is, I would fain hope," but here his face grew grave and sad, "good in the worst. But even allowing that we could draw the line, is it likely that the bad, even those who have all but lost the last spark, who don't want to be good, is it likely that they, if, as we must believe, under Divine control, would be allowed to leave their new life of punishment—punishment in the sense of *correction*, mind you—to come back here, wasting their time, one may say, to frighten perfectly innocent people for no purpose? No, I think I am quite consistent. Only try to get rid of all *fears*—that is what we can all do. But really I should apologise for all this lecture;" and he was turning to me with a smile, when his eyes fell on the cup which he had replaced on the table.

"I cannot get over the impression that I have seen that cup— no, not that cup, but one just like it, before. Not long ago, I fancy," he said.

"Oh, you must let us know if you find out anything," we all exclaimed.

"I certainly shall do so," he said, and a few minutes afterwards he and Mr. Grenfell took their leave.

But I had time for a word or two with the latter out of hearing of the others.

"Who is Sir Robert Masters?" I asked. "Have you known him long? He is a very uncommon and impressive sort of man."

"Yes, I thought you would like him. I have not personally known him long, but he is an old friend of friends of ours. He is of good family, an old baronetcy, but he is not much known in fashionable society. He travels a great deal, or has done so rather, and people say he has 'peculiar ideas,' though that would not go against him in the world. Peculiar ideas, or the cant of them, are rather the fashion it seems to me! But there is no cant about him. And whatever his ideas are," went on young Grenfell warmly, "he is one of the *best* men I ever knew. He has settled down for some years, and devotes his whole life to doing good, but so quietly and unostentatiously that no one knows how much he does, and others get the credit of it very often."

That was all I heard.

I have never seen Sir Robert again. Still I have by no means arrived yet at the end of my so-called ghost story.

The cup and saucer were carefully washed and replaced in the glass-doored cabinet. The summer gradually waned, and we all returned to our own home. It was at a considerable distance from my sister's, and we met each other principally in the summer time. So, though I did not forget Sir Robert Masters, or his somewhat strange conversation, amid the crowd of daily interests and pleasures, duties and cares, none of the incidents I have here recorded were much in my mind, and but that I had while still in Germany carefully noted the details of all bearing directly or indirectly on "Nora's ghost," as we had come to call it—though it was but rarely alluded to before the child herself—I should not now have been able to give them with circumstantiality.

Fully fifteen months after the visit to my sister, during which we had met Sir Robert, the whole was suddenly and unexpectedly recalled to my memory. Mark and Nora the elder—my sister, that is,—were in their turn staying with us, when one morning at breakfast the post brought for the latter an unusually bulky and important-looking letter. She opened it, glanced at an outer sheet enclosing several pages in a different handwriting, and passed it on to me.

"We must read the rest together," she said in a low voice, glancing at the children, who were at the table. "How interesting it will be!"

The sheet she had handed to me was a short note from Mr. Grenfell. It was dated from some place in Norway where he was fishing, and from whence he had addressed the whole packet to my sister's own home, not knowing of her absence.

My dear Mrs. Daventry, (—it began—), The enclosed will have been a long time of reaching its real destination, for it is, as you will see, really intended for your sister. No doubt it will interest you too, as it has done me, though I am too matter-of-fact and prosaic to enter into such things much. Still it is curious. Please keep the letter; I am sure my friend intends you to do so.

> Yours very truly,
> Ralph Grenfell.

The manuscript enclosed was, of course, from Sir Robert himself. It was in the form of a letter to young Grenfell; and after explaining that he thought it better to write to him, not having my address, he plunged into the real object of his communication.

You will not, (he said), have forgotten the incident of the 'ghost-cup,' in the summer of last year, and the curious story your friend was so good as to tell us about it. You may remember—Mrs. —— will, I am sure, do so—my strong impression that I had recently seen one like it. After I left you I could not get this feeling out of my head. It is always irritating not to be able, figuratively speaking, 'to lay your hand' on a recollection, and in this instance I really wanted to get the clue, as it might lead to some sort of 'explanation' of the little girl's strange experience. I cudgelled my brains, but all to no purpose; I went over in memory all the houses at which I had visited within a certain space of time; I made lists of all the people I knew interested in 'china,' ancient or modern, and likely to possess specimens of it. But all in vain.

All I got for my pains was that people began to think I was developing a new crotchet, or, as I heard one lady say to another, not knowing I was within earshot, 'the poor man must be a little off his head, though till now I have always denied it. But the revulsion from benevolent schemes to china-collecting shows it only too plainly.' So I thought I had better leave off cross-questioning my 'collecting' friends about porcelain and faïence, German ware in particular. And after a while I thought no more about it. Two months ago I had occasion to make a journey to the north—the same journey and to stay at the same house where I have been four or five times since I saw the 'ghost-cup.' But this was what happened *this* time. There is a junction by which one must pass on this journey.

I generally manage to suit my trains so as to avoid waiting there, but this is not always feasible. This time I found that an hour at the junction was inevitable. There is a very good refreshment room there, kept by very civil, decent people. They knew me by sight, and after I had had a cup of tea they proposed to me, as they have done before, to wait in their little parlour just off the public room. 'It would be quieter and more comfortable,' said either the mother or the daughter who manage the concern. I thanked them, and settled myself in an arm-chair with my book, when, looking up—there on the mantelpiece stood the fellow cup—the identical shape, pattern, and colour! It all flashed into my mind then. I had made this journey just before going into your neighbourhood last year, and had waited in this little parlour just as this time.

'Where did you get that cup, Mrs. Smith?' I asked.

There were two or three rather pretty bits of china about. The good woman was pleased at my noticing it.

'Yes, sir. Isn't it pretty? I've rather a fancy for china. That cup was sent me by my niece. She said she'd picked it up somewhere—at a sale, I think. It's foreign, sir; isn't it?'

'Yes, German. But can't you find out *where* your niece got it?' for at the word 'sale' my hopes fell.

'I can ask her. I shall be writing to her this week,' she replied; and she promised to get any information she could for me within a fortnight, by which time I expected to pass that way again. I did so, and Mrs. Smith proved as good as her word. The niece had got the cup from a friend of hers, an auctioneer, and he, not she, had got it at a sale. But he was away from home—she could hear nothing more at present. She gave his address, however, and assurances that he was very good-natured and would gladly put the gentleman in the way of getting china like it, if it was to be got. He would be home by the middle of the month. It was now the middle of the month. The auctioneer's town was not above a couple of hours off my line.

Perhaps you will all laugh at me when I tell you that I went those two hours out of my way, arriving at the town late that night and putting up at a queer old inn—worth going to see for itself—on purpose to find the man of the hammer. I found him. He was very civil, though rather mystified. He remembered the cup perfectly, but there was no chance of getting any like it where it came from!

'And where was that?' I asked eagerly.

'At a sale some miles from here, about four years ago,' he replied. 'It was the sale of the furniture and plate, and everything, in fact, of a widow lady. She had some pretty china, for she had a fancy for it. That cup was not of much value; it was quite modern. I bought it in for a trifle. I gave it to Miss Cross, and she sent it to her aunt, as you know. As for getting any like it——'

But I interrupted him by assuring him I did not wish that, but that I had reasons for wanting some information about the person who, I believed, had bought the cup. 'Nothing to do any harm to any one,' I said; 'a matter of feeling. A similar cup had been bought by a person I was interested in, and I feared that person was dead.'

The auctioneer's face cleared. He fancied he began to understand me.

'I am afraid you are right, sir, if the person you mean was young Mr. Paulet, the lady's son. You may have met him on his travels? His death was very sad, I believe. It killed his mother, they say—she never looked up after; and as she had no near relative to follow her, everything was sold. I remember I was told all that, at the sale, and it seemed to me particularly sad, even though one comes across many sad things in our line of business.'

'Do you remember the particulars of Mr. Paulet's death?' I asked.

'Only that it happened suddenly—somewhere in foreign parts. I did not know the family till I was asked to take charge of the sale,' he replied.

'Could you possibly get any details for me? I feel sure it is the same Mr. Paulet,' I said boldly.

The auctioneer considered.

'Perhaps I can. I rather think a former servant of theirs is still in the neighbourhood,' he replied.

I thanked him and left him my address, to which he promised to write. I felt it was perhaps better not to pursue my inquiries further in person; it might lead to annoyance, or possibly to gossip about the dead, which I detest. I jotted down some particulars for the auctioneer's guidance, and went on my way. That was a fortnight ago. Today I have his answer, which I transcribe:—

Sir—The servant I spoke of could not tell me very much, as she was not long in the late Mrs. Paulet's service. To hear more, she says, you must apply to the relations of the family. Young Mr. Paulet was tall and fair and very nice-looking. His mother and he were deeply attached to each other. He travelled a good deal and used to bring her home lots of pretty things. He met his death in some part of Germany where there are forests, for though it was thought at first he had died of heart disease, the doctors proved he had been struck by lightning, and his body was found in the forest, and the papers on him showed who he was. The body was sent home to be buried, and all that was found with it; a knapsack and its contents, among which was the cup I bought at the sale. His death was about the middle of August 18—.

I shall be glad if this information is of any service.

This, (continued Sir Robert's own letter), is all I have been able to learn. There does not seem to have been the very slightest suspicion of foul play, nor do I think it the least likely there was any ground for such. Young Paulet probably died some way farther in the forest than Silberbach, and it is even possible the surly landlord never heard of it. It *might* be worthwhile to inquire about it should your friends ever be there again. If I should be in the neighbourhood I certainly should do so; the whole coincidences are very striking.

Then followed apologies for the length of his letter which he had been betrayed into by his anxiety to tell all there was to tell. In return he asked Mr. Grenfell to obtain from me certain dates and particulars as he wished to note them down. It was the 18th of August on which "Nora's ghost" had appeared—just two years after the August of the poor young man's death!

There was also a postscript to Sir Robert's letter, in which he said, "I think, in Mrs. ——'s place, I would say nothing to the little girl of what we have discovered."

And I have never done so.

This is all I have to tell. I offer no suggestions, no theories in explanation of the facts. Those who, like Sir Robert Masters, are able and desirous to treat such subjects scientifically or philosophically will doubtless form their own. I cannot say that I find *his* theory a perfectly satisfactory one, perhaps I do not sufficiently understand it, but I have tried to give it in his own words. Should this matter-of-fact relation of a curious experience meet his eyes, I am sure he will forgive my having brought him into it. Besides, it is not likely that he would be recognised; men, and women too, of "peculiar ideas," sincere investigators and honest searchers after truth, as well as their superficial plagiarists, being by no means rare in these days.

# The Story of the Rippling Train
*A True Ghost Story*
(A story from *Four Ghost Stories*).


"Let's tell ghost stories, then," said Gladys.

"Aren't you tired of them? One hears nothing else nowadays. And they're all 'authentic,' really vouched for, only you never see the person who saw or heard or felt the ghost. It is always somebody's sister or cousin, or friend's friend," objected young Mrs. Snowdon, another of the guests at the Quarries.

"I don't know that that is quite a reasonable ground for discrediting them *en masse*," said her husband. "It is natural enough, indeed inevitable, that the principal or principals in such cases should be much more rarely come across than the stories themselves. A hundred people can repeat the story, but the author, or rather hero, of it, can't be in a hundred places at once. You don't disbelieve in any other statement or narrative merely because you have never seen the prime mover in it?"

"But I didn't say I discredited them on that account," said Mrs. Snowdon. "You take one up so, Archie. I'm not logical and reasonable; I don't pretend to be. If I meant anything, it was that a ghost story would have a great pull over other ghost stories if one could see the person it happened to. One does get rather provoked at *never* coming across him or her," she added a little petulantly.

She was tired; they were all rather tired, for it was the first evening since the party had assembled at the large country house known as "the Quarries" on which there was not to be dancing, with the additional fatigue of "ten miles there and ten back again"; and three or four evenings of such doings without intermission tell even on the young and vigorous.

Tonight various less energetic ways of passing the evening had been proposed,—music, games, reading aloud, recitation,—none had found favour in everybody's sight, and now Gladys Lloyd's proposal that they should "tell ghost stories" seemed likely to fall flat also.

For a moment or two no one answered Mrs. Snowdon's last remarks. Then, somewhat to everybody's surprise, the young daughter of the house turned to her mother.

"Mamma," she said, "don't be vexed with me—I know you warned me once to be careful how I spoke of it; but *wouldn't* it be nice if Uncle Paul would tell us his ghost story? And then, Mrs. Snowdon," she went on, "you could always say you had heard *one* ghost story at or from—which should I say?—head-quarters."

Lady Denholme glanced round half nervously before she replied.

"Locally speaking, it would not be *at* headquarters, Nina," she said. "The Quarries was not the scene of your uncle's ghost story. But I almost think it is better not to speak about it—I am not sure that he would like it mentioned, and he will be coming in a moment. He had only a note to write."

"I do wish he would tell it to us," said Nina regretfully. "Don't you think, mamma, I might just run to the study and ask him, and if he did not like the idea he might say so to me, and no one would seem to know anything about it? Uncle Paul is so kind—I'm never afraid of asking him any favour."

"Thank you, Nina, for your good opinion of me; you see there is no rule without exceptions; listeners do sometimes hear pleasant things of themselves," said Mr. Marischal, as he at that moment came round the screen which half concealed the doorway. "What is the special favour you were thinking of asking me?"

Nina looked rather taken aback.

"How softly you opened the door, Uncle Paul," she said. "I

would not have spoken of you if I had known you were there."

"But after all you were saying no harm," observed her brother Michael. "And for my part I don't believe Uncle Paul would mind our asking him what we were speaking of."

"What was it?" asked Mr. Marischal. "I think, as I have heard so much, you may as well tell me the whole."

"It was only——" began Nina, but her mother interrupted her.

"I have told Nina not to speak of it, Paul," she said anxiously; "but—it was only that all these young people are talking about ghost stories, and they want you to tell them your own strange experience. You must not be vexed with them."

"Vexed!" said Mr. Marischal, "not in the least." But for a moment or two he said no more, and even pretty, spoilt Mrs. Snowdon looked a little uneasy.

"You shouldn't have persisted, Nina," she whispered.

Mr. Marischal must have had unusually quick ears. He looked up and smiled.

"I really don't mind telling you all there is to hear," he said. "At one time I had a sort of dislike to mentioning the story, for the sake of others. The details would have led to its being recognised—and it might have been painful. But there is no one now living to whom it would matter—you know," he added, turning to his sister; "her husband is dead too."

Lady Denholme shook her head.

"No," she said, "I did not hear."

"Yes," said her brother, "I saw his death in the papers last year. He had married again, I believe. There is not now, therefore, any reason why I should not tell the story, if it will interest you," he went on, turning to the others. "And there is not very much to tell. Not worth making such a preamble about. It was—let me see—yes, it must be nearly fifteen years ago."

"Wait a moment, Uncle Paul," said Nina. "Yes, that's all right, Gladys. You and I will hold each other's hands, and pinch hard if we get very frightened."

"Thank you," Miss Lloyd replied. "On the whole I should

prefer for you not to hold my hand."

"But I won't pinch you so as to hurt," said Nina reassuringly; "and it isn't as if we were in the dark."

"Shall I turn down the lamps?" asked Mr. Snowdon.

"No, no," exclaimed his wife.

"There really is nothing frightening—scarcely even 'creepy,' in my story at all," said Mr. Marischal, half apologetically. "You make me feel like an impostor."

"Oh no, Uncle Paul, don't say that. It is all my fault for interrupting," said Nina. "Now go on, please. I have Gladys's hand all the same," she added *sotto voce*, "it's just as well to be prepared."

"Well, then," began Mr. Marischal once more, "it must be nearly fifteen years ago; and I had not seen her for fully ten years before that again! I was not thinking of her in the least; in a sense I had really forgotten her: she had quite gone out of my life; that has always struck me as a very curious point in the story," he added parenthetically.

"Won't you tell us who 'she' was, Uncle Paul?" asked Nina half shyly.

"Oh yes, I was going to do so. I am not skilled in story-telling, you see. She was, at the time I first knew her—at the only time, indeed, that I knew her—a very sweet and attractive girl, named Maud Bertram. She was very pretty—more than pretty, for she had remarkably regular features—her profile was always admired, and a tall and graceful figure. And she was a bright and happy creature too; that, perhaps, was almost her greatest charm. You will wonder—I see the question hovering on your lips, Miss Lloyd, and on yours too, Mrs. Snowdon—why, if I admired her and liked her so much, I did not go further. And I will tell you frankly that I did not because I dared not. I had then no prospect of being able to marry for years to come, and I was not very young. I was already nearly thirty, and Maud was quite ten years younger. I was wise enough and old enough to realise the situation thoroughly, and to be on my guard."

"And Maud?" asked Mrs. Snowdon.

"She was surrounded by admirers; it seemed to me then that

it would have been insufferable conceit to have even asked myself if it could matter to her. It was only in the light of after events that the possibility of my having been mistaken occurred to me. And I don't even now see that I could have acted otherwise——" Here Uncle Paul sighed a little. "We were the best of friends. She knew that I admired her, and she seemed to take a frank pleasure in its being so. I had always hoped that she really liked and trusted me as a friend, but no more. The last time I saw her was just before I started for Portugal, where I remained three years.

"When I returned to London Maud had been married for two years, and had gone straight out to India on her marriage, and except by some few friends who had known us both intimately, I seldom heard her mentioned. And time passed. I cannot say I had exactly forgotten her, but she was not much or often in my thoughts. I was a busy and much-absorbed man, and life had proved a serious matter to me. Now and then some passing resemblance would recall her to my mind—once especially when I had been asked to look in to see the young wife of one of my cousins in her court-dress; something in her figure and bearing brought back Maud to my memory, for it was thus, in full dress, that I had last seen her, and thus perhaps, unconsciously, her image had remained photographed on my brain.

"But as far as I can recollect at the time when the occurrence I am going to relate to you happened, I had not been thinking of Maud Bertram for months. I was in London just then, staying with my brother, my eldest brother, who had been married for several years, and lived in our own old town-house in —— Square. It was in April, a clear spring day, with no fog or half-lights about, and it was not yet four o'clock in the afternoon— not very ghost-like circumstances, you will admit. I had come home early from my club—it was a sort of holiday-time with me just then for a few weeks—intending to get some letters written which had been on my mind for some days, and I had sauntered into the library, a pleasant, fair-sized room lined with books, on the first-floor.

"Before setting to work I sat down for a moment or two in an easy-chair by the fire, for it was still cool enough weather to make a fire desirable, and began thinking over my letters. No thought, no shadow of a thought of my old friend Miss Bertram was present with me; of that I am perfectly certain. The door was on the same side of the room as the fireplace; as I sat there, half facing the fire, I also half faced the door. I had not shut it properly on coming in—I had only closed it without turning the handle—and I did not feel surprised when it slowly and noiselessly swung open, till it stood right out into the room, concealing the actual doorway from my view.

"You will perhaps understand the position better if you think of the door as just then acting like a screen to the doorway. From where I sat I could not have seen anyone entering the room till he or she had got beyond the door itself. I glanced up, half expecting to see someone come in, but there was no one; the door had swung open of itself. For the moment I sat on, with only the vague thought passing through my mind, 'I must shut it before I begin to write.'

"But suddenly I found my eyes fixing themselves on the carpet; something had come within their range of vision, compelling their attention in a mechanical sort of way. What was it?

"'Smoke,' was my first idea. 'Can there be anything on fire?' But I dismissed the notion almost as soon as it suggested itself. The something, faint and shadowy, that came slowly rippling itself in as it were beyond the dark wood of the open door, was yet too material for 'smoke.' My next idea was a curious one. 'It looks like soapy water,' I said to myself; 'can one of the housemaids have been scrubbing, and upset a pail on the stairs?' For the stair to the next floor almost faced the library door. But—no; I rubbed my eyes and looked again; the soapy water theory gave way.

"The wavy something that kept gliding, rippling in, gradually assumed a more substantial appearance. It was—yes, I suddenly became convinced of it—it was ripples of soft silken stuff, creeping in as if in some mysterious way unfolded or unrolled, not jerkily or irregularly, but glidingly and smoothly, like little wavelets on the sea-shore.

"And I sat there and gazed. 'Why did you not jump up and look behind the door to see what it was?' you may reasonably ask. That question I cannot answer. Why I sat still, as if bewitched, or under some irresistible influence, I cannot tell, but so it was.

"And it—came always rippling in, till at last it began to rise as it still came on, and I saw that a figure—a tall, graceful woman's figure—was slowly advancing, backwards of course, into the room, and that the waves of pale silk—a very delicate shade of pearly gray I think it must have been—were in fact the lower portion of a long court-train, the upper part of which hung in deep folds from the lady's waist. She moved in—I cannot describe the motion, it was not like ordinary walking or stepping backwards—till the whole of her figure and the clear profile of her face and head were distinctly visible, and when at last she stopped and stood there full in my view just, but only just beyond the door, I saw—it came upon me like a flash—that she was no stranger to me, this mysterious visitant! I recognised, unchanged it seemed to me since the day, ten years ago, when I had last seen her, the beautiful features of Maud Bertram."

Mr. Marischal stopped a moment. Nobody spoke. Then he went on again.

"I should not have said 'unchanged.' There was one great change in the sweet face. You remember my telling you that one of my girl-friend's greatest charms was her bright sunny happiness—she never seemed gloomy or depressed or dissatisfied, seldom even pensive. But in this respect the face I sat there gazing at was utterly unlike Maud Bertram's. Its expression, as she—or 'it'—stood there looking, not towards me, but out beyond, as if at some one or something outside the doorway, was of the profoundest sadness. Anything *so* sad I had never seen in a human face, and I trust I never may. But I sat on, as motionless almost as she, gazing at her fixedly, with no desire, no power perhaps, to move or approach more nearly to the phantom.

"I was not in the least frightened. I knew it *was* a phantom, but I felt paralysed, and as if I myself had somehow got outside of ordinary conditions. And there I sat—staring at Maud, and there she stood, gazing before her with that terrible, unspeakable sadness in her face, which, even though I felt no *fear*, seemed to freeze me with a kind of unutterable pity.

"I don't know how long I had sat thus, or how long I might have continued to sit there, almost as if in a trance, when suddenly I heard the front-door bell ring. It seemed to awaken me. I started up and glanced round, half-expecting that I should find the vision dispelled. But no; she was still there, and I sank back into my seat just as I heard my brother coming quickly upstairs. He came towards the library, and seeing the door wide open walked in, and I, still gazing, saw his figure *pass through that of the woman in the doorway* as you may walk through a wreath of mist or smoke—only, don't misunderstand me, the figure of Maud till that moment had had nothing unsubstantial about it. She had looked to me, as she stood there, literally and exactly like a living woman—the shade of her dress, the colour of her hair, the few ornaments she wore, all were as defined and clear as yours, Nina, at the present moment, and remained so, or perhaps became so again as soon as my brother was well within the room.

"He came forward addressing me by name, but I answered him in a whisper, begging him to be silent and to sit down on the seat opposite me for a moment or two. He did so, though he was taken aback by my strange manner, for I still kept my eyes fixed on the door. I had a queer consciousness that if I looked away *it* would fade, and I wanted to keep cool and see what would happen. I asked Herbert in a low voice if *he* saw nothing, but though he mechanically followed the direction of my eyes, he shook his head in bewilderment. And for a moment or two he remained thus.

"Then I began to notice that the figure was growing less clear, as if it were receding, yet without growing smaller to the sight; it grew fainter and vaguer, the colours grew hazy. I rubbed my eyes once or twice with a half idea that my long watching was making them misty, but it was not so. My eyes were not at fault—slowly but surely Maud Bertram, or her ghost, melted away, till all trace of her had gone. I saw again the familiar pattern of the carpet where she had stood and the objects of the room that had been hidden by her draperies—all again in the most commonplace way, but she was gone, quite gone.

"Then Herbert, seeing me relax my intense gaze, began to question me. I told him exactly what I have told you. He answered, as every "common-sensible" person of course would, that it was strange, but that such things did happen sometimes and were classed by the wise under the head of 'optical delusions.' I was not well, perhaps, he suggested. Been over-working? Had I not better see a doctor? But I shook my head. I was quite well, and I said so. And perhaps he was right, it might be an optical delusion only. I had never had any experience of such things.

"'All the same,' I said, 'I shall mark down the date.'

"Herbert laughed and said that was what people always did in such cases. If he knew where Mrs. —— then was he would write to her, just for the fun of the thing, and ask her to be so good as to look up her diary, if she kept one, and let us know what she had been doing on that particular day—'the 6th of April, isn't it?' he said—when I would have it her wraith had paid me a visit. I let him talk. It seemed to remove the strange painful impression—painful because of that terrible sadness in the sweet face. But we neither of us knew where she was, we scarcely remembered her married name! And so there was nothing to be done—except, what I did at once in spite of Herbert's rallying, to mark down the day and hour with scrupulous exactness in *my* diary.

"Time passed. I had not forgotten my strange experience, but of course the impression of it lessened by degrees till it seemed more like a curious dream than anything more real, when one day I *did* hear of poor Maud again. 'Poor' Maud I cannot help calling her. I heard of her indirectly, and probably, but for the sadness of her story, I should never have heard it at all. It was a friend of her husband's family who had mentioned the circumstances in the hearing of a friend of mine, and one day something brought round the conversation to old times, and he startled me by suddenly inquiring if I remembered Maud Bertram. I said, of course I did. Did he know anything of her? And then he told me.

"She was dead—she had died some months ago after a long and trying illness, the result of a terrible accident. She had caught fire one evening when dressed for some grand entertainment or other, and though her injuries did not seem likely to be fatal at the time, she had never recovered the shock.

"'She was so pretty,' my friend said, 'and one of the saddest parts of it was that I hear she was terrifically disfigured, and she took this most sadly to heart. The right side of her face was utterly ruined, and the sight of the right eye lost, though, strange to say, the left side entirely escaped, and seeing her in profile one would have had no notion of what had happened. Was it not sad? She was such a sweet, bright creature.'

"I did not tell him *my* story, for I did not want it chattered about, but a strange sort of shiver ran through me at his words. *It was the left side of her face only* that the wraith of my poor friend had allowed me to see."

"Oh, Uncle Paul!" exclaimed Nina.

"And—as to the dates?" inquired Mr. Snowdon.

"I never knew the exact date of the accident," said Mr. Marischal, "but that of her death was fully six months after I had seen her. And in my own mind, I have never made any doubt that it was at or about, probably a short time after, the accident, that she came to me. It seemed a kind of appeal for sympathy—and—a farewell also, poor child."

They all sat silent for some little time, and then Mr. Marischal got up and went off to his own quarters, saying something vaguely about seeing if his letters had gone.

"What a touching story!" said Gladys Lloyd. "I am afraid, after all, it has been more painful than he realised for Mr. Marischal to tell it. Did you know anything of Maud's husband, dear Lady Denholme? Was he kind to her? Was she happy?"

"We never heard much about her married life," her hostess replied. "But I have no reason to think she was unhappy. Her husband married again two or three years after her death, but that says nothing."

"N—no," said Nina. "All the same, mamma, I am sure she really did love Uncle Paul very much,—much more than he had any idea of. Poor Maud!"

"And he has never married," added Gladys.

"No," said Lady Denholme, "but there have been many practical difficulties in the way of his doing so. He has had a most absorbingly busy life, and now that he is more at leisure he feels himself too old to form new ties."

"But," persisted Nina, "if he had had any idea at the time that Maud cared for him so?"

"Ah well," Lady Denholme allowed, "in that case, in spite of the practical difficulties, things would probably have been different."

And again Nina repeated softly, "Poor Maud!"

# Old Gervais

Penforres Hall, Carmichael, N.B.,
Jan. 17th, 188—.

. . . And now, as to your questions about that long-ago story. What put it into your head, I wonder? You have been talking "ghosts" like everybody else nowadays, no doubt, and you want to have something to tell that you had at "first hand." Ah well, I will try to recall my small experience of the kind as accurately as my old brain is capable of doing at so long a distance. Though, after all, that is scarcely a correct way of putting it. For, like all elderly people, I find it true, strikingly true, that the longer ago the better, as far as memory is concerned. I can recollect events, places—nay, words and looks and tones, material impressions of the most trivial, such as scents and tastes, of forty or fifty years ago, far more vividly, more minutely, than things of a year or even a month past. It is strange, but I like it. There is something consolatory and suggestive about it. It seems to show that we are still all there, or all here, rather; that there is a something—an innermost "I"—which goes on, faithful and permanent, however rusty and dull the machinery may grow with the wear and tear of time and age.

But you won't thank me for reflections of this kind. You want my little personal experience of the "more things," and you shall have it.

You know, of course, that by birth—by descent, that is to say—I am a little, a quarter or half a quarter, French, And by affection I have always felt myself much more than that. It is often so; there is a sort of loyalty in us to the weaker side of things. Just because there is really so much less French than English in me, because I have spent nearly all my threescore and —! years in Great Britain, I feel bound to stand up for the Gallic part of me, and to feel quite huffed and offended if France or "Frenchness" is decried. It is silly, I dare say; but somehow I cannot help it. We don't know, we can't say in what proportions our ancestors are developed in us. It is possible that I am really, paradoxical as it may sound, more French than English, after all.

*You* know all about me, but if you want to tell my bit of a ghost-story to others, you will understand that I am not actuated by egotism in explaining things. It was through my being a little French that I came to pay long visits to old friends of my mother's in Normandy. *They* were not relations, but connections by marriage, and bound by the closest ties of association and long affection to our cousins. And the wife of the head of the family, dear Madame de Viremont, was my own godmother. She had visited us in England and Scotland—she loved both, and she was cosmopolitan enough to think it only natural that even as a young girl I should be allowed to cross the channel to stay with her for weeks, nay, months at a time, in her old *château* of Viremont-les-bocages.

Not that I travelled over there *alone*—ah no, indeed! Girls, even of the unmistakably upper classes, *do* travel alone now, I am assured, still I can't say that it has ever come within my own knowledge that a young lady should journey by herself to Normandy, though I believe such things are done. But it was very different in my young days. My father himself took me to Paris—I am speaking just now of the first time I went, with which indeed only, I am at present concerned—and after a few days of sightseeing there, Madame de Viremont's own maid came to escort me to my destination—the *château*.

We travelled by diligence, of course—the journey that five or six hours would now see accomplished took us the best part of two days. At Caen, my godmother met us, and I spent a night in her "hotel" there—the town residence of the family—dear old house that it was! Many a happy day have I spent there since. And then, at Caen, I was introduced for the first time to my godmother's granddaughters, her son's children, Albertine and Virginie. Albertine was older than I, Virginie two years younger. We were dreadfully shy of each other, though Albertine was too well bred to show it, and talked formalities in a way that I am sure made her grandmother smile. Virginie, dear soul, did not speak at all, which you must remember is *not* bad manners in a French girl before she is out, and I, as far as I recollect, spoke nonsense in very bad French, and blushed at the thought of it afterwards. It was stupid of me, for I really could speak the language very decently.

But that all came right. I think we took to each other in spite of our shyness and awkwardness, at once. It must have been so, for we have remained friends ever since, staunch friends, though Albertine's life has been spent among the great ones of the earth (she is a great-grandmother now) and I only see my Virginie once a year, or once in two or three years, for a few hours, at the convent of which she has long, long been the head; and *I* am an old-fashioned, narrow-minded perhaps, Scotch maiden lady of a very certain age, who finds it not always easy to manage the journey to France even to see her dear old friends.

How delightful, how unspeakably exciting and interesting and fascinating that first real glimpse into the home life of another nation was! The queernesses, the extraordinary differences, the indescribable mingling of primitiveness with ultra refinement, of stateliness and dignity of bearing and customs with odd unsophisticatedness such as I had imagined mediaeval at least—all added to the charm.

How well I remember my first morning's waking in my bedroom at the *château*! There was no carpet on the floor; no looking-glass, except a very black and unflattering one which might have belonged to Noah's wife, over the chimney-piece; no attempt at a dressing-table; a ewer and basin in the tiny *cabinet-de-toilette* which would have delighted my little sister for her dolls. Yet the cup in which old Désirée brought me my morning chocolate was of almost priceless china, and the chocolate itself such as I do not think I ever have tasted elsewhere, so rich and fragrant and steaming hot—the roll which accompanied it, though sour, lying on a little fringed doyley marked with the Viremont crest in embroidery which must have cost somebody's eyes something.

It seemed to me like awaking in a fairytale in a white cat's *château*. And the charm lasted till I had come to feel so entirely at home with my dear, courteous, kindly hosts, that I forgot to ask myself if I were enjoying myself or no. Nay, longer than till then, did it last—indeed, I have never lost the *feeling* of it—at any moment I can hear the tapping of my godmother's stoutly shod feet as she trotted about early in the morning, superintending her men and maidens, and giving orders for the day; I can scent the perfume of *Monsieur's* pet roses; I can hear the sudden wind, for we were not far from the sea, howling and crying through the trees as I lay in my alcove bed at night.

It was not a great house, though called a *château*. It was one of the still numerous moderate-sized old country houses which escaped the destruction of that terrible time now nearly a century past. The De Viremonts were of excellent descent, but they had never been extremely wealthy, nor very prominent. They were pious, home-loving, cultivated folk—better read than most of their class in the provinces, partly perhaps thanks to their English connections which had widened their ideas, partly because they came of a scholarly and thoughtful race. The house was little changed from what it must have been for a century or more.

The grounds, so Madame de Viremont told me, were less well tended than in her husband's childhood, for it was increasingly difficult to get good gardeners, and she herself had no special gift in that line, such as her mother-in-law had been famed for. And though *Monsieur* loved his roses, his interest in horticulture began and ended with them. I don't think he minded how untidy and wilderness-like the grounds were, provided the little bit near the house was pretty decent. For there, round the "lawn" which he and *Madame* fondly imagined was worthy of the name, bloomed his beloved flowers.

If it had been my own home, the wildness of the unkempt grounds would have worried me sadly. I have always been old-maidish about neatness and tidiness, I think. But as it was not my home, and I therefore felt no uncomfortable responsibility, I think I rather liked it. It was wonderfully picturesque—here and there almost mysterious. One terrace I know, up and down which Virginie and I were specially fond of pacing, always reminded me of the garden in George Sand's *Château de Pictordu,* if only there had been a broken statute at one end!

The time passed quickly, even during the first two or three weeks, when my only companions were "Marraine," as *Madame* made me call her, and her husband. I was not at all dull or bored, though my kind friends would scarcely believe it, and constantly tried to cheer my supposed loneliness by telling me how pleasant it would be when *les petites*—Albertine and Virginie—joined us, as they were to do before long. I didn't feel very eager about their coming. I could not forget my shyness; though, of course, I did not like to say so. I only repeated to my godmother that I *could* not feel dull when she and Monsieur de Viremont were doing so much to amuse me.

And for another reason I was glad to be alone with my old friends at first. I was very anxious to improve my French, and I worked hard at it under *Monsieur's* directions. He used to read aloud to us in the evenings; he read splendidly, and besides the exercises and dictations he gave me, he used to make me read aloud too. I hated it at first, but gradually I improved very much, and then I liked it.

So passed three or four weeks; then at last one morning came a letter announcing the grand-daughters' arrival on the following day. I could not but try to be pleased, for it was pretty to see how delighted everyone at the *château* was, to hear the news.

"They must be nice girls," I thought, "otherwise all the servants and people about would not like them so much," and I made myself take an interest in going round with my godmother superintending the little preparations she was making for the girls.

They were to have separate rooms. Albertine's was beside mine, Virginie's on the floor above. There was a good deal of excitement about Virginie's room, for a special reason. Her grandmother was arranging a surprise for her, in the shape of a little oratory. It was a tiny closet—a dark closet it had been, used originally for hanging up dresses, in one corner of her room, and here on her last visit, the girl had placed her *prie-Dieu*, and hung up her crucifix. Madame de Viremont had noticed this, and just lately she had had the door taken away, and the little recess freshly painted, and a small window knocked out, and all made as pretty as possible for the sacred purpose.

I felt quite interested in it. It was a queer little recess—almost like a turret—and *Madame* showed me that it ran up the whole height of the house from the cellars where it began, as an out-jut, with an arched window to give light to one end of the large "cave" at that side, which would otherwise have been quite dark.

"The great cellar used to be a perfect rat-warren," she told me, "till light and air were thus thrown into it. What that odd out-jut was originally, no one knows. There goes a story that a secret winding-staircase, very, very narrow, of course, once ran up it to the roof. There were some doubts, I know, as to the solidity of the masonry—it has sunk a little at one side, you can see it in the cellar. But I expect it has all 'settled,' as they call it, long ago. Old Gervais, whom we employed to knock out the new window in Virginie's little oratory, had no doubt about it, and he is a clever mason."

"Old Gervais," I repeated; "who is he, Marraine? I don't think I have seen him, have I?"

For she had spoken of him as if I must have known whom she meant.

"Have you not?" she said. "He is a dear old man—one of our great resources. He is so honest and intelligent. But no I dare say you have not seen him. He does not live in our village, but at Plaudry, a mere hamlet about three miles off. And he goes about a good deal; the neighbouring families know his value, and he is always in request for some repairs or other work. He is devout, too," my godmother added; "a simple, sincere, and yet intelligent Christian. And that is very rare nowadays: the moment one finds a thoughtful or intelligent mind among our poor, it seems to become the prey of all the sad and hopeless teaching so much in the air."

And Madame de Viremont sighed. But in a moment or two she spoke again in her usual cheerful tone.

"It was quite a pleasure to see Gervais' interest in this little place," she said—we were standing in the oratory at the time. "He has the greatest admiration for our Virginie, too," she added, "as indeed everyone has who knows the child."

"She does look *very* sweet," I said, and truly. But as I had scarcely heard Virginie open her lips, I could not personally express admiration of anything *but* her looks! In those days too, the reputation of unusual "goodness"—as applied to Virginie de Viremont, I see now that the word "sanctity" would scarcely be too strong to use—in one so young, younger than myself, rather alarmed than attracted me.

But her grandmother seemed quite pleased.

"You will find the looks a true index," she said.

I was examining the oratory—and wondering if there was any little thing I could do to help to complete it. Suddenly I exclaimed to my godmother—

"Marraine, the floor does sink decidedly at one side—just move across slowly, and you will feel it."

"I know," she replied composedly, "that is the side of the settling I told you of It is the same in the two intermediate stories—one of them is my own *cabinet-de-toilette*. If Virginie does not observe it at once, we shall have Albertine discovering it someday, and teasing the poor child by saying she has weighed down the flooring by kneeling too much—it is just where she will kneel."

"Is Albertine a tease?" I asked; and in my heart I was not sorry to hear it.

"Ah, yes indeed," said *Madame.* "She is full of spirits. But Virginie, too, has plenty of fun in her."

My misgivings soon dispersed.

The two girls had not been forty-eight hours at Viremont before we were the best of friends, Virginie and I especially. For though Albertine was charming, and truly high-principled and reliable, there was not about her the quite indescribable fascination which her sister has always possessed for me. I have never known anyone like Virginie, and I am quite sure I never shall. Her character was the most childlike one in certain ways that you could imagine—absolutely single-minded, unselfish, and sunny—and yet joined to this a strength of principle like a rock, a resolution, determination, and courage, once she was convinced that a thing was *right,* such as would have made a martyr of her without a moment's flinching. I have often tried to describe her to you; and the anecdote of her childhood, which at last I am approaching—she was barely out of childhood—shows what she was even then.

Those were very happy days. Everything united to make them so. The weather was lovely, we were all well, even *Monsieur's* gout and *Madame's* occasional rheumatism having for the time taken to themselves wings and fled, while we girls were as brilliantly healthful and full of life as only young things can be. What fun we had! Games of hide-and-seek in the so-called garden—much of it better described as a wilderness, as I have said—races on the terrace; explorations now and then, on the one or two partially rainy days, of *Madame's* stores—from her own treasures of ancient brocades and scraps of precious lace and tapestry, to the "rubbish," much of it really rubbish, though some of it quaint and interesting, hoarded for a century or two in the great "*grenier*" which extended over a large part of the house under the rafters. I have by me now, in this very room where I write, some precious odds and ends which we extracted from the collection, and which my godmother told me I might take home with me to Scotland, if I thought it worth the trouble.

One day we had been running about the grounds till, breathless and tired, we were glad to sit down on the seat at the far end of the terrace. And, while there, we heard someone calling us.

"Albertine, Virginie, Jeannette," said the voice.

"It is grandpapa," said Virginie, starting up, and running in the direction indicated, Albertine and I following her more leisurely.

"Where have you been, my children? "said the old gentleman, as we got up to him. "I have been seeking you—what are your plans for the afternoon? Your grandmother is going to pay some calls, and proposes that one of you should go with her, while I invite the other two to join me in a good walk—a long walk, I warn you—to Plaudry. What do you say to that?"

The two girls looked at me. As the stranger, they seemed to think it right that I should speak first.

"I should like the walk best," I said with a smile. "I have not been to Plaudry, and they say it is so pretty. And—perhaps Marraine would prefer one of you two to pay calls—I have already visited most of your neighbours with her before you came, and everyone was asking when you were coming."

"Albertine, then," said her grandfather. "Yes, that will be best. And you two little ones shall come with me."

The arrangement seemed to please all concerned, especially when *Monsieur* went on to say that the object of his expedition was to see Gervais the mason.

"Oh," said Virginie, "I am so glad. I want to thank him for all the interest he took in my dear little oratory. Grandmamma told me about it."

Her eyes sparkled. I think I have omitted to say that Madame de Viremont had been well rewarded for her trouble by Virginie's delight in the little surprise prepared for her.

"I want him to see to the arch of the window in the 'cave,'" said *Monsieur*. "Some stones are loosened, one or two actually dropped out. Perhaps his knocking out of your little window, Virginie, has had to do with it. In any case, it must be looked to, without delay. Come round that way, and you shall see what I mean."

He led us to the far side of the house. The window in question had been made in the out-jut I have described; but as it was below the level of the ground, a space had been cleared out in front of it, making a sort of tiny yard, and two or three steps led down to this little spot. It seemed to have been used as a receptacle for odds and ends—flower-pots, a watering-can, etc., were lying about. *Monsieur* went down the steps to show us the crumbling masonry. He must have had good eyes to see it, I thought, for only by pushing aside with his stick the thickly growing ivy, could he show us the loosened and falling stones. But then in a moment he explained.

"I saw it from the inside. I was showing the men where to place some wine I have just had sent in, in the wood. And the proper cellar is over-full—yes, it must certainly be seen to. Inside it looks very shaky."

So we three walked to Plaudry that afternoon. It was a lovely walk, for *Monsieur* knew the shortest way, partly through the woods, by which we avoided the long, hot stretch of high-road. And when we reached our destination—a hamlet of only half a dozen cottages at most—by good luck Gervais was at home, though looking half ashamed to be caught idle, in spite of his evident pleasure at the visit.

He had not been very well lately, his good wife explained, and she had insisted on his taking a little rest. And though I had never seen him before, it seemed to me I could have discerned a worn look—the look of pain patiently borne—in the old man's quiet, gentle face and eyes.

"Gervais not well!" said *Monsieur*. "Why, that is something new. What's been the matter, my friend? "

Oh, it was nothing—nothing at all. The old wife frightened herself for nothing, he said. A little rheumatism, no doubt— a pain near the heart. But it was better, it would pass. What was it *Monsieur* wanted? He would be quite ready to see to it by tomorrow.

Then *Monsieur* explained, and I could see that at once the old mason's interest was specially aroused. "Ah yes, certainly," he interjected. It must be seen to—he had had some misgivings, but had wished to avoid further expense. But all should be put right. And he was so glad that Mademoiselle was pleased with the little oratory, his whole face lighting up as he said it. Tomorrow by sunrise, or at least as soon as possible after, he would be at the *château*.

Then we turned to go home again, though not till Madame Gervais had fetched us a cup of milk, to refresh us after our walk; for they were well to do, in their way, and had a cow of their own, though the bare, dark kitchen, which in England would scarcely seem better than a stable, gave little evidence of any such prosperity. I said some words to that effect to my companions, and then I was sorry I had done so.

"Why, did you not see the armoire?" said Virginie. "It is quite a beauty."

"And the bed and bedding would put many such commodities in an English cottage to shame, I fancy," added *Monsieur*, which I could not but allow was probably true.

Gervais kept his word. He was at his post in the "cave" long before any of us were awake, and Virginie's morning devotions must have been disturbed by the knocking and hammering far below.

He was at it all day. *Monsieur* went down to speak to him once or twice, but Gervais had his peculiarities. He would not give an opinion as to the amount of repair necessary till he was sure. And that afternoon we all went for a long drive—to dine with friends, and return in the evening. When we came home, there was a message left for *Monsieur* by the old mason to the effect that he would come again "tomorrow," and would then be able to explain all. *Monsieur* must not mind if he did not come early, as he would have to get something made at the forge— something iron, said the young footman who gave the message.

"Ah, just so," said *Monsieur*. "He has found it more serious than he expected, I fancy; but it will be all right, now it is in his hands."

So the next morning there was no early knocking or tapping to be heard in the old cellar. Nor did Gervais return later, as he had promised.

"He must have been detained at the forge," said *Monsieur*. "No doubt he will come tomorrow."

Tomorrow came, but with it no Gervais. And Monsieur de Viremont, who was old and sometimes a little irascible, began to feel annoyed. He went down to the cellar, to inspect the work.

"It is right enough," he said, when he came up stairs to the room where we four ladies were sitting—there had been a change in the weather, and it was a stormily rainy day—"I see he has got out the loose stones, and made it all solid enough, but it looks unsightly and unfinished. It wants pointing, and—"

"What was it Alphonse said about an iron band or something?" said *Madame*. "Perhaps Gervais is getting one made, and it has taken longer than he expected."

"It is not necessary," said the old gentleman. "Gervais is over-cautious. No—a girder would be nonsense; but I do not like to see work left so untidy; and it is not his usual way."

So little indeed was it the old mason's way, that when another day passed, and there was no news of Gervais, *Monsieur* determined to send in the morning to hunt him up.

"I would have walked over this afternoon myself," he said, "if the weather had been less terrible."

For it really was terrible—one of those sudden storms to which, near the sea, we are always liable, even in summer—raging wind, fierce beating, dashing rain, that take away for the time all sensation of June or July.

But whatever the weather was, orders were given that night that one of the outdoor men was to go over to Plaudry first thing the next morning.

*Monsieur* had a bad night, a touch of gout, and he could not get to sleep till very late, or rather early. So *Madame* told us when we met at table for the eleven o'clock *big* breakfast.

"He only awoke an hour ago, and I wanted him to stay in

bed all day," she said. "But he would not consent to do so. Ah! there he comes," as our host at that moment entered the room with apologies for his tardiness.

The wind had gone down, though in the night it had been fiercer than ever; but it was still raining pitilessly.

"I do hope the storm is over," said Virginie. "Last night, when I was saying my prayers, it almost frightened me. I really thought I felt the walls rocking."

"Nonsense, child!" said her grandfather, sharply. Incipient gout is not a sweetener of the temper. But Virginia's remark had reminded him of something.

"Has Jean Pierre come back from Plaudry?" he asked the servant behind his chair; "and what message did he bring?"

Alphonse started. He had been entrusted with a message, though not the one expected, but had forgotten to give it.

"He did not go, *Monsieur*," he said; hastily adding, before there was time for his master to begin to storm. "There was no need. Old Gervais was here this morning—very early, before it was light almost; so Nicolas"—Nicolas was the bailiff—"said no one need go."

"Oh—ah, well," said *Monsieur*, mollified. "Then tell Gervais I want to speak to him before he leaves."

Then Alphonse looked slightly uneasy.

"He is gone already, unfortunately—before *Monsieur's* bell rang. He must have had but little to do—by eight o'clock, or before, he was gone."

Monsieur de Viremont looked annoyed.

"Very strange," he said, "when he left word he would explain all to me. Did you see him? did he say nothing?"

No, Alphonse had not seen him—he had only heard him knocking. But he would inquire more particularly if there was no message.

He came back in a few moments, looking perplexed. *No one*, it appeared, had really seen the mason; no one, at least, except a little lad, Denis by name—who worked in the garden—"the little fellow who sings in the choir," said Alphonse. He—Denis—

had seen Gervais' face from the garden, at the window. And he had called out, "Good morning," but Gervais did not answer.

"And the work is completed? Has he perhaps left his tools? if so, he may be coming back again," asked *Monsieur*.

Alphonse could not say. Impatient, the old gentleman rose from the table, and went off to make direct inquiry.

"Very odd, very odd indeed," he said when he returned and sat down again. "To all appearance, the work is exactly as it was when he left it three days ago. Not tidied up or finished. And yet the cook and all heard him knocking for two hours certainly, and the child, Denis, saw him."

"I dare say he will be returning," said *Madame*, soothingly. "Let us wait till this evening."

So they did; but no Gervais came back, and the rain went on falling, chill, drearily monotonous.

Just before dinner *Monsieur* summoned the bailiff.

"Someone must go first thing tomorrow," he began at once, when Nicolas appeared, "and tell Gervais sharply that I won't be played the fool with. What has come over the old fellow?"

"No, *Monsieur*, certainly not. *Monsieur's* orders must be treated with respect," replied Nicolas, ignoring for the moment his master's last few words. "But" and then we noticed that he was looking pale, "Someone has just called in from Plaudry—a neighbour—he thought we should like to know. Gervais is dead—he died last night. He has been ill these three days—badly ill; the heart, they say. And the weather has stopped people coming along the roads as much as usual, else we should have heard. Poor old Gervais—peace to his soul." And Nicolas crossed himself.

"Dead!" *Monsieur* repeated.

"Dead!" we all echoed.

It seemed incredible. *Monsieur*, I know, wished he had not spoken so sharply.

"Virginie, Jeannette," whispered Albertine. "It must have been his ghost!"

But she would not have dared to say so to her grandfather.

"It is sad, very sad," said *Monsieur* and *Madame*. Then a few directions were given to the bailiff, to offer any help she might be in want of, to the poor widow, and Nicolas was dismissed.

"It just shows what imagination will do," said *Monsieur*, "all these silly servants believing they heard him, when it was *impossible*."

"Yes," whispered Albertine again, "and Denis Blanc, who saw him. And Denis, who is so truthful; a little saint indeed! You know, Virginia, the boy with the lovely voice."

Virginie bent her head in assent, but said nothing. And the subject was not referred to again that evening.

But—

The storm was over, next day was cloudless, seeming as if such things as wind and rain and weather fury had never visited this innocent-looking world before. Again we went off to a neighbouring *château*, returning late and tired, and we all slept soundly. Again an exquisite day. *Monsieur* was reading aloud to us in the *salon* that evening; it was nearly bedtime, when a sort of skirmish and rush—hushed, yet excited voices, weeping even, were heard outside.

*Monsieur* stopped. "What is it? "he said Then rising, he went to the door.

A small crowd of servants was gathered there, arguing, vociferating, yet with a curious hush over it all.

"What is it?" repeated the master sternly.

Then it broke out. They could stand it no longer; something must be done; though *Monsieur* had forbidden them to talk nonsense—it was not nonsense, only too true.

"*What?*" thundered the old gentleman.

About Gervais. He was there again—at the present moment. He had been there the night before, but no one had dared to tell. He had returned, no notice having been taken of his first warning. And he *would* return. There now, if everyone would be perfectly still, even here, his knockings could be heard."

The speaker was the cook. And truly, as an uncanny silence momentarily replaced the muffled hubbub, far-off yet distinct taps, coming from below, were to be heard.

"Some trick," said *Monsieur*. "Let us go down, all of us together, and get to the bottom of this affair."

He led the way; we women, and after us the crowd of terrified servants, following. *Monsieur* paused at the kitchen door.

"It is dark in the 'cave,'" he said.

"No, no," cried the cook. "There is a beautiful moon. Not a light, pray *Monsieur*; he might not like it."

All was silent.

We reached the cellar, and entered it a little way. Quite a distance off, so it seemed, was the arched window, the moonlight gleaming through it eerily, the straggling ivy outside taking strange black shapes; but no one to be seen, nothing to be heard. Ah, what was that? The knocking again, unmistakable, distinct, *real*. And why did one side of the window grow dark, as if suddenly thrown into shadow? Was there *something* intercepting the moonlight? It seemed misty, or was it partly that we scarcely dared look? Then, to our surprise, the grandfather's voice sounded out clearly.

"Virginie, my child," he said, "you are the youngest, the most guileless, perhaps the one who has least cause for fear. Would you dread to step forward and—*speak*? If so be it is a message from the poor fellow, let him tell it. Show every one that those who believe in the good God need not be afraid."

Like a white angel, Virginie, in her light summer dress, glided forward, silent. She walked straight on; then, rather to our surprise, she crossed the floor, and stood almost out of sight in the dark corner, at the further side of the window. Then she spoke—

"Gervais, my poor Gervais," she said. "Is it you? I think I see you, but I cannot be sure. What is troubling you, my friend? What is keeping you from your rest?"

Then all was silent again. I should have said that as Virginie went forward, the knocking ceased—*so* silent that we could almost hear our hearts beat. And then—Virginie was speaking again, and *not repeating her questions*! When we realized this, it did seem awful. She was carrying on a conversation. *She had been answered.*

What she said I cannot recall. Her voice was lower now; it sounded almost dreamy. And in a moment or two she came back to us, straight to her grandfather.

"I will tell you all," she said. "Come upstairs—all will be quiet now," she added, in a tone almost of command, to the awestruck servants. And upstairs she told.

"I do not know if he spoke," she said, in answer to Albertine's eager inquiries. "I cannot tell. I know what he wanted, that is enough. No; I did not *exactly* see him; but—he was there."

And this was the message, simple enough. The wall was not safe, though he had done what could be done to the stonework. Iron girders must be fixed, and that without delay. He had felt too ill to go to the forge that night as he had intended, and the unfinished work, the possible danger, was sorely on his mind.

"He thanked me," said Virginie, simply. "He feared that grandfather would think all the solid work was done, and that the wall only needed finishing for appearance."

As, indeed, Monsieur de Viremont *had* thought.

Afterwards the old woman told us a little more. Gervais had been alternately delirious and unconscious these two or three days. He had talked about the work at Viremont, but she thought it raving, till just at the last he tried to whisper something, and she saw he was clear-headed again, about letting *Monsieur* know. She had meant to do so when her own first pressure of grief and trouble was over. She never knew that the warning had been forestalled.

That is all. And it was long ago, and there are thrillingly sensational ghost-stories to be had by the score nowadays. It seems nothing. But I have always thought it touching and impressive, knowing it to be true.

If I have wearied you by my old woman's garrulity, forgive it. It has been a pleasure to me to recall those days.

Your ever affectionate,

Janet Marie Bethune.

# At the Dip of the Road

(A story from *Uncanny Tales*)

Have I ever seen a ghost? I do not know.

That is the only reply I can truthfully make to the question nowadays so often asked. And sometimes, if enquirers care to hear more, I go on to tell them the one experience which makes it impossible for me to reply positively either in the affirmative or negative, and restricts me to "I do not know."

This was the story.

I was staying with relations in the country. Not a very isolated or out-of-the-way part of the world, and yet rather inconvenient of access by the railway, for the nearest station was six miles off. Though the family I was visiting were nearly connected with me I did not know much of their home or its neighbourhood, as the head of the house, an uncle of mine by marriage, had only come into the property a year or two previously to the date of which I am writing, through the death of an elder brother.

It was a nice place. A good comfortable old house, a prosperous, satisfactory estate. Everything about it was in good order from the farmers—who always paid their rents—to the shooting—which was always good—and from the vineries—which were noted—to the woods, where the earliest primroses in all the countryside were to be found each year.

And my uncle and aunt and their family deserved these pleasant things and made a good use of them.

But there was a touch of the commonplace about it all. There was nothing picturesque or romantic. The country was flat though fertile, and the house, though old, was conveniently modern in its arrangements, airy, cheery and bright.

"Not even a ghost, or the shadow of one," I remember saying one day with a faint grumble.

"Ah, well—as to that," said my uncle, "perhaps we—" but just then something interrupted him, and I forgot his unfinished speech.

Into the happy party of which for the time being I was one, there fell one morning a sudden thunderbolt of calamity. The post brought news of the alarming illness of the eldest daughter, Frances, married a year or two ago and living—as the crow flies—at no very great distance. But as the crow flies is not always as the railroad runs, and to reach the Aldoyn's home from Fawne Court, my uncle's place, was a complicated business. In fact it was scarcely possible to go and return in a day.

"Can one of you come over?" wrote the young husband. "She is already out of danger, but longing to see her mother or one of you. She is worrying about the baby"—a child of a few months old—"and wishing for a nurse."

We looked at each other.

"Nurse must go at once," said my uncle to me, as the eldest of the party. Perhaps I should here say that I am a widow, though not old, and with no close ties or responsibilities. "But for your aunt it is impossible."

"Quite so," I agreed. For she was at the moment painfully lamed by rheumatism.

"And the other girls are almost too young at such a crisis," my uncle continued. "Would you Charlotte—" and he hesitated. "It would be such a comfort to have personal news of her."

"Of course I will go," I said. "Nurse and I can start at once. I will leave her there, and return alone to give you, I have no doubt, better news of poor Frances."

He was full of gratitude. So were they all.

"Don't hurry back tonight," said my uncle. "Stay till—till Monday if you like." But I could not promise. I knew they would be glad of news at once, and in a small house like my cousin's, at such a time, an inmate the more might be inconvenient.

"I will try to return tonight," I said. And as I sprang into the carriage I added: "Send someone to meet the last train, unless I telegraph to the contrary."

My uncle nodded; the boys called after me, "All right"; the old butler bowed assent, and I was satisfied.

Nurse and I reached our journey's end promptly, considering the four or five junctions at which we had to change carriages. But on the whole, the trains fitted astonishingly.

We found Frances better, delighted to see us, eager for news of her mother, and, finally, disposed to sleep peacefully now that she knew that there was an experienced person in charge.

And both she and her husband thanked me so much that I felt ashamed of the little I had done. Mr Aldoyn begged me to stay till Monday—but the house was upset and I was eager to carry back my good tidings.

"They are meeting me from the last train," I said. "No thank you, I think it is best I go."

"You will have an uncomfortable journey," he replied. "It is Saturday, and the trains will be late, and the stations crowded with the market people. It will be horrid for you, Charlotte."

But I persisted.

It *was* rather horrid. And it was queer. There was a sort of uncanny eeriness about that Saturday evening's journey that I have never forgotten. The season was very early spring. It was not very cold, but chilly and ungenial. And there were such odd sorts of people about. I travelled second-class; for I am not rich and I am very independent. I did not want my uncle to pay my fare, for I liked the feeling of rendering some small service in return for his steady kindness to me. The first stage of my journey was performed in the company of two old naturalists travelling to Scotland to look for some small plant which was to be found only in one spot in the Highlands. This I gathered from their talk to each other. You never saw two such extraordinary creatures as they were. They both wore black kid gloves much too large for them, and the ends of their fingers waved about like feathers.

Then followed two or three short transits, interspersed with weary waitings at stations. The last of these was the worst and tantalising too, for by this time I was within a few miles of Moore. The station was crowded with rough folk, all, it seemed to me, more or less tipsy. So I took refuge in a dark waiting-room on the small side of the line by which I was to proceed, where I felt I might have been robbed and murdered and no one the wiser.

But at last came my slow train and I jumped in—to jump out more joyfully some fifteen minutes later when we drew up.

I peered about for the carriage. It was not to be seen; only two or three tax-carts or dog-carts, farmer's vehicles, standing about, while their owners, it was easy to hear, were drinking far more than was good for them in the taproom of the Unicorn. Thence, nevertheless—not to the taproom, but to the front of the inn—I made my way, though not undismayed by the shouts and roars breaking the stillness of the quiet night. "Was the Fawne Court carriage not here?" I asked.

The landlady was a good-natured woman, especially civil to any member of the "Court" family. But she shook her head.

"No, no carriage has been down today. There must be some mistake."

There was nothing for it but to wait till she could somehow or other disinter a fly and horse, and, worst of all a driver. For the men she had to call were all rather . . . . "well, ma'am, you see it's Saturday night. We weren't expecting anyone."

And when, after waiting half an hour, the fly at last emerged, my heart almost failed me. Even before he drove out of the yard, it was very plain that if we ever reached Fawne Court alive, it would certainly be more thanks to good luck than to the driver's management.

But the horse was old and the man had a sort of instinct about him. We got on all right till we were more than half way to our journey's end. The road was straight and the moonlight bright, especially after we had passed a certain corner, and got well out of the shade of the trees which skirted the first part of the way.

Just past this turn there came a dip in the road. It went down, down gradually, for a quarter of a mile or more, and I looked up anxiously, fearful of the horse taking advantage of the slope. But no, he jogged on, if possible more slowly than before, though new terrors assailed me when I saw that the driver was now fast asleep, his head swaying from side to side with extraordinary regularity. After a bit I grew easier again; he seemed to keep his equilibrium, and I looked out at the side window on the moon-flooded landscape, with some interest. I had never seen brighter moonlight.

Suddenly from out of the intense stillness and loneliness a figure, a human figure, became visible. It was that of a man, a young and active man, running along the footpath a few feet to our left, apparently from some whim, keeping pace with the fly. My first feeling was of satisfaction that I was no longer alone, at the tender mercies of my stupefied charioteer. But, as I gazed, a slight misgiving came over me. Who could be running along this lonely road so late, and what was his motive in keeping up with us so steadily. It almost seemed as if he had been waiting for us, yet that, of course, was impossible. He was not very highwayman—like certainly; he was well dressed—neatly dressed that is to say, like a superior gamekeeper—his figure was remarkably good, tall and slight, and he ran gracefully. But there was something queer about him, and suddenly the curiosity that had mingled in my observation of him was entirely submerged in alarm, when I saw that, as he ran, he was slowly but steadily drawing nearer and nearer the fly.

"In another moment he will be opening the door and jumping in," I thought, and I glanced before me only to see that the driver was more hopelessly asleep than before; there was no chance of his hearing if I called out. And get out I could not without attracting the strange runner's attention, for as ill-luck would have it, the window was drawn up on the right side and I could not open the door without rattling the glass. While, worse and worse, the left-hand window was down! Even that slight protection wanting!

I looked out once more. By this time the figure was close—very close to the fly. Then an arm was stretched out and laid along the edge of the door, as if preparatory to opening it, and then, for the first time, I saw his face.

It was a young face, but terribly, horribly pale and ghastly, and the eyes—all was so visible in the moonlight—had an expression such as I had never seen before or since. It terrified me, though afterwards on recalling it, it seemed to me it might have been more a look of agonised appeal than of menace of any kind.

I cowered back into my corner and shut my eyes, feigning sleep. It was the only idea that occurred to me. My heart was beating like a sledge hammer. All sorts of thoughts rushed through me; amongst them I remember saying to myself: "He must be an escaped lunatic—his eyes are so awfully wild."

How long I sat thus I don't know—whenever I dared to glance out furtively he was still there. But all at once a strange feeling of relief came over me. I sat up—yes, he was gone! And though, as I took courage, I leant out and looked round in every direction, not a trace of him was to be seen, although the roads and fields were bare and clear for a long distance around.

When I got to Fawne Court I had to wake the lodge-keeper—everyone was asleep. But my uncle was still up, though not expecting me, and very distressed he was at the mistake about the carriage.

"However," he concluded, "all's well that ends well. It's delightful to have your good news. But you look sadly pale and tired, Charlotte."

Then I told him of my fright—it seemed now so foolish of me, I said. But my uncle did not smile—on the contrary.

"My dear," he said, "it sounds very like our ghost, though, of course, it may have been only one of the keepers."

He told me the story. Many years ago in his grandfather's time, a young and favourite gamekeeper had been found dead in the field skirting the road down there. There was no sign of violence upon the body; it was never explained what had killed him. But he had in his charge a watch—a very valuable one—

which his master for some reason or other had handed him to take home to the house, not wishing to keep it on him. And when the body was found late that night, the watch was not on it. Since then, the story goes, on a moonlight night the spirit of the poor fellow haunts the spot. It is supposed that he wants to tell what had become of his master's watch, which was never found. But no one has ever had the courage to address him.

"He never comes farther than the dip in the road," said my uncle. "If you had spoken to him, Charlotte, I wonder if he would have told you his secret?"

He spoke half laughingly, but I have never quite forgiven myself for my cowardice. It was the look in those terrible eyes.

# The Man With The Cough

(A story from *Uncanny Tales*)

## 1

I am a German by birth and descent. My name is Schmidt. But by education I am quite as much an Englishman as a '*Deutscher*', and by affection much more the former. My life has been spent pretty equally between the two countries, and I flatter myself I speak both languages without any foreign accent.

I count England my headquarters now: it is 'home' to me. But a few years ago I was resident in Germany, only going over to London now and then on business. I will not mention the town where I lived. It is unnecessary to do so, and in the peculiar experience I am about to relate I think real names of people and places are just as well, or better avoided.

I was connected with a large and important firm of engineers. I had been bred up to the profession, and was credited with a certain amount of talent; and I was considered—and, with all modesty, I think I deserved the opinion—steady and reliable, so that I had already attained a fair position in the house, and was looked upon as a 'rising man'. But I was still young, and not quite so wise as I thought myself. I came very near once to making a great mess of a certain affair. It is this story which I am going to tell.

Our house went in largely for patents—rather too largely, some thought. But the head partner's son was a bit of a genius in his way, and his father was growing old, and let Herr Wilhelm—Moritz we will call the family name—do pretty much as he chose. And on the whole Herr Wilhelm did well. He was cautious, and he had the benefit of the still greater caution and larger experience of Herr Gerhardt, the second partner in the firm.

Patents and the laws which regulate them are queer things to have to do with. No one who has not had personal experience of the complications that arise could believe how far these spread and how entangled they become. Great acuteness as well as caution is called for if you would guide your patent bark safely to port—and perhaps more than anything, a power of holding your tongue. I was no chatterbox, nor, when on a mission of importance, did I go about looking as if I were bursting with secrets, which is, in my opinion, almost as dangerous as revealing them.

No one, to meet me on the journeys which it often fell to my lot to undertake, would have guessed that I had anything on my mind but an easy-going young fellow's natural interest in his surroundings, though many a time I have stayed awake through a whole night of railway travel if at all doubtful about my fellow-passengers, or not dared to go to sleep in a hotel without a ready-loaded revolver by my pillow. For now and then—though not through me—our secrets did ooze out. And if, as has happened, they were secrets connected with Government orders or contracts, there was, or but for the exertion of the greatest energy and tact on the part of my superiors, there would have been, to put it plainly, the devil to pay.

## 2

One morning—it was nearing the end of November—I was sent for to Herr Wilhelm's private room. There I found him and Herr Gerhardt before a table spread with papers covered with figures and calculations, and sheets of beautifully executed diagrams.

'Lutz,' said Herr Wilhelm. He had known me from childhood, and often called me by the abbreviation of my Christian name, which is Ludwig, or Louis. 'Lutz, we are going to confide to you a matter of extreme importance. You must be prepared to start for London tomorrow.'

'All right, sir,' I said, 'I shall be ready.'

'You will take the express through to Calais—on the whole it is the best route, especially at this season. By travelling all night you will catch the boat there, and arrive in London so as to have a good night's rest, and be clear-headed for work the next morning.'

I bowed agreement, but ventured to make a suggestion.

'If, as I infer, the matter is one of great importance,' I said, 'would it not be well for me to start sooner? I can—yes,' throwing a rapid survey over the work I had before me for the next two days—I can be ready tonight.' Herr Wilhelm looked at Herr Gerhardt. Herr Gerhardt shook his head.

'No,' he replied, 'tomorrow it must be,' and then he proceeded to explain to me why.

I need not attempt to give all the details of the matter with which I was entrusted. Indeed, to 'lay' readers it would be impossible. Suffice it to say, the whole concerned a patent—that of a very remarkable and wonderful invention, which it was hoped and believed the Government of both countries would take up. But to secure this being done in a thoroughly satisfactory manner it was necessary that our firm should go about it in concert with an English house of first-rate standing. To this house—the firm of Messrs Bluestone & Fagg I will call them—I was to be sent with full explanations.

And the next half-hour or more passed in my superiors going minutely into the details, so as to satisfy themselves that I understood. The mastering of the whole was not difficult, for I was well grounded technically; and like many of the best things the idea was essentially simple, and the diagrams were perfect. When the explanations were over, and my instructions duly noted, I began to gather together the various sheets, which were all numbered. But, to my surprise, Herr Gerhardt, looking over me, withdrew two of the most important diagrams, without which the others were valueless, because inexplicable.

# 3

'Stay,' he said; 'these two, Ludwig, must be kept separate. These we send today, by registered post, direct to Bluestone & Fagg. They will receive them a day before they see you, and with them a letter announcing your arrival.'

I looked up in some disappointment. I had known of precautions of the kind being taken, but usually when the employee sent was less reliable than I believed myself to be. Still, I scarcely dared to demur.

'Do you think that necessary?' I said respectfully. 'I can assure you that from the moment you entrust me with the papers they shall never quit me day or night. And if there were any postal delay—you say time is valuable in this case—or if the papers were stolen in the transit—such things have happened—my whole mission would be worthless.'

'We do not doubt your zeal and discretion, my good Schmidt,' said Herr Gerhardt. 'But in this case we must take even extra precautions. I had not meant to tell you, fearing to add to the certain amount of nervousness and strain unavoidable in such a case, but still, perhaps it is best that you should know that we have reason for some special anxiety. It has been hinted to us that some breath of this'—and he tapped the papers—'has reached those who are always on the watch for such things. We cannot be too careful.'

'And yet', I persisted, 'you would trust the post?'

'We do not trust the post,' he replied. 'Even if these diagrams were tampered with, they would be perfectly useless. And tampered with they will not be. But even supposing anything so wild, the rogues in question knowing of your departure (and they are more likely to know of it than of our packet by post), were they in collusion with some traitor in the post office, are sharp enough to guess the truth—that we have made a Masonic secret of it—the two separate diagrams are valueless without your papers; your papers reveal nothing without Nos. 7 and 13.'

I bowed in submission. But I was, all the same, disappointed, as I said, and a trifle mortified.

Herr Wilhelm saw it, and cheered me up.

'All right, Lutz, my boy,' he said. 'I feel just like you—nothing I should enjoy more than a rush over to London, carrying the whole documents, and prepared for a fight with anyone who tried to get hold of them. But Herr Gerhardt here is cooler-blooded than we are.'

## 4

The elder man smiled.

'I don't doubt your readiness to fight, nor Ludwig's either. But it would be by no such honestly brutal means as open robbery that we should be outwitted. Make friends readily with no one while travelling, Lutz, yet avoid the appearance of keeping yourself aloof. You understand?'

'Perfectly,' I said. 'I shall sleep well tonight, so as to be prepared to keep awake throughout the journey.'

The papers were then carefully packed up. Those consigned to my care were to be carried in a certain light, black handbag with a very good lock, which had often before been my travelling companion. And the following evening I started by the express train agreed upon. So, at least, I have always believed, but I have never been able to bring forward a witness to the fact of my train at the start being the right one, as no one came with me to see me off. For it was thought best that I should depart in as unobtrusive a manner as possible, as, even in a large town such as ours, the members and employees of an old and important house like the Moritzes' were well known.

I took my ticket then, registering no luggage, as I had none but what I easily carried in my hand, as well as the bag. It was already dusk, if not dark, and there was not much bustle in the station, nor apparently many passengers. I took my place in an empty second-class compartment, and sat there quietly till the train should start. A few minutes before it did another man got in. I was somewhat annoyed at this, as in my circumstances nothing was more undesirable than travelling alone with one other. Had there been a crowded compartment, or one with three or four passengers, I would have chosen it; but at the moment I got in, the carriages were all either empty or with but one or two occupants. Now, I said to myself, I should have done better to wait till nearer the time of departure, and then chosen my place.

I turned to reconnoitre my companion, but I could not see his face clearly, as he was half leaning out of the window. Was he doing so on purpose? I said to myself, for naturally I was in a suspicious mood. And as the thought struck me I half started up, determined to choose another compartment. Suddenly a peculiar sound made itself heard. My companion was coughing. He drew his head in, covering his face with his hand, as he coughed again. You never heard such a curious cough. It was more like a hen clucking than anything I can think of. Once, twice he coughed; then, as if he had been waiting for the slight spasm to pass, he sprang up, looked eagerly out of the window again, and, opening the door, jumped out, with some exclamation, as if he had just caught sight of a friend.

## 5

And in another moment or two—he could barely have had time to get in elsewhere—much to my satisfaction, the train moved off.

'Now,' thought I, 'I can make myself comfortable for some hours. We do not stop till M——: it will be nine o'clock by then. If no one gets in there I am safe to go through till tomorrow alone; then there will only be —— Junction, and a clear run to Calais.'

I unstrapped my rug and lit a cigar—of course I had chosen a smoking-carriage—and, delighted at having got rid of my clucking companion, the time passed pleasantly till we pulled up at M——. The delay there was not great, and to my enormous satisfaction no one molested my solitude. Evidently the express to Calais was not in very great demand that night. I now felt so secure that, notwithstanding my intention of keeping awake all night, my innermost consciousness had not I suppose quite resigned itself to the necessity, for, not more than a hour or so after leaving M——, possibly sooner, I fell fast asleep.

It seemed to me that I had slept heavily, for when I awoke I had great difficulty in remembering where I was. Only by slow degrees did I realise that I was not in my comfortable bed at home, but in a chilly, ill-lighted railway-carriage. Chilly—yes, that it was—very chilly; but as my faculties returned I remembered my precious bag, and forgot all else in a momentary terror that it had been taken from me. No; there it was my elbow had been pressed against it as I slept. But how was this? The train was not in motion. We were standing in a station; a dingy deserted looking place, with no cheerful noise or bustle; only one or two porters slowly moving about, with a sort of sleepy 'night duty', surly air. It could not be the Junction? I looked at my watch. Barely midnight! Of course, not the Junction. We were not due there till four o'clock in the morning or so.

What, then, were we doing here, and what was 'here'? Had there been an accident—some unforeseen necessity for stopping? At that moment a curious sound, from some yards' distance only it seemed to come, caught my ear. It was that croaking, cackling cough!—the cough of my momentary fellow-passenger, towards whom I had felt an instinctive aversion. I looked out of the window—there was a refreshment room just opposite, dimly lighted, like everything else, and in the doorway, as if just entering, was a figure which I felt pretty sure was that of the man with the cough.

## 6

'Bah!' I said to myself, 'I must not be fanciful. I dare say the fellow's all right. He is evidently in the same hole as myself. What in Heaven's name are we waiting here for?'

I sprang out of the carriage, nearly tumbling over a porter slowly passing along.

'How long are we to stay here?' I cried. 'When do we start again for ——?' and I named the Junction.

'For ——,' he repeated in the queerest German I ever heard—was it German? or did I discover his meaning by some preternatural cleverness of my own? 'There is no train for —— for four or five hours, not till ——' and he named the time; and leaning forward lazily, he took out my larger bag and my rug, depositing them on the platform. He did not seem the least surprised at finding me there—I might have been there for a week, it seemed to me.

'No train for five hours? Are you mad?' I said.

He shook his head and mumbled something, and it seemed to me that he pointed to the refreshment-room opposite. Gathering my things together I hurried thither, hoping to find some more reliable authority. But there was no one there except a fat man with a white apron, who was clearing the counter—and—yes, in one corner was the figure I had mentally dubbed 'The man with the cough'.

I addressed the cook or waiter—whichever he was. But he only shook his head—denied all knowledge of the trains, but informed me that—in other words—I must turn out; he was going to shut up.

'And where am I to spend the night, then?' I said angrily, though clearly it was not the aproned individual who was responsible for the position in which I found myself.

There was a '*Restauration*', he informed me, near at hand, which I should find still open, straight before me on leaving the station, and then a few doors to the right, I would see the lights.

Clearly there was nothing else to be done. I went out, and as I did so the silent figure in the corner rose also and followed me. The station was evidently going to bed. As I passed the porter I repeated the hour he had named, adding: 'That is the first train for —— Junction?'

## 7

He nodded, again naming the exact time. But I cannot do so, as I have never been able to recollect it.

I trudged along the road—there were lamps, though very feeble ones; but by their light I saw that the man who had been in the refreshment-room was still a few steps behind me. It made me feel slightly nervous, and I looked round furtively once or twice; the last time I did so he was not to be seen, and I hoped he had gone some other way.

The '*Restauration*' was scarcely more inviting than the station-room. It, too, was very dimly lighted, and the one or two attendants seemed half asleep and were strangely silent. There was a fire of a kind, and I seated myself at a small table near it and asked for some coffee, which would, I thought, serve the double purpose of warming me and keeping me awake.

It was brought me, in silence. I drank it, and felt the better for it. But there was something so gloomy and unsociable, so queer and almost weird about the whole aspect and feeling of the place, that a sort of irritable resignation took possession of me. If these surly folk won't speak, neither will I, I said to myself childishly. And, incredible as it may sound, I did not speak. I think I paid for the coffee, but I am not quite sure. I know I never asked what I had meant to ask—the name of the town—a place of some importance, to judge by the size of the station and the extent of twinkling lights I had observed as I made my way to the '*Restauration*'. From that day to this I have never been able to identify it, and I am quite sure I never shall.

What was there peculiar about that coffee? Or was it something peculiar about my own condition that caused it to have the unusual effect I now experienced? That question, too, I cannot answer. All I remember is feeling a sensation of irresistible drowsiness creeping over me—mental, or moral I may say, as well as physical. For when one part of me feebly resisted the first onslaught of sleep, something seemed to reply: 'Oh, nonsense! you have several hours before you. Your papers are all right. No one can touch them without awaking you.'

### 8

And dreamily conscious that my belongings were on the floor at my feet—the bag itself actually resting against my ankle—my scruples silenced themselves in an extraordinary way. I remember nothing more, save a vague consciousness through all my slumber of confused and chaotic dreams, which I have never been able to recall.

I awoke at last, and that with a start, almost a jerk. Something had awakened me—a sound—and as it was repeated to my now aroused ears I knew that I had heard it before, off and on, during my sleep. It was the extraordinary cough!

I looked up. Yes, there he was! At some two or three yards' distance only, at the other side of the fireplace, which, and this I have forgotten to mention as another peculiar item in that night's peculiar experiences, considering I have every reason to believe I was still in Germany, was not a stove, but an open grate.

And he had not been there when I first fell asleep; to that I was prepared to swear. 'He must have come sneaking in after me,' I thought, and in all probability I should neither have noticed nor recognised him but for that traitorous cackle of his.

Now, my misgivings aroused, my first thought, of course, was for my precious charge. I stooped. There were my rugs, my larger bag, but—no, not the smaller one; and though the other two were there, I knew at once that they were not quite in the same position—not so close to me. Horror seized me. Half wildly I gazed around, when my silent neighbour bent towards me. I could declare there was nothing in his hand when he did so, and I could declare as positively that I had already looked under the small round table beside which I sat, and that the bag was not there. And yet when the man, with a slight cackle, caused, no doubt, by his stooping, raised himself, the thing was in his hand!

Was he a conjuror, a pupil of Maskelyne and Cook? And how was it that, even as he held out my missing property, he managed, and that most cleverly and unobtrusively, to prevent my catching sight of his face! I did not see it then—I never did see it!

## 9

Something he murmured, to the effect that he supposed the

bag was what I was looking for. In what language he spoke I know not; it was more that by the action accompanying the mumbled sounds, I gathered his meaning, than that I heard anything articulate.

I thanked him, of course, mechanically, so to say, though I began to feel as if he were an evil spirit haunting me. I could only hope that the splendid lock to the bag had defied all curiosity, but I felt in a fever to be alone again, and able to satisfy myself that nothing had been tampered with.

The thought recalled my wandering faculties. How long had I been asleep? I drew out my watch. Heavens! It was close upon the hour named for the first train in the morning. I sprang up, collected my things, and dashed out of the '*Restauration*'. If I had not paid for my coffee before, I certainly did not pay for it then. Besides my haste, there was another reason for this—there was no one to pay to! Not a creature was to be seen in the room or at the door as I passed out—always excepting the man with the cough.

As I left the place and hurried along the road, a bell began, not to ring, but to toll. It sounded most uncanny. What it meant, of course, I have never known. It may have been a summons to the workpeople of some manufactory, it may have been like all the other experiences of that strange night. But no; this theory I will not at present enter upon.

Dawn was not yet breaking, but there was in one direction a faint suggestion of something of the kind not far off. Otherwise all was dark. I stumbled along as best as I could, helped in reality, I suppose, by the ugly yellow glimmer of the woebegone street, or road lamps. And it was not far to the station, though somehow it seemed farther than when I came; and somehow, too, it seemed to have grown steep, though I could not remember having noticed any slope the other way on my arrival. A nightmare-like sensation began to oppress me. I felt as if my luggage was growing momentarily heavier and heavier, as if I should never reach the station; and to this was joined the agonising terror of missing the train.

# 10

I made a desperate effort. Cold as it was, the beads of perspiration stood out upon my forehead as I forced myself along. And by degrees the nightmare feeling cleared off. I found myself entering the station at a run just as—yes, a train was actually beginning to move! I dashed, baggage and all, into a compartment; it was empty, and it was a second-class one, precisely similar to the one I had occupied before; it might have been the very same one. The train gradually increased its speed, but for the first few moments, while still in the station and passing through its immediate entourage, another strange thing struck me—the extraordinary silence and lifelessness of all about. Not one human being did I see, no porter watching our departure with the faithful though stolid interest always to be seen on the porter's visage. I might have been alone in the train—it might have had a freight of the dead, and been itself propelled by some supernatural agency, so noiselessly, so gloomily did it proceed.

You will scarcely credit that I actually and for the third time fell asleep. I could not help it. Some occult influence was at work upon me throughout those dark hours, I am positively certain. And with the daylight it was dispelled. For when I again awoke I felt for the first time since leaving home completely and normally myself, fresh and vigorous, all my faculties at their best.

But, nevertheless, my first sensation was a start of amazement, almost of terror. The compartment was nearly full! There were at least five or six travellers besides myself, very respectable, ordinary-looking folk, with nothing in the least alarming about them. Yet it was with a gasp of extraordinary relief that I found my precious bag in the corner beside me, where I had carefully placed it. It was concealed from view. No one, I felt assured, could have touched it without awaking me.

It was broad and bright daylight. How long had I slept?

'Can you tell me,' I enquired of my opposite neighbour, a cheery-faced compatriot—'Can you tell me how soon we get to —— Junction by this train? I am most anxious to catch the evening mail at Calais, and am quite out in my reckonings, owing to an extraordinary delay at —— I have wasted the night by getting into a stopping train instead of the express.'

## 11

He looked at me in astonishment. He must have thought me either mad or just awaking from a fit of intoxication—only I flatter myself I did not look as if the latter were the case.

'How soon we get to —— Junction?' he repeated. 'Why, my good sir, you left it about three hours ago! It is now eight o'clock. We all got in at the Junction. You were alone, if I mistake not?'—he glanced at one or two of the others, who endorsed his statement. 'And very fast asleep you were, and must have been, not to be disturbed by the bustle at the station. And as for catching the evening boat at Calais'—he burst into a loud guffaw— 'why, it would be very hard lines to do no better than that! We all hope to cross by the midday one.'

'Then—what train is this?' I exclaimed, utterly perplexed.

'The express, of course. All of us, excepting yourself, joined it at the Junction,' he replied.

'The express?' I repeated. 'The express that leaves ——'—and I named my own town, 'at six in the evening?'

'Exactly. You have got into the right train after all,' and here came another shout of amusement. 'How did you think we had all got in if you had not yet passed the Junction? You had not the pleasure of our company from M——, I take it? M——, which you passed at nine o'clock last night, if my memory is correct.'

'Then', I persisted, this is the double-fast express, which does not stop between M—— and your Junction?'

'Exactly,' he repeated; and then, confirmed most probably in his belief that I was mad, or the other thing, he turned to his newspaper, and left me to my extraordinary cogitations.

Had I been dreaming? Impossible! Every sensation, the very taste of the coffee, seemed still present with me—the curious accent of the officials at the mysterious town, I could perfectly recall. I still shivered at the remembrance of the chilly waking in the 'Restauration'; I heard again the cackling cough.

But I felt I must collect myself, and be ready for the important negotiation entrusted to me. And to do this I must for the time banish these fruitless efforts at solving the problem.

## 12

We had a good run to Calais, found the boat in waiting, and a fair passage brought us prosperously across the Channel. I found myself in London punctual to the intended hour of my arrival.

At once I drove to the lodgings in a small street off the Strand which I was accustomed to frequent in such circumstances. I felt nervous till I had an opportunity of thoroughly overhauling my documents. The bag had been opened by the Custom House officials, but the words 'private papers' had sufficed to prevent any further examination; and to my unspeakable delight they were intact. A glance satisfied me as to this the moment I got them out, for they were most carefully numbered.

The next morning saw me early on my way to—No. 909, we will say—Blackfriars Street, where was the office of Messrs Bluestone & Fagg. I had never been there before, but it was easy to find, and had I felt any doubt, their name stared me in the face at the side of the open doorway. 'Second-floor' I thought I read; but when I reached the first landing I imagined I must have been mistaken. For there, at a door ajar, stood an eminently respectable-looking gentleman, who bowed as he saw me, with a discreet smile.

'Herr Schmidt?' he said. 'Ah, yes; I was on the lookout for you.'

I felt a little surprised, and my glance involuntarily strayed to the doorway. There was no name upon it, and it appeared to have been freshly painted. My new friend saw my glance.

'It is all right,' he said; 'we have the painters here. We are using these lower rooms temporarily. I was watching to prevent your having the trouble of mounting to the second-floor.'

And as I followed him in, I caught sight of a painter's ladder—a small one—on the stair above, and the smell was also unmistakable. The large outer office looked bare and empty, but under the circumstances that was natural. No one was, at the first glance, to be seen; but behind a dulled glass partition screening off one corner I fancied I caught sight of a seated figure. And an inner office, to which my conductor led the way, had a more comfortable and inhabited look. Here stood a younger man. He bowed politely.

## 13

'Mr Fagg, my junior,' said the first individual airily. 'And now, Herr Schmidt, to business at once, if you please. Time is everything. You have all the documents ready?'

I answered by opening my bag and spreading out its contents. Both men were very grave, almost taciturn; but as I proceeded to explain things it was easy to see that they thoroughly understood all I said.

'And now,' I went on, when I had reached a certain point, 'if you will give me Nos. 7 and 13 which you have already received by registered post, I can put you in full possession of the whole. Without them, of course, all I have said is, so to say, preliminary only.'

The two looked at each other.

'Of course,' said the elder man, 'I follow what you say. The key of the whole is wanting. But I was momentarily expecting you to bring it out. We have not—Fagg, I am right, am I not—we have received nothing by post?'

'Nothing whatever,' replied his junior. And the answer seemed simplicity itself. Why did a strange thrill of misgiving go through me? Was it something in the look that had passed between them? Perhaps so. In any case, strange to say, the inconsistency between their having received no papers and yet looking for my arrival at the hour mentioned in the letter accompanying the documents, and accosting me by name, did not strike me till some hours later.

I threw off what I believed to be my ridiculous mistrust, and it was not difficult to do so in my extreme annoyance.

'I cannot understand it,' I said. 'It is really too bad. Everything depends upon 7 and 13. I must telegraph at once for enquiries to be instituted at the post office.'

'But your people must have duplicates,' said Fagg eagerly. 'These can be forwarded at once.'

'I hope so,' I said, though feeling strangely confused and worried.

'They must send them direct here,' he went on.

I did not at once answer. I was gathering my papers together.

'And in the meantime,' he proceeded, touching my bag, you had better leave these here. We will lock them up in the safe at once. It is better than carrying them about London.'

It certainly seemed so. I half laid down the bag on the table, but at that moment from the outer room a most peculiar sound caught my ears—a faint cackling cough! I think I concealed my start. I turned away as if considering Fagg's suggestion, which, to confess the truth, I had been on the very point of agreeing to. For it would have been a great relief to me to know that the papers were in safe custody. But now a flash of lurid light seemed to have transformed everything.

## 14

'I thank you,' I replied, 'I should be glad to be free from the responsibility of the charge, but I dare not let these out of my own hands till the agreement is formally signed.'

The younger man's face darkened. He assumed a bullying tone.

'I don't know how it strikes you, Mr Bluestone,' he said, 'But it seems to me that this young gentleman is going rather too far. Do you think your employers will be pleased to hear of your insulting us, sir?'

But the elder man smiled condescendingly, though with a touch of superciliousness. It was very well done. He waved his hand.

'Stay, my dear Mr Fagg; we can well afford to make allowance. You will telegraph at once, no doubt, Herr Schmidt, and—

let me see—yes, we shall receive the duplicates of Nos. 7 and 13 by first post on Thursday morning.'

I bowed.

'Exactly,' I replied, as I lifted the now locked bag. 'And you may expect me at the same hour on Thursday morning.'

Then I took my departure, accompanied to the door by the urbane individual who had received me.

The telegram which I at once dispatched was not couched precisely as he would have dictated, I allow. And he would have been considerably surprised at my sending off another, later in the day, to Bluestone & Fagg's telegraphic address, in these words:

Unavoidably detained till Thursday morning.—Schmidt.

This was after the arrival of a wire from home in answer to mine. By Thursday morning I had had time to receive a letter from Herr Wilhelm, and to secure the services of a certain noted detective, accompanied by whom I presented myself at the appointed hour at 909. But my companion's services were not required. The birds had flown, warned by the same traitor in our camp through whom the first hints of the new patent had leaked out. With him it was easy to deal, poor wretch! but the clever rogues who had employed him and personated the members of the honourable firm of Bluestone & Fagg were never traced.

The negotiation was successfully carried out. The experience I had gone through left me a wiser man. It is to be hoped, too, that the owners of 909 Blackfriars Street were more cautious in the future as to whom they let their premises to when temporarily vacant. The repainting of the doorway, etc., at the tenant's own expense had already roused some slight suspicion.

### 15

It is needless to add that Nos. 7 and 13 had been duly received on the second-floor.

I have never known the true history of that extraordinary night. Was it all a dream, or a prophetic vision of warning? Or was it in any sense true? Had I, in some inexplicable way, left my own town earlier than I intended, and really travelled in a slow train?

Or had the man with a cough, for his own nefarious purposes, mesmerised or hypnotised me, and to some extent succeeded? I cannot say. Sometimes, even, I ask myself if I am quite sure that there ever was such a person as 'the man with the cough'!

# The Abbaye de Cérisy

[1]In the spring of this present year—1889—two ladies were seated together one afternoon talking comfortably, as they sipped their "five-o'clock tea." Five-o'clock tea is, or was, at least, a thoroughly English institution, but it is no longer unknown to our neighbours across the Channel. And a glance—a glance of the slightest and shortest, would have shown any one that this special refection was not being enjoyed in an English drawing-room or *boudoir*.

The room was small, oblong in shape, the whole of one end being occupied by a rather large window, or glazed door, opening on to a balcony. From this balcony one had a good view of a wide, quaint, hilly street, with high walls on each side, in which, at irregular intervals, were visible the great *portes-cochères* leading into the coach-yards of the spacious old mansions or *hôtels*, of the gentry still resident in an old town of Normandy. Here and there stood a more modest dwelling-house, guiltless of *cour* (though not of *jardin* at the back), whose front-door steps ran straight down to the pavement. It was a very picturesque street, from every point of view, and the long, level rays of the afternoon sun showed it to peculiar advantage.

Inside the *boudoir*, it was difficult to believe one's self still in the nineteenth century. The room was entirely lined with wood—light-coloured brown wood—into the panels of which were inserted Louis XVI. paintings of the quaintest description:

---

1. The incident here related is perfectly true. The Abbaye de Cérisy is the real name of the place where the strange recluse was seen.

cupids, nymphs, garden and terrace landscapes, grotesque statues, grinning masks; all the well-known decorative designs of the period, from the *attributs de jardinage* and those of *musique* also, with their bows of impossible blue ribbon, to an armless satyr or a ring of dancing "loves." The furniture, of which there was not much, and indeed the space was very small, was mostly of the same date; a small brass-mounted, marble-topped *bureau* occupied one corner; two or three medallion-backed, white-painted chairs stood about.

With this background, the little English tea-table, and the two friends seated—on easier chairs than the Louis XVI. *fauteuils*—were scarcely in keeping. But the cups and saucers were of old Sèvres; and the snow-white hair, drawn back from the forehead, of the elder of the two ladies—a woman of sixty or thereabouts—simply though richly dressed in black, with touches of creamy old lace here and there, harmonized with the whole, or rather seemed a sort of meeting-point for the past and the present. This lady was the Marquise de Romars; her companion, considerably younger than herself, was her visitor, and an Englishwoman, by name Miss Poynsett.

Miss Poynsett was on her way home from a winter spent in the south; she had lingered, nothing loath, to pass a few days with her hospitable old friend.

"Then there is really no chance of my seeing you again this year, my dear Clemency?" said the old lady.

Miss Poynsett shook her head. "None whatever, unless you will come over to us."

"That I cannot. But I had hoped the exhibition, the Eiffel Tower, and all the rest of it, would have tempted some of you to Paris; and, of course, it is easy to make this a half-way, or three-quarters-way house," said Madame de Romars—who, by the way, spoke perfect English—insinuatingly.

Again Miss Poynsett shook her head, more vigorously this time.

"If a visit to you were not temptation enough, certainly Paris in a state of exhibition would not be," she said, half laughingly.

"I cannot bear exhibitions, and Paris, with a world's show going on, is worst of all. Just think of how one would be running up against everybody one had ever seen or heard of. Not that I am unsociable; but one doesn't leave one's own country to see one's own country-folk. When I travel, I like to see new things and people."

"The exhibition would be new, and the Eiffel Tower has certainly never been seen before," said Madame de Romars, in a matter-of-fact tone.

"Dear *madame*, I think the Eiffel Tower has bewitched you," replied her friend. "I have not the very slightest wish to see it nor the exhibition. And then the association. I should have thought you would have shrunk from any commemoration of the horrors of a hundred years ago."

The old lady did not at once reply.

"This year actually commemorates the destruction of the Bastille," she said, after a little pause. "With that one can have full sympathy. As for what came afterwards——" she sighed deeply.

"One of the most grievous thoughts about the great Revolution," she went on—"even, in the widest sense, more grievous than the terrible individual horrors, is what it might have been and done; what enormous opportunities for the world's good were lost at that time. For the individual suffering is over and past, and doubtless it made saints and martyrs of many who might otherwise have lived and died like soulless animals; but the misdirection, the fearful misuse and abuse of the powers at that time set free will never—while the world lasts, it sometimes seems to me—be, in their sad consequences, past and over."

Miss Poynsett listened attentively and respectfully, but scarcely as if she fully understood.

"I am no philosopher like you, dear *madame*," she said. "To me I own the story of the great Revolution is just like a very fearful though most fascinating tragedy; it is the personal histories mixed up in it that always come into my mind. And oh, by-the-by, I am so much obliged to you for lending me Monsieur de Beauchesne's book; it has interested me exceedingly. Indeed, for a time, some parts of it almost haunted me."

"You mean, of course, his Louis XVII. I forgot I had lent it you. Yes, it is a very impressive book, and a very exhaustive account of what is always full of fresh interest—the history of the Royal Family in the Temple. Of course the *dauphin* is the central figure. Monsieur de Beauchesne has really got together everything that is known about the poor little prince. One or two of the anecdotes are intensely touching."

"Almost too much so. I can't imagine ever being able to read them without tears," the English lady replied. "Monsieur de Beauchesne seems quite to set beyond a doubt the child's death in his prison," she went on, after a little pause. "It is almost disappointing, there is such a fascination about the subject. And one would fain have hoped that perhaps, after all, though his princeship was over forever, the poor boy had some peaceful years, even in a comparatively humble position."

The *Marquise* remained silent for a moment or two. When she spoke, her voice was very grave and almost solemn.

"I don't think it is to be hoped or wished that it was so," she said. "For my part, I would rather believe he died at the time generally supposed. Nothing in the annals of child saints or martyrs could be more beautiful, more holy, than those last days of his life in the Temple. One can scarcely think it possible that a soul so near heaven had longer to stay on earth. And yet No, Clemency, I hope he died that 8th of June. His life, had he lived, did he live, must have been too sad."

Something in her words and tone struck her companion. She looked up eagerly.

"There is a shade of uncertainty in your way of speaking, dear *madame*," she said. "You don't mean to say that you have any other theory on the subject, besides all the stories Monsieur de Beauchesne refutes so carefully?"

"No," said the old lady. "I have no theory, but—I had a strange adventure once, Clemency, and though I have told it to very few— no one now living remembers it—I have never lost the impression it left on my mind."

She stopped. Miss Poynsett opened her lips to speak, but hesitated. Her eager look and questioning eyes, however, told their own story. Madame de Romars understood her.

"I will tell it to you if you like," she said. "There is no reason why I should not; it can do no one any harm. And I fear you will be disappointed; there is so little to tell."

"No, no; whatever it is, it will interest me," said Clemency. "And thank you so much. I hope there is nothing painful to yourself in it?"

"Not exactly. Oh no; it only brings back past days, and sadder than that, past hopes and bright anticipations never to be realized. For I was very young then—not twenty-one—and I think nearly all the friends just at that time associated with me are dead—yes, all. But I will tell you my story. It was, as nearly as I can remember, in the year 1844. We, my husband and I, were staying with a party of friends, mostly young—I myself was little more than a bride—at a charming old *château* in the further extremity of Normandy. The *château* was old, but recently restored, so that, especially as the restoration had been carried out with the greatest care and good taste; it really combined the attractions of antiquity with those of modern life.

"It had been for centuries the home of our hosts' ancestors; the present festivities were a sort of "housewarming," after the restorations, as well as to do honour to the *finçailles* of the lovely young and only daughter of the family, a girl of eighteen, who was to be married a few weeks later in the season. All of these details are irrelevant to my little story, but they have remained in my memory as a sort of frame to it, or, one might say, a bright background to the strange sad impression my adventure left.

"Our days passed delightfully. The country was picturesque and beautiful. There were points of interest of various kinds, old Roman remains, famous 'views,' charming woods; every day some new excursion to one or other of these was planned, and, thanks to the quite exceptionally fine weather, these were successfully carried out. Yes, it was a very happy time." Madame de Romars stopped for a moment and sighed. Clemency waited in quiet sympathy. She did not know the whole details of her old friend's history, but she knew that trials and disappointments of no common severity had fallen to her share, and she felt half repentant that she had asked for the story. After a moment, the *Marquise* went on—

"One day, an expedition was arranged to visit the ancient Abbaye de Cérisy. I was delighted to make one of the party, especially as we were to stop at the Château de Selcourt on the way, which we did. This is one of the few remaining really Feudal Châteaux, interesting on that ground alone, though it is also worth visiting for its quantity of old tapestry, furniture, and some queer pictures. One I remember well, was a picture of the Blessed Virgin, surrounded by her *cousins*, knights in full 'Moyen Age' armour, and ladies in the garb of nuns. At Selcourt, too, there are seven fishponds, considered a unique curiosity. Then we drove on to Cérisy. We had spent more time than we intended at Selcourt, so that when we got to the Abbaye, it was already rather late afternoon.

"We hastened to visit the church, the old cloisters, etc., and the architectural connoisseurs among us were loud in their praise of the grandly simple Norman style. There was one fishpond at Cérisy too; a very large one, and there was a legend—I forget what—connected with it which interested some of our party. I got tired of the discussion about it, and wandered off by myself, choosing accidently a path which led, I found, to some old, half-ruinous buildings. This sort of thing has always had a great attraction for me, and I had a curiosity to find the building which, in former days, must have been the Abbot's house. I was really delighted when suddenly, at the angle of a wall which I had been skirting, I came upon a very massive and most curiously carved door, in an almost perfect state of preservation.

"I felt like the prince in the *Sleeping Beauty* story, only my door was not overgrown with nettles and brambles. On the contrary, it was slightly ajar, and had evidently been opened not long before, for a very slight touch made it turn on its hinges enough for me to see before me a large wide stone staircase, with handsome and curiously carved *rampe* also in stone. This was too enticing to resist. Up I mounted, pleasantly excited by a slight sense of impropriety in my proceedings, and had almost reached the small landing at the top of the staircase when I was confronted by a young peasant girl, who, startled and alarmed by my appearance, stood there as if to remonstrate against my going further.

"But, the blood of my curiosity and love of adventure was 'up' by this time; I moved on, taking no notice whatever of her evident terror and half-whispered, stammering remonstrances. My whole attention was absorbed by the strangeness of the interior which I began to catch sight of. The door of a room on my right was wide open, revealing a sort of thick hedge or wall of close-growing cactus and other unfamiliar, weird-looking exotic shrubs. They were of an unusual height, and though I have visited many botanical gardens in my time, and had even possessed, in my own conservatories, many curious foreign plants, I have never seen any to equal these, nor could I have given a name to any one of them. They must have been there, growing where they stood, for many and many a year; for their branches, in several cases, reached up to the old black beams of the apartment, and the lower part of this strange hedge, so to call it, quite concealed from view, where I first stood, the room behind.

"But a step or two forward and a slight turn to the right showed me more. I perceived that the hedge stopped, leaving an entrance way as it were, and standing just in it, most of the interior was revealed to me. I saw before me a fair-sized room, at once strongly impressing me by its ancient and old-world aspect. In one corner, that on my right, stood a large square black oak bedstead of the style known as 'Henri IV.,' the faded, though well-preserved hangings and coverlet were of the same period, for to an eye trained and accustomed to judge of such things almost from childhood, thus much can be perceived at a glance. The dark wooden chairs, their seats covered with tapestry, were of the same period; and had evidently, so bravely to stand the wear and tear of centuries, been of the very best materials.

"A fairly good fire was burning in the open stone hearth, and some preparation for a meal seemed to be simmering upon it, but my gaze was drawn upwards by the really splendid carving of the old mantelpiece and jambs, and I was on the point of moving forward to examine It more closely, when my presumption was suddenly arrested. From the further side of the room came a deep sepulchral voice.

"*Madame*," it said—I can hear it now—'*que demandez-vous?*' and turning towards the left, where the afternoon light happened to fall, I saw, half concealed by a large olive-green-coloured curtain of heavy cloth, the strangest being my eyes have ever rested upon. I did not see the whole of the figure; it remained half shrouded by the curtain, and by the screen of plants I have tried to describe, but the face was very plainly visible. Whether it was that of a man or a woman I have never been able to decide; the unuttered exclamation that rose to my lips was a strange one.

"'That is the face of a Bourbon!'

"For familiar to me from my earliest years have been the strongly marked, to me, *unmistakable* features of that unfortunate race.

"The snow-white hair of the mysterious being was drawn back from the forehead and concealed by some kind of skull cap or cowl, again covered in its turn by something black and floating like a veil; a black cape or mantle shrouded as much of the rest of the body as was visible. The figure neither rose nor moved, but remained seated in front of a small table covered with book, papers, writing materials, etc., and as I stood, half-stunned, '*interdite*, as we say, again came the deep voice, accompanied this time by a glance of the haughtiest and sternest—

"'*Que voulez-vous, Madame? On n'entre pas ici.*'

"My position was not a dignified one, only my curiosity had supported me so far! But, notwithstanding its increasing intensity, I dared not persist. With one glance round the extraordinary scene, a glance that has printed it forever on my memory, and hastily murmured words of respectful apology, I retreated, to find myself once more on the landing outside, where the peasant girl, by this time almost imbecile with terror, shiveringly awaited me. I don't know if she half pushed or pulled me down the stairs—but once outside, I turned and asked her the reason of her extraordinary behaviour. After all, I had done no harm; I was only interested in the old buildings; what was she afraid of, and who was the person she served?

"I could obtain no satisfactory reply. She had not been long there, she said; she belonged to a distant part of the country—as, indeed, her costume showed—and could tell me nothing of the Abbaye nor its inmates. Then she re-entered the building, and closed the door in my face—not rudely, but as if completely indifferent to any but the one idea of getting me off the premises. Poor girl, I dare say a reprimand of the sharpest was in store for her!

"I retraced my steps in the direction where I had left my friends. A few paces further on, I almost ran against an aged priest, evidently bound for the place I had just left. An expression of surprise and annoyance crossed his face on seeing me, or rather the direction whence I came. He did not speak, but stopped short, and stood there motionless, openly watching me till I passed through a great archway in a wall a little further on, and was lost to his sight.

"Close at hand were my friends, somewhat impatiently awaiting my return by the famous fishpond. Its legend—a gruesome one enough, of its having been used as a burial-place for their prisoners by some bloodthirsty monks of old, to the benefit of the fat carp and pike— had been discussed and quarrelled over sufficiently, and the whole party was now anxious to get home to the cheery *château*. During the drive thither, I told my story, which was received with great interest. Various plans were formed for revisiting Cérisy, and trying to solve the mystery, but somehow they were never carried out.

"Nor did the inquiries set on foot in the neighbourhood about the strange inhabitant of the ruined Abbaye, ever bring anything to light concerning him. Our party shortly after broke up. I never revisited my friends at their *château*. Something prevented my going to them the following year, and after that, I had no longer any reason for doing so. Troubles, as unexpected as undeserved, fell thickly on our kind hosts, the once happy family there—and but a few years after the merry gathering I have described, the poor mother, of all the group, was left to mourn alone the blighted hopes and vanished brightness.

"For such sorrows as hers there is no consolation in this world to be found, so you can understand that the associations of my one visit to that part of the country came to be sad enough. And notwithstanding my curiosity about the being I have described, I never could make up my mind to revisit the neighbourhood of Cérisy."

Madame de Romars stopped. Clemency Poynsett looked up inquiringly.

"How sad!" she said feelingly. "Yes, dear *madame*, I well understand. But, tell me, please—do you really think it *possible*—had you the feeling that the figure you saw was—was perhaps really Louis XVII.—the poor little prince, grown into——Stay *would* he have been as old as the recluse of the Abbaye at the time you named; about the year 1844, was it not?"

"He was born in 1785," said the *Marquise*. "He would have been, therefore, fifty-nine at the date of my adventure. Certainly, the person I saw looked much older than that, to judge in an ordinary way. But then—consider what the Prince went through! *Had* he lived, it is scarcely to be expected he would ever have recovered his health bodily or mental; at least, he could never have been like other people. No; *if* Louis XVII. lived, I can scarcely help picturing him to myself at sixty as at best much such a prematurely aged, fearfully *marked* human being as the strange vision I came across. I hope it was not he—I cannot endure to think it was—to picture the long monotonous years that must have passed in that sad captivity of concealment, and, in all probability, in great physical suffering too.

"For I *think* the poor creature I saw must have been paralyzed or something of that kind. Yet there was such dignity, such reserve and *presence* about the strange being—no angry chatter of scolding; just the few cold, haughty, yet not uncourteous words I have repeated."

"Whoever it was—man or woman—must have been quite of the upper classes," said Miss Poynsett.

"Oh dear, yes—a thousand times yes. The tone, the accent, the manner—all showed it. *Poor* old man, for I think it was a man, Louis XVII. or not—there was a sad story shut up in that strange room—a story almost certainly connected with that awful time a century ago. How often since, I have wished I could have shown some kindness to the recluse, infused some little brightness into that almost unearthly life! But it could not have been. And whoever it was, it is all over now——"

"I, too, hope it was not the Prince," said Clemency, "strangely fascinating though the idea is. But there were the Bourbon features."

"Yes," agreed her old friend. "There were those undoubtedly: the unmistakable Bourbon features."

# "Half-Way Between the Stiles"
## (A Right-of-Way Incident.)
### (A story from *Uncanny Tales*)

By the road, Scarby village is good three miles from Collet-wood, the nearest town and railway station. But there is a short cut over the hills for foot passengers. *Over* the hills they call it, but *between* the hills would be more correct, for there is a sort of tableland once you have climbed a short, steep bit up from the town, which extends nearly to Scarby, sloping gradually down to the village.

And on each side of this tableland the hills rise again, north and south, much higher to the north than to the south. So this flat stretch, though at some considerable height, is neither bleak nor exposed, being sheltered on the colder side, and fairly open to the sunshine south and west.

It is a pleasant place, and so it must have been considered in the old days; for a large monastery stood there once, of which the ruins are still to be seen, and of which the memory is still preserved in the name—"Monksholdings".

Pleasant, but a trifle inconvenient, as the only carriage-road makes a great round from Colletwood, winding along the base of the hill on the north side till it reaches the village, then up again by the gradual slope, half a mile or so—a drive in all of three to four miles, whereas, as the bird flies or the pedestrian walks, the distance from the town is barely a quarter of that.

In the old days there was probably no road at all, the hill-path doubtless serving all requirements. Naturally enough, therefore, it came to be looked upon as entirely public property, and people forgot—if, indeed, any one had ever thought of it—that though the monastery was a ruin, the once carefully kept land round about the old dwelling-place of Monksholdings was still private property.

And the sensation was great when suddenly the news reached the neighbourhood that this "unique estate," as the agents called it, was sold—sold by the old Duke of Scarshire, who scarcely remembered that he owned it, to a man who meant to live on it, to build a house which should be a home for several months of the year for himself and his family.

There was considerable growling and grumbling; and this rose to its height when a rumour got about that the hill-path—such part of it, that is to say, as lay within the actual demesne—was to be closed—*must* be closed, if the site already chosen for the new house was to be retained; for the house would actually stand upon the old foot-track, and there could be no two opinions that this position had been well and wisely selected.

Things grew warlike, boding no agreeable reception for the newcomers—a Mr. Raynald and his family, newcomers to England, it was said, as well as to Scarshire. Every one plunged into questions of right-of-way; the local legalities raised and discussed knotty points; Colletwood and Scarby were aflame. But it all ended, flatly enough, in a compromise!

Mr. Raynald turned out to be one of the most reasonable and courteous of men. He came, saw, and—conquered. The goodwill of his future neighbours was won e'er he knew he had risked its loss. Henceforward congratulations, reciprocated and repeated, on the charming additions to Scarby society were the order of the day, and the *détour*, skirting the south boundary of the Monksholdings grounds, which the footpath was now inveigled into making, was voted "a great improvement".

And in due time the mansion rose.

"A great improvement" also, to the aspect of the surrounding landscape. It was in perfectly good taste—unpretentious and quietly picturesque. It might have been there always for any jarring protest to the contrary.

And just half-way along the old foot-track, that is to say, between the two stiles which let the traveller to or from Scarby in or out of the Monksholdings *demesne*, stood Sybil Raynald's grand piano!

The stiles remained as an interesting survival; but they were made use of by no one not bound for the house itself. And beside each was a gate—a good oaken gate, that suited the place, as did everything about it; and beside each gate a quaint miniature dwelling, one of which came to be known as the east, and the other as the west, Monksholdings lodge.

The first time the Raynalds came down to their new home they made but a short stay there. It was already late in the season, and though the preceding summer had been a magnificent one for drying fresh walls and plaster, it would scarcely have done to risk damp or chilly weather in so recently-built a house.

They stayed long enough to confirm the favourable impression the head of the family had already made, and to lead themselves to look forward with pleasure to a less curtailed stay in Scarshire.

The last morning of their visit, Sybil, the eldest daughter, up and about betimes, turned to her father, when she had taken her place beside him at the breakfast-table, with a suspicion of annoyance on her usually cheerful face.

"Papa," she said, "I have seen that old man *again*, leaning on the stile by the Scarby lodge and looking in—along the drive—*so* queerly. I don't quite like it. It gave me rather a ghosty feeling; or else he is out of his mind."

Her brother, Mark by name, began to laugh, after the manner of brothers.

"How very oddly you express yourself!" he said. "I should like to experience 'a ghosty feeling'. A ghost is just what this place wants to make it perfect. But it should be the spirit of one of the original monks."

Mr. Raynald turned to his son rather sharply.

"I don't want any nonsense of that kind set about, Mark," he said. "It would frighten the younger children when they come down here. I will ask about the old man. It is quite possible he is half-witted, or something of that sort. I forgot about it when Sybil mentioned it before. But no doubt he is perfectly harmless. Has no one seen him but you, Sybil?"

The girl shook her head.

"None of *us*," she replied. "And I wasn't exactly frightened. There was something very pathetic about him. He looked at me closely, murmuring some words, and then shook his head. That was all."

But just then her father was called away to give some last directions, and in the bustle of hurry to catch their train the matter passed from the minds of the younger as well as the elder members of the family.

It returned to Sybil's memory, however, when she found herself in their London house again, and called upon by her younger sisters to relate every detail of Monksholdings and its neighbourhood. But mindful of her father's warning, she said nothing to Esther or Annis of the figure at the gate. It was only to Miss March—Ellinor March—the dearly-loved governess, who was more friend than teacher to her three pupils, that she spoke of it, late in the evening, when the younger ones had gone to bed, and her father and mother were busy with Indian letters in Mr. Raynald's study.

The two girls, we may say—for Ellinor was still some years under thirty—were alone in the drawing-room. Ellinor had been playing something tender and faintly weird—it died away under her fingers, and she sat on at the piano in silence.

Sybil spoke suddenly.

"That is *so* melancholy," she said, "something so long ago about it, like the ghost of a sorrow rather than a sorrow itself. I know—I know what it makes me think of. Listen, Ellinor."

For out of school hours the two threw formality aside. And Sybil told of the sad, wistful old face looking over the stile.

"Now it has come back to me," she said, "I can't forget it."

Ellinor, too, was impressed.

"Yes," she said, "it sounds very pitiful. Who knows what tragedy is bound up in it?" and she sighed.

Sybil understood her. Miss March's own history was a strange one.

"We must find out about it when we go down to Monksholdings next year," she said.

"And perhaps," added Ellinor, "even if he is half-witted, we might do something to comfort the poor man."

Sybil hesitated.

"Then you don't think he can be a ghost?" she said, looking half ashamed of the suggestion.

Miss March smiled—her smile was sad.

"In one sense, no, I should think it highly improbable; in another, yes, there must be the ghost of some great sorrow about the face you describe," she said.

So there was.

This is the story.

At the farther end of Scarby village—the farther end, that is to say, from Monksholdings and the path between the hills—the road drops again somewhat suddenly. Only for a short distance, however; Mayling Farm—"Giles's" as it is colloquially called—which is the first house you come to when you reach level ground again, being by no means low lying.

On the contrary, the west windows command a grand view of the great Scarshire plain beneath, bordered by the faint hazy blue, scarcely to be distinguished from clouds, of the long range of hills concealing the far-off glimmer of the ocean, which otherwise might sometimes be perceptible.

Mayling is a very old place, and the Giles's had been there "always," so to speak—steady-going, unambitious, save as regards their farming and its success; they had been just the make of men to settle on to their ground as if it and they could have no existence apart. A fine race physically as well as morally, though some twenty-five years or so before the Raynalds bought Monksholdings, a run of ill luck, a whole chapter of casualties, had brought them down to but one representative, and he scarcely the typical

Farmer Giles of Mayling.

This was Barnett, the youngest of four stalwart sons; the youngest and the only survivor. He was already forty when his father died, earnestly commending to him the "old place," which even at eighty the aged farmer felt himself better fitted to manage than the somewhat delicate, sensitive man whom his brothers had made good-natured fun of in his youth as a "bookworm."

But Barnett was intelligent and sensible, and he rose to the occasion. Circumstances helped him. The year after old Giles's death Barnett for the first time fell in love, wisely and well. His affection was bestowed on a worthy object—Marion Grover, the daughter of a yeoman in the next county—and was fully returned.

Marion was years younger than her lover, fifteen at least, eminently practical, healthy, and pretty. She brought her husband just exactly what he was most in need of—brightness, energy, and youth. It was an ideal marriage, and everything prospered at Mayling. Four years after the advent of the new Mrs. Giles you would scarcely have recognised the farmer, he seemed another man.

He adored his wife, and could hardly find it in his heart to regret that their child was not a son, even though, failing an heir, the old name must die out; for if there was one creature the husband and wife loved more than each other it was their baby girl.

A month or two after this child's second birthday the singular catastrophe occurred which changed the world to poor Barnett Giles, leaving him but a wreck of his former self, physically and mentally.

Young Mrs. Giles was strong in every way, and from the first she took the line of saving her husband all extra fatigue or annoyance which she could possibly hoist on to her own brave shoulders. There was something quaint and even pathetic in the relations of the couple. For, notwithstanding Marion's being so much Barnett's junior, her attitude towards him had a decided suggestion of the maternal about it, though at times of real emergency his sound judgment and advice never failed her. It was within a week or two of Christmas; the weather was bitingly, raspingly cold. And though as yet no snow had fallen, the weather-wise were predicting it daily.

"I *must* go over to Colletwood this week," said Mrs. Giles, "and I must take Nelly. Her new coat is waiting to be tried at the dressmaker's, and I must get her some boots and several other things before Christmas. And there is a whole list of other shopping too—all our Christmas presents to see to."

Her husband was looking out of the window, it was still very early in the day.

"I doubt if the snow will hold off much longer," he said.

"And once it begins it may be heavy," his wife replied, "and then I might not be able to go for ever so long, even by the road,"—for a deep fall of snow at Scarby was practically a stoppage to all traffic. "I'll tell you what, Barnett, we'll go today and make sure of it. I will put other things aside and start before noon. A couple of hours, or three at the most, will do everything, and then Nelly and I will be back long before dark. You'll come to meet us, won't you?"

"Of course I will—if you go. But," and again he glanced at the sky. The morning was, so far, clear and bright, though very cold, but over towards the north there was a suspicious look about the blue-grey clouds. "I don't know," he said, "but that you'd better wait till tomorrow and see if it blows off again."

But Marion shook her head.

"I've a feeling," she said, "that if I don't go today, I won't go at all. And I really must. I'll take Betsy to carry the child till we're just above the town, and then send her home, so as not to be tired for coming back. Not that I'm *ever* tired, as you know," with a smile.

He gave in, only stipulating that at all costs they should start to return by a certain hour, unless the snow should have already begun, in which case Marion was to run no risks, but either to hire a fly to bring her home by the road, or to stay in the town

162

with some of her friends till the weather cleared again.

"And I'll meet you," he added. "Let us set our watches to-gether—I'll start from here so as to be at—let me see——"

"Half-way between the stiles," said Marion. "We can each see the other from one stile to the opposite one, you know, even though it's a good bit of a way. Yes, dear, I'll time it as near as I can to meet half-way between the stiles."

And with these words the last on her lips, she set off, a picture of health and happiness—little Nelly crowing back to "Dada" from over stout Betsy's shoulder.

Betsy was home again within the hour.

But the mother and child—alas and alas! It was the immortal story of "Lucy Gray" in an almost more pathetic shape.

Farmer Giles, as I have said, was a studious, often absent-minded man. There was not much to do at that season and in such weather, and what there was, some amount of supervision on his part was enough for. After his early dinner he got out his books for an hour or two's quiet reading till it should be time to set off to meet his darlings. No fear of his forgetting *that* time, but till the clock struck, and he saw it was approaching nearly, he never looked out—he was unconscious of the rapid growth of the lurid, steely clouds; he had no idea that the snowflakes were already falling, falling, more and more closely and thickly with each instant that passed.

Then rose the storm spirit and issued his orders—all too quickly obeyed. Before Barnett Giles had left the village street he found himself in what now-a-days would be called a "bliz-zard". And his pale face grew paler, and his heart beat as if to choke him, when at last he reached the first stile and stood there panting, to regain his breath. It was all he could do to battle on through the fury of the wind, the blinding, whirling snow, which seemed to envelop him as if in sheets. Not for many and many a day will that awful snowstorm be forgotten in Scarshire.

★★★★★★

It was at the appointed trysting place they found him—"half-way between the stiles." But not till late that evening, when

Betsy, more alarmed by his absence than by her mistress's not returning, at last struggled out through the deep-lying snow to alarm the nearest neighbours.

"The missis and Miss Nell will have stayed the night in the town," she said. "But I misdoubt me if the master will ever have got so far, though he may have been tempted on when he did not meet them."

By this time the fury of the storm had spent itself, and they found poor Giles after a not very protracted search, and brought him home—dead, they thought at first.

No, he was not dead, but it was less than half *life* that he returned to. For his first inquiry late the next day, when glimmering consciousness had begun to revive—"Marion, the baby?"—seemed by some subtle instinct to answer itself truthfully, in spite of the kindly endeavour to deceive him for the time.

"Dead!" he murmured. "I knew it. Half-way between the stiles," and he turned his face to the wall.

They almost wished he had died too—the rough but kind-hearted country-folk who were his neighbours. But he lived. He never asked and never knew the details of the tragedy, which, indeed, was never fully known by anyone.

All that came to light was that the dead body of Marion Giles was brought by some semi-gipsy wanderers to the workhouse of a town several miles south of Colletwood, early on the morning after the blizzard. They had found it, they said, at some little distance from the road along which they were journeying, so that she must have lost her way long before approaching the Monksholdings confines, not improbably, indeed, in attempting to retrace her steps to the town which she had so imprudently quitted. But of the child the tramps said nothing, and after making the above deposition, they were allowed to go on their way, which they expressed themselves as anxious to do; for reasons of their own, no doubt; possibly the same reasons which had prevented their returning to Colletwood with the young woman's corpse, as would have seemed more natural.

And afterwards no very special inquiry was made about the

baby. The father was incapable of it, and in those days people accepted things more carelessly, perhaps. It was taken for granted that "Little Nell" had fallen down some cliff, no doubt, and lay buried there, with the snow for her shroud, like a strayed lambkin. Her tiny bones might yet be found, years hence, maybe, by a shepherd in search of some bleating wanderer, or—no more might ever be known of the infant's fate!

Barnett Giles rose from his bed, after many weeks, with all the look of a very old man. At first it was thought that his mind was quite gone; but it did not prove to be so. After a time, with the help of an excellent foreman, or bailiff, he showed himself able to manage his farm with a strange, mechanical kind of intelligence. It seemed as if the sense of duty outlived the loss of other perceptions, though these, too, cleared by degrees to a considerable extent, and material things, curious as it may appear, prospered with him.

But he rarely spoke unless obliged to do so; and whenever he felt himself at leisure, and knew that his work was not calling for him, he seemed to relapse into the half-dreamy state which was his more real life. Then he would pass through the village and slowly climb the slope to the stile, where he would stand for hours together, patiently gazing before him, while he murmured the old refrain: "'Half-way between the stiles,' she said. I shall meet them there, 'half-way between the stiles'."

Fortunately, perhaps, it was not often he attempted to climb over; he contented himself with standing and gazing. Fortunately so, for otherwise the changes at Monksholdings would have probably terribly shocked his abnormally sensitive brain. But he did not seem to notice them, nor the new route of the old right-of-way agreed to by the compromise. He was content with his post—standing, leaning on the stile, and gazing before him.

His, of course, was the worn, wistful face which had half frightened, half appealed to Sybil Raynald.

But she forgot about it again, or other things put it temporarily aside, so that when the Raynalds came down to Monksholdings again the following Easter it did not at once occur to her to remind her father of the inquiry he had promised to make.

Miss March was not with her pupils and their parents at first. She had gone to spend a holiday week with the friends who had brought her up and seen to her education—good, benevolent people, if not specially sympathetic, but to whom she felt herself bound by ties of sincerest gratitude, though her five years with the Raynald family had given her more of the feeling of a "home" than she had ever had before.

And her arrival at Monksholdings was the occasion of much rejoicing. There was everything to show her, and everyone, from Mark down to little Robin, wanted to be her guide. It was not till the morning of the next day that Sybil managed to get her to herself for a *tête-à-tête* stroll.

Ellinor had some things to tell her quondam pupil. Mrs. Bellairs, her self-appointed guardian, was growing old and somewhat feeble.

"I fear she is not likely to live many years," said Miss March, "and she thinks so herself. She has a curious longing, which I never saw in her before, to find out my history—to know if there is no one really belonging to me to whom she can give me back, as it were, before she dies. She gave me the little parcel containing the clothes I had on when she rescued me from being sent to a workhouse. They are carefully washed and mended, and though I was a poor, dirty little object when I was found, they do not look really as if I had been a beggar child," with a little smile.

"You a beggar child!" exclaimed Sybil indignantly. "Of course not. Perhaps, on the contrary, you were somebody very grand."

"No, no," said Ellinor sensibly. "In that case I should have been advertised for and inquired after. No, I have never thought that, and I should not wish it. I should be more than thankful to know I came of good, honest people, however simple; to have some one of my very own."

"I forget the actual details," said Sybil, "though you have often told me about it. You were found—no, not literally in the workhouse, was it?"

"They were going to take me there," said Miss March. "It was at a village near Bath where Mr. and Mrs. Bellairs were then living, and one day, after a party of gipsies had been encamping on the common, a cottager's wife heard something crying in the night, and found me in her little garden. She was too poor to keep me herself, and felt certain I was a child the gipsies had stolen and then wanted to get rid of. I was fair-haired and blue-eyed, not like them. She was a friend or relation of some of Mrs. Bellairs's servants, and so the story got round to my kind old friend. And you know the rest—how they first thought of bringing me up in quite a humble way, and then finding me— well, intelligent and naturally rather refined, I suppose, I got a really good education, and my good luck did not desert me, dear, when I came to be your governess."

Sybil smiled.

"And can you remember *nothing*?"

Ellinor hesitated.

"Queer, dreamy fragments come back to me sometimes," she said. "I have a feeling of having seen hills long, long ago. It is strange," she went on, for by this time they had left the private grounds and were strolling along the hill-path in the direction of the town, "it is strange that since I came here I seem to have got hold of a tiny bit of these old memories, if they are such. It must be the hills," and she stood still and gazed round her with a deep breath of satisfaction, "I could only have been between two and three when I was found," she went on. "The only words I said were 'Dada' and 'Nennie'—it sounded like 'Nelly'. That was why Mrs. Bellairs called me 'Ellinor,' and 'March,' because it was in that month she took me to her house."

Sybil walked on in silence for a moment or two.

"It *is* such a romantic story," she said at last. "I am never tired of thinking about it."

They entered Monksholdings again from the east entrance, Ellinor glanced at the stile.

"By-the-bye," she said, "this is one of the two old stiles, I suppose. Have you ever seen your ghost again, Sybil? Have you found out anything about him?"

Sybil looked round her half nervously.

"It is the other stile he haunts," she said. "I rather avoid it, at least, I mean to do so now. It is curious you speak of it, for till yesterday I had not seen him again, and had almost forgotten about it. But yesterday afternoon, just before you came, there he was—exactly the same, staring in. I meant to speak to papa about it, but with the pleasure and bustle of your arrival, I forgot it. Remind me about it. I am afraid he is out of his mind."

"Poor old man!" said Ellinor. "I wish we could do something to comfort him. I feel as if everybody *must* be happy here. It is such a charming, exhilarating place. Dear me, how windy it is! The path is all strewn with the white petals of the cherry blossom."

"They have degenerated into wild cherry trees," said Sybil. "Long ago papa says these must have been good fruit trees of many kinds, and this is a great cherry country, you know."

The wind dropped that afternoon, but only temporarily. It rose again so much during the night that by the next morning the grounds looked, to use little Annis's expression, "quite untidy".

"And down in the village, or just beyond it," said Mark, who had been for an early stroll, "at one place it really looks as if it had been snowing. The road skirts that old farmhouse; you know it, father? I forget the name—there's a grand cherry orchard there."

"'Mayling Farm,' you must mean," said Mr. Raynald. "Farmer Giles's. Oh, by the way, that reminds me, Sybil," but a glance round the table made him stop short. They were at breakfast. He scarcely felt inclined to relate the tragic story before the younger children, "they might look frightened or run away if they came across the poor fellow," he reflected. "I will tell Sybil about it afterwards."

Easter holidays were not yet over, though the governess had returned, so regular routine was set aside, and the whole of the young party, Ellinor included, spent that morning in a scramble among the hills.

The children seemed untirable, and set off again somewhere or other in the afternoon. Sybil was busy with her mother, writing letters and orders to be despatched to London, so that towards four o'clock or so, when Miss March, having finished her own correspondence, entered the drawing-room, she found it deserted.

Sybil had promised to practise some duets with her, and while waiting on the chance of her coming, Ellinor seated herself at the piano and began to play—nothing very important—just snatches of old airs which she wove into a kind of half-dreamy harmony, one melting into another as they occurred to her.

All at once a shadow fell on the keys, and then she remembered having heard the door softly open a moment or two before—so softly, that she had not looked round, imagining it to be the wind, which, though fallen now, still lingered about.

Now her ideas took another shape.

"It is Sybil, no doubt," she thought with a smile. "She is going to make me jump," and she waited, half expecting to feel Sybil's hands suddenly clasped over her eyes from behind.

But this was not to be the mode of attack, apparently, though she heard what sounded like stealthy footsteps.

"You need not try to startle me, Sybbie," she exclaimed laughingly, without turning or ceasing to play, "I hear you."

It was no laughing voice which replied.

On the contrary, a sigh, almost a groan, close to her made her look up sharply—a trifle indignant perhaps at the joke being carried so far—and she saw, a pace or two from her only, the figure of an old man—a white-haired, somewhat bent form, a worn face with wistful blue eyes—gazing at her.

She had scarcely time to feel frightened, for almost instantaneously Sybil's "ghost" recurred to her memory.

"He has found his way in, then," she thought, not without a slight and natural tremor, which, however, disappeared as she gazed, so pathetically gentle was the whole aspect of the intruder.

But—his face changed curiously—the sight of hers, now fully in his view, seemed strangely to affect him. With a gesture of utter bewilderment he raised his hand to his forehead as if to brush something away—the cloud still resting on his brain—then a smile broke over the old face, a wonderful smile.

"Marion," he said, "at last? I—I thought I was dreaming. I heard you playing in my dream. It is the right place though, 'Half-way between the stiles,' you said. I have waited so long and come so often, and now it is snowing again. Just a little, dear, nothing to hurt. Marion, my darling, why don't you speak? Is it all a dream—this fine room, the music and all? Are *you* a dream?"

He closed his eyes as if he were fainting. Inexpressibly touched, all Ellinor's womanly nature went out to him. She started forward, half leading, half lifting him to a seat close at hand.

"I—I am not Marion," she said, and afterwards she wondered what had inspired the words, "but I am"—not "Ellinor," something made her change the name as he spoke—"I am Nelly."

He opened his eyes again.

"Little Nell," he said, "has she sent you down to me from heaven? My little Nell!"

And then he fell back unconscious—this time he had fainted.

She thought he was dead, but it was not so—her cries for help soon brought her friends, Mr. Raynald first of all. He did not seem startled, he soothed Ellinor at once.

"It is poor old Giles," he said. "I know all about him, he has found his way in at last."

"But—but——," stammered the girl, "there is something else, Mr. Raynald. I—I seem to remember something."

She looked nearly as white as their poor visitor, and as Mr. Raynald glanced at her, a curious expression flitted across his own face.

Could it be so? He knew all her story.

"Wait a little, my dear," he said. "We must attend to poor Giles first."

They were very kind and tender to the old man, but he seemed to be barely conscious, even after restoratives had brought him out of the actual fainting fit. Then Mrs. Raynald proposed that his servants—his housekeeper if he had one—should be sent for.

And when faithful Betsy, stout as of old, though less nimble, made her appearance, her irrepressible emotion at the sight of Ellinor, pale and trembling though the young governess was, gave form and substance to Mr. Raynald's suspicions.

Yes, they had met at last—father and daughter—"half-way between the stiles". He was "Dada," she was little "Nell." Might it not be that Marion's prayers had brought them together?

Every reasonable proof was forthcoming—the little parcel of clothes, the correspondence in the dates, the strong resemblance to her mother.

And—joy does not often kill. Barnett was able to understand it all better than might have been expected. He was never *quite* himself, but infinitely better both in mind and body than poor old Betsy had ever dreamt of seeing him. And he was perfectly content—content to live as long as it should please God to spare him to his little Nell; ready to go to his Marion when the time should come.

And Ellinor had her wish—a home, though not a "grand" one; some one of her "very own" to care for; a father's devoted love, and, to complete her happiness, the friends who had grown so dear to her close at hand.

More may yet be hers in the future, for she is still young. Her father may live to see his grandchildren playing about the farmstead at Mayling, so that, though the name be changed, the old stock will still nourish where so many generations of its ancestors have sown and reaped.

# The Clock that Struck Thirteen

(A story from *Uncanny Tales*)

"You misunderstand me wilfully, Helen. I neither said nor inferred anything of the kind."

"What did you mean then, for if words to you bear a different interpretation from what they do to me, I must trouble you to speak in *my* language when addressing me," angrily retorted a young girl, with what nature had intended to be a very pretty face with a charming expression, but which at the present moment was far from deserving the latter part of the description. Eyes flashing, cheeks burning and hands clenched in the excess of her indignation, stood Helen Beaumont by the window of her pretty little sitting-room, or "studio" as she loved to call it, presenting a striking contrast to the peaceful scene without; where a carefully tended garden still looked bright with the remaining flowers of late September.

Her companion, standing in the attitude invariably assumed now-a-days by novelists' heroes, namely, leaning against the mantelpiece, was a young man of equally prepossessing appearance with her own. At first glance no one would have suspected him of sharing any of the young lady's excitement, for his expression was so calm as almost to merit the description of sleepy. Looking more closely, however, the signs of some unusual disturbance or annoyance were to be descried, for his face was slightly flushed and his blue eyes had lost the look of sweet temper evidently their ordinary expression.

"What I meant to say, Helen, was not, as you choose to misinterpret it, that I blame you for proper womanly courage and spirit, than which, I consider few things more admirable, nor as you are well aware do I admire the sweetly silly and affectedly timid order of young ladies. But this I do mean and repeat, that I think your persistence in this foolish scheme a piece of sheer bravado and foolhardiness, totally unworthy of any sensible person's approval, and what is more——"

"Thank you, Malcolm, or rather Mr. Willoughby, I have heard quite enough,"—and as she spoke, Helen turned from the window out of which she had been gazing while Malcolm spoke, with, it must be confessed, very little interest in the varied tints of the dahlias blooming in all their rich brilliance on the terrace,—"I have heard quite enough, and think myself exceedingly fortunate in having heard it now before it is too late. You may imagine," she continued, "that I am speaking in temper, but it is not so. I have for some time suspected, and now feel convinced, that we are not suited to each other. Your own words bear witness to your opinion of me, 'self-willed, foolhardy, unwomanly,' and I know not what other pretty expressions you have applied to me, and for my part I tell you simply that I cannot and will not marry a man whose opinion of what a woman should be is like yours; and who insults me constantly as you do, by telling me how far short I fall of his ideal. Marry your ideal, Malcolm Willoughby, and I shall wish you joy of her. Some silly little fool who dares not move a step alone in her bewitching helplessness. But do not think to convert *me* into such a piece of contemptible inanity," and so saying she turned towards the door.

"Helen," said Malcolm quietly, so quietly that Helen was arrested in spite of herself, "you are unjust, unreasonable and ungenerous. You know that I never cared for any woman but you, you know that nothing pleases me more than to witness your superiority in numberless particulars to the general run of girls, and you know too the pride and pleasure I take in your skill as an artist; but blinded by self-will you will not see the perfect reasonableness of my request that you will abandon this absurd expedition. If not for your own sake, at least do so for Edith's, who is as you know left in your special charge by Leonard."

The first part of this speech seemed, to judge by Helen's transparent countenance, likely to soften and move her, but the unlucky word "absurd" and the tone in which Malcolm spoke, as if it was necessary to remind her of her duty, effectually did away with any good result that his remonstrance might have worked. She turned, with her hand on the door, and saying, "I have told you my decision, Mr. Willoughby, and I wish you good-evening," left the room. Malcolm remained behind, lost in thought of no pleasurable nature. At last he too left the little sitting-room, after first ringing the bell and ordering his horse to be brought round. Making his way to the front entrance he there "mounted and rode away," his spirits, poor fellow, by no means the better for his visit.

It is time, I think, to explain the cause of the lovers' quarrel above described. Helen and Edith Beaumont were orphans, left to the guardianship of their brother Leonard, in whose house we have seen the former. Delicacy, induced by a severe illness some months previously, had obliged Mr. Beaumont, accompanied by his wife, to go for the autumn and winter months to the south of France, leaving his sisters at home under the nominal chaperonage of an elderly aunt, who performed her duty to the perfect satisfaction of her nieces by letting them do exactly as they liked.

More correctly speaking, perhaps, exactly as Helen liked, for the younger of the two, Edith, a girl of seventeen and four years her sister's junior, could hardly be said to have likes or dislikes distinct from those of Helen. Possibly Mr. Beaumont might not have left the two to their own devices with so easy a mind, had he not quitted home happy in the knowledge of Helen's engagement to his friend and neighbour Malcolm Willoughby. The gentleman in question lived within a few miles of our heroine's home, having succeeded some years before to his father's property. His only sister, Mrs. Lindsay, was at this time living with him for a few months while awaiting her husband's return from India, and though some years older, was, next to her sister, Helen's most valued friend and companion.

Malcolm Willoughby was a man of high character, peculiarly fitted, by his unusual amount of sterling good sense, to be the guide of an impulsive, enthusiastic girl like pretty Helen Beaumont, whom to know was to love, and who would have been altogether charming but for her inordinate amount of self-will and inveterate dislike to being, as she expressed it, "ordered" to do or not to do whatever came into her head. She and her sister had real talent as artists, and their spirited and well-executed landscapes bore but little resemblance to the insipid productions of most young lady painters. To improving herself in this direction Helen had devoted much time and labour. Unfortunately, it had so absorbed her thoughts and desires that in its pursuance she was inclined sometimes to forget what were for her more important avocations.

Helen's fortunate engagement to Mr. Willoughby had for some time past corrected these only objectionable tendencies in her character, and all had gone smoothly and happily till the date at which our story commences, when, unluckily, some artist friends had filled her head with their descriptions of the exquisite autumn scenery, "effects of foliage," etc., to be seen in a mountainous and hitherto little explored part of Wales. Her imagination, and through her that of her sister Edith, ran wild on the subject, and now nothing would satisfy her but a journey to the spot in question, by themselves, in order that they might enjoy their freedom to the utmost, and revel in the delight of painting some of the wonderful Welsh scenery described to them. The idea had at first been mooted half in joke, but an impolitic expression of strong disapprobation on the part of Mr. Willoughby had done more to determine Helen on carrying it out than all the anticipated artistic enjoyment.

"It will be just the opportunity I wanted," thought the foolish girl, "of showing him that I do not intend to be a silly nonentity of a wife with no opinion of my own, and hedged in by all the absurd old-fashioned conventionalities which will not allow a woman to have an existence of her own or give her opportunity to cultivate what talents she may possess."

And once determined, Miss Helen remained inflexible. In vain Mr. Willoughby remonstrated, in vain even their indulgent old aunt expressed her horror at the idea of "two young girls scouring the country by themselves," her own feebleness rendering her accompanying them out of the question. Go to Wales Helen and Edith must, and go they would, till at last the discussion with her *fiancé* terminated in the disastrous manner above recorded.

I will not undertake to describe Helen's feelings, when, in the solitude of her own room, she thought over what she had done. Had she herself been obliged to put them into words, I believe she would have repeated that she had not acted in temper and that the stand she had made for her womanly freedom, as she would have expressed it, had been an act of supreme heroism and devotion to the cause of right. She said all this to herself and tried hard, very hard to believe it; and to stifle the little voice at the very bottom of her heart which whispered that she had behaved like a silly, self-willed, petted child, and shown herself undeserving of so good a gift as the love of a man like Malcolm Willoughby. The little voice was smothered for the time by exaggerated anticipations of the delights of their tour and attempted self-congratulations at her newly regained liberty to do as she chose; for Malcolm did not come near her again, and it took all her pride to hide from herself and others the shock she felt through all her being when, in the course of a few days, she heard accidentally that Mr. Willoughby was leaving home for an uncertain length of time.

"He has taken me at my word," thought she, "but of course I meant him to do so," and she hurried on the preparations for their journey which they were now on the eve of.

"You will at least take Maxwell," said Aunt Fanny timidly.

"Maxwell, aunt! No, thank you," said Helen ironically; "she would be crying for her spring mattress the first night and thinking she was going to die if she heard the wind howl. No, thank you, I mean to be independent for once in my life, and so does Edith."

Other twenty-four hours saw our two young ladies on their way. Unaccustomed as they were to travelling alone they got on very well for the greater part of their journey, till they arrived at a certain railway station in Wales, of name unpronounceable by civilised tongue, but which sounded to them like that of the place where they were to leave the railway. Never doubting but what they were right in so doing Helen and Edith calmly descended from their carriage, watched the train disappear in the tunnel hard by, and then began to make inquiries for a conveyance to transport themselves and their luggage, white umbrellas, easels and all, the five or six miles which they imagined were all that divided them from their destination.

A colloquy ensued with the most intelligible of two or three fly-drivers, carmen, or whatever these personages are called in Wales; but what was Helen's consternation on learning that fifteen miles at least remained to be traversed; they having left the railway at Llanfar, two stations too soon, instead of remaining in it till they reached Llanfair, the point nearest to the farmhouse where lodgings had been taken for them. No chance of a train to Llanfair till tomorrow morning, for the line was a new one, and the traffic as yet but small. No prospect of a night's accommodation where they were. Nothing for it but to trust to the driver's assurance that he and his unpromising-looking horse could easily convey them to the farmhouse, with the inevitably unpronounceable name. With some unconfessed misgivings Helen and Edith mounted the vehicle awaiting them, and drove off along a muddy, jolting lane into the quickly gathering gloom.

Shivering on her uncomfortable seat, did Helen wish herself at home again in her own little sitting-room, with Aunt Fanny peacefully knitting, Edith kneeling on the hearth-rug, and Malcolm's face bright with the reflection of the ruddy log fire so welcome in autumn evenings; all together as was their wont, enjoying "blind man's holiday"?

177

I think we had better not press the question too closely. However, "it's a long lane that has no ending," and even this dreary journey gradually drew to a close. They passed but few houses of any kind, one or two straggling hamlets were left behind, and for some two or three miles the road had been perfectly solitary, when they suddenly heard wheels advancing to meet them, and in a few minutes a car like their own drove towards them, and being hailed by their driver, drew up at their side. A jabbering ensued of directions asked and given, and they again drove on.

"Are you sure you know the way?" said Helen timidly.

"Oh yes, miss," the driver answered confidently, and further informed them that the car they had met, had just returned from their own destination (being translated), the Black Nest Farm, having there deposited a traveller who had taken the middle course of leaving the railway at the intermediate stoppage between Llanfar and Llanfair. Other three-quarters of an hour and they pulled up at last before a house which the darkness prevented their seeing more of than that it was long and low.

They stumbled up the rough garden path, and in answer to their knock, the door was opened by a tidy, clean-looking old woman, with a flickering candle in her hand, evidently surprised at their appearance. She had, she said, quite given up thoughts of their coming that night, and feared the fire in the sitting-room was out. Thankful to have reached the Black Nest at last, a chilly room seemed a smaller evil than the two girls would have considered it at home; and after all, things were not so bad, for the fire in the little farmhouse parlour, to which their landlady conducted them, was not quite out, and a little judicious coaxing soon brought it round.

Their hostess's and their own first idea was of course *tea*. What a blessing, by the way, it is that British womankind in general, high and low, rich and poor, old and young, have this *one* taste in common! Refreshed by the homely meal speedily set before them, Helen and Edith proceeded, under the guidance of the old woman (apparently the only inhabitant of the house), and the flickering candle, to inspect their sleeping apartment.

The result was not eminently satisfactory, for it struck them as gloomy, ill-ventilated, and a long way from their parlour, though but few rooms appeared to intervene between the two. This puzzled them at the time, but was afterwards explained by the fact that Black Nest Farmhouse had originally consisted of two one-storeyed cottages standing at some yards distance from each other, and which, on becoming the property of one owner, had been united by a long passage; which arrangement was looked upon in the neighbourhood as a triumph of architectural ingenuity.

On returning to their sitting-room Helen's eye fell on a door beside their own which she had not before noticed, and she inquired if that was a bedroom. To which the old woman replied in the affirmative, but added that they could not have it, as it and a small sitting-room opening out of it were engaged by a "strange gentleman." And besides this, she added, the bedroom was not so desirable for ladies, having a second, or rather third door to the outside of the house. The only other room they could have was so small that she did not think they would like it, but they should see for themselves, and so saying she turned towards a recess in the passage. Helen followed her, but the flickering candle suddenly throwing light in a new direction, she gave a little exclamation of alarm at what appeared at the first moment to be a very ugly grinning portrait high up on the wall.

"It's only the clock, miss," said the old woman. "Though, to be sure, it is quare," and as she spoke she threw the light more fully upon the object that had startled Helen, which she now perceived to be a very antique clock, standing high in a dark wooden case, and with the face she had seen, peeping at you as it were from behind the dial-plate. An ugly, coarsely painted face, with a disagreeably mocking expression it seemed to Helen; nor was it the only repulsive feature in this very remarkable clock, for the artist appeared to have outdone himself in the grotesquely hideous devices at the bottom of the dial.

Death's heads, cross-bones, and other equally unpleasant objects of various kinds, curiously intermingled with a condensed solar system, in which sun, moon and stars appeared jumbled together haphazard. The general object of the whole evidently being to bring before the spectator the ghastly side of his future, and to read him a wholesome, but certainly not attractive, homily on the shortness of life, and the speed with which time was ticking away. Helen felt half fascinated by its hideousness.

"Dear me, what a very curious clock!" she ejaculated, and the old woman repeated, with a little inward chuckle at what she evidently considered the admiration drawn forth by her heirloom:—

"Yes, sure it *is* quare."

An uncanny object it certainly was, and Helen felt relieved that the room in its immediate vicinity was so small as to be out of the question for the accommodation of her sister and herself. Re-entering the sitting-room she found poor Edith looking so utterly worn-out that she proposed that they should at once go to bed; which they accordingly did, followed by the old woman with offers of assistance. Passing the door of "the strange gentleman's" room, they heard sounds of someone moving inside, and Edith sleepily remarked that she wondered what could have brought a gentleman to an outlandish place like the Black Nest, unless, like themselves, he came to take views in the neighbourhood. Helen pricked up her ears at this and inquired of Mrs. Jones if their fellow-lodger was an artist.

Mrs. Jones thought not, but seemed unwilling to pursue the topic of the strange gentleman further. In rather a forced manner she changed the subject by inquiring if the young ladies would like to hire her pony while there, as it was rough walking, and her grandson Griffith, the only other inhabitant of the cottage, a little lad of twelve, could lead it for them, and show them the way whenever they chose. Helen gladly closed with the offer.

"Dear me, Mrs. Jones," she exclaimed "how very lonely you must be living here with no one but a little boy. Have you no near neighbours?"

"None nearer than three miles ma'am, for the farm-men live at a distance, save old Thomas in the last cottage you passed, but he is bed-ridden. My widow daughter, Griffith's mother, was with me till she took ill, two winters ago, and died before the doctor could get to her. Yes, it is lonesome like in winter to be sure. It's not often that gentry like you, miss, care to be in these parts so late in the year."

Further inquiries elicited that the nearest church was a good five miles off, that there was no doctor nearer than Llanfar, that the butcher only came in the winter once a fortnight and that irregularly; in consequence of which the Black Nesters had often to depend upon their own scanty resources, the roads being almost impassable in stormy weather.

"Don't you think it feels rather dreary, Helen?" said Edith, as she was falling asleep.

"*Eerie*, rather, I should say," replied her sister, "but that, you know, is the beauty of it. In the morning, I daresay, it will look bright enough, but I confess I do not like that clock. Listen, can't you hear its ticking, faintly, even here, at the end of that long passage?"

"What clock do you mean? I saw no clock," said Edith, but almost before Helen could answer, her soft regular breathing told that she was asleep. Helen however, could not so quickly compose herself. She felt excited and vaguely uneasy; and when she at last fell asleep, it was only to have her discomfort increased, by absurd, yet alarming dreams. With them all the ugly clock was grotesquely intermingled. Sometimes it was herself, sometimes Edith, and once Malcolm, whom she fancied in some position of terrible peril, always associated with the clock, and at last she awoke with a half-smothered scream of horror at the most frightful dream of all; in which the "strange gentleman," their fellow-lodger, was pursuing her with a veil over his face, which just as he caught her fell off, and disclosed, horrible to relate, the face on the clock.

Edith started up as Helen convulsively clutched her, and exclaiming, "What in the world is the matter?" really thought Helen was going out of her mind when she replied, "That horrible clock;" and as she spoke, as if invoked, the clock began to strike: "One, two, three, four," and so on. "Is it never going to stop?" said Helen. Poor Edith, half asleep still, listened with her.

"Edith, I am almost certain that clock struck *thirteen*," said Helen in an awestruck voice; and then they heard a door shut at the end of the passage.

"Helen, you have been dreaming, and you are only half awake now," said Edith. "It is not like you to waken me in this frightening way, please let me go to sleep."

"I am very sorry," said Helen penitently, and she too closed her eyes and tried hard to go to sleep, which of course she did, as soon as she left off trying, and had made up her mind to lie awake till daylight.

The morning broke clear and fresh; and, as Helen had said, things in general bore a very different aspect to that of the night before. Indoors, the quaint old house now looked simply picturesque, and Mrs. Jones the *beau idéal* of a cheery old hostess. Even the face of the clock, when Helen pointed it out to Edith, seemed to have lost its mocking grin, and to be merely bidding them good-morning, with a comical smile at the consternation it had awakened the night before.

Out-of-doors they soon turned their steps. There was no view from the house, but a short voyage of discovery quickly explained to them their locality. Black Nest Farm stood at the foot of a hill close on to the high road, or what passed for such in that hitherto little frequented neighbourhood. On the opposite side of the road but little was to be seen, as the meadows were soon lost in a thick belt of wood; but immediately behind the house was a tempting prospect, for there a little winding path led up the hill to one of the spots Helen and Edith most ardently desired to paint, and of which their friends had given them a glowing description.

It was rather a long walk to the Black Lake, Mrs. Jones informed them, but their enthusiasm knew no bounds, and hardly permitted them to do justice to their breakfast of ham and eggs, home-made bread and home-churned butter. See them then starting on their expedition,—their painting materials, and some creature comforts in the shape of sandwiches and hard-boiled eggs, safely packed on the pony's back, Griffith leading him and acting as guide. A pretty stiff pull it was, enthusiasm notwithstanding, and rather hard work for the little feet, sensibly shod in good strong boots it is true, but unaccustomed nevertheless to mountain scrambling. But at last their circuitous path brought them to the summit, and there a curious prospect broke upon them.

They stood at the edge of the great Welsh tableland. There it stretched away before them, miles and miles beyond their view; a vast expanse of wild, brown moor, unrelieved by tree or shrub, but here and there dotted by great patches of what Edith at first sight took to be "lovely emerald moss." Treacherous loveliness, for it told, as they learnt from Griffith, of fearful bog-pits, down whose slimy sides once slipped no man or beast could ever regain firm ground.

"What a horrible death that would be," said Helen, shuddering, "far worse than regular drowning in clean water. It would be slow suffocation in nasty, dirty mud."

A few minutes' careful walking brought them in sight of the Black Lake, the special object of their excursion. And it certainly was well worth coming to see, if not to paint; probably too, better seen in the greyness of a late autumn day than in the summer sun, whose bright rays reflected on its surface would have little harmonised with its character of gloom and loneliness. The lake was equal to several acres in extent, but from where they stood could not all be seen, as its farther end was hidden by the undulations of the land. In colour it was a dull, leaden grey, and looking at it, one's mind spontaneously reverted to travellers' descriptions of the Dead Sea, for *dead* was essentially the word by which to describe it.

There were no fish to be caught in it Griffith told them, and as for its depth he had never heard tell of any one's sounding it. The effect of the whole scene was very peculiar, and so Helen and Edith felt it to be, as they stood gazing at the leaden water and the great, apparently boundless moorland. It was difficult to realise that they were so far above the ordinary haunts of men, for there was nothing in that great plain to remind them of the existence even of hills and mountains, except a steady-blowing breeze of that peculiar freshness pertaining only to sea or mountain air. Pleasantly invigorating at first, but soon becoming too chilly to make one care to stand about, or, worse still, to *sit*, as our young ladies now prepared to do.

"We are very lucky in the weather," remarked Helen, as they prepared for their sketching. "I should fancy it is just the day to see the lake to the best advantage."

"Or disadvantage," said Edith, "for I do think it is the most horrible place I ever saw. I don't know," added she dreamily, "but what it would seem even more desolate on a bright, sunny day. I don't know why."

"I understand how you mean," replied her sister, "the contrast would be so strange. Like a skeleton dressed in a golden robe. Dear me, I am becoming quite poetical. But look, Edith, how do you like this?" And a consultation on their work ensued.

Very cold work it became, as it grew to afternoon, notwithstanding the pleasurable excitement of their occupation, and Edith, for one, was not sorry when Helen at last thought it time to pack up their painting materials and turn homewards. A drizzling rain began to fall as they neared the foot of the hill, and they both felt thankful to reach the farmhouse,—tired, muddy and damp, and in not *quite* such high spirits as when they set off on their expedition. A savoury odour meeting them on their entrance, Helen suddenly bethought herself that she had utterly forgotten to order anything for their "high tea," or whatever one likes to call the said incongruous meal.

It was therefore an agreeable surprise to her after remembering her neglect to see on entering their little sitting-room the brightest of fires, and the table daintily set out with evident preparation for a tempting repast; part of which, in the shape of a delicious-looking ham, "a new-made pat of butter and a wheaten loaf so fine," had already made its appearance. Damp clothes and muddy boots discarded, they sat down with an excellent appetite to their meal, and the savoury odour which had greeted them was soon explained by the appearance of Mrs. Jones bearing a chicken stewed in mushrooms.

"Mushrooms!" exclaimed Helen, "the thing of all others I like. How clever you are, Mrs. Jones, to get us all these good things! I shall leave our food to your providing, I think, in future."

Mrs. Jones laughed and said a friend had sent some things from Llanfar, and a friend also had gathered the mushrooms, the last of their season, thinking the young ladies might like them.

"Your friends are as good as yourself then, Mrs. Jones," said Helen; but as she spoke she was startled by what sounded like a half-smothered laugh or exclamation of some kind just outside the door. Almost at the same moment her friend the clock began to strike, and she therefore fancied the sound she had heard must have come from it. "Its internal arrangements are, I daresay, as peculiar as its outside," thought she to herself, and refrained therefore from mentioning to Edith what she thought she had heard. All the rest of the evening, however, though she would hardly have owned it to herself, she felt a little nervous and uneasy, particularly when she heard the clock strike.

"I wonder what our fellow-lodger does with himself all day," said Edith that evening.

"I am sure I don't know, or care either," said Helen, "indeed, I hardly believe there is such a being at all."

They went early to bed, and fell quickly asleep. After having slept, it seemed to her for several hours, Helen woke suddenly with the feeling that something had wakened her, and found that the clock was busy striking, and to her confused fancy had been striking for ever so long before she woke. Its strokes ceased before she was sufficiently awake to count them, but a moment or two afterwards she heard a door shut as it had done the night before.

"It is very annoying that I can't get a good night's rest here," thought she. A whispered "Helen," told her that Edith too was awake.

"The clock *did* strike thirteen," said Edith, "and there *must* be somebody in that room, for I heard the door shut again."

"And so did I," said Helen, whereupon they lay still in awe-struck silence, till they both fell fast asleep again.

The next day was Saturday, and though somewhat stiff and tired with their exertions, Friday's programme was repeated. The sketches proceeded satisfactorily, but our heroines were less fortunate in other respects, for just as they were about to leave the Black Lake in the afternoon, the rain came on in torrents. Long before they got back to the farmhouse the poor girls were thoroughly drenched. Edith escaped with no ill results, but Helen sat shivering over the fire all the evening, passed an uneasy night in which it seemed to her that the clock never left off striking at all, and woke on Sunday morning with every symptom of a delightfully bad cold.

The prospect outside was not cheering. Rain, rain, rain. Down it came in torrents. No chance of making their way to the five miles' off church, no chance even of a quiet stroll along the lanes; and, worst of all, no books to read, for such a possibility as a whole day in the house had never presented itself to their inexperienced imaginations! It was very dull. Helen was almost cross with Edith for being so exceedingly sympathetic. It was kind of course, but provoking nevertheless, as to Helen's sensitiveness it seemed to convey a tacit reproach. She would not allow to herself that they were at all to be pitied. All the same she was not sorry when the time came at last for them to go to bed.

"I wish we had brought some sherry with us," said Edith. "A little white wine whey would have been the very thing for your cold."

"What's the good of wishing," replied her sister rather snappishly, "you had better call Mrs. Jones and ask her to make me some gruel." But on Mrs. Jones's appearance, and when the request had been made, both the girls felt rather surprised at her volunteering the very thing they had been wishing for.

She had, she said, "some very nice sherry wine, given her by a friend," and many years ago, when she was in service in

Chester, she had learnt to make white wine whey. Sure enough a tempting-looking basinful shortly after made its appearance.

Thanks to its soporific influence Helen soon fell asleep, but woke (as she had got strangely into the habit of doing) just at midnight, or as Edith had taken to calling it, "thirteen o'clock." The clock was half-way through its striking when she woke, and a sudden impulse seized her to jump up, and, opening the door slightly, to peep out and either see who it was that always shut a door after the clock struck, or, by seeing nothing, satisfy herself that the sound had all along been merely the creation of her own and Edith's imagination.

She opened the door very cautiously, and instantly perceived that there was a light at the end of the passage in the recess where stood the clock. Helen's heart beat more loudly, and she wished devoutly that she had allowed her curiosity to remain unsatisfied, when to her horror the light moved out of the recess, and she saw that it was held by a tall dark figure with its back turned towards her. The passage was so long and the light flickered so much that it was impossible for her to distinguish anything but the general outline of the person who held it.

Not Mrs. Jones or Griffith, assuredly, but poor Helen was too frightened to do more than lock the door with her trembling fingers and leap back into bed, thereby awakening Edith, who on hearing Helen's story calmly assured her that she had either been dreaming, or had seen the strange gentleman their fellow-lodger whose existence Helen had rashly dared to question. Oddly enough she had forgotten all about him, and felt somewhat relieved by Edith's matter-of-fact solution.

"Only what should he be doing at the clock at this time of night? I hope he is not out of his mind;"—to which Edith replied:—

"I do believe he gets up to make it strike thirteen on purpose to tease us."

Monday morning wore a more promising aspect than Sunday, for such clouds as there were, bespoke nothing worse than showers, and our young ladies succeeded in obtaining an hour or two's sketching at the lake. Helen, however, felt still considerably the worse of her terrible wetting, and was actually the first to propose that they should return to the farmhouse. Somewhat weakened by her cold, and tired too, she mounted the little pony at Edith's suggestion, and they were proceeding cheerily enough on their way—Griffith, loaded with their painting materials, some little distance behind—when a stumble on the pony's part brought him suddenly to the ground. Helen had been paying little attention to her steed, and, unprepared for the shock, fell on her side with some little force.

A most undignified procedure had there been any one to witness it, but which would have drawn forth nothing but a laugh had it not been that in the fall her foot caught in the stirrup. Her sharp cry of pain terrified Edith, who, however, soon succeeded in disentangling her, as the poor little pony remained perfectly quiet, but a moment's examination, and a vain attempt to stand, showed them that the ankle was badly sprained. All that could be done was to mount Helen again as well as Edith and Griffith could manage, and to make the best of their way home. Arrived there, hot applications soon reduced the pain, but it was easy to be seen, even by their inexperienced eyes, that Helen must not attempt to move for several days to come.

Here was a charming ending to their expedition! Helen, even, felt woefully disconcerted, and poor Edith fairly began to cry.

"If it were not that you would not like it, I would write to Mrs. Lindsay to come and nurse you," said Edith, "she is so good and kind, and I know she would come in a minute, for she has nothing to prevent her."

"Mrs. Lindsay! Edith," exclaimed Helen indignantly, "the very last person I would apply to, however good and kind she may be. Do you really think that. I would put myself under such an obligation to the sister of the man I have——"

"Quarrelled with for nothing at all," said the little voice at the bottom of her heart. Edith said nothing, but for the first time in her life took an independent resolution and acted upon it. Her love for Helen conquered her fear of displeasing her. What this resolution was we shall not disclose, nor shall we tell whose hand addressed a letter to Mrs. Lindsay carried that evening by the post-boy to Llanfar. The strangest coincidence was that *two* letters bearing the same direction left the Black Nest Farm that evening.

Tired out with the pain of her ankle, Helen, for the first time since their arrival, slept past midnight and only woke to hear the clock strike five. All too soon for her comfort, for her thoughts were none of the brightest, as she lay waiting for the daylight. Her folly, her headstrong determination, right or wrong, to carry out her own way, began to show themselves to her more clearly; or rather, she began to allow herself to see them in their true light. And when at last the morning came, and she was established for the day on the hard little horse-hair sofa in their sitting-room, her spirits were not improved by the perusal of a letter from her Aunt Fanny.

The good old lady, after deploring their absence and pathetically describing her anxiety on their behalf, made mention of a visit from Mrs. Lindsay, who had come to tell her how unhappy she was about her brother. "He left home," wrote Aunt Fanny, "two days after that unfortunate conversation with you without telling his sister what was the matter. At least she only gathered that something unpleasant had happened from his saying that you were leaving home, and that he did not expect to see you before you went. He left no direction beyond telling her to write to his club, which she has done two or three times, but got no answer. She says he looked so unlike himself that she fears he has fallen ill somewhere and cannot write to tell her. Oh, Helen, I do wish you had never thought of this expedition."

"How very silly Mrs. Lindsay is to be so fanciful," said Helen, in which view of the case tender-hearted little Edith did not at all agree, though she hardly dared to say so. They spent a dull day, for Edith would not consent to leave her sister, and their paintings were at a standstill for want of another day's sketching from the original.

"Tomorrow, Edith," said Helen, "you might go to the lake for an hour or so without me and finish your sketch, and I might go on with mine from yours," to which Edith made no objection.

By night Helen's feverish uneasiness had increased, and Edith secretly congratulated herself on her resolute step of the day before. And a wretched night followed. In reality Helen was very anxious and unhappy about Malcolm Willoughby, and her dreams were full of terrors that something had befallen him. Through all, the disagreeable clock again thrust forward its ugly face, and she woke in an indescribable state of horror, fancying that the clock was standing by her bedside, striking loudly in her ears to a kind of "refrain" of the words: "I told you so. I told you so." Of course the clock *was* striking, and had evidently awakened her by so doing.

"Thirteen again," whispered Edith, "it is really very disagreeable."

"It sounds to *me* like the voice of my conscience," said Helen, "warning me that some terrible punishment is coming upon me for my wicked folly. Yes, Edith, I see it all now, and as soon as ever I can move we shall go home, and I shall ask poor Aunt Fanny to forgive me. I wish every other consequence of my wrong-doing could be done away with as easily as her displeasure." And all her pride broken down, poor Helen burst into tears, and Edith's affectionate words of soothing were of no avail to stop her sobs. She felt rather better in the morning however, partly, perhaps, because the day was bright and sunny. About mid-day she fell into a doze on her sofa, and waking after an hour's sleep was surprised to miss Edith. A note in pencil pinned to the table-cover caught her attention. It bore these words:

You are so nicely asleep I don't like to waken you. I shall come back as early as I can, but don't be alarmed if I am a little later than you expect.

"She has gone to finish the sketch," thought Helen uneasily. "I wish I had not asked her to do so, it looks dull and overcast."

She rang the hand-bell for Mrs. Jones, who appeared with a basin of soup, and told her that the young lady had set off a quarter of an hour before.

"It can't be helped now," said Helen, "but I wish I had not proposed it."

The afternoon seemed long and dull, and yet Helen felt sorry when it began to close in, for no Edith had yet appeared. Still it was not later than they had been out together more than once. Helen tried to think it was not yet dusk outside, but felt this comfort fail her when it gradually grew so indisputably dark that Mrs. Jones brought in candles without her asking for them.

"Are you not uneasy about my sister and Griffith, Mrs. Jones?" said Helen; but her anxiety was tenfold increased when Mrs. Jones replied calmly:—

"Griffith is not with the young lady today. I had to send him a message to Llanfair, and as like as not he will stay at his uncle's till the morning. The young lady said it did not matter, and I saddled the pony for her myself."

"Griffith not with her!" exclaimed Helen. "Oh, Mrs. Jones, what will become of her?"

"Don't be alarmed, miss," said the old woman, "the pony is very steady, and the darkness comes on so sudden-like, it seems later than it is."

And with this scanty consolation Helen was obliged to remain satisfied. Mrs. Jones stirred up the fire and set the tea all ready, but Helen grew sick at heart as the time went on, and still no Edith. Six, struck the clock, and ticked on again to seven. Helen could bear it no longer.

"Mrs. Jones," cried she, "can you not get anyone to go to look for my sister? She may be on her way down the hill, and have got into some difficulty with the pony."

"Indeed, miss, I don't know what I can do. There's no one nearer than old Thomas and he can't move."

"The strange gentleman!" said Helen suddenly; "your other lodger. Would he not help me?"

"He has been out since early this morning," replied Mrs. Jones, "and he told me he was not sure of being back tonight. He has gone to meet a friend."

Helen felt more in despair than before. It seemed an aggrava-tion of her anxiety to have to lie still on the sofa doing nothing. Indeed had she been able to do so, nothing would have pre-vented her making her way to the Black Lake, and too probably losing her own life in the endeavour to save her sister's. As it was, she managed at last to drag herself to the door in hopes of hear-ing footsteps up the path, but nothing broke the silence save the tick, tick of the clock. It wore on to nine, despite her wretched-ness and indescribable anxiety. She pictured to herself her sister, her dear little Edith, left so specially in her charge, cowering on the moor, alone in that dreary darkness, sobbing in despair of ever finding her way out of that frightful desert.

Or, worse still, lying cold and dead in one of those fearful pits under the mockingly beautiful moss; whence, in all probability, her poor body even would never be recovered. It was too fright-ful. Helen almost shrieked aloud: "Oh, my darling, my little sis-ter, come back, do come back. Oh, Malcolm, if only you were here. How terribly I am punished for my self-will!" And terribly punished she was, for the memory of that night's suffering was too painful to recall in after years without a shudder. Mrs. Jones was in helpless distress, though in hopes of every moment hear-ing the pony and the young lady at the gate, and she returned to her own domains saying she had better have hot water ready as Miss Edith would be fainting for her tea. Helen remained alone at the window of the sitting-room.

The night was fine but very dark. Darker than she had ever seen a night before, it seemed to Helen. She was almost in a stupor of despair. She sank down half-unconsciously before the fire and never knew how long she had lain there when she was roused by the clock striking. "One, two, three, four,"—she counted aloud as if bewitched, till when it got to the fatal *thir-teen*, her over-strained nerves gave way, and with a scream she ran or stumbled, she knew not how, along the passage to seek for Mrs. Jones. As she passed the front-door she was arrested by the sharp sounds of steps coming quickly up the garden path. The door was pushed open.

The only light was what came through the open door of the room she had just left, and she could distinguish nothing but a tall dark figure hurrying towards her. She screamed with terror but stood, unable to move, when to her intense relief a voice from behind the person she saw, exclaimed eagerly: "Helen, dearest Helen, don't be frightened. I am quite safe," and some one rushed past the tall person, now close to her, and kissing her passionately, Helen felt, rather than saw, that it was Edith.

"Malcolm! Malcolm! she is fainting!" called Edith, and the tall person pressed forward, caught her up in his arms like a baby, and, unconscious now of everything, Helen was carried back into the sitting-room, laid on the hard little sofa, and there held tenderly by the strong yet gentle arms whose protecting care she, poor foolish child, had fancied she could so well dispense with.

It was the first time in her life that Helen Beaumont had ever fainted, and it was not long before she began to recover.

"Malcolm! oh, Malcolm!" were her first words on returning consciousness (and it seemed to her afterwards as if someone else had spoken them for her, her good angel perhaps!), "can you ever forgive me?"

"My darling," was the whispered answer, "you know you need not ask it." And then Helen felt as if she were just going to die, but was too happy to care, and too languid to ask even how all this had come about. But now a third person came forward saying:—

"Malcolm, let me stay beside her," and, wonderful to tell, the sweet voice and kind face were Mrs. Lindsay's. Helen thought she must be dreaming, but lay still as she was told, and then drank something or other Mrs. Lindsay brought her; so before long she was able to sit up and begin to wonder what was the meaning of it all.

"Are you not amazed, Helen?" said Edith; "but first of all you must forgive me for frightening you so, for indeed I have been nearly as wretched as you, thinking of what you must have been feeling." And before Helen could reply the eager girl ran on with her explanations. "Who do you think has been our fellow-lodger all this time, Helen? Who do you think is the 'strange gentleman'? Only fancy Malcolm's having been here ever since we came! It was he that travelled by the same train, and seeing as it moved off at Llanfar that we had got out, he did so at the next station, and arrived here before us. He had inquired about Mrs. Jones, and heard what a good creature she was; and he had time to have a talk with her, and to take her to some extent into his confidence."

Helen looked at first, as this recital went on, as if she were wavering between a return to her old dislike to being interfered with, and gratitude to Malcolm for his undeserved devotion. The good angel triumphed, as Malcolm, who was watching her anxiously, quickly perceived.

"I did not interfere with you, Helen," he said in a low voice, "but it was the greatest comfort to me to be able to protect and care for you, even though you did not know it."

The tears started to Helen's eyes.

"Oh, Malcolm, I know how good you are, but——"

"Never mind any 'buts,'" said Mrs. Lindsay brightly, catching the last word. "'All's well, that ends well.'"

"I know now who foraged for us so successfully," said Edith. "Who was the mysterious friend that gave Mrs. Jones the mushrooms!"

"And nearly betrayed myself by laughing at the door, when passing I heard Helen's enthusiastic thanks to Mrs. Jones," said Malcolm.

"Yes, and frightened me horribly by so doing," added Helen, "as I really began to think that clock was bewitched, and had a special ill-will against me. In fact it took the place of my conscience for the time being."

"I have the very greatest regard for the clock," said Malcolm demurely, "and I intend to make Mrs. Jones an offer for it forthwith."

"Please don't," said Helen piteously. "I daresay it is very silly, but I really don't quite like that clock, though, after all, its warning of ill-luck has brought the very reverse to me. But I have not heard yet what kept Edith out so late, or how in the world you and Mrs. Lindsay met her at the Black Lake."

"The Black Lake?" said Mrs. Lindsay, "what do you mean?"

Whereupon Edith hastened on with that part of her story relating to her own adventures. She, it appeared, feeling confident in Mrs. Lindsay's ready kindness, and never doubting but what she would at once respond to her appeal by coming to nurse Helen, instead of going to the Black Lake to sketch, as Helen imagined, set off on the pony to meet her friend at the station, having proposed to her to come by a certain train. Overtaking Griffith on the road to Llanfair, as she expected from Mrs. Jones's account, he accompanied her to the village, where she gave over the pony to his care.

As she entered the station she saw a return train about to start for the Junction about half an hour's journey from where she was. Finding by her watch that she was in ample time, it struck her that she might as well go so far to meet her friend, but on arriving at the Junction she was startled to find that with the new month a change had taken place in the trains, and that consequently Mrs. Lindsay could not arrive till late in the evening. Worse still she herself could not now get back to Helen till she was frightened to think what hour, the evening train in question not going farther than Llanfar, the station near the Junction at which she and her sister had by mistake got out on their arrival, and which was fifteen miles from the Black Nest.

It is needless to describe her distress of mind all the long hours she had to sit in the little waiting-room at the Junction; or her corresponding delight when, on the train coming up, she descried looking out of a window the familiar face of Malcolm Willoughby, and found that he was accompanied by his sister whom he had gone to meet half-way on her journey.

Helen woke at noon the next day feeling indescribably happy, she could not tell why till the sight of Mrs. Lindsay's sweet face recalled to her mind all her misery of the night before and the relief and happiness with which it had ended.

"How little I deserve it!" thought she humbly and gratefully, "and how can I ever repay Malcolm for his goodness?"

Their dull little parlour looked very different now that it was enlivened by the presence of the two newcomers; and Helen could scarcely believe it to be the same room in which, but yesterday, she had passed hours of such agonising suspense. So thoroughly penitent and softened did she feel that she offered no opposition to anything proposed, and it was therefore arranged that as soon as Helen was well enough to travel they should all return home together to relieve poor Aunt Fanny's anxiety.

"I wonder," said Helen, with a little sigh, a few days afterwards, when they were packing up their painting materials, "I wonder if I shall ever finish my sketch of the Black Lake."

"I don't like to make rash promises," said Malcolm, "but if somebody I know is *very* good perhaps next summer she may see the Black Lake again, provided she will neither catch cold nor tumble off her pony."

Edith laughed and Helen blushed.

"But there's one thing still," said Edith, "which I don't understand. Why, Malcolm, did you always shut your door as the clock struck thirteen?"

"Very simply explained," replied he. "The first night I was here I was sitting up reading till midnight and thought I heard it strike thirteen. I thought it very odd, and for a night or two I listened till it began to strike and then opened my door to make sure I was not mistaken. And one night I went out with my candle to examine the clock, trying to make out the cause of it, and to see if I could put it right. No man, they say, can resist meddling with a clock even though he is no mechanical genius."

"All the same," said Edith triumphantly, "notwithstanding your examinations, you and no one else can tell the reason why that clock does strike thirteen."

# The Shadow in the Moonlight
(A story from *Uncanny Tales*)

## PART 1

We never thought of Finster St. Mabyn's being haunted. We really never did.

This may seem strange, but it is absolutely true. It was such an extremely interesting and curious place in many ways that it required nothing extraneous to add to its attractions. Perhaps this was the reason.

Now-a-days, immediately that you hear of a house being "very old," the next remark is sure to be "I hope it is"—or "is not"—that depends on the taste of the speaker—"haunted".

But Finster was more than very old; it was *ancient* and, in a modest way, historical. I will not take up time by relating its history, however, or by referring my readers to the chronicles in which mention of it may be found. Nor shall I yield to the temptation of describing the room in which a certain royalty spent one night, if not two or three nights, four centuries ago, or the tower, now in ruins, where an even more renowned personage was imprisoned for several months. All these facts—or legends—have nothing to do with what I have to tell. Nor, strictly speaking, has Finster itself, except as a sort of prologue to my narrative.

We heard of the house through friends living in the same county, though some distance farther inland. They—Mr. and Miss Miles, it is convenient to give their name at once—knew that we had been ordered to leave our own home for some months, to get over the effects of a very trying visitation of influenza, and that sea-air was specially desirable.

We grumbled at this. Seaside places are often so dull and commonplace. But when we heard of Finster we grumbled no longer.

"Dull" in a sense it might be, but assuredly not "commonplace". Janet Miles's description of it, though she was not particularly clever at description, read like a fairy tale, or one of Longfellow's poems.

"A castle by the sea—how perfect!" we all exclaimed. "Do, oh, do fix for it, mother!"

The objections were quickly over-ruled. It was rather isolated, said Miss Miles, standing, as was not difficult to trace in its name, on a point of land—a corner rather—with sea on two sides. It had not been lived in, save spasmodically, for some years, for the late owner was one of those happy, or unhappy people, who have more houses than they can use, and the present one was a minor. Eventually it was to be overhauled and some additions and alterations made, but the trustees would be glad to let it at a moderate rent for some months, and had intended putting it into some agents' hands when Mr. Miles happened to meet one of them, who mentioned it to him.

There was nothing against it; it was absolutely healthy. But the furniture was old and shabby, and there was none too much of it. If we wanted to have visitors we should certainly require to add to it. This, however, could easily be done, our informant went on to say. There was a very good upholsterer and furniture dealer at Raxtrew, the nearest town, who was in the habit of hiring out things to the officers at the fort. "Indeed," she added, "we often pick up charming old pieces of furniture from him for next to nothing, so you could both hire and buy."

Of course, we should have visitors—and our own house would not be the worse for some additional chairs and tables here and there, in place of some excellent monstrosities Phil and Nugent and I had persuaded mother to get rid of.

"If I go down to spy the land with father," I said, "I shall certainly go to the furniture dealer's and have a good look about me."

I did go with father. I was nineteen—it is four years ago—and a capable sort of girl. Then I was the only one who had not been ill, and mother had been the worst of all, mother and Dormy—poor little chap—for *he* nearly died.

He is the youngest of us—we are four boys and two girls. Sophy was then fifteen. My own name is Leila.

If I attempted to give any idea of the impression Finster St. Mabyn's made upon us, I should go on for hours. It simply took our breath away. It really felt like going back a few centuries merely to enter within the walls and gaze round you. And yet we did not see it to any advantage, so at least said the two Miles's who were our guides. It was a gloomy day, with the feeling of rain not far off, early in April. It might have been November, though it was not cold.

"You can scarcely imagine what it is on a bright day," said Janet, eager, as people always are in such circumstances, to show off her *trouvaille*. "The lights and shadows are so exquisite."

"I love it as it is," I said. "I don't think I shall ever regret having seen it first on a grey day. It is just perfect."

She was pleased at my admiration, and did her utmost to facilitate matters. Father was taken with the place, too, I could see, but he hummed and hawed a good deal about the bareness of the rooms—the bedrooms especially. So Janet and I went into it at once in a business-like way, making lists of the actually necessary additions, which did not prove very formidable after all.

"Hunter will manage all that *easily*," said Miss Miles, upon which father gave in—I believe he had meant to do so all the time. The rent was really so low that a little furniture-hire could be afforded, I suggested. And father agreed.

"It is extremely low," he said, "for a place possessing so many advantages."

But even then it did not occur to any of us to suggest "suspiciously low."

We had the Miles's guarantee for it all, to begin with. Had there been any objection they must have known it.

We spent the night with them and the next morning at the furniture dealer's. He was a quick, obliging little man, and took in the situation at a glance. And *his* terms were so moderate that father said to me amiably: "There are some quaint odds and ends here, Leila. You might choose a few things, to use at Finster in the first place, and then to take home with us."

I was only too ready to profit by the permission, and with Janet's help a few charmingly quaint chairs and tables, a three-cornered wall cabinet, and some other trifles were soon put aside for us. We were just leaving, when at one end of the shop some tempting-looking draperies caught my eye.

"What are these?" I asked the upholsterer. "Curtains! Why, this is real old tapestry!"

The obliging Hunter drew out the material in question.

"They are not exactly curtains, miss," he said. "I thought they would make nice *portières*. You see the tapestry is set into cloth. It was so frail when I got it that it was the only thing to do with it."

He had managed it very ingeniously. Two panels, so to say, of old tapestry, very charming in tone, had been lined and framed with dull green cloth, making a very good pair of *portières* indeed.

"Oh, papa!" I cried, "do let us have these. There are sure to be draughty doors at Finster, and afterwards they would make *perfect "portières"* for the two side doors in the hall at home."

Father eyed the tapestry appreciatively, but first prudently inquired the price. It seemed higher in proportion than Hunter's other charges.

"You see, sir," he said half apologetically, "the panels are real antique work, though so much the worse for wear."

"Where did they come from?" asked father.

Hunter hesitated.

"To tell you the truth, sir," he replied, "I was asked not to name the party that I bought it from. It seems a pity to part with *heir*-looms, but—it happens sometimes—I bought several things together of a family quite lately. The *portières* have only come out of the workroom this morning. We hurried on with them to stop them fraying more—you see where they were before, they must have been nailed to the wall."

Janet Miles, who was something of a connoisseur, had been examining the tapestry.

"It is well worth what he asks," she said, in a low voice. "You don't often come across such tapestry in England."

So the bargain was struck, and Hunter promised to see all that we had chosen, both purchased and hired, delivered at Finster the week before we proposed to come.

Nothing interfered with our plans. By the end of the month we found ourselves at our temporary home—all of us except Nat, our third brother, who was at school. Dormer, the small boy, still did lessons with Sophy's governess. The two older "boys," as we called them, happened to be at home from different reasons—one, Nugent, on leave from India; Phil, forced to miss a term at college through an attack of the same illness which had treated mother and Dormy so badly.

But now that everybody was well again, and going to be very much better, thanks to Finster air, we thought the ill wind had brought us some very distinct good. It would not have been half such fun had we not been a large family party to start with, and before we had been a week at the place we had added to our numbers by the first detachment of the guests we had invited.

It was not a very large house; besides ourselves we had not room for more than three or four others. For some of the rooms—those on the top story—were really too dilapidated to suit any one but rats—"rats or ghosts," said someone laughingly one day, when we had been exploring them.

Afterwards the words returned to my memory.

We had made ourselves very comfortable, thanks to the invaluable Hunter. And every day the weather grew milder and more spring-like. The woods on the inland side were full of primroses. It promised to be a lovely season.

There was a gallery along one side of the house, which soon became a favourite resort; it made a pleasant lounging-place, in the day-time especially, though less so in the evening, as the fireplace at one end warmed it but imperfectly, and besides this it was difficult to light up. It was draughty, too, as there was a superfluity of doors, two of which, one at each end, we at once condemned. They were not needed, as the one led by a very long spiral staircase, to the unused attic rooms, the other to the kitchen and offices. And when we did have afternoon tea in the gallery, it was easy to bring it through the dining or drawing-rooms, long rooms, lighted at their extreme ends, which ran parallel to the gallery lengthways, both of which had a door opening on to it as well as from the hall on the other side. For all the principal rooms at Finster were on the first-floor, not on the ground-floor.

The closing of these doors got rid of a great deal of draught, and, as I have said, the weather was really mild and calm.

One afternoon—I am trying to begin at the beginning of our strange experiences; even at the risk of long-windedness it seems better to do so—we were all assembled in the gallery at tea-time. The "children," as we called Sophy and Dormer, much to Sophy's disgust, and their governess, were with us, for rules were relaxed at Finster, and Miss Larpent was a great favourite with us all.

Suddenly Sophy gave an exclamation of annoyance.

"Mamma," she said, "I wish you would speak to Dormer. He has thrown over my tea-cup—only look at my frock!"

"If you cannot sit still," she added, turning herself to the boy, "I don't think you should be allowed to come to tea here."

"What is the matter, Dormy?" said mother.

Dormer was standing beside Sophy, looking very guilty, and rather white.

"Mamma," he said, "I was only drawing a chair out. It got so dreadfully cold where I was sitting, I really could not stay there," and he shivered slightly.

He had been sitting with his back to one of the locked-up

doors. Phil, who was nearest, moved his hand slowly across the spot.

"You are fanciful, Dormy," he said, "there is really no draught whatever."

This did not satisfy mother.

"He must have got a chill, then," she said, and she went on to question the child as to what he had been doing all day, for, as I have said, he was still delicate.

But he persisted that he was quite well, and no longer cold.

"It wasn't exactly a draught," he said, "it was—oh! just icy, all of a sudden. I've felt it before—sitting in that chair."

Mother said no more, and Dormer went on with his tea, and when bed-time came he seemed just as usual, so that her anxiety faded. But she made thorough investigation as to the possibility of any draught coming up from the back stairs, with which this door communicated. None was to be discovered—the door fitted fairly well, and beside this, Hunter had tacked felt round the edges—furthermore, one of the thick heavy *portières* had been hung in front.

An evening or two later we were sitting in the drawing room after dinner, when a cousin who was staying with us suddenly missed her fan.

"Run and fetch Muriel's fan, Dormy," I said, for Muriel felt sure it had slipped under the dinner table. None of the men had as yet joined us.

"Why, where are you going, child?" as he turned towards the farther door. "It is much quicker by the gallery."

He said nothing, but went out, walking rather slowly, by the gallery door. And in a few minutes he returned, fan in hand, but by the *other* door.

He was a sensitive child, and though I wondered what he had got into his head against the gallery, I did not say anything before the others. But when, soon after, Dormy said "Good night," and went off to bed, I followed him.

"What do you want, Leila?" he said rather crossly.

"Don't be vexed, child," I said. "I can see there is something the matter. Why do you not like the gallery?"

He hesitated, but I had laid my hand on his shoulder, and he knew I meant to be kind.

"Leila," he said, with a glance round, to be sure that no one was within hearing—we were standing, he and I, near the inner dining-room door, which was open—"you'll laugh at me, but—there's something queer there—sometimes!"

"What? And how do you mean 'sometimes'?" I asked, with a slight thrill at his tone.

"I mean not always, I've felt it several times—there was the cold the day before yesterday, and besides that, I've felt a—a sort of *breaving*"—Dormy was not perfect in his "th's"—"like somebody very unhappy."

"Sighing?" I suggested.

"Like sighing in a whisper," he replied, "and that's always near the door. But last week—no, not so long ago, it was on Monday—I went round that way when I was going to bed. I didn't want to be silly. But it was moonlight—and—Leila, a shadow went all along the wall on that side, and stopped at the door. I saw it waggling about—its *hands*," and here he shivered—"on that funny curtain that hangs up, as if it were feeling for a minute or two, and then——"

"Well,—what then?"

"It just went out," he said simply. "But it's moonlight again tonight, sister, and I daren't see it again. I just *daren't*."

"But you did go to the dining-room that way," I reminded him.

"Yes, but I shut my eyes and ran, and even then I felt as if something cold was behind me."

"Dormy, dear," I said, a good deal concerned, "I do think it's your fancy. You are not *quite* well yet, you know."

"Yes, I am," he replied sturdily. "I'm not a bit frightened anywhere else. I sleep in a room alone you know. It's not *me*, sister, its somefing in the gallery."

"Would you be frightened to go there with me now? We can run through the dining-room; there's no one to see us," and I turned in that direction as I spoke.

Again my little brother hesitated.

"I'll go with you if you'll hold hands," he said, "but I'll shut my eyes. And I won't open them till you tell me there's no shadow on the wall. You must tell me truly."

"But there must be some shadows," I said, "in this bright moonlight, trees and branches, or even clouds scudding across—something of that kind is what you must have seen, dear."

He shook his head.

"No, no, of course I wouldn't mind that. I know the difference. No—you couldn't mistake. It goes along, right along, in a creeping way, and then at the door its hands come farther out, and it *feels*."

"Is it like a man or a woman?" I said, beginning to feel rather creepy myself.

"I think it's most like a rather little man," he replied, "but I'm not sure. Its head has got something fuzzy about it—oh, I know, like a sticking out wig. But lower down it seems wrapped up, like in a cloak. Oh, it's *horrid*."

And again he shivered—it was quite time all this nightmare nonsense was put out of his poor little head.

I took his hand and held it firmly; we went through the dining-room. Nothing could have looked more comfortable and less ghostly. For the lights were still burning on the table, and the flowers in their silver bowls, some wine gleaming in the glasses, the fruit and pretty dishes, made a pleasant glow of colour. It certainly seemed a curiously sudden contrast when we found ourselves in the gallery beyond, cold and unillumined, save by the pale moonlight streaming through the unshuttered windows. For the door closed with a bang as we passed through—the gallery *was* a draughty place.

Dormy's hold tightened.

"Sister," he whispered, "I've shut my eyes now. You must stand with your back to the windows—between them, or else you'll think it's our own shadows—and watch."

I did as he said, and I had not long to wait.

It came—from the farther end, the second condemned door, whence the winding stair mounted to the attics—it seemed to begin or at least take form there. Creeping along, just as Dormy said—stealthily but steadily—right down to the other extremity of the long room. And then it grew blacker—more concentrated—and out from the vague outline came two bony hands, and, as the child had said, too, you could see that they were *feeling*—all over the upper part of the door.

I stood and watched. I wondered afterwards at my own courage, if courage it was. It was the shadow of a small man, I felt sure. The head seemed large in proportion, and—yes—it—the original of the shadow—was evidently covered by an antique wig. Half mechanically I glanced round—as if in search of the material body that *must* be there. But no; there was nothing, literally *nothing*, that could throw this extraordinary shadow.

Of this I was instantly convinced; and here I may as well say once for all, that never was it maintained by any one, however previously sceptical, who had fully witnessed the whole, that it could be accounted for by ordinary, or, as people say, "natural" causes. There was this peculiarity at least about our ghost.

Though I had fast hold of his hand, I had almost forgotten Dormy—I seemed in a trance.

Suddenly he spoke, though in a whisper.

"You see it, sister, I know you do," he said.

"Wait, wait a minute, dear," I managed to reply in the same tone, though I could not have explained why I waited.

Dormer had said that after a time—after the ghastly and apparently fruitless *feeling* all over the door—"it"—"went out".

I think it was this that I was waiting for. It was not quite as he had said. The door was in the extreme corner of the wall, the hinges almost in the angle, and as the shadow began to move on again, it *looked* as if it disappeared; but no, it was only fainter. My eyes, preternaturally sharpened by my intense gaze, still saw it, working its way round the corner, as assuredly no *shadow* in the real sense of the word ever did nor could do. I realised this, and the sense of horror grew all but intolerable; yet I stood still, clasping the cold little hand in mine tighter and tighter. And an instinct of protection of the child gave me strength. Besides, it was coming on so quickly—we could not have escaped—it was coming, nay, it *was behind* us.

"Leila!" gasped Dormy, "the cold—you feel it now?"

Yes, truly—like no icy breath that I had ever felt before was that momentary but horrible thrill of utter cold. If it had lasted another second I think it would have killed us both. But, mercifully, it passed, in far less time than it has taken me to tell it, and then we seemed in some strange way to be released.

"Open your eyes, Dormy," I said, "you won't see anything, I promise you. I want to rush across to the dining-room."

He obeyed me. I felt there was time to escape before that awful presence would again have arrived at the dining-room door, though it was *coming*—ah, yes, it was coming, steadily pursuing its ghastly round. And, alas! the dining-room door was closed. But I kept my nerve to some extent. I turned the handle without over much trembling, and in another moment, the door shut and locked behind us, we stood in safety, looking at each other, in the bright cheerful room we had left so short a time ago.

*Was* it so short a time? I said to myself. It seemed hours!

And through the door open to the hall came at that moment the sound of cheerful laughing voices from the drawing-room. Someone was coming out. It seemed impossible, incredible, that within a few feet of the matter-of-fact pleasant material life, this horrible inexplicable drama should be going on, as doubtless it still was.

Of the two I was now more upset than my little brother. I was older and "took in" more. He, boy-like, was in a sense triumphant at having proved himself correct and no coward, and though he was still pale, his eyes shone with excitement and a queer kind of satisfaction.

But before we had done more than look at each other, a figure appeared at the open doorway. It was Sophy.

"Leila," she said, "mamma wants to know what you are doing with Dormy? He is to go to bed at once. We saw you go out of the room after him, and then a door banged. Mamma says if you are playing with him it's very bad for him so late at night."

Dormy was very quick. He was still holding my hand, and he pinched it to stop my replying.

"Rubbish!" he said. "I am speaking to Leila quietly, and she is coming up to my room while I undress. Good night, Sophy."

"Tell mamma Dormy really wants me," I added, and then Sophy departed.

"We musn't tell *her*, Leila," said the boy. "She'd have 'sterics."

"Whom shall we tell?" I said, for I was beginning to feel very helpless and upset.

"Nobody, tonight," he replied sensibly. "You *mustn't* go in there," and he shivered a little as he moved his head towards the gallery; "you're not fit for it, and they'd be wanting you to. Wait till the morning and then I'd—I think I'd tell Philip first. You needn't be frightened tonight, sister. It won't stop you sleeping. It didn't me the time I saw it before."

He was right. I slept dreamlessly. It was as if the intense nervous strain of those few minutes had utterly exhausted me.

## PART 2

Phil is our soldier brother. And there is nothing fanciful about *him*! He is a rock of sturdy commonsense and unfailing good nature. He was the very best person to confide our strange secret to, and my respect for Dormy increased.

We did tell him—the very next morning. He listened very attentively, only putting in a question here and there, and though, of course, he was incredulous—had I not been so myself?—he was not mocking.

"I am glad you have told no one else," he said, when we had related the whole as circumstantially as possible. "You see mother is not very strong yet, and it would be a pity to bother father, just when he's taken this place and settled it all. And for goodness' sake, don't let a breath of it get about among the servants; there'd be the—something to pay, if you did."

"I won't tell anybody," said Dormy.

"Nor shall I," I added. "Sophy is far too excitable, and if she knew, she would certainly tell Nannie." Nannie is our old nurse.

"If we tell anyone," Philip went on, "that means," with a rather irritating smile of self-confidence, "if by any possibility I do not succeed in making an end of your ghost and we want another opinion about it, the person to tell would be Miss Larpent."

"Yes," I said, "I think so, too."

I would not risk irritating him by saying how convinced I was that conviction awaited *him* as surely it had come to myself, and I knew that Miss Larpent, though far from credulous, was equally far from stupid scepticism concerning the mysteries "not dreamt of" in ordinary "philosophy".

"What do you mean to do?" I went on. "You have a theory, I see. Won't you tell me what it is?"

"I have two," said Phil, rolling up a cigarette as he spoke. "It is either some queer optical illusion, partly the effect of some odd reflection outside—or it is a clever trick."

"A trick!" I exclaimed; "what *possible* motive could there be for a trick?"

Phil shook his head.

"Ah," he said, "that I cannot at present say."

"And what are you going to do?"

"I shall sit up tonight in the gallery and see for myself."

"Alone?" I exclaimed, with some misgiving. For big, sturdy fellow as he was, I scarcely liked to think of him—of *anyone*—alone with that awful thing.

"I don't suppose you or Dormy would care to keep me company," he replied, "and on the whole I would rather not have you."

"I wouldn't do it," said the child honestly, "not for—for nothing."

"I shall keep Tim with me," said Philip, "I would rather have him than anyone."

Tim is Phil's bull-dog, and certainly, I agreed, much better than nobody.

So it was settled.

Dormy and I went to bed unusually early that night, for as the day wore on we both felt exceedingly tired. I pleaded a headache, which was not altogether a fiction, though I repented having complained at all when I found that poor mamma immediately began worrying herself with fears that "after all" I, too, was to fall a victim to the influenza.

"I shall be all right in the morning," I assured her.

I knew no further details of Phil's arrangements. I fell asleep almost at once. I usually do. And it seemed to me that I had slept a whole night when I was awakened by a glimmering light at my door, and heard Philip's voice speaking softly.

"Are you awake, Lel?" he said, as people always say when they awake you in any untimely way. Of course, *now* I was awake, very much awake indeed.

"What is it?" I exclaimed eagerly, my heart beginning to beat very fast.

"Oh, nothing, nothing at all," said my brother, advancing a little into the room. "I just thought I'd look in on my way to bed to reassure you. I have seen *nothing*, absolutely nothing."

I do not know if I was relieved or disappointed.

"Was it moonlight?" I asked abruptly.

"No," he replied, "unluckily the moon did not come out at all, though it is nearly at the full. I carried in a small lamp, which made things less eerie. But I should have preferred the moon."

I glanced up at him. Was it the reflection of the candle he held, or did he look paler than usual?

"And," I added suddenly, "did you *feel* nothing?"

He hesitated.

"It—it was chilly, certainly," he said. "I fancy I must have dosed a little, for I did feel pretty cold once or twice."

"Ah, indeed!" thought I to myself. "And how about Tim?"

Phil smiled, but not very successfully.

"Well," he said, "I must confess Tim did not altogether like it. He started snarling, then he growled, and finished up with whining in a decidedly unhappy way. He's rather upset—poor old chap!"

And then I saw that the dog was beside him—rubbing up close to Philip's legs—a very dejected, reproachful Tim—all the starch taken out of him.

"Goodnight, Phil," I said, turning round on my pillow. "I'm glad you are satisfied. Tomorrow morning you must tell me which of your theories holds most water. Goodnight, and many thanks."

He was going to say more, but my manner for the moment stopped him, and he went off.

Poor old Phil!

We had it out the next morning. He and I alone. He was *not* satisfied. Far from it. In the bottom of his heart I believe it was a strange yearning for a breath of human companionship, for the sound of a human voice, that had made him look in on me the night before.

*For he had felt the cold passing him.*

But he was very plucky.

"I'll sit up again tonight, Leila," he said.

"Not tonight," I objected. "This sort of adventure requires one to be at one's best. If you take my advice you will go to bed early and have a good stretch of sleep, so that you will be quite fresh by tomorrow. There will be a moon for some nights still."

"Why do you keep harping on the moon?" said Phil rather crossly, for him.

"Because—I have some idea that it is only in the moonlight that—that anything is to be *seen*."

"Bosh!" said my brother politely—he was certainly rather discomposed—"we are talking at cross-purposes. You are satis-fied——"

"Far from satisfied," I interpolated.

"Well, convinced, whatever you like to call it—that the whole thing is supernatural, whereas I am equally sure it is a trick; a clever trick I allow, though I haven't yet got at the mo-tive of it."

"You need your nerves to be at their best to discover a trick of this kind, if a trick it be," I said quietly.

Philip had left his seat, and walked up and down the room; his way of doing so gave me a feeling that he wanted to walk off some unusual consciousness of irritability. I felt half provoked and half sorry for him.

At that moment—we were alone in the drawing-room—the door opened, and Miss Larpent came in.

"I cannot find Sophy," she said, peering about through her rather short-sighted eyes, which, nevertheless, see a great deal sometimes; "do you know where she is?"

"I saw her setting off somewhere with Nugent," said Philip, stopping his quarter-deck exercise for a moment.

"Ah, then it is hopeless. I suppose I must resign myself to very irregular ways for a little longer," Miss Larpent replied with a smile.

She is not young, and not good looking, but she is gifted with a delightful way of smiling, and she is—well, the dearest and almost the wisest of women.

She looked at Philip as he spoke. She had known us nearly since our babyhood.

"Is there anything the matter?" she said suddenly. "You look fagged, Leila, and Philip seems worried."

I glanced at Philip. He understood me.

"Yes," he replied, "I am irritated, and Leila is——" he hesitated.

"What?" asked Miss Larpent.

"Oh, I don't know—obstinate, I suppose. Sit down, Miss Larpent, and hear our story. Leila, you can tell it."

I did so—first obtaining a promise of secrecy, and making Phil relate his own experience.

Our new *confidante* listened attentively, her face very grave. When she had heard all, she said quietly, after a moment's silence:—

"It's very strange, very. Philip, if you will wait till tomorrow night, and I quite agree with Leila that you had better do so, I will sit up with you. I have pretty good nerves, and I have always wanted an experience of that kind."

"Then you don't think it is a trick?" I said eagerly. I was like Dormer, divided between my real underlying longing to explain the thing, and get rid of the horror of it, and a half childish wish to prove that I had not exaggerated its ghastliness.

"I will tell you that the day after tomorrow," she said. I could not repress a little shiver as she spoke.

She *had* good nerves, and she was extremely sensible.

But I almost blamed myself afterwards for having acquiesced in the plan. For the effect on her was very great. They never told me exactly what happened; "You *know*," said Miss Larpent. I imagine their experience was almost precisely similar to Dormy's and mine, intensified, perhaps, by the feeling of loneliness. For it was not till all the rest of the family was in bed that this second vigil began. It was a bright moonlight night—they had the whole thing complete.

It was impossible to throw off the effect; even in the daytime the four of us who had seen and heard, shrank from the gallery, and made any conceivable excuse for avoiding it.

But Phil, however convinced, behaved consistently. He examined the closed door thoroughly, to detect any possible trickery. He explored the attics, he went up and down the staircase leading to the offices, till the servants must have thought he was going crazy. He found *nothing*—no vaguest hint even as to why the gallery was chosen by the ghostly shadow for its nightly round.

Strange to say, however, as the moon waned, our horror faded, so that we almost began to hope the thing was at an end, and to trust that in time we should forget about it. And we congratulated ourselves that we had kept our own counsel and not disturbed any of the others—even father, who would, no doubt, have hooted at the idea—by the baleful whisper that our charming castle by the sea was haunted!

And the days passed by, growing into weeks. The second detachment of our guests had left, and a third had just arrived, when one morning as I was waiting at what we called "the sea-door" for some of the others to join me in a walk along the sands, some one touched me on the shoulder. It was Philip.

"Leila," he said, "I am not happy about Dormer. He is looking ill again, and———"

"I thought he seemed so much stronger," I said, surprised and distressed, "quite rosy, and so much merrier."

"So he was till a few days ago," said Philip. "But if you notice him well you'll see that he's getting that white look again. And—I've got it into my head—he is an extraordinarily sensitive child, that it has something to do with the moon. It's getting on to the full."

For the moment I stupidly forgot the association.

"Really, Phil," I said, "you are too absurd! Do you actually—oh," as he was beginning to interrupt me, and my face fell, I feel sure—"you don't mean about the gallery."

"Yes, I do," he said.

"How? Has Dormy told you anything?" and a sort of sick feeling came over me. "I had begun to hope," I went on, "that somehow it had gone; that, perhaps, it only comes once a year at a certain season, or possibly that newcomers see it at the first and not again. Oh, Phil, we *can't* stay here, however nice it is, if it is really haunted."

"Dormy hasn't said much," Philip replied. "He only told me he had *felt the cold* once or twice, 'since the moon came again,' he said. But I can see the fear of more is upon him. And this determined me to speak to you. I have to go to London for ten days or so, to see the doctors about my leave, and a few other things. I don't like it for you and Miss Larpent if—if this thing is to return—with no one else in your confidence, especially on Dormy's account. Do you think we must tell father before I go?"

I hesitated. For many reasons I was reluctant to do so. Father would be exaggeratedly sceptical at first, and then, if he were convinced, as I *knew* he would be, he would go to the other extreme and insist upon leaving Finster, and there would be a regular upset, trying for mother and everybody concerned. And mother liked the place, and was looking so much better!

"After all," I said, "it has not hurt any of us. Miss Larpent got a shake, so did I. But it wasn't as great a shock to us as to you, Phil, to have to believe in a ghost. And we can avoid the gallery while you are away. No, except for Dormy, I would rather keep it to ourselves—after all, we are not going to live here always. Yet it is so nice, it seems such a pity."

It was such an exquisite morning; the air, faintly breathing of the sea, was like elixir; the heights and shadows on the cliffs, thrown out by the darker woods behind, were indeed, as Janet Miles had said, "wonderful".

"Yes," Phil agreed, "it is an awful nuisance. But as for Dormy," he went on, "supposing I get mother to let me take him with me? He'd be as jolly as a sand-boy in London, and my old landlady would look after him like anything if ever I had to be out late. And I'd let my doctor see him—quietly, you know—he might give him a tonic or something."

I heartily approved of the idea. So did mamma when Phil broached it—she, too, had thought her "baby" looking quite pale lately. A London doctor's opinion would be such a satisfaction. So it was settled, and the very next day the two set off. Dormer, in his "old-fashioned," reticent way, in the greatest delight, though only by one remark did the brave little fellow hint at what was, no doubt, the principal cause of his satisfaction.

"The moon will be long past the full when we come back," he said. "And after that there'll only be one other time before we go, won't there, Leila? We've only got this house for three months?"

"Yes," I said, "father only took it for three," though in my heart I knew it was with the option of three more—six in all.

And Miss Larpent and I were left alone, not with the ghost, certainly, but with our fateful knowledge of its unwelcome proximity.

We did not speak of it to each other, but we tacitly avoided the gallery, even, as much as possible, in the daytime. I felt, and so, she has since confessed, did she, that it would be impossible to endure *that cold* without betraying ourselves.

And I began to breathe more freely, trusting that the dread of the shadow's possible return was really only due to the child's overwrought nerves.

Till—one morning—my fool's paradise was abruptly destroyed.

Father came in late to breakfast—he had been for an early walk, he said, to get rid of a headache. But he did not look altogether as if he had succeeded in doing so.

"Leila," he said, as I was leaving the room after pouring out his coffee—mamma was not yet allowed to get up early—"Leila, don't go. I want to speak to you."

I stopped short, and turned towards the table. There was something very odd about his manner. He is usually hearty and eager, almost impetuous in his way of speaking.

"Leila," he began again, "you are a sensible girl, and your nerves are strong, I fancy. Besides, you have not been ill like the others. Don't speak of what I am going to tell you."

I nodded in assent; I could scarcely have spoken. My heart was beginning to thump. Father would not have commended my nerves had he known it.

"Something odd and inexplicable happened last night," he went on. "Nugent and I were sitting in the gallery. It was a mild night, and the moon magnificent. We thought the gallery would be pleasanter than the smoking-room, now that Phil and his pipes are away. Well—we were sitting quietly. I had lighted my reading-lamp on the little table at one end of the room, and Nugent was half lying in his chair, doing nothing in particular except admiring the night, when all at once he started violently with an exclamation, and, jumping up, came towards me. Leila, his teeth were chattering, and he was *blue* with cold. I was very much alarmed—you know how ill he was at college. But in a moment or two he recovered.

"'What on earth is the matter?' I said to him. He tried to laugh.

"'I really don't know,' he said; 'I felt as if I had had an electric shock of *cold*—but I'm all right again now.'

"I went into the dining-room, and made him take a little brandy and water, and sent him off to bed. Then I came back, still feeling rather uneasy about him, and sat down with my book, when, Leila—you will scarcely credit it—I myself felt the same shock exactly. A perfectly *hideous* thrill of cold. That was how it began. I started up, and then, Leila, by degrees, in some instinctive way, I seemed to realise what had caused it. My dear child, you will think I have gone crazy when I tell you that there was a shadow—a shadow in the moonlight—*chasing* me, so to say, round the room, and once again it caught me up, and again came that appalling sensation. I would not give in. I dodged it after that, and set myself to watch it, and then——"

I need not quote my father further; suffice to say his experience matched that of the rest of us entirely—no, I think it surpassed them. It was the worst of all.

Poor father! I shuddered for him. I think a shock of that kind is harder upon a man than upon a woman. Our sex is less sceptical, less entrenched in sturdy matters of fact, more imaginative, or whatever you like to call the readiness to believe what we cannot explain. And it was astounding to me to see how my father at once capitulated—never even *alluding* to a possibility of trickery. Astounding, yet at the same time not without a certain satisfaction in it. It was almost a relief to find others in the same boat with ourselves.

I told him at once all *we* had to tell, and how painfully exercised we had been as to the advisability of keeping our secret to ourselves. I never saw father so impressed; he was awfully kind, too, and so sorry for us. He made me fetch Miss Larpent, and we held a council of—I don't know what to call it!—not "war," assuredly, for none of us thought of fighting the ghost. How could one fight a shadow?

We decided to do nothing beyond endeavouring to keep the affair from going further. During the next few days father arranged to have some work done in the gallery which would prevent our sitting there, without raising any suspicions on mamma's or Sophy's part.

"And then," said father, "we must see. Possibly this extraordinary influence only makes itself felt periodically."

"I am almost certain it is so," said Miss Larpent.

"And in this case," he continued, "we may manage to evade it. But I do not feel disposed to continue my tenancy here after three months are over. If once the servants get hold of the story, and they are sure to do so sooner or later, it would be unendurable—the worry and annoyance would do your mother far more harm than any good effect the air and change have had upon her."

I was glad to hear this decision. Honestly, I did not feel as if I could stand the strain for long, and it might kill poor little Dormy.

But where should we go? Our own home would be quite uninhabitable till the autumn, for extensive alterations and repairs were going on there. I said this to father.

"Yes," he agreed, "it is not convenient,"—and he hesitated. "I cannot make it out," he went on, "Miles would have been *sure* to know if the house had a bad name in any way. I think I will go over and see him today, and tell him all about it—at least I shall inquire about some other house in the neighbourhood—and *perhaps* I will tell him our reason for leaving this."

He did so—he went over to Raxtrew that very afternoon, and, as I quite anticipated would be the case, he told me on his return that he had taken both our friends into his confidence.

"They are extremely concerned about it," he said, "and very sympathising, though, naturally, inclined to think us a parcel of very weak-minded folk indeed. But I am glad of one thing—the Rectory there, is to be let from the first of July for three months. Miles took me to see it. I think it will do very well—it is quite out of the village, for you really can't call it a town—and a nice little place in its way. Quite modern, and as unghost-like as you could wish, bright and cheery."

"And what will mamma think of our leaving so soon?" I asked.

But as to this father reassured me. He had already spoken of it to her, and somehow she did not seem disappointed. She had got it into her head that Finster did not suit Dormy, and was quite disposed to think that three months of such strong air were enough at a time.

"Then have you decided upon Raxtrew Rectory?" I asked.

"I have the refusal of it," said my father. "But you will be almost amused to hear that Miles begged me not to fix absolutely for a few days. He is coming to us tomorrow, to spend the night."

"You mean to see for himself?"

Father nodded.

"Poor Mr. Miles!" I ejaculated. "You won't sit up with him, I hope, father?"

"I offered to do so, but he won't hear of it," was the reply. "He is bringing one of his keepers with him—a sturdy, trustworthy young fellow, and they two with their revolvers are going to nab the ghost, so he says. We shall see. We must manage to prevent our servants suspecting anything."

This *was* managed. I need not go into particulars. Suffice to say that the sturdy keeper reached his own home before dawn on the night of the vigil, no endeavours of his master having succeeded in persuading him to stay another moment at Finster, and that Mr. Miles himself looked so ill the next morning when he joined us at the breakfast-table that we, the initiated, could scarcely repress our exclamations, when Sophy, with the curious instinct of touching a sore place which some people have, told him that he looked exactly "as if he had seen a ghost".

His experience had been precisely similar to ours. After that we heard no more from him—about the pity it was to leave a place that suited us so well, etc., etc. On the contrary, before he left, he told my father and myself that he thought us uncommonly plucky for staying out the three months, though at the same time he confessed to feeling completely nonplussed.

"I have lived near Finster St. Mabyn's all my life," he said, "and my people before me, and *never*, do I honestly assure you, have I heard one breath of the old place being haunted. And in a shut-up neighbourhood like this, such a thing would have leaked out."

We shook our heads, but what could we say?

## Part 3

We left Finster St. Mabyn's towards the middle of July.

Nothing worth recording happened during the last few weeks. If the ghostly drama were still re-enacted night after night, or only during some portion of each month, we took care not to assist at the performance. I believe Phil and Nugent planned another vigil, but gave it up by my father's expressed wish, and on one pretext or another he managed to keep the gallery locked off without arousing any suspicion in my mother or Sophy, or any of our visitors.

It was a cold summer,—those early months of it at least—and that made it easier to avoid the room.

Somehow none of us were sorry to go. This was natural, so far as several were concerned, but rather curious as regarded those of the family who knew no drawback to the charms of the place. I suppose it was due to some instinctive consciousness of the influence which so many of the party had felt it impossible to resist or explain.

And the Rectory at Raxtrew was really a dear little place. It was so bright and open and sunny. Dormy's pale face was rosy with pleasure the first afternoon when he came rushing in to tell us that there were tame rabbits and a pair of guinea-pigs in an otherwise empty loose box in the stable-yard.

"Do come and look at them," he begged, and I went with him, pleased to see him so happy.

I did not care for the rabbits, but I always think guinea-pigs rather fascinating, and we stayed playing with them some little time.

"I'll show you another way back into the house," said Dormy, and he led me through a conservatory into a large, almost un-furnished room, opening again into a tiled passage leading to the offices.

"This is the Warden boys' playroom," he said. "They keep their cricket and football things here, you see, and their tricycle. I wonder if I might use it?"

"We must write and ask them," I said. "But what are all these big packages?" I went on. "Oh, I see, its our heavy luggage from Finster. There is not room in this house for our odds and ends of furniture, I suppose. It's rather a pity they have put it in here, for we could have had some nice games in this big room on a wet day, and see, Dormy, here are several pairs of roller skates! Oh, we must have this place cleared."

We spoke to father about it—he came and looked at the room and agreed with us that it would be a pity not to have the full use of it. Roller skating would be good exercise for Dormy, he said, and even for Nat, who would be joining us before long for his holidays.

So our big cases, and the chairs and tables we had bought from Hunter, in their careful swathings of wisps and matting, were carried out to an empty barn—a perfectly dry and weather-tight barn—for everything at the Rectory was in excellent repair. In this, as in all other details, our new quarters were a complete contrast to the picturesque abode we had just quitted.

The weather was charming for the first two or three weeks— much warmer and sunnier than at Finster. We all enjoyed it, and seemed to breathe more freely. Miss Larpent, who was staying through the holidays this year, and I congratulated each other more than once, when sure of not being overheard, on the cheerful, wholesome atmosphere in which we found ourselves.

"I do not think I shall ever wish to live in a very old house again," she said one day. We were in the play-room, and I had been persuading her to try her hand—or feet—at roller skating. "Even now," she went on, "I own to you, Leila, though it may sound very weak-minded, I cannot think of that horrible night without a shiver. Indeed, I could fancy I feel that thrill of indescribable cold at the present moment."

She *was* shivering—and, extraordinary to relate, as she spoke, her tremor communicated itself to me. Again, I could swear to it, again I felt that blast of unutterable, unearthly cold.

I started up. We were seated on a bench against the wall—a bench belonging to the play-room, and which we had not thought of removing, as a few seats were a convenience.

Miss Larpent caught sight of my face. Her own, which was very white, grew distressed in expression. She grasped my arm.

"My dearest child," she exclaimed, "you look blue, and your teeth are chattering! I do wish I had not alluded to that fright we had. I had no idea you were so nervous."

"I did not know it myself," I replied. "I often think of the Finster ghost quite calmly, even in the middle of the night. But just then, Miss Larpent, do you know, I really *felt* that horrid cold again!"

"So did I—or rather my imagination did," she replied, trying to talk in a matter-of-fact way. She got up as she spoke, and went to the window. "It can't be *all* imagination," she added. "See, Leila, what a gusty, stormy day it is—not like the beginning of August. It really is cold."

"And this play-room seems nearly as draughty as the gallery at Finster," I said. "Don't let us stay here—come into the drawing-room and play some duets. I wish we could quite forget about Finster."

"Dormy has done so, I hope," said Miss Larpent.

That chilly morning was the commencement of the real break-up in the weather. We women would not have minded it so much, as there are always plenty of indoor things we can find to do. And my two grown-up brothers were away. Raxtrew held no particular attractions for them, and Phil wanted to see some of our numerous relations before he returned to India. So he and Nugent started on a round of visits. But, unluckily, it was the beginning of the public school holidays, and poor Nat—the fifteen-year-old boy—had just joined us. It was very disappointing for him in more ways than one. He had set his heart on seeing Finster, impressed by our enthusiastic description of

222

it when we first went there, and now his anticipations had to come down to a comparatively tame and uninteresting village, and every probability—so said the wise—of a stretch of rainy, unsummerlike weather.

Nat is a good-natured, cheery fellow, however—not nearly as clever or as impressionable as Dormy, but with the same common sense. So he wisely determined to make the best of things, and as we were really sorry for him, he did not, after all, come off very badly.

His principal amusement was roller-skating in the play-room. Dormy had not taken to it in the same way—the greater part of *his* time was spent with the rabbits and guinea-pigs, where Nat, when he himself had had skating enough, was pretty sure to find him.

I suppose it is with being the eldest sister that it always seems my fate to receive the confidences of the rest of the family, and it was about this time, a fortnight or so after his arrival, that it began to strike me that Nat looked as if he had something on his mind.

"He is sure to tell me what it is, sooner or later," I said to myself. "Probably he has left some small debts behind him at school—only he did not look worried or anxious when he first came home."

The confidence was given. One afternoon Nat followed me into the library, where I was going to write some letters, and said he wanted to speak to me. I put my paper aside and waited.

"Leila," he began, "you must promise not to laugh at me."

This was not what I expected.

"Laugh at you—no, certainly not," I replied, "especially if you are in any trouble. And I have thought you were looking worried, Nat."

"Well, yes," he said, "I don't know if there is anything coming over me—I feel quite well, but—Leila," he broke off, "do you believe in ghosts?"

I started.

"Has anyone——" I was beginning rashly, but the boy interrupted me.

"No, no," he said eagerly, "no one has put anything of the kind into my head—no one. It is my own senses that have seen—felt it—or else, if it is fancy, I must be going out of my mind, Leila—I do believe there is a ghost here *in the play-room.*"

I sat silent, an awful dread creeping over me, which, as he went on, grew worse and worse. Had the thing—the Finster shadow—attached itself to us—I had read of such cases—had it journeyed with us to this peaceful, healthful house? The remembrance of the cold thrill experienced by Miss Larpent and myself flashed back upon me. And Nat went on.

Yes, the cold was the first thing he had been startled by, followed, just as in the gallery of our old castle, by the consciousness of the terrible shadow-like presence, gradually taking form in the moonlight. For there had been moonlight the last night or two, and Nat, in his skating ardour, had amused himself alone in the play-room after Dormy had gone to bed.

"The night before last was the worst," he said. "It stopped raining, you remember, Leila, and the moon was very bright—I noticed how it glistened on the wet leaves outside. It was by the moonlight I saw the—the shadow. I wouldn't have thought of skating in the evening but for the light, for we've never had a lamp in there. It came round the walls, Leila, and then it seemed to stop and fumble away in one corner—at the end where there is a bench, you know."

Indeed I did know; it was where our governess and I had been sitting.

"I got so awfully frightened," said Nat honestly, "that I ran off. Then yesterday I was ashamed of myself, and went back there in the evening with a candle. But I saw nothing: the moon did not come out. Only—I felt the cold again. I believe it was there—though I could not see it. Leila, what *can* it be? If only I could make you understand! It is so *much* worse than it sounds to tell."

I said what I could to soothe him. I spoke of odd shadows thrown by the trees outside swaying in the wind, for the weather was still stormy. I repeated the time-worn argument about optical illusions, etc., etc., and in the end he gave in a little. It *might* have been his fancy. And he promised me most faithfully to breathe no hint—not the very faintest—of the fright he had had, to Sophy or Dormy, or any one.

Then I had to tell my father. I really shrank from doing so, but there seemed no alternative. At first, of course, he pooh-poohed it at once by saying Dormy must have been talking to Nat about the Finster business, or if not Dormy, *some one*—Miss Larpent even! But when all such explanations were entirely set at nought, I must say poor father looked rather blank. I was sorry for him, and sorry for myself—the idea of being *followed* by this horrible presence was too sickening.

Father took refuge at last in some brain-wave theory—involuntary impressions had been made on Nat by all of us, whose minds were still full of the strange experience. He said he felt sure, and no doubt he tried to think he did, that this theory explained the whole. I felt glad for him to get any satisfaction out of it, and I did my best to take it up too. But it was no use. I felt that Nat's experience had been an "objective" one, as Miss Larpent expressed it—or, as Dormy had said at the first at Finster: "No, no, sister—it's something *there*—it's nothing to do with *me*."

And earnestly I longed for the time to come for our return to our own familiar home.

"I don't think I shall ever wish to leave it again," I thought.

But after a week or two the feeling began to fade again. And father very sensibly discovered that it would not do to leave our spare furniture and heavy luggage in the barn—it was getting all dusty and cobwebby. So it was all moved back again to the play-room, and stacked as it had been at first, making it impossible for us to skate or amuse ourselves in any way there, at which Sophy grumbled, but Nat did not.

Father was very good to Nat. He took him about with him as much as he could to get the thought of that horrid thing out of his head. But yet it could not have been half as bad for Nat as for the rest of us, for we took the greatest possible precautions against any whisper of the dreadful and mysterious truth reaching him, that the ghost had *followed us* from Finster.

Father did not tell Mr. Miles or Jenny about it. They had been worried enough, poor things, by the trouble at Finster, and it would be too bad for them to think that the strange influence was affecting us in the *second* house we had taken at their recommendation.

"In fact," said father with a rather rueful smile, "if we don't take care, we shall begin to be looked upon askance as a haunted family! Our lives would have been in danger in the good old witchcraft days."

"It is really a mercy that none of the servants have got hold of the story," said Miss Larpent, who was one of our council of three. "We must just hope that no further annoyance will befall us till we are safe at home again."

Her hopes were fulfilled. Nothing else happened while we remained at the Rectory—it really seemed as if the unhappy shade was limited locally, in one sense. For at Finster, even, it had never been seen or felt save in the one room.

The vividness of the impression of poor Nat's experience had almost died away when the time came for us to leave. I felt now that I should rather enjoy telling Phil and Nugent about it, and hearing what *they* could bring forward in the way of explanation.

We left Raxtrew early in October. Our two big brothers were awaiting us at home, having arrived there a few days before us. Nugent was due at Oxford very shortly.

It was very nice to be in our own house again, after several months' absence, and it was most interesting to see how the alterations, including a good deal of new papering and painting, had been carried out. And as soon as the heavy luggage arrived we had grand consultations as to the disposal about the rooms of the charming pieces of furniture we had picked up at Hunter's. Our rooms are large and nicely shaped, most of them. It was not difficult to make a pretty corner here and there with a quaint old chair or two and a delicate spindle-legged table, and when we had arranged them all—Phil, Nugent, and I, were the movers—we summoned mother and Miss Larpent to give their opinion.

They quite approved, mother even saying that she would be glad of a few more odds and ends.

"We might empower Janet Miles," she said, "to let us know if she sees anything very tempting. Is that really all we have? They looked so much more important in their swathings."

The same idea struck me. I glanced round.

"Yes," I said, "that's all, except—oh, yes, there are the tapestry *portières*—the best of all. We can't have them in the drawing-room, I fear. It is too modern for them. Where shall we hang them?"

"You are forgetting, Leila," said mother. "We spoke of having them in the hall. They will do beautifully to hang before the two side doors, which are seldom opened. And in cold weather the hall is draughty, though nothing like the gallery at Finster."

Why did she say that? It made me shiver, but then, of course, she did not know.

Our hall is a very pleasant one. We sit there a great deal. The side doors mother spoke of are second entrances to the dining-room and library—quite unnecessary, except when we have a large party, a dance or something of that sort. And the "*portières*" certainly seemed the very thing, the mellow colouring of the tapestry showing to great advantage. The boys—Phil and Nugent, I mean—set to work at once, and in an hour or two the hangings were placed.

"Of course," said Philip, "if ever these doors are to be opened, this precious tapestry must be taken down, or very carefully looped back. It is very worn in some places, and in spite of the thick lining it should be tenderly handled. I am afraid it has suffered a little from being so long rolled up at the Rectory. It should have been hung up!"

Still, it looked very well indeed, and when father, who was away at some magistrates' meeting, came home that afternoon, I showed him our arrangements with pride.

He was very pleased.

"Very nice—very nice indeed," he said, though it was almost too dusk for him to judge quite fully of the effect of the tapestry. "But, dear me, child, this hall is very cold. We must have a larger fire. Only October! What sort of a winter are we going to have?"

He shivered as he spoke. He was standing close to one of the *portières*—smoothing the tapestry half absently with one hand. I looked at him with concern.

"I *hope* you have not got a chill, papa," I said.

But he seemed all right again when we went into the library, where tea was waiting—an extra late tea for his benefit.

The next day Nugent went to Oxford. Nat had already returned to school. So our home party was reduced to father and mother, Miss Larpent, Phil and I, and the children.

We were very glad to have Phil settled at home for some time. There was little fear of his being tempted away, now that the shooting had begun. We were expecting some of our usual guests at this season; the weather was perfect autumn weather; we had thrown off all remembrance of influenza and other depressing "influences," and were feeling bright and cheerful, when again—ah, yes, even now it gives me a faint, sick sensation to recall the horror of that *third* visitation!

But I must tell it simply, and not give way to painful remembrances.

It was the very day before our first visitors were expected that the blow fell, the awful fear made itself felt. And, as before, the victim was a new one—the one who, for reasons already mentioned, we had specially guarded from any breath of the gruesome terror—poor little Sophy!

What she was doing alone in the hall late that evening I cannot quite recall—yes, I think I remember her saying she had run downstairs when half-way up to bed, to fetch a book she had left there in the afternoon. She had no light, and the one lamp in the hall—we never sat there after dinner—was burning feebly.

*It was bright moonlight.*

I was sitting at the piano, where I had been playing in a rather sleepy way—when a sudden touch on my shoulder made me start, and, looking up, I saw my sister standing beside me, white and trembling.

"Leila," she whispered, "come with me quickly. I don't want mamma to notice."

For mother was still nervous and delicate.

The drawing-room is very long, and has two or three doors. No-one else was at our end. It was easy to make our way out unperceived. Sophy caught my hand and hurried me upstairs without speaking till we reached my own room, where a bright fire was burning cheerfully.

Then she began.

"Leila," she said, "I have had such an awful fright. I did not want to speak until we were safe up here."

"What was it?" I exclaimed breathlessly. Did I already suspect the truth? I really do not know, but my nerves were not what they had been.

Sophy gasped and began to tremble. I put my arm round her.

"It does not sound so bad," she said. "But—oh, Leila, what *could* it be? It was in the hall," and then I think she explained how she had come to be there. "I was standing near the side door into the library that we never use—and—all of a sudden a sort of darkness came along the wall, and seemed to settle on the door—where the old tapestry is, you know. I thought it was the shadow of something outside, for it was bright moonlight, and the windows were not shuttered. But in a moment I saw it could not be that—there is nothing to throw such a shadow. It seemed to wriggle about—like—like a monstrous spider, or—" and there she hesitated—"almost like a deformed sort of human being. And all at once, Leila, my breath went and I fell down. I really did. I was *choked* with cold. I think my senses went away, but I am not sure. The next thing I remember was rushing across the hall and then down the south corridor to the drawing-room, and then I was so thankful to see you there by the piano."

I drew her down on my knee, poor child.

"It was very good of you, dear," I said, "to control yourself, and not startle mamma."

This pleased her, but her terror was still uppermost.

"Leila," she said piteously, "can't you explain it? I did so hope you could."

What *could* I say?

"I—one would need to go to the hall and look well about to see what could cast such a shadow," I said vaguely, and I suppose I must involuntarily have moved a little, for Sophy started, and clutched me fast.

"Oh, Leila, don't go—you don't mean you are going now?" she entreated.

Nothing truly was farther from my thoughts, but I took care not to say so.

"I won't leave you if you'd rather not," I said, "and I tell you what, Sophy, if you would like very much to sleep here with me tonight, you shall. I will ring and tell Freake to bring your things down and undress you—on one condition."

"What?" she said eagerly. She was much impressed by my amiability.

"That you won't say *one word* about this, or give the least shadow of a hint to any one that you have had a fright. You don't know the trouble it will cause."

"Of course I will promise to let no one know, if you think it better, for you are so kind to me," said Sophy. But there was a touch of reluctance in her tone. "You—you mean to do something about it though, Leila," she went on. "I shall never be able to forget it if you don't."

"Yes," I said, "I shall speak to father and Phil about it tomorrow. If anyone has been trying to frighten us," I added unguardedly, "by playing tricks, they certainly must be exposed."

"Not *us*," she corrected, "it was only me," and I did not reply. Why I spoke of the possibility of a trick I scarcely know. I had no hope of any such explanation.

But another strange, almost incredible idea was beginning to take shape in my mind, and with it came a faint, very faint touch of relief. Could it be not the *houses*, nor the *rooms*, nor, worst of all, we ourselves that were haunted, but something or things among the old furniture we had bought at Raxtrew?

And lying sleepless that night a sudden flash of illumination struck me—could it—whatever the "it" was—could it have something to do with the tapestry hangings?

The more I thought it over the more striking grew the coincidences. At Finster it had been on one of the closed doors that the shadow seemed to settle, as again here in our own hall. But in both cases the *portières* had hung in front!

And at the Rectory? The tapestry, as Philip had remarked, had been there rolled up all the time. Was it possible that it had never been taken out to the barn at all? What *more* probable than that it should have been left, forgotten, under the bench where Miss Larpent and I had felt for the second time that hideous cold? And, stay, something else was returning to my mind in connection with that bench. Yes—I had it—Nat had said "it seemed to stop and fumble away in one corner—at the end where there is a bench, you know."

And then to my unutterable thankfulness at last I fell asleep.

## PART 4

I told Philip the next morning. There was no need to bespeak his attention. I think he felt nearly as horrified as I had done myself at the idea that our own hitherto bright, cheerful home was to be haunted by this awful thing—influence or presence, call it what you will. And the suggestions which I went on to make struck him, too, with a sense of relief.

He sat in silence for some time after making me recapitulate as precisely as possible every detail of Sophy's story.

"You are sure it was the door into the library?" he said at last.

"Quite sure," I replied; "and, oh, Philip," I went on, "it has just occurred to me that *father* felt a chill there the other evening."

For till that moment the little incident in question had escaped my memory.

"Do you remember which of the *portières* hung in front of the door at Finster?" said Philip.

I shook my head.

"Dormy would," I said, "he used to examine the pictures in the tapestry with great interest. I should not know one from the other. There is an old castle in the distance in each, and a lot of trees, and something meant for a lake."

But in his turn Philip shook his head.

"No," he said, "I won't speak to Dormy about it if I can possibly help it. Leave it to me, Leila, and try to put it out of your own mind as much as you possibly can, and don't be surprised at anything you may notice in the next few days. I will tell you, first of any one, whenever I have anything to tell."

That was all I could get out of him. So I took his advice.

Luckily, as it turned out, Mr. Miles, the only outsider, so to say (except the unfortunate keeper), who had witnessed the ghostly drama, was one of the shooting party expected that day. And him Philip at once determined to consult about this new and utterly unexpected manifestation.

He did not tell me this. Indeed, it was not till fully a week later that I heard anything, and then in a letter—a very long letter from my brother, which, I think, will relate the sequel of our strange ghost story better than any narration at second-hand, of my own.

Mr. Miles only stayed two nights with us. The very day after he came he announced that, to his great regret, he was obliged—most unexpectedly—to return to Raxtrew on important business.

"And," he continued, "I am afraid you will all feel much more vexed with me when I tell you I am going to carry off Phil with me."

Father looked very blank indeed.

"Phil!" he exclaimed, "and how about our shooting?"

"You can easily replace us," said my brother, "I have thought of that," and he added something in a lower tone to father. He—Phil—was leaving the room at the time. *I* thought it had reference to the real reason of his accompanying Mr. Miles, but I was mistaken. Father, however, said nothing more in opposition to the plan, and the next morning the two went off.

We happened to be standing at the hall door—several of us—for we were a large party now—when Phil and his friend drove away. As we turned to re-enter the house, I felt some one touch me. It was Sophy. She was going out for a constitutional with Miss Larpent, but had stopped a moment to speak to me.

"Leila," she said in a whisper, "why have they—did you know that the tapestry had been taken down?"

She glanced at me with a peculiar expression. I had not observed it. Now, looking up, I saw that the two locked doors were visible in the dark polish of their old mahogany as of yore—no longer shrouded by the ancient *portières*. I started in surprise.

"No," I whispered in return, "I did not know. Never mind, Sophy. I suspect there is a reason for it which we shall know in good time."

I felt strongly tempted—the moon being still at the full—to visit the hall that night—in hopes of feeling and seeing—*nothing*. But when the time drew near, my courage failed; besides I had tacitly promised Philip to think as little as I possibly could about the matter, and any vigil of the kind would certainly not have been acting in accordance with the spirit of his advice.

I think I will now copy, as it stands, the letter from Philip which I received a week or so later. It was dated from his club in London.

My Dear Leila,

I have a long story to tell you and a very extraordinary one. I think it is well that it should be put into writing, so I will devote this evening to the task—especially as I shall not be home for ten days or so.

You may have suspected that I took Miles into my confidence as soon as he arrived. If you did you were right. He was the best person to speak to for several reasons. He looked, I must say, rather—well 'blank' scarcely expresses it—when I told him of the ghost's re-appearance, not only at the Rectory, but in our own house, and on both occasions to persons—Nat, and then Sophy—who had not heard a breath of the story. But when I went on to propound your suggestion, Miles cheered up. He had been, I fancy, a trifle touchy about our calling Finster haunted, and it was evidently a satisfaction to him to start another theory. We talked it well over, and we decided to test the thing again—it took some resolution, I own, to do so.

We sat up that night—bright moonlight luckily—and—well, I needn't repeat it all. Sophy was quite correct. It came again—the horrid creeping shadow—poor wretch, I'm rather sorry for it now—just in the old way—quite as much at home in ——shire, apparently, as in the Castle. It stopped at the closed library door, and fumbled away, then started off again—ugh! We watched it closely, but kept well in the middle of the room, so that the cold did not strike us so badly. We both noted the special part of the tapestry where its hands seemed to sprawl, and we meant to stay for another round; but—when it came to the point we funked it, and went to bed.

Next morning, on pretence of examining the date of the tapestry, we had it down—you were all out—and we found—*something*. Just where the hands felt about, there had been a cut—three cuts, three sides of a square, as it were, making a sort of door in the stuff, the fourth side having evidently acted as a hinge, for there was a mark where it had been folded back. And just where—treating the thing as a door—you might expect to find a handle to open it by, we found a distinct dint in the tapestry, as if a button or knob had once been there. We looked at each other. The same idea had struck us. The tapestry had been used to conceal a small door in the wall—the door of a secret cupboard probably. The ghostly fingers had been vainly seeking for the spring which in the days of their flesh and bone they had been accustomed to press.

'The first thing to do,' said Miles, 'is to look up Hunter and make him tell where he got the tapestry from. Then we shall see.'

'Shall we take the *portières* with us?' I said.

But Miles shuddered, though he half laughed too.

'No, thank you,' he said. 'I'm not going to travel with the evil thing.'

'We can't hang it up again, though,' I said, 'after this last experience.'

In the end we rolled up the two *portières*, not to attract attention by only moving one, and—well, I thought it just possible the ghost might make a mistake, and I did not want any more scares while I was away—we rolled them up together, first carefully measuring the cut, and its position in the curtain, and then we hid them away in one of the lofts that no one ever enters, where they are at this moment, and where the ghost may have been disporting himself, for all I know, though I fancy he has given it up by this time, for reasons you shall hear.

Then Miles and I, as you know, set off for Raxtrew. I smoothed my father down about it, by reminding him how good-natured they had been to us, and telling him Miles really needed me. We went straight to Hunter. He hummed and hawed a good deal—he had not distinctly promised not to give the name of the place the tapestry had come from, but he knew the gentleman he had bought it from did not want it known.

'Why?' said Miles. 'Is it some family that has come down in the world, and is forced to part with things to get some ready money?'

'Oh, dear no!' said Hunter. 'It is not that, at all. It was only that—I suppose I must give you the name—Captain Devereux—did not want any gossip to get about, as to ____'

'Devereux!' repeated Miles, 'you don't mean the people at

Hallinger?'

'The same,' said Hunter. 'If you know them, sir, you will be careful, I hope, to assure the captain that I did my best to carry out his wishes?'

'Certainly,' said Miles, 'I'll exonerate you.'

And then Hunter told us that Devereux, who only came into the Hallinger property a few years ago, had been much annoyed by stories getting about of the place being haunted, and this had led to his dismantling one wing, and—Hunter thought, but was not quite clear as to this—pulling down some rooms altogether. But he, Devereux, was very touchy on the subject—he did not want to be laughed at.

'And the tapestry came from him—you are certain as to that?' Miles repeated.

'Positive, sir. I took it down with my own hands. It was fitted on to two panels in what they call the round room at Hallinger—there were, oh, I daresay, a dozen of them, with tapestry nailed on, but I only bought these two pieces—the others were sold to a London dealer.'

'The round room,' I said. Leila, the expression struck me. Miles, it appeared, knew Devereux fairly well. Hallinger is only ten miles off. We drove over there, but found he was in London. So our next move was to follow him there. We called twice at his club, and then Miles made an appointment, saying that he wanted to see him on private business.

He received us civilly, of course. He is quite a young fellow—in the Guards. But when Miles began to explain to him what we had come about, he stiffened.

'I suppose you belong to the Psychical Society?' he said. 'I can only repeat that I have nothing to tell, and I detest the whole subject.'

'Wait a moment,' said Miles, and as he went on I saw that Devereux changed. His face grew intent with interest and a queer sort of eagerness, and at last he started to his feet.

'Upon my soul,' he said, 'I believe you've run him to earth for me—the ghost, I mean, and if so, you shall have my endless gratitude. I'll go down to Hallinger with you at once—this afternoon, if you like, and see it out.'

He was so excited that he spoke almost incoherently, but after a bit he calmed down, and told us all he had to tell—and that was a good deal—which would indeed have been nuts for the Psychical Society. What Hunter had said was but a small part of the whole. It appeared that on succeeding to Hallinger, on the death of an uncle, young Devereux had made considerable changes in the house. He had, among others, opened out a small wing—a sort of round tower—which had been completely dismantled and bricked up for, I think he said, over a hundred years. There was some story about it. An ancestor of his—an awful gambler—had used the principal room in this wing for his orgies. Very queer things went on there, the finish up being the finding of old Devereux dead there one night, when his servants were summoned by the man he had been playing with—with whom he had had an awful quarrel. This man, a low fellow, probably a professional cardsharper, vowed that he had been robbed of a jewel which his host had staked, and it was said that a ring of great value had disappeared. But it was all hushed up—Devereux had really died in a fit—though soon after, for reasons only hinted at, the round tower was shut up, till the present man rashly opened it again.

Almost at once, he said, the annoyances, to use a mild term, began. First one, then another of the household were terrified out of their wits, just as we were, Leila. Devereux himself had seen it two or three times, the 'it,' of course, being his miserable old ancestor. A small man, with a big wig, and long, thin, claw-like fingers. It all corresponded. Mrs. Devereux is young and nervous. She could not stand it. So in the end the round tower was shut up again, all the furniture and hangings sold, and locally speaking, the ghost laid. That was all Devereux knew.

We started, the three of us, that very afternoon, as excited as a party of schoolboys. Miles and I kept questioning Devereux, but he had really no more to tell. He had never thought of examining the walls of the haunted room—it was wainscotted, he said—and might be lined all through with secret cupboards, for all he knew. But he could not get over the extraordinariness of the ghost's sticking to the *tapestry*—and indeed it does rather lower one's idea of ghostly intelligence.

We went at it at once—the tower was not *bricked* up again, luckily—we got in without difficulty the next morning—Devereux making some excuse to the servants, a new set who had not heard of the ghost, for our eccentric proceedings. It was a tiresome business. There were so many panels in the room, as Hunter had said, and it was impossible to tell in which *the* tapestry had been fixed. But we had our measures, and we carefully marked a line as near as we could guess at the height from the floor that the cut in the *portières* must have been. Then we tapped and pummelled and pressed imaginary springs till we were nearly sick of it—there was nothing to guide us. The wainscotting was dark and much shrunk and marked with age, and full of joins in the wood any one of which might have meant a door.

It was Devereux himself who found it at last. We heard an exclamation from where he was standing by himself at the other side of the room. He was quite white and shaky. 'Look here,' he said, and we looked.

Yes—there was a small deep recess, or cupboard in the thickness of the wall, excellently contrived. Devereux had touched the spring at last, and the door, just matching the cut in the tapestry, flew open.

Inside lay what at first we took for a packet of letters, and I hoped to myself they contained nothing that would bring trouble on poor Devereux. They were not letters, however, but two or three incomplete packs of cards—grey and dust-thick with age—and as Miles spread them out, certain markings on them told their own tale. Devereux did not like it, naturally—their supposed owner had been a member of his house.

'The ghost has kept a conscience,' he said, with an attempt at a laugh. 'Is there nothing more?'

Yes—a small leather bag—black and grimy, though originally, I fancy, of chamois skin. It drew with strings. Devereux pulled it open, and felt inside.

'By George!' he exclaimed. And he held out the most magnificent diamond ring I have ever seen—sparkling away as if it had only just come from the polisher's. 'This must be *the* ring,' he said.

And we all stared—too astonished to speak.

Devereux closed the cupboard again, after carefully examining it to make sure nothing had been left behind. He marked the exact spot where he had pressed the spring so as to find it at any time. Then we all left the round room, locking the door securely after us.

Miles and I spent that night at Hallinger. We sat up late talking it all over. There are some queer inconsistencies about the thing which will probably never be explained. First and foremost—why has the ghost stuck to the tapestry instead of to the actual spot he seemed to have wished to reveal? Secondly, what was the connection between his visits and the full moon—or is it that only by the moonlight the shade becomes perceptible to human sense? Who can say?

As to the story itself—what was old Devereux's motive in concealing his own ring? Were the marked cards his, or his opponent's, of which he had managed to possess himself, and had secreted as testimony against the other fellow?

I incline, and so does Miles, to this last theory, and when we suggested it to Devereux, I could see it was a relief to him. After all, one likes to think one's ancestors were gentlemen!

'But what, then, has he been worrying about all this century or more?' he said. 'If it were that he wanted the ring returned to its real owner—supposing the fellow *had* won it—I could understand it, though such a thing would be impossible. There is no record of the man at all—his name was never mentioned in the story.'

'He may want the ring restored to its proper owner all the same,' said Miles. 'You are its owner, as the head of the family, and it has been your ancestor's fault that it has been hidden all these years. Besides, we cannot take upon ourselves to explain motives in such a case. Perhaps—who knows?—the poor shade could not help himself. His peregrinations may have been of the nature of punishment.'

'I hope they are over now,' said Devereux, 'for his sake and everybody else's. I should be glad to think he wanted the ring restored to us, but besides that, I should like to do something—something *good* you know—if it would make him easier, poor old chap. I must consult Lilias.' Lilias is Mrs. Devereux.

This is all I have to tell you at present, Leila. When I come home we'll have the *portières* up again and see what happens. I want you now to read all this to my father, and if he has no objection—he and my mother, of course—I should like to invite Captain and Mrs. Devereux to stay a few days with us—as well as Miles, as soon as I come back.

Philip's wish was acceded to. It was with no little anxiety and interest that we awaited his return.

The tapestry *portières* were restored to their place—and on the first moonlight night, my father, Philip, Captain Devereux and Mr. Miles held their vigil.

What happened?

*Nothing*—the peaceful rays lighted up the quaint landscape of the tapestry, undisturbed by the poor groping fingers—no gruesome unearthly chill as of worse than death made itself felt to the midnight watchers—the weary, may we not hope repentant, spirit was at rest at last!

And never since has anyone been troubled by the shadow in the moonlight.

"I cannot help hoping," said Mrs. Devereux, when talking it over, "that what Michael has done may have helped to calm the poor ghost."

And she told us what it was. Captain Devereux is rich, though not immensely so. He had the ring valued—it represented a very large sum, but Philip says I had better not name the figures—and then he, so to say, bought it from himself. And with this money he—no, again, Phil says I must not enter into particulars beyond saying that with it he did something very good, and very useful, which had long been a pet scheme of his wife's.

Sophy is grown up now and she knows the whole story. So does our mother. And Dormy too has heard it all. The horror of it has quite gone. We feel rather proud of having been the actual witnesses of a ghostly drama.

# "———Will Not Take Place"

(A story from *Uncanny Tales*)

"'Lingard,' 'Trevannion,'" murmured Captain Murray, as he ran his eye down the column of the morning paper specially devoted to so-called fashionable intelligence, "Lingard, Arthur Lingard; yes, I've met him; a very good fellow. And Trevannion; don't you know a Miss Trevannion, Bessie?"

Mrs. Murray glanced up from her teacups.

"What do you say, Walter? Trevannion; yes, I have met a girl of the name at my aunt's. A pretty girl, and I think I heard she was going to be married. Is that what you are talking about?"

"No," her husband replied. "It's the other way—broken off, I wonder why."

"What an old gossip you are," said Mrs. Murray. "No good reason at all, I daresay. People are so capricious now-a-days."

"Still, they don't often announce a marriage till it's pretty certain to come off. This sort of thing," tapping the paper as he spoke, "isn't exactly pleasant."

"Very much the reverse," agreed Mrs. Murray, and then they thought no more about it.

"I wonder why," said a good many people that morning, when they caught sight of the announcement. For the two principals it concerned—Arthur Lingard, especially—had a large circle of friends and acquaintances, and their engagement had been the subject of much and hearty congratulation. It seemed so natural and fitting that these two should marry. Both young, amiable, good-looking, and sufficiently well off. Even the most cynical could discern no cloud in the bright sky of their future, no crook in the lot before them.

And now—

No marvel that Captain Murray's soliloquy was repeated by many.

But who would have guessed that in one heart it was ever ringing with maddening anguish?

"I wonder why, oh, I wonder why he has done it. Oh, if he would but tell me, it could not surely seem quite so unendurable."

And Daisy Trevannion pressed her aching head, and her poor swollen eyes on to her mother's loving bosom in a sort of wild despair.

"Mamma, mamma," she cried, "help me. I cannot be angry with him. I wish I could. He was so gentle, so sweet—and he is so heartbroken, I can see by his letter. Oh, mamma, what can it be?"

But to this, even the devoted mother, who would gladly have given her own life to save her child this misery, could find no answer.

This was what had happened.

They had been engaged about three months, the wedding day was approximately fixed, when one morning the blow fell.

A letter to Daisy's father, enclosing one to herself—a letter which made Mr. Trevannion draw his brows together in instinctive indignation, and then as the first impulse cooled a little, caused him to turn to his daughter with a movement of irritation, underneath which, hope had, nevertheless, found time to reassert itself.

"Daisy," he exclaimed sharply, "what is the meaning of all this nonsense? Have you been quarrelling with Lingard? You're a bit of a spoilt child I know, my dear, but I don't like playing with edged tools—a man like Arthur won't stand being trifled with. Do you hear, Daisy—eh, what?"

For the girl had scarcely caught the sense of his words, so absorbed was she in those of the short, all too short, but terrible letter she had just read—the letter addressed to herself, which began "Daisy, my Daisy, for the last time," and ended abruptly with the simple signature, "Arthur Lingard".

She gazed up at her father—her white face all drawn, and as it were, withered with that minute's agony—her eyes dulled and yet wild. Never was there such a metamorphosis from the happy, laughing girl who had hurried in with some pretty excuse for her unpunctuality.

"Daisy, my child! Daisy," her father repeated, repenting already of his hasty remarks, "don't take it so seriously. Margaret," to his wife, "speak to her."

And Mrs. Trevannion, as pale almost as her daughter, drew the sheet of note-paper from the girl's unresisting hands, while her husband held out to her his own letter.

"Some complete mistake," she said, "some misplaced quixotry. Daisy, my own darling, do not take it so seriously. Your father will see him—you will, will you not, Hugh?" detecting the proud hesitation in her husband's face. "It is not as if we did not know him well, and all about him. Your father will find out, Daisy, and make it all right."

Mr. Trevannion did not contradict her, but murmured some consolatory words, and then the mother led Daisy away, and to a certain extent the girl allowed herself to be reassured.

"I will consult Keir if necessary," said the father when out of hearing of his daughter. "He is the natural person, both as our own connection and because he introduced Lingard, and thinks so highly of him. But first I will see Arthur alone. The fewer mixed up in such a case the better."

Mrs. Trevannion agreed. She was constitutionally sanguine, but a painful idea struck her as her husband spoke.

"Hugh," she said hesitatingly, "you don't think—it surely is not possible that his—that Arthur's brain is affected?"

"His brain—tut, nonsense! What a woman's idea!" replied Mr. Trevannion irritably. "Why, he is receiving compliments on every side, from the very highest quarters, too, on that article of his on the Capricorn Islands. Brain affected, indeed!"

And to a whisper of, "I was thinking of over-work," which

followed him apologetically, he vouchsafed no reply.

Some intensely trying days passed. Mr. Trevannion's interview with his recalcitrant son-in-law-to-be, proved a complete failure. Nothing, absolutely nothing was to be "got out of the fellow," he told his wife in mingled anger and wretchedness, for the poor man was a devoted father. Arthur was gentleness itself, respectful, deferential even, to the man whose peculiarly disagreeable position he felt for inexpressibly. But he was as firm, as hard in his decision that all should be, must be, over between Miss Trevannion and himself, as if his own heart had suddenly turned to iron, as if he possessed no feelings at all.

He grew white to the lips, with a terrible death-like whiteness, when he named her; he said with a quiet, deliberate emphasis, more impressive by far than any passionate declaration, that never, never while he lived, would he forgive himself for the trouble he had brought into her young life, but that he was powerless to do otherwise, he was absolutely without a choice. As to the reason for the breaking off of the engagement to be given to the world, he left it entirely in the Trevannions' own hands; he would contradict nothing they thought it best to say; but, if possible, he grew still whiter when his visitor from under his shaggy eyebrows glanced at him with a look of contempt while he replied cuttingly that he had no love of falsehood. For his part he would tell the truth, and in the end he believed it would be best for Daisy that all the world should know the way in which she had been treated.

"Best for her and worst for you," he repeated.

And Arthur only said:—

"I hope so. It must be as you think well."

Then Trevannion softened again a little.

"I shall say nothing to any one at present," he went on. "I must see Keir; possibly he may understand you better than I can."

But, "No, it will be no use," the young man repeated coldly, though his very heart was wrung for the father, crushing down his own pride while he thought he saw still the ghost of a hope.

"It will be no use. No one can do anything."

"And you adhere to your determination not to see my—not to see Daisy again?"

Lingard bowed his head.

And Mr. Trevannion left him.

Philip Keir was no blood relation of the Trevannions, but a cousin by marriage and a very intimate friend. He was some years older than Mr. Lingard, and it was through him that the acquaintance resulting in Daisy's engagement had begun. He was a reserved man, with a frank and cordial manner. Daisy thought she knew him well, but as to this she was in some directions entirely mistaken.

He was away from home when Mr. Trevannion called on him, driving straight to his chambers from the fruitless interview with Lingard. Philip did not return for a couple of days, and had left no address. Hence ensued the painful interval of suspense alluded to.

But on the third evening a hansom dashed up to the Trevannions' door, and Mr. Keir jumped out. It was late, but there was no hesitation as to admitting him.

"I found your note," he said, as he grasped his host's hand, "and came straight on. I have only just got back. What is the matter? Tell me at once."

He was a self-controlled man, but his agitation was evident. "Daisy?" he added hastily.

"Yes," replied the father. The two were alone in his study. "Poor Daisy!" And then he told the story.

Keir listened, though not altogether in silence, for broken exclamations, which he seemed unable to repress, broke out from him more than once.

"Impossible—-inconceivable!" he muttered, "Lingard, of all men, to behave like a——" he stopped short, at a loss for a comparison.

"Then you can throw no light upon it—none whatever?" said Mr. Trevannion. "We had hoped—foolishly, perhaps—I had somehow hoped that you might have helped us. You know him well, you see, you have been so much together, your acquaintance is of old date, and you must understand any peculiarities of his character."

His tone still sounded as if he could not bring himself finally to accept the position. Keir was inexpressibly sorry for him.

"I know of none," he said. "Frankly, I know of nothing about him that is not estimable. And, as you say, we have been much and most intimately associated. We have travelled together half over the world, we have been dependent on each other for months at a time, and the more I have seen of him the more I have admired and—yes—loved him. If I had to pick a fault in him I would say it is a curious spice of obstinacy—I have seen it very strongly now and then. Once," and his face grew grave, "once, we nearly quarrelled because he would not give in on a certain point. It was in Siberia, not long ago," and here Philip gave a sort of shiver, "it was very horrible—no need to go into details. He, Arthur, got it into his head that a particular course of action was called for, and there was no moving him. However it ended all right. I had almost forgotten it. But he was determined."

Mr. Trevannion listened, but vaguely. Keir's remarks scarcely seemed to the point.

"Obstinate!" he repeated. "Yes, but that doesn't explain things. There was no question of giving in. They had had no quarrel. Daisy was perfectly happy. The only thing she can say on looking back over the last week or two closely, is that Arthur had seemed depressed now and then, and when she taxed him with it he evaded a reply. You don't think, Philip, that there is anything of that kind—melancholia, you know—in his family?"

"Bless you, no, my dear sir. He comes of the healthiest stock possible. People one knows all about for generations. No, no, it's nothing of that kind," Keir replied. "And—what man ever had such happy prospects?"

"Then what in heaven's name is it?" said Mr. Trevannion, bringing his hand down violently on the table beside which they were sitting. "Can you get it out of him, if you can do nothing else for us, Philip? It is our right to know; it is—it is due to my child, it is———" he stopped, his face working with emotion. "He won't see her, you know," he added disconnectedly.

"I will try," said Philip. "It is indeed the least I can do. If—if I could get him to see her—Daisy; surely that would be the best chance."

Mr. Trevannion looked at him sharply, scrutinisingly.

"You—you are satisfied then—entirely satisfied that there is nothing we need dread her being mixed up in, so to say? Nothing wrong—nothing to shock a girl like her? You see," half apologetically, "his refusing to see her makes one afraid———"

"I am as sure of him as of myself—surer," said Philip earnestly. "There is nothing in his past to explain it—nothing."

"An early secret marriage; a wife he thought dead turning up again," suggested the father. "It sounds absurd, sensational—but after all—there must be some reason."

"Not that," said Keir, getting up as he spoke. "Well then, I will see him first thing in the morning, and communicate with you as soon as possible after I have done so. You will tell Mrs. Trevannion and—and Daisy that I will do my best?"

"My wife is still in the drawing-room. Will you not see her tonight?"

Philip shook his head.

"It is late," he said, "and I am dusty and unpresentable. Besides, there is really nothing to say. Tomorrow it shall be as you all think best. I will see Mrs. Trevannion—and Daisy," here he flushed a little, but his host did not observe it, "if you like and if she wishes it. Heaven send I may have better news than I expect."

And with a warm pressure of his old friend's hand, Mr. Keir left him.

The two younger men met the next morning. There was no difficulty about it, for Lingard, knowing by instinct that the interview must take place, had determined to face it. So of the two he was the more prepared, the more forearmed.

The conversation was long—an hour, two hours passed before poor Philip could make up his mind to accept the ultimatum contained in the few hard words with which Arthur Lingard first greeted him.

"I know what you have come about. I knew you must come. You could not help yourself. But, Philip, it will save you pain—I don't mind for myself; nothing can matter now—if you will at once take my word for it that nothing you can say will do the least shadow of good. No, don't shake hands with me. I would rather you didn't."

And he put his right arm behind his back and stood there, leaning against the mantelpiece, facing his friend.

Philip looked up at him grimly.

"No," he said, "I've given my word to—to these poor dear people, and I'll stick to it. You've got to make up your mind to a cross-examination, Lingard."

But through or below the grimness was a terrible pity. Philip's heart was very tender for the man whose inexplicable conduct was yet filling him with indignation past words. Arthur was so changed—the last week or two had done the work of years—all the youthfulness, the almost boyish brightness, which had been one of his charms, was gone, dead. He was pale with a strange indescribable pallor, that told of days, and worse still, of nights of agony; the lines of his face were hardened; the lips spoke of unalterable determination. Only once had Philip seen him look thus, and then it was but in expression—the likeness and the contrast struck him curiously. The other time it had been resolution temporarily hardening a youthful face; now—what did it remind him of? A monk who had gone through a life-time of spiritual struggle alone, unaided by human sympathy? A martyr—no, there was no enthusiasm. It was all dull, dead anguish of unalterable resolve.

There was silence for a moment. Keir was choking down an uncomfortable something in his throat, and bracing himself to the inquisitorial torture before him to perform.

"Well," said Arthur, at last.

And Philip looked up at him again.

How queer his eyes were—they used to be so deeply blue.

Daisy had often laughed at his changeable eyes, as she called them—blue in the daytime, almost black at night, but always lustrous and liquid. Now, they were glassy, almost filmy. What was it? A sudden thought struck Philip.

"Arthur!" he exclaimed, "Arthur, old fellow, are you going blind? Is that the mystery? If it is that, good Lord, how little you know her, if you think that——"

Arthur's pale lips grew visibly paler. He had been unprepared for attack in this direction, and for the moment he quailed before it.

"No," he whispered hoarsely, "it is not that. Would to God it were!"

But almost instantly he had mastered himself, and from that moment throughout the interview not even the mention of Daisy's name had power to stir him.

And Philip, annoyed with his own impulsiveness, stiffened again.

"You are determined not to reveal your secret," he began, "but I want to come to an understanding with you on one point. If I guess it, if I put my finger on it, will you give me the satisfaction of owning that I have done so."

Lingard hesitated.

"Yes," he said, "I will do so on one condition—your word of honour, your oath, never to tell it to any human being."

"Not to—her—Daisy?"

"Least of all."

Philip groaned. This did not look very promising for the meeting with Daisy, which at the bottom of his heart he believed in as his last—his trump card.

Still, he had gained something.

"Then, my first question seems, in the face of that, almost a mockery. I was going to ask you," and he half gasped—"it is nothing—nothing about her that is at the root of all this misery? No fancy," again the gasp, "that—that she doesn't care for you, or love you enough? No nonsense about your not being suited to each other, or that you couldn't make a girl of her sensitive, high-strung nature happy?"

"No," said Arthur, and the word seemed to ring through the room. "No, I know she loves me as I love her. Oh, no, not quite like that, I trust," and his voice was firm through all the tragedy of the last sentence. "And I believe I could have made her very happy. Leave her name out of it now, Phil, once for all. It has nothing to do personally with the woman who is, and always will be, to me my perfect ideal of sweetness and excellence and truth and beauty."

"Then it has to do with yourself," murmured Keir. "Come, the radius is narrowing. I flew out at poor Trevannion when he suggested it, but all the same, it's nothing in your past you're ashamed of that's come to light, is it? The best fellows in the world make fools of themselves sometimes, you know. Don't mind my asking."

"I don't mind," said Arthur wearily, "but it's no use. No, it's nothing like that. I have done nothing I am ashamed of. I am not secretly married, nor have I committed forgery," with a very ghastly attempt at a smile.

"Then," said Philip, "is it something about your family. Have you found out that there's a strain of insanity in the Lingards perhaps? People exaggerate that kind of thing now-a-days. There's a touch of it in us all, I take it."

"No," said Arthur, again "my family's all right. I've no very near relations except my sister, but you know her, and you know all about us. We're not adventurers in any sense of the word."

"Far from it," agreed Philip warmly. Then for a moment or two he relapsed into silence. "Does your sister—does Lady West know about—about this mysterious affair?" he asked abruptly, after some pondering.

"Nothing whatever. I, of course, was bound by every consideration not to tell her—to tell no one anything till it was understood by—the Trevannions. And I had no reason for consulting her or—any friend," Arthur replied.

He spoke jerkily and with effort, as if he were putting force on himself to endure what yet he was convinced was absolutely useless torture.

But his words gave Keir a new opening, which he was quick to seize.

"That's just it," he exclaimed eagerly. "That's just where it strikes me you've gone wrong. You should have consulted some one—not myself, not your sister even; I don't say whom, but someone sensible and trustworthy. I believe your mind has got warped. You've been thinking over this trouble, whatever it is, till you can't see it rightly. You've exaggerated it out of all proportion, and you shouldn't trust your own morbid judgment."

Lingard did not answer. He stood motionless, his eyes fixed upon the ground. For an instant a wild hope dashed through Philip that at last he had made some impression. But as Arthur slowly raised his dim, worn eyes, and looked him in the face, it faded again, even before the young man spoke.

"To satisfy you, I will tell you this much. I have consulted one person—a man whom you would allow was trustworthy and wise and good. From him I have hidden nothing whatever, and he agrees with me that I have no choice—that duty points unmistakably to the course I am pursuing."

Again a flash of suggestion struck his hearer.

"One person—a man," he repeated. "Arthur, is it some priest? Have they been converting or perverting you, my boy? Are you going over to Rome, fancying yourself called to be a Trappist, or a—those fellows at the Grande Chartreuse, you remember?"

For the second time during the interview, Arthur smiled, and his smile was a trifle less ghastly this time.

"No, again," he said. "You're quite on a wrong tack. I have not the slightest inclination that way. I—I wish I had. No, my adviser is no priest. But he's one of the best of men, all the same, and one of the wisest."

"You won't tell me who he is?"

"I cannot."

"And"—Philip was reluctant to try his last hope, and felt conscious that he would do it clumsily—"Arthur," he burst out, "you will see her—Daisy—once more? She has a right to it. You are putting enough upon her without refusing this one request of hers."

He stood up as he spoke. He himself had grown strangely pale, and seeing this, as he glanced at him, Lingard's own face became ashen.

He shook his head.

"Good God!" he said, "I think this might have been spared me. No, I will not see her again. The only thing I can do for her is to refuse this last request. Tell her so, Philip—tell her what I say. And now leave me. Don't shake hands with me. I don't wish it, and I daresay you don't. If—if we never meet again, you and I—and who knows?—if this is our goodbye, thank you, old fellow, thank you for all you have tried to do. Perhaps I know the cost of it to you better than you imagine. Good-bye, Phil!"

Keir turned towards the door. But he looked back ere he reached it. Arthur was standing as he had been—motionless.

"You're not thinking of killing yourself, are you?" he said quietly.

Arthur looked at him. His eyes had a different expression now—or was it that something was gleaming softly in them that had not been there before?

"No, no—I am not going to be false to my colours. I—I don't care to talk much about it, but—I am a Christian, Phil."

"At least I can put that horrid idea out of the poor child's head, then," thought Keir to himself. Though to Arthur he did not reply, save by a bend of his head.

★★★★★★

Time passed. And in his wings there was healing.

At twenty-four, Daisy Trevannion, though her face bore traces of suffering of no common order, was yet a sweet and serene woman. To some extent she had outlived the strange tragedy of her earlier girlhood.

It had never been explained. The one person who might naturally have been looked to, to throw some light on the mystery, Lingard's sister, Lady West, was, as her brother had stated, completely in the dark. At first she had been disposed to blame Daisy,

253

or her family; and though afterwards convinced that in so doing she was entirely mistaken, she never became in any sense confidential with them on the matter. And after a few months they met no more. For her husband was sent abroad, and detained there on an important diplomatic mission.

Now and then, in the earlier days of her broken engagement, Daisy would ask Philip to "try to find out if Mary West knows where he is". And to please her he did so. But all he learnt was—what indeed was all the sister had to tell—that Arthur was off again on his old travels—to the Capricorn Islands or to the moon, it was not clear which.

"He has promised that I shall hear from him once a year—as near my birthday as he can manage. That is all I can tell you," she said, trying to make light of it.

And whether this promise was kept or no, one thing was certain—Arthur Lingard had entirely disappeared from London society.

At twenty-five, Daisy married Philip. He had always loved her, though he had never allowed her to suspect it; and knowing herself and her history as he did, he was satisfied with the true affection she could give him—satisfied, that is to say, in the hope and belief that his own devotion would kindle ever-increasing response on her side. And his hopes were not disappointed. They were very happy.

Now for the sequel to the story—such sequel, that is to say, as there is to give—a suggestion of explanation rather than any positive *dénoument* of the mystery.

They—Philip and Daisy—had been married for two or three years when one evening it chanced to them to dine at the house of a rather well-known literary man with whom they were but slightly acquainted. They had been invited for a special reason; their hosts were pleasant and genial people who liked to get those about them with interests in common. And Keir, though his wings were now so happily clipt, still held his position as a traveller who had seen and noted much in his former wanderings.

"We think your husband may enjoy a talk with Sir Abel Maynard, who is with us for a few days," Mrs. Thorncroft had said in her note.

And Sir Abel, not being of the surly order of lions who refuse to roar when they know that their audience is eager to hear them, made himself most agreeable. He appreciated Mr. Keir's intelligence and sympathy, and was by no means indifferent to Mrs. Keir's beauty, though "evidently," he thought to himself, "she is not over fond of reminiscences of her husband's travels. Perhaps she is afraid of his taking flight again."

During dinner the conversation turned, not unnaturally, on a subject just at that moment much to the fore. For it was about the time of the heroic Damien's death.

"No," said Sir Abel, in answer to some inquiry, "I never visited his place. But I have seen lepers—to perfection. By-the-by," he went on suddenly, "I came across a queer, a very queer, story a while ago. I wonder, Keir, if you can throw any light upon it?"

But at that moment Mrs. Thorncroft gave the magic signal and the women left the room.

By degrees the men came straggling upstairs after them, then a little music followed, but it was not till much later in the evening than was usual with him that Philip made his appearance in the drawing-room, preceded by Sir Abel Maynard. Philip looked tired and rather "distrait," thought Daisy, whose eyes were keen with the quick discernment of perfect affection, and she was not sorry when, before very long, he whispered to her that it was getting late, might they not leave soon? Nor was she sorry that during the interval before her husband made this suggestion, Sir Abel, who had been devoting himself to her, had avoided all mention of his travels, and had been amusing her with his criticism of a popular novel instead. She could never succeed altogether in banishing the painful association of Arthur Lingard from allusion to her husband's old wanderings.

Poor Arthur! Where was he now?

"Philip, dear," she said, slipping her hand into his when they found themselves alone, and with a longish drive before them, in their own little brougham, "there is something the matter. You have heard something? Tell me what it is."

Keir hesitated.

"Yes," he said, "I suppose it is best to tell you. It is the strange story Sir Abel alluded to before you left the room."

"About—about Arthur? Is it about Arthur?" whispered she, shivering a little.

Philip put his arm round her.

"I can't say. We shall perhaps never know certainly," he replied. "But it looks very like it. Listen, dear. Some little time ago—two or three years ago—Maynard spent some days at one of those awful leper settlements—never mind where. I would just as soon you did not know. There, to his amazement, among the most devoted of the attendants upon the poor creatures he found an Englishman, young still, at least by his own account, though to judge by his appearance it would have been impossible to say. For he was himself far gone, very far gone in some ways, in the disease. But he was, or had been, a man of strong constitution and enormous determination. Ill as he was, he yet managed to tend others with indescribable devotion. They looked upon him as a saint.

"Maynard did not like to inquire what had brought him to such a pass—he, the poor fellow, was a perfect gentleman. But the day Sir Abel was leaving, the Englishman took him to some extent into his confidence, and asked him to do him a service. This was his story. Some years before, in quite a different part of the world, the young man had nursed a leper—a dying leper—for some hours. He believed for long that he had escaped all danger, in fact he never thought of it; but it was not so. There must have been an unhealed wound of some kind—a slight scratch would do it—on his hand. No need to go into the details of his first misgivings, of the horror of the awful certainty at last. It came upon him in the midst of the greatest happiness; he was going to be married to a girl he adored."

"Oh, Philip, Philip, why did he not tell?" Daisy wailed.

"He consulted the best and greatest physician, who—as a

friend, he said—approved of the course he had mapped out for himself. He decided to tell no one, to break off his engagement, and die out of her—the girl's—life; not once, after he was sure, did he see her again. He would not even risk touching her hand. And he believed that telling would only have brought worse agony upon her in the end than the agony he was forced to inflict. For he was a doomed man, though they gave him a few years to live. And he did the only thing he could do with those years. He set off to the settlement in question. Maynard was to call there some months later on his way home, and the young man knew he would be dead then, and so he was.

"But he showed Maynard a letter explaining all, that he had got ready—all but the address—*that*, he would not add till he was in the act of dying. There must be no risk of her knowing till he was dead. And this letter Maynard was to fetch on his return. He did so, but—there had been no time to add the address—death had come suddenly. All sorts of precautions had been ordered by the poor fellow as to disinfecting the letter and so on. But it did not seem to Maynard that these had been taken. So he contented himself by spreading out the paper on the seashore and learning it by heart, and then leaving it. The sum total of it was what I have told you, but not one name was named."

Daisy was sobbing quietly.

"Was it he?" she said.

"Yes, I feel sure of it," Philip replied. "For I can supply the missing link. The one time I really quarrelled with Arthur was when we were in Siberia. He *would* spend a night in a dying leper's hut. I would have done it myself, I believe and hope, had it been necessary. But by riding on a few miles we could have got help for the poor creature—which indeed I did—and more efficient help than ours. But Lingard was determined, and no ill seemed to come of it. I had almost forgotten the circumstance. I never associated it with the mystery that caused you such anguish, my poor darling."

"It was he," whispered Daisy. "Philip, he was a hero after all."

"Not even you can feel that, as I do," Keir replied.

Then they were silent.

★★★★★★

A few weeks afterwards came a letter from Lady West, in her far-off South American home. Daisy had not heard from her for years.

"By circuitous ways, I need not explain the details," she wrote, "I have learnt that my darling brother is dead. I thought I had better tell you. I am sure his most earnest wish was that you should live to be happy, dear Daisy, as I trust you are. And I know you have long forgiven him the sorrow he caused you—it was worse still for him."

"I wonder," said Daisy, "if she knows more?"

But the letter seemed to add certainty to their own conviction.

# "Not Exactly A Ghost Story"
(A tale from *Summer Stories*)

*I know not by what name beside*
*I shall it call,*

C. Lamb.

We talked a good deal about the story Leonard had read
aloud to us. He wouldn't let us call it a story—"a sketch" he said
it was. We all agreed that it was very prettily told, though some
of the boys said it was meant for much younger children than
any of us. "But there were rather long words in it," said Frances.
"I peeped over Leonard's shoulder once or twice when he was
reading it. I assure you there were a good many words *I* couldn't
have read easily."

"Really," said Leslie, "that decides it. Any literary production
which *Frances* cannot read easily must be learned indeed."

"Leslie!" said Frances, growing very red, poor little thing. It
was truly a shame of Leslie to tease the little ones so.

"Supposing," said Honor—it was the next morning at breakfast now, you understand—"supposing, instead of wasting your
time by disputing, you were to begin to consider about the *next*
story. Who is to take Leonard's place this afternoon?"

Several faces grew rather long.

"*I* can't," said one, and "I'm quite sure *I* can't," said another.
Then a brilliant idea struck a third, and it was echoed by several
others. "You, Honor," was the cry. "It's your turn now, and you
can't get out of it."

"I haven't the very least wish to get out of it, I assure you,"

259

said Honor good-naturedly. "But I would much *rather* someone else would take the place of honour," she laughed at the pun—"I really didn't mean it—you must forgive me," she said. "If someone else would follow Leonard before me I'll try to be ready by Monday; but I am not clever at telling stories right off, as Di calls it, and I am not ready yet."

"Well, then, we'll have to skip today, for nobody's ready," said Leslie. Everybody looked disappointed. "It's such a pity to miss at the very beginning," we said. And so it seemed. Certainly the idea of the stories had given us something to talk about which was better than idling about and quarrelling.

"Never you mind," said Honor cheerfully. "Try to get on with your stories for next week, and I'll see if I can't find *something* for this evening."

"I believe she has got something, do you know?" Di said to me confidentially. "I know she wrote to mamma last night, and I shouldn't wonder if it was to ask her for something, for you know she and papa are coming this afternoon to stay till Monday or Tuesday. Mamma has got some nice stories, I know, and I think she has some of them written out. It will be rather a shame, won't it, if Honor gets one from her, for you know Honor could far better make one up than *we* could?" But she said it quite good-naturedly.

"I don't know," I said. "I think you and I together can manage something—what we thought of, you know; and if your mother stays a day or two longer I daresay she'll help us with it."

"That would be a good idea," she said; "but we'd better get on with it as much as we can before she comes."

Di's mother did come that afternoon, and in good time. She was quite ready to make one of the Dingle tea-party, and congratulated us all on the good idea we had had! But it was not till tea was over that anything was said about the entertainment in store for us, and I think we all felt very curious, for Honor looked quite cool and comfortable. Di's suspicion proved correct. When the tea-things had been cleared away and we were all settled in our places, Honor drew out a paper from her pocket.

"I am happy to say I have got something to read to you," she said, "but it is no thanks to any exertions of my own. It is thanks to Aunt Anna."

Di glanced at me. "I told you so," she whispered.

"But," continued Honor, "I daresay that won't make it any the less interesting. The title is—

### NOT EXACTLY A GHOST STORY.

Shall I go on?"

And as we all nodded eager assent, for the title sounded very fascinating, she went on.

★★★★★★

I cannot explain it in the least. If I could I do not suppose I should care to write it out for other people to read. If any of *them* can explain it I shall be delighted, but somehow I do not expect ever to have it cleared up in a sensible, matter-of-fact way. And after all, there is not much to tell. I daresay many people could tell of much more "thrilling" experiences, but I suppose I am doubly interested in my little adventure, or whatever you like to call it—perhaps, indeed, in my secret heart a little proud of it, like a hen with one chicken, because it is the *only* experience of the kind that has fallen to my share.

And from another point of view I don't know but that my pride is legitimate, for, though there may be—doubtless are—many men and women who have been more favoured than I, yet again, on the other hand, there are to my certain knowledge numbers who have been less so. For, after making every reasonable deduction, after allowing that someone *may* have been playing a trick on me, for instance, or that I *may* have been dreaming, still the fact—can I call it a fact?—yes, I think I may—still the fact remains that I *may* have seen a ghost. And it is not everybody that can say that!

It is not *likely* that I was dreaming. you will, I am sure, allow. For it was not in the middle of the night—not even late in the evening, but still early, about four o'clock or thereabouts on a peculiarly lovely summer afternoon.

We were in the country, in the house which we were already—though it had not long been ours, and though none of our family had ever before lived in it learning to call "home." A dear old house it was still is; and dearer and pleasanter I think it every time we return to it after sometimes prolonged absences. It is not very large, but it is charmingly straggly, and therefore seems larger than it is, for there are two or three ways of getting to every room, and till one learns to know it well it is really rather puzzling. It has been added to and altered till the original owner, could he return to it, would assuredly not know it again. It has been lived in for a couple of centuries or more by many people, young and old, for, as seems the fate of certain houses, it has very often changed hands. Could stone walls tell tales, *these* would doubtless have many interesting ones to relate; but, unfortunately, they are dumb, and so we must draw upon our imagination if we want to picture to ourselves anything of the past of our old house.

And from the very fact of its having been the home of so many different families, we know peculiarly little about any of these predecessors of ours. It is said to be haunted by a tall lady dressed in white I believe, but *that* has nothing to do with what happened to me that bright summer afternoon. I was in the garden; the garden too is in its way delightful—quaint and old-fashioned, and yet not too prim to ramble about in. You enter the house by a sort of covered-in terrace which runs along one side, and this adds to the eccentricity of the place, for, on first coming, there is no front door to be seen! It is perfectly secure, for, though the door opening from the house into this verandah is only a glass one, you cannot get into the verandah except through the garden and by another door, which is always kept locked, and has a bell which rings into the house. I have to trouble you with these details as you will see, and I must also mention that this verandah entrance was not the original entrance, but was a whim of one of the several owners of the house, who appear to have had a mania for reconstructing it.

I remember being told, on first going to our new home and

remarking on this odd kind of entrance, that in former times there had been a different "approach," as they call it a much more imposing one somewhere away at what is now the back of the house, though *where* I never had thought or cared to inquire.

Well, as I was saying, I was in the garden. It was rather hot, and I had been resting a little after my labours among my roses, under the shade of one of the big elms of which we are so proud. And here I suppose *some* people would suggest that I had there fallen asleep, and that what followed was a dream! But it just *wasn't*—that is all I can say about it. I got up at last and sauntered slowly towards the house, along the verandah to the front door, which I opened and went into the hall. It looked dark after the light outside; my eyes felt a little dazzled, and for half a moment I thought they were playing me false when, from the gloom at the farther end of the hall, I saw a figure approaching me.

"Who is there?" I called out. What made me say that, I can't tell, for there was nothing the least remarkable in one of the servants my maid, perhaps crossing the hall, or coming to meet me.

"Is it you, Fanny?" I said, for I saw it was a woman. But there was no reply, and, slightly rubbing my eyes to get the sunshine out of them, I looked again. Yes, it was no fancy. A small, neat figure in black was noiselessly approaching me, and, as she drew nearer, I saw that she was an elderly, not to say a very old, woman. She was very small—much smaller than my maid Fanny or than anyone in the house except my baby daughter!—very, very neat and trim, though even in the half-light I could see that her clothes had a painfully cared-for look about them; that they would have been threadbare on anyone *less* careful; and more than that, that the fashion of them was curiously antique—more ancient than I have ever seen clothes worn by even the oldest or oldest-fashioned of my old lady friends.

Yet she looked like a lady. Her face, from beneath the shade of her large bonnet, was very pale and wrinkled; two or three queer little prim curls of gray hair were carefully arranged at each side; the eyes had a sad, *tired* look—an indescribably pathetic look it was; and yet when she smiled, as she did when she drew still nearer, the sadness melted into a real sweetness of expression which curiously attracted me. I did not speak—I don't know why. Was I frightened? No, I do not think so. I felt *strange*; that is all I can vouch for, except one other thing I felt *cold*. It was natural, *perhaps*. The shady hall could not but feel cold in comparison with the sun-bright garden outside, but *yet*—the cold seemed to have come suddenly; I had not felt it when I first came in, and certainly never before or since, in spring or autumn, midsummer or mid-winter, have I felt that same kind of cold in our hall or any part of the house.

And I just stood there without speaking, staring at her, and she stood there smiling that strange sweet smile at me. And then she spoke. And this, you see, goes greatly *against* the ghost story theory, for everyone knows that a ghost never does—*can't*, in fact—speak to any human being till the human being speaks to *it*. But my old lady *did* speak.

"I beg your pardon, madam," she said; and her voice was very low and soft, though with an accent I could not define or recognise. It was not a foreign accent; it was not a provincial one such as *I* had ever heard. I know *now* what I think it was. I think it was the accent of fifty or sixty or a hundred years ago; but I did not then think of this. "I beg your pardon, madam," said the clear, soft, strange voice. "I most humbly ask your pardon for presuming, but perhaps you may be in need of someone to repair your laces. I have great experience. May I show you some of my work?"

Then for the first time, as she brought it forward, I noticed that my queer visitor had a bag on her arm—a small bag, almost small enough to be described by the old-fashioned word "reticule," and quite in accordance with the old lady's own appearance, for it was worked in faded wools, and the piece of black silk which drew it together at the top was of that blue-black shade that our grandmothers so much affected. I had found my voice by this time.

"Thank you," I said courteously; "I do not require anything of the kind at present." But she paid no attention to my words. She proceeded quietly to unfasten her bag, and from it she drew forth a long piece of the very queerest, yellowest lace I ever saw. She held it towards me, and I took hold of it.

"See, madam," she repeated, "you will find it impossible to discern the repairs." I certainly did. It just looked to me a mass of confused yellow thread. I am no great *connoisseur* in lace; had I been so, very likely I should have burst into enthusiastic admiration, but I only thought it very queer-looking stuff. And I felt anxious to dismiss my odd visitor. It began to occur to me that perhaps she had designs on some of the valuables in the house, and that the lace-repairing was only a blind.

"Thank you," I said again. It would have been almost impossible to speak to her otherwise than courteously; besides she was old—yes, indeed, I have said to myself since, Heaven only knows *how* old! "Thank you; I have no doubt it is very beautifully done, but I don't know much about lace, and I have certainly none to repair. But," I added, fancying that a disappointed look came into the old face, and that the eyes grew sadder—they had brightened up a little with pride as she drew out the lace— "if you will leave me your address I will not forget you in case I ever have any lace to repair, or my friends, perhaps—"

"I thank you, madam," she replied with dignity; "I will leave you my card;" and again the reticule came into service, for she extracted from it the most astonishing calling card I ever saw, perfectly matching its owner and her old lace. "Thick" was no word for it; it was as hard as a piece of wood, highly glazed and yellow, and with a browny look round the edges as if it had been locked up in a drawer for a few score years. And on this wonderful card were inscribed the words:

*Mrs. Kirtin,*
*14 Crossway.*

"Fourteen Crossway," I read aloud. "Where is that? You don't live at Northsprings, then?" Northsprings is the name of the neighbouring little watering-place—half town, half village, but, whichever you like to call it, venerable of its kind. Indeed there *are* antiquaries who maintain that it is one of the most ancient little towns in England! Again my odd visitor looked at me with her queer smile.

"Oh, yes," she said; "the Crossway is well known at North-springs. Perhaps, madam, you have not been long here?"

"Not very long," I said; "but I certainly thought I knew all the streets in Northsprings."

She did not reply to this remark, but turned as if to go. "I thank you, madam, for your courtesy, and I wish you farewell," she said. But to my surprise, instead of going towards the door—the door by which I had come in—she moved away in the opposite direction, *the same direction from which she had come forward to meet me,* as if there lay the way out.

"Stop!" I exclaimed; "you are going into the dining-room. *There* is the front door," and I pointed towards it. The old woman turned.

"Ah," she said, half under her breath, "I forgot!" Then swiftly and silently more swiftly than I would have expected she moved away in the right direction this time. Only, *just* as she reached the door, she stopped again one instant. "It has been such a pleasure to see it all again," she said softly, more as if speaking to herself than to me, and yet with a sort of tone of thanking me too, which touched me.

I followed her in a half mechanical way; she was already at the farther end of the verandah. I went on slowly,—I don't quite know why,—and watched her making her way down the garden path. But again I was on the point of exclaiming, "Stop! that is not the right way," for instead of directing her steps towards the garden door or gate, which she *could* not have mistaken—it was just before her—she turned straight off to the left, crossing a piece of grass which lay between the path and a belt of very thickly growing shrubs, and—that was the queerest part of it all—suddenly *disappearing* in the heart of these same shrubs. I rubbed my eyes—I could not believe their testimony; I was too confused and amazed for the first moment to reflect clearly—to say to myself that my old woman *could* not be among the shrubs; that they were far too closely planted for even a tiny child to get in among them without difficulty; and that as for easily stepping in among them—melting into them as she had to me appeared to do—it was, for a creature of flesh and bones, a physical impossibility.

All this I said to myself afterwards, and say it still, whenever I think over my adventure, but just then at the moment it did not come into my mind. A new idea seized me, and filled me with an unreasoning terror. "She is a madwoman," I said to myself; "she must have escaped from the asylum," (for there *is* one not far from Northsprings), "and she will hide among the bushes and make her way into the house again when no one is about."

I rushed off to the servants' quarters.

"Fanny—Roberts—all—any of you," I exclaimed; "there is an old madwoman hiding in the garden. Go and watch the door, and let no one out till I see who it is. And stay—she *may* have got out in this moment. You run round to the front gate, James, and Fanny come out at the back with me. If she *has* got out she *cannot* pass down the road without our seeing her."

This was perfectly true. But see her we did not. Up and down the road we stared in vain. There was not a creature to be seen except some of our own ducks which had escaped, and were quacking along the edge of the footpath in search of some dirty water—for of course the more beautifully clean you keep ducks the more delighted they are with dirty water when they can find it—and a cart just coming into sight round the turn more than a quarter of a mile off, for we can see quite half a mile up and down the road from our back gate, and there is not a corner where anyone could hide—no hedge or ditch of any kind just about there. I strained my eyes in vain; the sun was beating down on my uncovered head, for it was a very hot, bright day. *Imagine* thinking of a ghost in such surroundings!

"Fanny," I said, "she must be still in the garden;" but hardly had I said the words when the other servants came running towards us.

"There is no one in the garden, ma'am," said James; "and no one has gone out neither."

He looked at me with puzzled inquiry.

"But among the shrubs," I said; "over there by the wall. She *must* be there."

James looked at me now with an increasingly odd expression.

"Among the shrubs over there," he said, following me as I hastily led the way; "why no one could hide there—not Tiny, let alone a woman."

And when I myself got to the place, and stood gazing at the very spot where my queer visitor had disappeared, I could not but be sure he was right. *No one* could be hidden there! But, allowing this—and I was very ready to allow it; I had no wish to have an old maniac hidden in the garden, and to be wakened up in the middle of the night perhaps to find her dangling her bit of yellow lace over my nose—allowing this, the question remained—"Where was she?"

"I cannot make it out," I said; "but at least I will try to do so. I have her card and address, though for that matter I know it by heart,—

*Mrs. Kirtin,*
*14 The Crossway.*

Fanny, fetch me a calling-card—a very queer, yellow, old-looking card that you will see lying on the hall table. I just laid it down there." Fanny hastened off. She was a quick, ready girl, with, as the saying is, "*all her eyes about her,*" but this time she was slower than usual of executing her message. She appeared in a few minutes looking rather perplexed, and with no card in her hand.

"I cannot find it, ma'am," she said, "and I have looked all over the hall—under the table and everywhere. It is really not there."

"Not there," I repeated; "but I am *sure* I left it there." Still

I mechanically put my hand in my pocket. There was no card forthcoming! And I remembered the exact spot on the hall table where I had laid it. The whole affair grew queerer and queerer.

"I will go and look myself," I said. But as I was turning away, another idea struck me.

"Which of you opened the door to the old woman?" I said to the assembled servants. "And whom did she ask for? Did she know my name?"

They all stared at each other and then at me.

"It wasn't I" "I never saw her" "The bell never rang," I heard repeated in various tones.

"You none of you let her in?" I exclaimed. "Then how did she get in? When I saw her first she appeared to be coming out of the dining-room. Who could have shown her in there?"

They all shook their heads. Somehow I did not feel surprised. Everything that had happened this afternoon had been so strange and disjointed that I began to feel as if ordinary rules of possibility and impossibility were not to be taken into account. I too shook my head, and made my way to the house to *look* for the card, as I had said, but with faint hopes of finding it. And I did *not* find it, though I searched most thoroughly.

There remained but one thing to do. The name and address of my queer visitor were firmly engraved on my memory. I would not give up my "adventure" as an insoluble mystery without at least an attempt at throwing some light on it.

"Fanny," I said again, "I want you to go off to Northsprings at once and inquire for this person. If you find her; and yet, how you possibly *can* find her, how she can possibly be there to be found, passes my comprehension; but *if* you find her, make any excuse you like—say that I *have* some old lace to repair, and wanted to be sure of her address—ask her for another card—anything you like. James will drive you in the pony-carriage. Don't forget the address: 'Mrs. Kirtin, 14 The Crossway.' Stay, I'll write it down. James is sure to say he doesn't know it—he never does know any place that isn't straight before him but never mind. It will be some old-fashioned little place. Inquire all about till you find it."

"Oh yes, ma'am," said Fanny confidently. And, armed with my written direction, off she set.

It was late when she came back late, that is to say, considering the comparatively short distance she had to go; I was dressing for dinner when her tap came to the door.

"Well?' I said, "have you found her? You've been a good while about it."

"Yes, ma'am," said Fanny; "I'm sorry to be so late, but I knew you would be better pleased to hear all I could find out. It's very odd, ma'am—*very* odd; but,"—she lowered her voice a little and spoke slowly,—"there's *no* such place as The Crossway at North-springs, and—"

"Then it's a regular imposture," I exclaimed, starting up; "or else," I added—"or else the old woman's an escaped lunatic, as I half feared. I wish I were *quite* sure she was out of our premises."

"You may be quite sure of that, ma'am," said Fanny; "least-ways as sure as anyone can be with—with things like that. No, ma'am, she wasn't a lunatic; but I know what I think she was," and here Fanny grew quite pale and lowered her voice again, with a timid glance around her. "I think she was a *ghost.*"

"A ghost, and in broad daylight! A ghost—on a midsummer sunshiny afternoon! Oh, Fanny, what nonsense!" And yet, as I said it, there returned to my memory the strangeness of the old woman's first appearance—the indescribable feeling that had gone through me—above all, the sudden sensation of *cold*, and my last words faltered on my lips.

"Yes, ma'am, a *ghost,*" repeated Fanny impressively; "and I'll tell you why. I did find out something. I asked right and left—at all the shops, and even at the post-office for The Crossway—thinking perhaps it might be some out of the way place that was little known, though that wasn't very likely in so small a town. But no one had ever heard of it, till at last an old man—quite an old man—who was smoking his pipe in the kitchen behind the greengrocer's shop—that neat-looking little shop at the corner, where they have such nice fruit, you know, ma'am—called out that there *had* been such a street in Northsprings—right across where the market-hall stands now; it ran, he said, from Green Bank Terrace to the Bexley Road. He remembered when he was a boy—nigh upon sixty-five years ago, he said—he remembered them pulling down the last of the row of old houses that had been called 'The Crossways.'—Nigh upon sixty-five years ago, he said, ma'am."

A strange, giddy feeling came over me, and for a moment I could not answer Fanny. The face and figure of my old visitor seemed to rise before me. *Could* it be?—*were* such things possible?—*had* I seen, spoken to, *touched*—yes, I remember her gown had come in contact with mine as she passed me—a being no longer of this world of ours, a poor stray wanderer from some other state of existence, drawn back by heaven knows what mysterious attraction, what imperfectly severed ties, to the scenes of her earthly life? Poor old ghost, poor pathetic old face—how sad it seemed! My fear melted into a strange pity. "I wonder if I could have done anything to satisfy the troubled spirit,?" I said to myself. "There was nothing evil in those sad old eyes—no unatoned-for crime. Why should she not be allowed to rest? Why should she thus revisit the haunts of her flesh-and-blood life?"

"Was that all you heard ?" I said at last.

"All," said Fanny. "I did ask the old man if he remembered ever to have heard speak of a family called Kirtin in these parts; but he shook his head, and said his memory was not as good as it had been. But there had been a street, or a row of houses, called The Crossways—of that he was sure. So I thanked him, and said there must have been a mistake someway—I thought my mistress had found the name in an old book, or something of that sort, and that we hadn't been long here. I didn't want to make any story about it—it was better, wasn't it?"

"Much better," I said, "and thank you, Fanny, for all the trouble you have taken. I won't say anything more about it to the other servants; just tell them you couldn't find out anything, and

271

that I think the old woman must have been some harmless old body, not quite right in the head. But it is *very* strange."

"*Very* strange," repeated Fanny. But she said nothing else. She seemed to understand that I preferred to discuss it no more. That was the seventh of July. I marked the date in my pocket-book, but after a while I began to forget about it, for my old visitor never came back again, and the yellow card never turned up. I felt a little nervous, just a very little, for a week or two, but the feeling passed off; and the following summer the seventh of July went by without my even recalling the date till some days after!

Only once again a circumstance brought my queer adventure back to my memory. "It was in the autumn of the following year; we were thinking of altering the approach to our house,— we have never done it by-the-by, for we found it would have been more troublesome and expensive than we had imagined, and would also have disturbed some of the finest of the fine old shrubs of which we are so proud,—we were thinking, I say, of altering the approach, and for this purpose we sent for some workmen to discuss the matter. Among them was an old man who had now and then done odd work for us, and seemed to think he had a sort of right about the place. He was very, very deaf, and stood by leaning on his spade while my husband talked to a clever young foreman mason, or whatever you call that kind of workman, about it all.

"We are thinking of enlarging the walk in the front of the house, making it wide enough for a carriage to drive up, and carrying it round to the left there," etc. etc., my husband was saying, when old Mike broke in:

"Werst you thinking o' running th' road whur werst afore?" he said suddenly.

"Where it was before? What does he mean?" I exclaimed; and my husband, who could better make himself heard by the deaf old man than I could, cross-questioned him. He explained clearly enough what he meant. Long ago, when he was a boy, he remembered his father talking of a piece of work *he* had had to do with at Eastedge, as our house is called, and that it had been rather a troublesome business—namely, the doing away with the gravel drive leading up to the house, and altering the principal entrance to suit the fancy of the then owner. Mike pointed out as near as he could the place where the former drive "had used to run;" and my husband, curious to find if "what he said were correct, made the workmen examine it. One or two of the smaller shrubs had to be displaced, and then their pickaxes soon struck on hard ground, and very little more research proved the truth of Mike's statement: the former drive ran right up to what had then been the front door—right through the thick-growing belt of shrubs *where my old woman had disappeared.*

"Nay, more, it became evident,—and Mike's memory again corroborated the fact—that the former entrance to the house, the front hall, had been round at the other side, and that our present dining-room had been this hall.

And—it was from the dining-room, if you remember, that the old woman had come out to meet me, exactly as if she and not I had been entering the house.

This is all I have to tell. Not worth telling, perhaps, but some wiser person than I *may* be able to answer the question that has often puzzled me—*Was* she a ghost?"

★★★★★★

"What do *you* think?" we all exclaimed. "Aunt Anna, it is your story—you should tell. *Was* she a ghost?"

Aunt Anna shook her head, smiling.

"My dears," she said. "I have told you all I know. I cannot say more."

"But what do you *think?*" we persisted.

"Well, if you mean do I think the old woman was a ghost, I certainly do *not* think so. Still the adventure was a curious one, and not very easy to explain."

"And nothing more was ever heard or o found out?"

"Nothing. It remains what it is called—*Not exactly a ghost story.*"

"It's very queer," said Leslie, who had been remarkably attentive. "It's not so easy to say what it was, after all. Now, Honor, remember, you're down for Monday on your own account."

"And if we go by ages," replied Honor, "as we have clone hitherto, you, my dear brother, may consider yourself down for Tuesday."

Upon this Leslie subsided.

# A Strange Messenger

(A story from *The Wrong Envelope and Other Stories*)

Late in the afternoon of a dull autumn day a man was walking briskly along a hilly road in one of the northern Welsh counties. It was at all times a gloomy part of the world, yet not without a certain picturesqueness of its own, enhanced perhaps by its very grimness—grimness more the work of human hands than of nature, for it was a mining district.

The man, a fairly young man—my story dates back fully twenty years—stood still for a moment and looked about him. He was not a native of the place, and, comparatively speaking, a newcomer. But he was growing to feel at home in it, and he was grateful for the position he had come thither to hold, that of manager to the important mine not far from where he stood—a position which had enabled him to marry sooner than at one time he had dared to hope would be possible.

'Yes,' he thought, 'it has turned out very well. Margaret is so sensible and adaptable. She never seems to feel it dull, as I feared she might. I remember how I felt like a fish out of water at first, scarcely understanding what the people said, nor their queer ways'; then a shadow crossed his face. 'It is very sad about Brough,' he went on thinking. 'I wonder if I shall find him any better today. I fear not. He has been such a good steady fellow, and being an Englishman, made him enter into my difficulties, in his quiet way,' and with these thoughts he hurried on again, till he reached a row of small houses occupied by some of the many miners, at a short distance from the pit's mouth.

At the door of one of these he stopped and knocked. It was opened by a tidy-looking elderly woman, the wife of the man to whom the cottage belonged, and with whom Brough, unmarried and with no relations in the place, had lodged for several years.

She shook her head in reply to the manager's unspoken inquiry.

'No better, sir. Step in; he'll be pleased to see you. It's the master, Brough,' she went on in a louder voice as she showed Mr. Heald into a small room opening out of the kitchen.

'No better' was plainly written on the worn thin face of the man who tried to raise himself on his pillows as the manager entered, and gently, very gently, shook the big hand, once brown and rough, now pathetically smooth and white, held out to him.

'So good of you, sir,' the sick man murmured. 'Indeed, I don't know how to thank you for coming so regular, and you so busy,' a cough stopped him and he lay back exhausted.

'I wish I could do more for you,' said Mr. Heald very kindly, with a sigh.

'Nay, sir,' Brough went on again, and his honest blue eyes gazed into his friend's face with the indescribable, mysterious intentness of the dying, 'Nay, sir, if I could but have done something in return—you and the lady too—sending me soup and fruit and the best of everything—if I could have done something for you, I feel as if I'd die easier.'

Mr. Heald gently touched the thin hand again.

'Don't speak that way, my dear fellow,' he said. 'If we have been able to cheer you a little, we are only too glad.'

But Brough's expression did not change. He murmured something inaudible, and lay still. The manager did not stay long; he saw that the patient was very weak. He just waited to tell the poor fellow that a few details as to his little possessions—the sending some money that the miner had saved, to a sister in Australia, and so on, were all carefully noted and should be attended to, and then with a 'I'll come again tomorrow,' he left, the blue eyes, faithful and devoted, following him to the door.

And when, true to his promise, he came again next day, Brough was dead.

★★★★★★

Time passed. The winter—a very severe one that year—came on, and now and then, when the thought of Brough crossed his mind, the manager would say to his wife that he was glad the poor fellow had not lingered; 'it would have been terribly trying for him in that cottage in such weather.'

Then slowly and half reluctantly, as it were, followed the spring. The snowdrops, and, later on, the primroses and violets—faithful little friends as ever—began to peep out in the lanes and copses among the valleys between the great grim hills—for there were still green oases even in that black country. Then a short but glowing summer, and 'again,' said Margaret Heald to herself, with a little sigh, as she stood one dull morning look-ing after her husband as he set off to his day's work, 'again it is autumn and the long winter before us.'

But the sigh was quietly replaced by a smile. 'We are so hap-py,' she murmured, 'so very happy. What do outside things like the weather matter ?'

That very afternoon, as the doctor of the district returned to his own house after a long round, he was met at the door by an unexpected summons. He was tired and hungry, and, being no longer a young man, these sensations were less easy to bear with philosophy than formerly. And his work was arduous, for he was the only medical man within a circuit of five miles, and, excepting for the cluster of dwellings in the neighbourhood of the mine, his patients were scattered at considerable distances, in that sparsely-populated corner of the world.

'I really think I shall have to get a partner, or at least a thor-oughly efficient assistant,' he was saying to himself, as he got down from his dog-cart at the gate, and his 'Well, what's the matter, Eliza?' to the servant who opened the door before he had time to take out his latch-key, was perhaps, excusably, a little irritable.

277

Eliza was a newcomer—a capable and intelligent girl, for she came from a suburb of London and was not without 'cockney' acuteness, but as yet unaccustomed to the conditions of a doctor's house and scarcely acclimatised to the place.

'What's the matter now?' said her master, for the girl looked startled and anxious.

'Oh, if you please, sir, will you go at once, *at once,*' with emphasis, 'to the manager's house, Mr. Heald's. I've been watching to catch you before the horse was taken out. The messenger's not been gone five minutes.'

Dr. Warden's face lengthened.

'Did he not say what was wrong ? Who brought the message ?' he inquired, sharply.

'Oh yes, sir. It's an accident—very bad he seemed to think— to the manager himself. He was one of the workmen, the miners, I mean. He said his name was——,' but by this time she was speaking to the air, for the doctor had rushed to the stable-yard, calling to his man that he must have the trap again at once—yes, *at once—* Eliza's emphasis on the words seemed to have pressed them on to his brain.

He had a most hearty and sincere regard—affection indeed, one might say—for both Heald and his sweet wife, but as he drove along, his anxiety had time to cool a little, for his destination was between two and three miles away.

'I daresay that girl has exaggerated,' he thought. 'She's nervous and excitable, though sharp enough. It was a fad of the missus's to have a servant from such a distance, because the girls hereabouts are rough and clumsy—however, this air will put some colour into Eliza's cheeks. I daresay there's not much wrong with Heald—it may be all a mistake, and they will laugh at me for coming.'

But as he entered the village—for village of a kind had grown up near the mine—his fears returned. For, grouped round the gate of the manager's pretty little house at the far end of the street, stood a number of men—miners of course, with grave faces and apprehensive looks. They would have spoken to the doctor, but he, springing from his cart with the alacrity of twenty years ago, pushed his way through them, eager to get to headquarters at once.

The door was closed, but almost before his knock had ceased sounding, it was opened, and at the same moment Margaret Heald came out into the little hall. Her face was deadly pale, her eyes full of anguish, but at the sight of the newcomer a look of intense relief overspread her whole countenance; she almost smiled.

'Oh Dr. Warden, oh dear doctor,' she exclaimed. 'What a mercy! Thank God, what a blessed chance! Come in at once. You may, you *must* be in time. He is scarcely conscious; he is bleeding to death. We have done all we could, but we *cannot* stop it. Oh come.'

She caught hold of the doctor's sleeve and pulled him into the room, where, on a couch, for they had not dared to take him upstairs, lay poor Robert Heald—more dead than alive, for in fact it was getting to be a question of minutes for him. And yet the actual accident had not been a very serious one. He had caught his foot somehow when examining some new tools or machinery just being unpacked, and had fallen, cutting his wrist on a piece of sharp jagged iron lying about, and all but completely severing the artery. But had medical skill been instantly available, he need scarcely have run any risk. As it was, the more experienced as to wounds and injuries, among the miners, had done their best, and temporarily stopped the bleeding, which had, however, burst out again as they carried him to his home, fortunately close at hand.

It took but a short time for Dr. Warden's clever surgery to save the situation, and with an ejaculation of profoundest thankfulness, Margaret saw her husband open his eyes and try to smile at her, while a little colour came back into his face.

'He will do now,' said the doctor,' give him what I have ordered from time to time,' referring to certain restoratives, 'and keep him absolutely quiet and still, till I look in again this evening. He will probably sleep a good deal. Don't talk to him more than you can help.'

Margaret followed the doctor out into the hall. Her eyes were full of tears, yet shining with happiness.

'You have saved his life,' she said. 'But oh, how unspeakably grateful we should be that you happened to be passing ! I suppose you saw the men at the gate. Collins'—the Healds' groom—'was just starting on the pony to fetch you. But,' and she shivered, 'it would have been too late, I feel certain.'

'Yes,' was the reply,' there was assuredly terrible risk. I was only just in time, but—' and he looked puzzled. 'How do you mean that I happened to be passing ? I came all the way from home—as soon as I got your message, of course ?'

The puzzled expression moved on to Margaret's face and intensified there.

'I did not send for you,' she exclaimed. 'There had not been time. Robert had not been five minutes in the house when you came.'

'Then one of the men must have gone straight from the mine the moment it happened,' the doctor replied, but Mrs. Heald still shook her head.

'No, no, impossible,' she maintained. 'For you to have got a message to bring you here so soon, you must have heard of the accident almost simultaneously with its occurring. It must have been a brain-wave, doctor,' and she smiled.

'A very substantial one,' he said. 'It *was* one of the men, sent, I understood, by you. Still,' he added, reflectively, '*you* wouldn't have sent on foot. Ah well,' as he went off, 'I'll inquire about it and tell you this evening.'

He returned within a few hours, and much to Margaret's delight volunteered to stay all night, 'just in case of anything going wrong.'

But nothing did go wrong, though both doctor and wife sat up; in turn watching by the patient, who slept fairly quietly.

And at breakfast the next morning Dr. Warden told his hostess a strange story.

'I waited till the night was over—not to excite or startle you, my dear,' he began, 'to tell you the result of my cross-questioning of Eliza, my servant. I had not misunderstood what she said. It *was* one of the miners—a workman, she called him, who summoned me, and by putting things together, he must have been at my door *almost,* as you said, simultaneously with Heald's accident——'

'But,' interrupted Margaret, 'how—how *could*——'

Dr. Warden in his turn broke into her speech.

'Stay,' he said, 'I must remind you of the old quotation *More things in heaven and earth.* Yes, it was one of the miners, or should I say one who *had* been such—but,' and he half murmured the next words—'rest his soul, he's dead.'

'Margaret,' he went on, 'the girl described him closely. He was pale—"delicate-like, for a rough sort of man, and he had a nice voice and very blue eyes," etc. "To make it still surer, as he turned to go, something seemed to strike him, 'Tell them,' he added, 'tell them as it was Brough, Laurence Brough, that fetched the doctor.' "Then," continued Eliza, "I was going to ask him to say it again, but he was gone—I don't know how he managed to slip off so quickly—and I said the name over to myself, not to forget it." That is, all she has to tell, and all *she* need ever know. It might upset her.'

Margaret had grown very, very white; but it was the whiteness of awe, not of fear.

'Doctor,' she said in a whisper, ' what do you think? *Can* such things be?'

His voice was very reverent as he replied, 'Far be it from me to say they cannot.'

It was not till some days' quiet had completely restored Robert Heald to his usual health that they told him the story. And after a moment or two's deep silence he looked up and said gently, 'I remember the last words I heard him speak, "If I could do something in return for you, I feel as if I'd die easier."'

'And how little we had done, or been able to do,' added Margaret. 'Such faithfulness of gratitude makes one ashamed—gratitude reaching not till, but beyond, death.'

Like the Last Minstrel,

*I say the tale as 'twas said to me,*

but as to its truth, I go further. The facts of the incident I have related are facts, not fiction.

# A Ghost of the Pampas

(A story from *The Wrong Envelope and Other Stories*—
Written by the Author's Son Bevil R. Molesworth, who died in
1899, aged 27, seven years before the book's first publication.)

'Then we'll go down to The Chase together—meet at Paddington, eh? The 1.45 is my usual train—brings one in just about
the right time of the day.'

'All right, I'll be there.'

'Mind you don't fail me,' returned the first speaker, Charles
Maud by name, as he drew out a small pocket diary of some
novel and specially convenient make, in which he carefully inscribed the appointment. 'Paddington, December 23rd, 1.45.
Meet Darcy,' he read aloud. 'You're such an uncivilised fellow
nowadays, you see—accustomed to diggings where there are no
times or tides—no, I'm making a mess of it. There are tides, I
suppose, as you weren't far from the coast; but *time* doesn't count
for much, I fancy.'

'No, not for much,' replied the other. But he spoke absently.
'December 23rd, you said, Maud? December 23rd,' and then he
relapsed into silence and sat with his eyes fixed on the glowing
recesses of the brightly-burning fire, in the snug smoking-room
of the club, where the two old companions, schoolfellows and
college friends in past days, had met again.

'December 23rd. Naturally—the day but one before Christmas. Has it any tender reminiscences for you?' asked Maud in a
rallying tone.

He was a cheery, good-hearted young fellow, whose life

had in no way diverged from the ordinary lives of his class, nor brought him in contact with the underlying *strata* of existence. Roger Darcy, on the other hand, was a very different type of man—quiet—considerate, somewhat taciturn, with a touch of melancholy in his dark eyes, and the look of one who has been used to depend on himself and himself alone. It was barely a twelvemonth since the death of an uncle—preceded by that of this uncle's only son—to whose title and property he had thus succeeded, had recalled him to England and civilisation. For several years before that he had been working hard, and that not unsuccessfully, in the southern States of the Argentine Republic, in various ways, dealing with cattle, sheep and horses. At Maud's remark, Darcy looked up, with a slow smile.

'Tender reminiscences,' he repeated. 'No, I haven't gone in much for that sort of thing. It's more in your way, Charley. Yet the 23rd of December is and always will be a marked day for me. It saw the death of a true friend of mine—true, yes indeed that sounds a cold word for what he was to me—my poor old Dorotéo—*that a man should give his life for his friend*—and he'd have done that any day. And—*he did more than that.*'

His voice sank. A strange expression stole into his deep eyes, and Maud, heedless rattle though he was, felt curiously impressed—something almost like a shiver passed through him as he caught sight of Roger's eyes, and heard his mysterious words.

'*More than that,*' he repeated. 'What can you mean, Darcy?'

Darcy glanced round. They were alone in the room. It was getting late. For an hour or so it was probable they would be undisturbed.

'I'll tell you, if you like,' he said quietly. 'But mind you, old fellow—it's—it's sacred to me. I couldn't stand you mocking or making light of it. It did more for me than I could easily express.'

'I won't make light of it—give you my word,' said Maud, whose curiosity, and perhaps some worthier feelings, were by this time aroused. 'I'm not such a fool as you take me for, on the whole, Roger.'

'Well then—listen. You know, or perhaps you don't know, that when by two successive mails—practically to me by the same mail, for I got the letters all at once—I learnt the extraordinary change that had come over my fortunes, I was some way up from the coast, to the north of the Rio Negro, where, after lots of ups and downs, I had at last settled on a good stretch of land. I had had infinite difficulty in getting it, and I could have made a good thing of it. So that it was not without a mixture of feelings that I saw before me no choice. I must sell up and come home. There were new duties and responsibilities before me which I had no right to evade. But I'd got to love the life— much of it, that is to say. There is—no, no words of mine can describe the extraordinary charm of that strange country. I mustn't let myself go on the subject, or I shall never get my story told. I'd got to love the life, I say, and I'd got some friends, real friends there; horses and dogs as well as human beings! A queer medley. And among the human beings there was no one I trusted more—till I lost him I didn't realise how he had wound himself round my heart—than one of my *guachos,* named Dorotéo. I had made him into a sort of head man, or as we call it out there, *capitas,* or *major-domo.* And it was he I chose to accompany me in an expedition I planned for myself, as a sort of compromise—a softener of the sharp abruptness of giving up my new country. There was no extreme hurry for my return home, so instead of making my way straight to Buenos Ayres—I resolved to strike into the very heart of Patagonia, south of the Rio Negro, and there to spend some three or four months in exploring what was to me, and indeed is to almost all Europeans, entirely new ground. The season was in my favour—by the time I had made all arrangements for disposing of my land and stock, we were at the end of October—that is to say, the Patagonian spring. No, I wasn't going to be troubled with any *impedimenta.* One pack horse could carry all we needed, for *we* meant only Dorotéo and myself, old and tried *campanisteros.*'

'Old and tried how much?' interposed Maud.

Darcy smiled.

'I'll avoid local terms in future—as much as I can, that's to say. "Camp-men" is the nearest translation of the word you object to. Well, to return to our preparations. Sixteen horses exclusive of the *madrina* mare—oh, by the by, I must explain. In the Argentine, and indeed all over those southern republics, every troop of horses, from seven to twenty, are kept together by the bell mare, to whom they are hefted, following her, as her name implies, as if she were their mother. So whenever the tinkle of her *cencesso* is heard, you may be sure her *tropilla* is round her. All you have to do at night to keep the troop from straying, is to *mancar*—*Anglice* "hobble"—the *madrina*. Well, as I was saying, sixteen horses were to form our troop—among them, I remember, a *bahio*; the word is used for a colour you never see in England, a curious yellowish shade horse, belonging to Dorotéo himself.

'He had had him as a colt, had broken him, and had come to love the creature so, that no offers, however tempting, had ever prevailed with him to part with his *bahio*— not even when he was drunk—for, alas, it would not be true to life if I made out that my friend, good as he was, was *always* sober—would Dorotéo have listened to such for a moment! Many a ten-dollar—ten, nay, fifty dollars, had he won on him, a *pellejo*,—bareback, that is to say. And he *was* a wonderful beast. You could literally do anything with him. He could *cinchar*—drag, I mean—a dead cow by himself; he could run out a young colt like no other horse I ever saw. I have known him, riderless, "work" the biggest bull I ever—with one exception—came across; what couldn't he do? By Jove—no, Charley, you have no idea, you *can* have no idea to what point a horse's intelligence can be developed if you take him the right way, and get him straight from nature, so to say, before generations of European management have driven all the individuality out of the breed. But I must hurry up, or I shall never have finished.

'Well—to make a long story short—we started, and knocked about the part of the country I wanted to see, crossing the Chupat River, bearing south till within seven or eight days' journey of the dry bed of the Rio Desideo; then striking westward towards the Cordilleras, we moved on in a north-easterly direction, intending to rejoin the Rio Negro at some point not so very far from the coast. But mind you, Charley, simple as this sounds, it took some real travel—we did travel, there was no dawdling or loitering—to cover the ground we did. We camped every night, sitting round the fire—sometimes a poor one enough, when fuel was extra scarce—with our *maté* and *bombilla*, as happy as kings, Dorotéo strumming on his guitar, to which the *madrina's* bell some little distance off tinkled an accompaniment. I knew it was for the last time—that added to the marvellous charm of it all. Ah me,'—and here Darcy rose from his seat and strolled to the window, from whence the lights and movement of Piccadilly were vaguely visible through the medium of a London fog—'I can't put it into fine words, but it comes upon me almost unbearably sometimes that there is more in *that*, after all, than in what such as you call "life." Ask any fellow who knows the Pampas if it doesn't seem so.'

He came back to his seat.

'Yes,' he went on, 'I knew it was for the last time. But yet I little thought how it was to be. It was the night of the twenty - second of December. We were within eight days' ride of the Rio Negro again, and comparative civilisation, when it happened. Sitting by the fire that night before turning in, he asked me— Dorotéo, I mean—if I had noticed fresh tracks of cattle late that afternoon.

'"If it please the Patron," he went on, " we will leave the troop here in the morning and ride about half a league towards where I saw the tracks. About there the plain dips a little, and there is a spring. The cattle will be there. We should like fresh beef."

'This for a *guacho* was a long speech. And the proposal did please me. I liked the idea of another go at wild cattle—another "last time." So, early in the morning we rode off in the direction Dorotéo proposed, and there sure enough we found the spring—and the cattle. There were about nine of them all told. On hearing us they cleared, all except one, a bull—the hugest

287

monster!—which stood there pawing the ground and lashing his tail in fury. He had a hump on his back almost as big as a camel's; two men could certainly have scarcely joined hands round his neck.

'"We'll cut him up," said Dorotéo "Plenty of him, though it may be tough. No use turning the others," and in half a minute his lasso was round the brute's horns.

'I never saw Dorotéo miss!

'He moved on—he was on his *bahio*, of course—tightening the lasso. But even he and his *bahio* could not uproot that bull. I hurried up, intending to throw my own lasso over the brute's hindquarters, but before I had time to do so the *guacho* called out—

'"Let him stand," he shouted. "He is all the easier cut up."

'And so saying he dropped off his horse, and making a detour came up from behind, meaning to hamstring the monster, when away went the bull, almost dragging the little *bahio* off his legs, but a whistle and an encouraging *"pingo"* from his master steadied him. Then suddenly the bull, feeling himself so far mastered, charged full tilt at the *bahio*, and, before the gallant little horse could swerve round, the huge brute's horns were through him—and down he went with a cry—a dreadful cry—almost like a child's. For one second, Dorotéo changed colour.

'"*Madre de Dios*" he shouted. " He has killed my *bahio*."

Then "*Carajo*," he hissed, "*Animal de mierda*, you shall follow him," and, driven reckless by grief and rage, he flung himself, as it were, upon the brute, stabbing him repeatedly in the throat, at the fatal spot well known to a *guacho*.

'For a moment the bull seemed to stare at him, as if too astonished to feel. Another second and there was a struggling mass on the ground, Dorotéo still working the knife in the gaping wound; all happening so quickly that the describing it takes far longer than the thing itself. I was off my horse in a moment, and with some difficulty managed to extricate him from beneath the still heaving body of the bull, which had partially fallen upon him, only to find, to my horror, that he was fearfully crushed—

not dead nor unconscious, but the blood pouring out of his mouth telling its deadly tale.

'He stretched out his arm and pointed to the sky, "Before the sun is overhead," he murmured, "I shall be gone."

'In a sort of agony, still striving to hope, I cut open his clothes, drawing them apart as tenderly as I could to examine his injured chest. It was worse than I could have imagined—mangled and crushed in. I tried to staunch the blood, it was useless, it streamed on, though more slowly than at first.

'He opened his eyes again and struggled to speak, while he glanced round.

'"Your horse, Patron," he whispered. "He has cleared. You will have to walk to where we left the others."

'I had forgotten all about my horse—sure enough he was gone! At first I did not seem to care, till there came over me with a rush the horror of it—the being there alone, on foot on the tremendous Pampas. You can't understand what it means unless you've gone through it.

'He died, as he had said, before noon.

'"*Amigo*," I heard him whisper, and I bent down lower to catch his words, "take courage. Find the horses and make for the coast."

'I was dazed and reckless.

'"Never mind about me," I said. "What does it matter? There is no one to care much whether I live or die."

'A troubled look crossed his poor face. Then a smile broke through it.

'"You shall live," he breathed. "You shall be glad to live."

'I think he murmured something more, but I could not catch it. And then all was still.

'I must have lain there beside him for some time in a sort of stupor. When I roused myself the sun was some way down. I got on my feet and set to work to skin the bull. There was no question of burying my poor old friend, all I could do was to wrap him in the hide with his *poncho* over his shoulders, and his *bolar* round his waist, and thus I laid him beside his dead *bahio*, rolling up his lasso neatly, and tying it to his saddle. And then I left him.

'Late that evening I reached our camping place of the night before. Our baggage was still there as we had left it in the morning, but nothing more. No sign of the horses. I was too dead beat quite to take it in. I think I cooked a slice of the meat I had brought with me, and then I lay down and slept—from utter exhaustion—till morning. And with the light came back the realisation of it all. If I did not find the horses, what was before me? Death—in one of its most awful forms—lingering death; or else—I would not let myself think of that just yet.

'I started off, carrying only my *poncho*, my revolver, and a little meat. All that day and the next I wandered about in search of the horses, listening intently every now and then for the faintest far-off tinkle of the bell. By the end of the third day my meat was finished. Of the fourth day I have only the vaguest recollection, and all through the fifth I lay on the same spot. It is no good trying to describe what I suffered. By fits and starts I must have been delirious, but towards evening I woke up clearer-headed. Perhaps I had slept a little.

'And then it is that I remembered praying—really praying, as I had not done for years.

'"O God," I cried, adding in a sort of frenzy, "if there is a God, help me. Dorotéo, can *you* hear me? You said I should live—look at me now."

'Then I took out my revolver. There were four cartridges left. I remember counting them. That would be more than enough.

'I stood straight up—an unnatural strength seemed to come to me. Should I do it now? Best be over with it. I could not stand another night.

'"Talk of God—Providence and all such fables," I thought. "What power can stop my shooting myself?"

'I held the revolver out at arm's length, the muzzle towards me. I looked up—once more—for the last time, at the darkening sky and as my eyes fell again, there—there, just in front of me, only a few yards off, was Dorotéo, on his *bahio*, just as I had seen him scores, hundreds of times. I could distinguish his features and everything about him down to the smallest detail. He was looking at me—with an expression of affectionate reproach, mingled almost with something of contempt. I took it all in. It was, and it was not Doroteo.

'I started towards him; he moved on then, slowly, I following. I remember how the *bahio's* queer yellow coat seemed to shine out in the lingering light, as we went—on and on. I had lost all sensation of fatigue, though every now and then I felt him glance towards me over his shoulder with a sort of kindly encouragement. I almost think he smiled.

'I don't know how long this lasted. The stars came out and went in again—it must have been hours and hours. For dawn was breaking when at last he pulled up, beckoning me forward—I found myself on the edge of a little ravine, there down below, not twenty yards from where I stood, were the horses feeding quietly, all—except the *bahio* —and he too was still within sight, now, with his silent rider, a few yards off to my right.

'Half mechanically, as if obeying the mysterious influence that had brought me so far, I ran down the ravine, caught the horse which had still my saddle on—nothing was missing of the gear. I unsaddled him, caught another, geared him up, and drove the troop, by a less steep side of the ravine, up on to the plain again. There still stood Doroteo, motionless, but the smile on his face was now unmistakable. He wheeled round slowly, stretching out his arm before him, as if to direct me. I rode on—I could not have done otherwise—driving the horses before me; once I glanced backwards—yes, there still stood the silent sentinel. I could feel he was watching me; I almost could feel he was smiling. But the next time I looked back he was gone.'

'Practically from that moment my troubles were over. That very morning I balled an ostrich, which gave me plenty of food till I reached a farm, a day or two's distance from the Rio Negro.

'A fortnight later I was on my way to England. That's all my story. Tomorrow is the anniversary of Doroteo's death.'

Charles Maud was silent.

'Thank you for telling it to me, old fellow,' he said at last. 'And—may I ask you one thing? The *guacho's* prophecy came true—the first part of it. And how about the second?'

Darcy smiled.

'Yes,' he said. 'I was going to tell you. That's why I'm going down to The Chase. I'm going to be married soon—to—you know whom. . . .Yes, I *am* glad to live—*now*—thank God.'

.

LEONAUR

# ALSO FROM LEONAUR

## AVAILABLE IN SOFTCOVER OR HARDCOVER WITH DUST JACKET

**THE FIRST BOOK OF AYESHA** *by H. Rider Haggard*—Contains *She & Ayesha: the Return of She.*

**THE SECOND BOOK OF AYESHA** *by H. Rider Haggard*—Contains *She and Allan & Wisdom's Daughter.*

**QUATERMAIN: THE COMPLETE ADVENTURES—1** *by H. Rider Haggard*—Contains *King Solomon's Mines & Allan Quatermain.*

**QUATERMAIN: THE COMPLETE ADVENTURES—2** *by H. Rider Haggard*—Contains *Allan's Wife, Maiwa's Revenge & Marie.*

**QUATERMAIN: THE COMPLETE ADVENTURES—3** *by H. Rider Haggard*—Contains *Child of Storm & Allan and the Holy Flower.*

**QUATERMAIN: THE COMPLETE ADVENTURES—4** *by H. Rider Haggard*—Contains *Finished & The Ivory Child.*

**QUATERMAIN: THE COMPLETE ADVENTURES—5** *by H. Rider Haggard*—Contains *The Ancient Allan & She and Allan.*

**QUATERMAIN: THE COMPLETE ADVENTURES—6** *by H. Rider Haggard*—Contains *Heu-Heu or, the Monster & The Treasure of the Lake.*

**QUATERMAIN: THE COMPLETE ADVENTURES—7** *by H. Rider Haggard*—Contains *Allan and the Ice Gods, Four Short Adventures & Nada the Lily.*

**TROS OF SAMOTHRACE 1: WOLVES OF THE TIBER** *by Talbot Mundy*—55 B.C.--an adventurer set during the Roman invasion of Britain.

**TROS OF SAMOTHRACE 2: DRAGONS OF THE NORTH** *by Talbot Mundy*—55 B.C. —Caesar plots, Britons war among themselves and the Vikings are coming.

**TROS OF SAMOTHRACE 3: SERPENT OF THE WAVES** *by Talbot Mundy*—55 B.C.--Caesar is poised to invade Britain—only a grand strategy can foil him!.

**TROS OF SAMOTHRACE 4: CITY OF THE EAGLES** *by Talbot Mundy*—54 B.C.—Rome—Tros treads in the streets of his sworn enemies!.

**TROS OF SAMOTHRACE 5: CLEOPATRA** *by Talbot Mundy*—Tros and the Roman Empire turn to the Egypt of the Pharaohs.

**TROS OF SAMOTHRACE 6: THE PURPLE PIRATE** *by Talbot Mundy*—The epic saga of the ancient world—Tros of Samothrace—draws to a conclusion in this sixth—and final—volume.

**LEONAUR**

# ALSO FROM LEONAUR
## AVAILABLE IN SOFTCOVER OR HARDCOVER WITH DUST JACKET

**THE CIVIL WAR NOVELS: 1** *by Joseph A. Altsheler*—*The Guns of Bull Run &
The Guns of Shiloh*—the first and second novels of a series of eight adventures which
follow the momentous events, campaigns and battles of the great American Civil War
between the Northern and Southern states.

**THE CIVIL WAR NOVELS: 2** *by Joseph A. Altsheler*—*The Scouts of Stonewall
& The Sword of Antietam*—the third and fourth novels of a series of nine adventures
which follow the momentous events, campaigns and battles of the great American
Civil War between the Northern and Southern states.

**THE CIVIL WAR NOVELS: 3** *by Joseph A. Altsheler*—*The Star of Gettysburg
& The Rock of Chickamauga*—the fifth and sixth novels of a series of nine adventures
which follow the momentous events, campaigns and battles of the great American
Civil War between the Northern and Southern states.

**THE CIVIL WAR NOVELS: 4** *by Joseph A. Altsheler*—*The Shades of the Wilderness & The Tree of Appomattox*—the seventh and eighth novels of a series of nine
adventures which follow the momentous events, campaigns and battles of the great
American Civil War between the Northern and Southern states.

**THE CIVIL WAR NOVELS: 5** *by Joseph A. Altsheler*—*Before the Dawn: a Story
of the Fall of Richmond*—the last of a series of nine adventures which follow the momentous events, campaigns and battles of the great American Civil War between the
Northern and Southern states.

**THE FRENCH & INDIAN WAR NOVELS: 1** *by Joseph A. Altsheler*—*The
Hunters of the Hills & The Shadow of the North*—In this three volume, six novel set the
story of the war, with many of its real life characters, is told through the adventures
of its principal characters, Robert Lennox, the hunter Willet and his Indian companion Tayoga.

**THE FRENCH & INDIAN WAR NOVELS: 2** *by Joseph A. Altsheler*—*The
Rulers of the Lakes & The Masters of the Peaks*—In this three volume, six novel set the
story of the war, with many of its real life characters, is told through the adventures
of its principal characters, Robert Lennox, the hunter Willet and his Indian companion Tayoga.

**THE FRENCH & INDIAN WAR NOVELS: 1** *by Joseph A. Altsheler*—*The Lords
of the Wild & The Sun of Quebec*—In this three volume, six novel set the story of the
war, with many of its real life characters, is told through the adventures of its principal
characters, Robert Lennox, the hunter Willet and his Indian companion Tayoga.

LEONAUR

# ALSO FROM LEONAUR
## AVAILABLE IN SOFTCOVER OR HARDCOVER WITH DUST JACKET

**THE LONG PATROL** by George Berrie—A Novel of Light Horsemen from Gallipoli to the Palestine campaign of the First World War.

**NAPOLEONIC WAR STORIES** by Arthur Quiller-Couch—Tales of soldiers, spies, battles & sieges from the Peninsular & Waterloo campaingns.

**THE FIRST DETECTIVE** by Edgar Allan Poe—The Complete Auguste Dupin Stories—The Murders in the Rue Morgue, The Mystery of Marie Rogêt & The Purloined Letter.

**THE COMPLETE DR NIKOLA—MAN OF MYSTERY: 1** by Guy Boothby—A *Bid for Fortune* & *Dr Nikola Returns*—Guy Boothby's Dr.Nikola adventures continue to fascinate readers and enthusiasts of crime and mystery fiction because—in the manner of Raffles, the gentleman cracksman—here is character far removed from the uncompromising goodness of Holmes and Watson or the uncompromising evil of Professor Moriarty.

**THE COMPLETE DR NIKOLA—MAN OF MYSTERY: 2** by Guy Boothby— *The Lust of Hate, Dr Nikola's Experiment* & *Farewell, Nikola*—Guy Boothby's Dr.Nikola adventures continue to fascinate readers and enthusiasts of crime and mystery fiction because—in the manner of Raffles, the gentleman cracksman—here is character far removed from the uncompromising goodness of Holmes and Watson or the uncompromising evil of Professor Moriarty.

**THE CASEBOOKS OF MR J. G. REEDER: BOOK 1** by Edgar Wallace— *Room 13, The Mind of Mr J. G. Reeder* and *Terror Keep*—Edgar Wallace's sleuth—whose territory is the London of the 1920s—is an unlikely figure, more bank clerk than detective in appearance, ever wearing his square topped bowler, frock coat, cravat and muffler, Mr Reeder is usually inseparable from his umbrella.

**THE CASEBOOKS OF MR J. G. REEDER: BOOK 2** by Edgar Wallace— *Red Aces, Mr J. G. Reeder Returns, The Guv'nor* and *The Man Who Passed*—Edgar Wallace's sleuth—whose territory is the London of the 1920s—is an unlikely figure, more bank clerk than detective in appearance, ever wearing his square topped bowler, frock coat, cravat and muffler, Mr Reeder is usually inseparable from his umbrella.

**THE COMPLETE FOUR JUST MEN: VOLUME 1** by Edgar Wallace—*The Four Just Men, The Council of Justice* & *The Just Men of Cordova*—disillusioned with a world where the wicked and the abusers of power perpetually go unpunished, the Just Men set about to rectify matters according to their own standards, and retribution is dispensed on swift and deadly wings.

LEONAUR

# ALSO FROM LEONAUR
### AVAILABLE IN SOFTCOVER OR HARDCOVER WITH DUST JACKET

**THE COMPLETE FOUR JUST MEN: VOLUME 2** *by Edgar Wallace—The Law of the Four Just Men & The Three Just Men*—disillusioned with a world where the wicked and the abusers of power perpetually go unpunished, the Just Men set about to rectify matters according to their own standards, and retribution is dispensed on swift and deadly wings.

**THE COMPLETE RAFFLES: 1** *by E. W. Hornung—The Amateur Cracksman & The Black Mask*—By turns urbane gentleman about town and accomplished cricketer, life is just too ordinary for Raffles and that sets him on a series of adventures that have long been treasured as a real antidote to the 'white knights' who are the usual heroes of the crime fiction of this period.

**THE COMPLETE RAFFLES: 2** *by E. W. Hornung—A Thief in the Night & Mr Justice Raffles*—By turns urbane gentleman about town and accomplished cricketer, life is just too ordinary for Raffles and that sets him on a series of adventures that have long been treasured as a real antidote to the 'white knights' who are the usual heroes of the crime fiction of this period.

**THE COLLECTED SUPERNATURAL AND WEIRD FICTION OF WILKIE COLLINS: VOLUME 1** *by Wilkie Collins*—Contains one novel 'The Haunted Hotel', one novella 'Mad Monkton', three novelettes 'Mr Percy and the Prophet', 'The Biter Bit' and 'The Dead Alive' and eight short stories to chill the blood.

**THE COLLECTED SUPERNATURAL AND WEIRD FICTION OF WILKIE COLLINS: VOLUME 2** *by Wilkie Collins*—Contains one novel 'The Two Destinies', three novellas 'The Frozen deep', 'Sister Rose' and 'The Yellow Mask' and two short stories to chill the blood.

**THE COLLECTED SUPERNATURAL AND WEIRD FICTION OF WILKIE COLLINS: VOLUME 3** *by Wilkie Collins*—Contains one novel 'Dead Secret,' two novelettes 'Mrs Zant and the Ghost' and 'The Nuns Story of Gabriel's Marriage' and five short stories to chill the blood.

**FUNNY BONES** *selected by Dorothy Scarborough*—An Anthology of Humorous Ghost Stories.

**MONTEZUMA'S CASTLE AND OTHER WEIRD TALES** *by Charles B. Cory*—Cory has written a superb collection of eighteen ghostly and weird stories to chill and thrill the avid enthusiast of supernatural fiction.

**SUPERNATURAL BUCHAN** *by John Buchan*—Stories of Ancient Spirits, Uncanny Places & Strange Creatures.

LEONAUR

# ALSO FROM LEONAUR
## AVAILABLE IN SOFTCOVER OR HARDCOVER WITH DUST JACKET

**MR MUKERJI'S GHOSTS** by S. *Mukerji*—Supernatural tales from the British Raj period by India's Ghost story collector.

**KIPLINGS GHOSTS** by *Rudyard Kipling*—Twelve stories of Ghosts, Hauntings, Curses, Werewolves & Magic.